just not mine

just not mine

escape to new zealand book six

ROSALIND JAMES

ISBN-10: 098876198X
ISBN-13: 9780988761988

author's note

table of contents

new zealand map

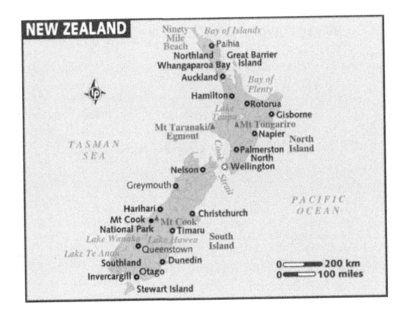

A New Zealand glossary appears at the end of this book

the combat zone

♡

Hugh Latimer had his eye on the ball. Fifteen minutes left in the deciding game of the Rugby Championship, the score, despite every desperate effort, stuck at 14 to 6 in favor of the Springboks, and the capacity crowd of fifty thousand South Africans at Loftus Verfeld was sniffing victory, baying for All Black blood.

The noise was a physical thing, an assault, but it didn't matter. There was no pain, no sweat, no fear. Only one thing mattered. Where was the ball, and how could he get to it and take it back.

The Boks were moving fast. Jan Strauss, the blazing winger, took the pass and was off with a burst of acceleration. Hugh read the tiny movement of his head that signaled one of his deceptive jukes, saw the line he was aiming for, and was into space in that fraction of a second to cut him off. He brought him down in a bone-jarring tackle a bare five meters from the tryline, sprang to his feet and went for the ball, keeping his balance to avoid the penalty that would put the chance of victory beyond reach. He planted both feet hard and solid, kept his body weight low, and used every bit of strength in his hands, arms, and shoulders to wrest the ball loose from Jan's grasp.

He was aware of Liam Mahaka barreling in in support, his ferocity, as always, undiminished by the gash to his head that had sent him to the blood bin for stapling minutes earlier. But Hugh wasn't thinking about that either. He kept his focus on the ball. That was his target. That was his only goal.

He felt the moment when he won, began to pull the ball to his side of the line even as he saw all hundred-twenty kilos of Flip van der Jongh bearing down on him in a desperate attempt to wrest it back. Flip's right eye was nearly closed, the area around it angry, red, and swollen, the injury only increasing his determination. Flip dove, his elbow cracked into Hugh's left hand where he had the ball in a death grip, and Hugh didn't let go, because that wasn't an option.

He barely felt the impact at all, because the ref was blowing his whistle, and the ball belonged to the All Blacks, and he had won. He sent the ball fast to Nate Torrance for distribution, and saw, as he got himself back into position, that Toro had immediately offloaded it himself to Nic Wilkinson behind the tryline, who got it off his left foot and safely to midfield. The try was saved, the disaster averted. For now.

Hugh wasn't celebrating. He was sprinting the moment the ball left Nico's foot, calculating angles, assessing the Boks' positions. Jean le Vieux, the centre, was running straight at Kevin McNicholl as Hugh had expected, testing the buggered foot that had been obvious from twenty minutes into the match. Kevin threw himself in for the tackle with undiminished courage, and Hugh was there in support, going for the ball again.

Except that he couldn't, because his left hand was crocked. He'd hardly noticed the pain, but he couldn't move his thumb, couldn't grab at all, couldn't tackle. He was useless.

No hope. No choice. He was jogging off the field, his replacement running on. His game was over, and he was on the sideline with an ice pack strapped to his hand, ten minutes left in the match and the big screen still showing 14 to 6, two scores away from a win, and nothing left to do but watch.

He had something cheering to watch, for a while. Four minutes out, and the All Blacks were driving. Koti James had the ball, was breaking the line, throwing a head-fake one way, making a couple seemingly impossible changes of direction, drawing three tacklers and offloading the ball at the last possible half-second out the back door, a quick flip from his left hand to Nate. The ball in and out of the skipper's hands in a flash, and before the Springboks could react, Kevin again, somehow still managing to run on that foot, crashing his big frame over the tryline in the corner, miraculously keeping his left foot off the chalk that marked the touchline, and Hugh was rising with the rest of the men on the bench in exultation, because that was surely a try, and they were in with a chance.

But both men had paid the price. Koti had been hit so hard his mouthpiece had gone flying, he'd crashed to the turf in a heap and hadn't risen again, and Kevin had pounded that foot once too often and was hobbling up now, trying to get back to midfield, but he wasn't going to make it. The trainer was bent over a still-prone Koti even as Nico was nailing the kick and making the score 14 to 13, which was so close, but Koti and Kevin were gone too, and the chances had just got even slimmer.

Every man on the field was digging deep, giving everything he had, but there wasn't enough time, and nothing the All Blacks could do to knock the ball loose from the Springboks' grip as they held on, this match as important to them as to their New Zealand counterparts, because if New Zealand's blood ran black, South Africa's ran green.

Three minutes. Two minutes. Sixty seconds. The clock ticked down, and still the Springboks held the ball. The hooter sounded, a Bok kicked the ball into touch, and the game was lost, and so was the Championship.

You played the match you got on the night, played what was in front of you with all your heart and all your passion and every last bit of drive and determination and strength you could screw out of your body and your soul. You played for your teammates, and for the jersey, and for your country, and for mana.

And sometimes, it wasn't enough.

a trained professional

♡

Dr. Eva Parker opened her white lab coat to reveal what she was wearing beneath it, smiled in slow satisfaction at the reaction in the shocked eyes that were definitely *not* staring into her own. Her outfit matched the coat, if sheer white lace could ever be said to match starched white cotton. A hard-working, low-cut demibra offered up her full, round breasts like treats on a shelf, while the tiniest thong curved over the perfectly smooth, perfectly moisturized skin of her rigorously-dieted hips, highlighted her absolutely, positively flat stomach. A diamond winked from the concave slit that was her navel, and a suspender belt kept her stockings clinging to the endless legs that tapered to the exclamation point of the killer black heels she always wore at work. Unless she was in the operating room, of course.

"Eva." Bruce Dixon, the hospital's administrative officer, groaned out the word. "I'm a married man."

"My favorite kind," she purred. Her fingers worked through his neatly combed blond hair, lingered on his smoothly shaved cheek, then traveled downward to splay against his chest. But not for long, because her hand was on a mission now, a heat-seeking missile homing in on its target, stroking down and down as she watched his eyes glaze, as she touched his abdomen with the lightest of caresses, landing at last on his belt buckle, her long, slim fingers with their red-polished nails playing with the leather strip, letting him know that she was more than ready to take it off, that he was well and truly hers.

"Ah, yes. My *very* favorite kind." Her voice was low, sensuous, full of promise. "The *talented* kind. Because I can tell you've got a major talent right here. Talents are meant to be used, you know. I can't wait to see how you'll use yours. I plan to use it myself, too, be warned. And be afraid." She smiled, a red-lipsticked thing that was pure predator. "Because I plan to use it, to use you, until you're begging for mercy."

"I can't just make ethics charges go away," he protested, sounding weaker by the moment.

"Of course you can." She took hold of his necktie, leaned against his desk, and pulled him into her. She gave him a long, slow kiss, saw his eyes closing, felt every lingering bit of his reserve weakening, and smiled again. She was seductive, oh, yes, she was. She was deadly. She was a man-eater, a Black Widow, and she loved it.

"A man as powerful as you," she told him, sweeping an arm behind her to send his pile of files tumbling to the floor, "can do anything. Anything you like."

"And...cut!" Mike said with satisfaction. "That one's in the can."

Josie sat up, let go of Clive's tie, and grinned at him. "Got you going there, didn't I?"

"I am a trained professional," he said, grinning back at her. "Just like you."

flight of the hummingbirds

♡

The Dance of the Ladybugs was cute enough. Six or seven three-year-olds wandered around the stage seemingly at random, bumping into each other to the accompaniment of clearly audible hisses from the wings. By the time the Waltz of the Butterflies came around, though, Hugh was bored. And endless minutes—or hours—later, when a bunch of little girls in pink tutus were earnestly performing the Flight of the Hummingbirds, he was just about catatonic.

"How long till Amelia's?" he muttered to his Aunt Cora under cover of the applause as the latest group trooped off the stage.

"Next but three," she told him. "Takes a while to get to the twelve-year-olds."

"I'll come back for that," he started to say. "Sorry, but I can't take much more of this."

The brunette in the row ahead of him turned around, a frown drawing her dark eyebrows together, and he shut up and looked at her.

She was lost from sight, unfortunately, because sure enough, the music had started up again, and the lights were dimming. Hugh sat back with a sigh. More tinkly music, more birds, or bugs, or some damn thing with wings. Again.

There was normal time, which was...normal, he decided as girls came on and girls went off, as somebody lost her place and ran crying into the wings, as the music stopped and started. There was rugby time, which was fast. And there was Dance Recital time. Which was endless.

"This is it," Charlie told him from his other side. "This is Amelia's."

Hugh looked down at his half-brother. Leaning forward, every line of his eight-year-old body straining, that intense look on his finely-carved features. He could feel the tension from Charlie, sense his toe tapping out the rhythm as the music swelled, the girls danced onto the stage. He *cared*.

"Pas de bourré, pirouette," he heard Charlie mutter. "Too stiff, though." And indeed, Amelia's arms weren't curved into the graceful lines some of the other girls had achieved, even Hugh could tell that. The music picked up, and the girls started leaping about.

"Aw, she's wobbled," Charlie said. Sure enough, the sturdy figure of Amelia, her dark hair scraped back like the other girls' into a painfully tight knot at the back of her head, was losing its line, her pink-clad leg showing a distinct tendency to tremble as the girls stopped leaping and ended with a foot stuck out behind them, and Hugh watched his half-sister set her errant foot down a full second ahead of the other girls.

He sighed with relief when the piece was over, began to stand up.

"Still four more to go," Aunt Cora told him.

"I could come back and meet you," Hugh suggested. "After."

The brunette from the row ahead turned around again, Aunt Cora looked at him reprovingly again, and Hugh sat back again, sighed, closed his eyes, and surrendered to the inevitable.

♡

When the thing was over—he looked at his phone afterwards and was astonished to see it had actually only been a couple of hours, during which he may or may not have fallen asleep, because he wasn't telling—he wasn't quite so sorry. The little bunches of teachers, parents, heroic family friends, and excited girls were mingling in the church hall housing tonight's performance, drinking tea and eating biscuits that some of the mums had provided, and Amelia's teacher was pretty.

"Oh," Aunt Cora said. "You won't have met Chloe Donaldson, Hugh. My nephew Hugh, Amelia's brother. Chloe owns the dance studio, Hugh. Hasn't she done a good job tonight?"

Hugh waited for a look of recognition that didn't come, uttered a few words of congratulation, and shook hands with the petite brunette as she smiled politely back at him, nothing but wariness in the dark eyes. Her hair was a sleek cap, cut a little—raggedly, although he didn't think that was the right word, her figure was willowy, her features were fine, and she looked more like a wood elf than any woman really had a right to look. She looked like she should be wearing a green tunic and pointed shoes, and all *her* movements *were* graceful.

"How's Amelia getting on?" he asked her.

He could sense the hesitation. "She's a good hard worker," she said, and Hugh knew what that meant.

She smiled briefly at him again, turned for another introduction to a dad, and Hugh hadn't met many women who'd been as unimpressed by him as that. Oh, well. Probably had a partner.

He spotted the other woman, and forgot about the ballet teacher. Her face had looked good, even frowning over the back of her seat at him. Now, though, he was treated to the full picture, and it was a sight to see, even though he wouldn't have called her presentation anything spectacular. Black leggings and boots, and a dark blue knit dress over them. She was completely covered, completely sober, nothing flash, her hair pulled back into a knot. But she couldn't hide the flash of that figure. She was slim to the point of thinness, but not every part of her was thin.

Not at all. Some Maori there, clearly visible in the golden-brown skin, the aristocratically carved features. And all those curves, the dress working hard to accommodate them. Yeh, she was golden, all right.

She was in the middle of a fairly sizable group of women, a few men, too, and he sighed. Somebody's mum. This was clearly not his night.

She glanced at him across the gray head of a shorter woman, because she was tall. Her eyes widened for just a moment at what he realized was his stare, then her face went blank and she looked away, the dismissal clear.

She was the only one who wasn't interested, though, because one of the fellas with her looked over, nudged somebody else, and now the men's attention was divided between the brunette and Hugh, and Hugh braced himself.

Luckily, Amelia turned up with a couple of friends just then, Amelia whispering, the others giggling, arms wrapped around each others' shoulders, the stiff net of their tutus shoved up against each other. Their scraped-back hair and heavy makeup made them look oddly like very young...models, to put it politely, which wasn't a look he cared for much at all, not on his little sister.

Amelia detached herself from her friends. "You need to tell Aunt Cora that it's time to go," she informed her brother. "It's past Charlie's bedtime."

He'd seldom heard more welcome words. "Why don't you tell her?" His aunt was in a group of her friends, and if there was a way out of having a chat, he'd welcome it. He was knackered, and his hand was throbbing in its sling.

She sighed with the patronizing exasperation that was something new, but that he'd seen more than once in the short day and a half since he'd come back from South Africa. "Because it's not *polite* to interrupt. You need to tell her."

"Why's it polite for me to interrupt, then?"

"Because you're grown up, and I'm a *child*," she said, one hand on her pink-leotarded hip.

"Beginning to wonder about that," he muttered, but he went over and put a hand on Aunt Cora's elbow, smiled at the older ladies and a few men who had immediately drifted over to join the group at his approach, answered a few questions, accepted the bitter disappointment and galling commiserations over the loss of the Championship with as much grace as he could muster, and tried his level best to convey that he was teetering on the verge of leaving.

"Past Charlie's bedtime," he murmured in Cora's ear, gave another smile all around, and they were finally done.

Family obligations: complete. Progress toward female companionship during his enforced holiday: zero.

getting a life

♡

Except that his family obligations turned out not to be complete at all, because it appeared that they'd only just begun.

"What do you mean, back to the UK?" His body was telling him it was well past time to be in bed, his hand was aching badly now, and the news he'd just got was a blindside he didn't need.

"I need a holiday," his aunt said. "And I need to go back to the UK. It's still my home, I haven't been back in nearly eighteen months, and that's too long. You were just there last summer, and I haven't been."

"I was working," he said. "I wasn't touring, looking at Big Ben. And I know you haven't been back, and I'm sorry. But you must see that it's not the best time, not with my thumb broken."

"Sorry, but I'm going anyway," she said. "Because there's someone I need to be with."

"Someone you need to *be* with?" He struggled to focus. "What kind of someone?"

"What do you think?" She was looking at him with exasperation now. "The male kind. I know you think, 'Oh, Auntie Cora, she's past it, she's happy to look after the kids,' but I'm only forty-five. I was nine years younger than Edward. And all right," she went on, even though Hugh hadn't said anything, "I needed the change, being made redundant at the office on top of it, and that made it easier to come, but now I've got someone."

"Got someone how? Someone here?"

"No. Someone there. Henry Selfridge," she said, and the color was high in her somewhat homely face.

"Who?"

She sighed in exasperation. "The man who was here last summer, visiting, when you first came. I took him to Waiheke, remember?"

"I thought he was...an old friend or something."

"He was. At least, you could call him that. But he was married before, and so was I."

"*What?*"

"Of course it wasn't that," she said crossly. "I didn't mean an affair, I meant, I knew him a bit from when he had a shop near us, and we always...there was something there, all right? And now he's divorced as well, he came here on holiday, we reconnected, and we've stayed in touch. And he wants me to visit," she finished in a rush, "and I'm going. He visited me, and now I'm visiting him, seeing his shop, seeing what happens."

"What kind of shop?" he asked. "What does this bloke do, exactly?"

"He's a butcher."

"Oh, no," he groaned. "You're joking. I'm going to read about you being stuck into a box somewhere." This was why his long-divorced aunt had a new style to her hair, had lost the bit of gray, he realized, and why she was wearing makeup, too. For a *butcher* she barely knew, and what were the chances of that ending well?

"You've got no right to tell me that," she said, her face even redder. "It's none of your bloody business, and I'm not a fool, no matter what you think. We've talked a bit about him selling up and moving here, but who knows? We've both been around the block, and we've got our eyes open. And I want to see the family, my friends, anyway. It's been almost a year and a half, and I left in a hurry. I need to catch up. I was glad to come, but I need a break."

He scrubbed his hand over his jaw, the stubble, well on its way toward becoming a beard, still feeling alien. "And I'm glad you did come. I don't know what we'd have done without you. Don't know what we'll do now, come to that."

Both things were true. When he'd got the news that his father and stepmother were gone, his half-siblings orphaned, Aunt Cora's arrival had been the life preserver that had saved them all, allowed the kids to remain in their home, given them stability. Hugh had been able to play out his contract with the Hurricanes, accept his selection to the All Blacks during an all-important transition year, go on the multi-week tours required of an international before moving north to help out. He'd paid the bills, but that had been the easy part. He'd paid, but she'd stayed. But she wasn't staying now.

"You'll manage," she said. "You'll have to for the next little while, because I don't want to end my days as somebody's dear old auntie, without any life of my own. I want a man again. I want a *life* again."

That one stopped him, because what could he say? That if they were talking about lives, he didn't have much of one him-self? That wasn't her fault. It wasn't anybody's fault, at least not anybody's who was still alive to take the blame, it was just the way it was. And if she needed to take a holiday, she should have one, because he needed her back.

"All right, then," he said. "I mean," he went on hastily, "I don't mean 'all right,' as if I'm giving you permission. I mean, all right, I understand." He hefted the hand that he'd taken from its sling. "Be easier without this."

"It's your left hand, though. Not that bad, and you can hoover with one hand," she said briskly.

Hoover? Who was hoovering? He was, he guessed, even though he barely knew where the vacuum cleaner was.

"And you can drive," she went on. "I just saw you do it tonight, and it'll get easier. You said you'd only be in the cast for a few weeks. You're going to be out of rugby all the way until February. You're on holiday yourself, aren't you?"

Some holiday. "I don't know...their timetable," he said, hearing the weakness of it. "How it all works."

"So ask them. They're not babies."

"Right, then." It looked like there was nothing more to say, and time to move on, however he felt about it. "For how long, and when are you off?"

"Three months, and day after tomorrow," she said, and he could see her tensing for the reaction that she must have known he'd provide.

"Three *months?* And day after *tomorrow?* Could you have told me about this a couple weeks ago? Could we have talked about it?"

"I thought I'd be going after you'd got back from the Tour, and I thought I'd only have six weeks or so. When you broke your thumb, well, it's an ill wind that blows nobody good, isn't it? Maybe it was a sign that it was meant to be, that your injury happened just when it did, especially since there was a last-minute sale on the tickets. And now I've got a chance to make it longer. It's only until a bit after the New Year, hardly a few weeks out of their summer holidays. You'll barely have Christmas, and I'll be back. And all right," she went on with exasperation as he continued to stare at her, "I didn't want to feel guilty. What would be the point? You're fine, the kids are fine, everybody's going to be fine, and I'm going to the UK."

the black widow speaks

♡

"And that's that," Chloe sighed when the last overly-invested mum had at last finished discussing her little ballerina's progress, the last long-suffering dad had made his grateful exit. "Another one down."

"A rousing success, I'd say." Josie helped her friend gather discarded programs and left-behind headpieces, an orphaned pair of butterfly wings.

"Yeh, should do a bit toward keeping the doors open and the lights on," Chloe agreed, locking up the auditorium behind them. "Come back with me and open a bottle of wine? Post-mortem?"

"Why not," Josie decided. "I'm not called for tomorrow, may as well go for the wild life."

"Gone nine, and you're still vertical," Chloe said. "Living the dream."

♡

Back in Chloe's little apartment, Josie got the wine out while Chloe paid the babysitter and saw her out.

"Funny how life turns out, isn't it?" Chloe said when they were into their second glass, propped against opposite ends of the couch.

"You mean...?" Josie asked cautiously.

"When Zavy turned up, I thought it was the end. The final nail in the coffin."

"I remember."

"And now..." Chloe gestured, the fatigue of the past hours, the wine clearly taking their toll, "I'm so...invested. In both things, Zavy and the school. Literally. I always thought I'd be a star, can I confess? Used to fall asleep—not even dreaming of it. *Planning* it, it seemed so real. Now I just want to be...a success. But I do want that."

"A different kind of star, that's all," Josie suggested. "A businesswoman. But, yeh, I thought you'd be a star too. I was never as good as you. Never even close, was I?"

"No." Chloe smiled tiredly. "Just Head Girl, best in the netball and hockey, coming top in the prize-giving for the academics, that's all. Not a star at all."

"Not at dance, which was what I wanted," Josie countered.

"Such a thing as being too athletic," Chloe said. "I have a few students like that. Dead keen, hard workers, but they fling themselves about just the way you used to do. Can't make it look easy to save their lives."

"But I could leap about like nobody's business," Josie said with a grin. "Nobody jumped farther."

"But who turned out to be the star pupil all the same, in the end?" Chloe asked. "You found your way, and so did I, even if it wasn't the path we started out on. Talking of which, did you have the meeting with your agent?"

"Yeh," Josie said. "Yesterday."

After work, when she'd been tired already, and Geoff's reaction to her inquiries hadn't helped any. She'd ended up pretty discouraged, and that was the truth.

"No such thing out there, from what I know," he'd said. "En Zed television's a small market, and the film business is even smaller, you know that as well as I do. You're already a regular on the most-viewed non-sports program on air. No place to go but down, and why would you do that? Now, you want me to put you up for something in Aussie, even the UK, possibly, we could be in business. But you can't have it both ways."

"You know how I feel about that," she said. "I tried it, remember?"

She had. Three long years across the Ditch, starting with the odd part in a TV show and some modeling assignments that had paid the rent on the luxury flat in Bondi, had got her into the papers, into the public eye. And then her big break, the regular spot on the courtroom drama playing a shark of a lawyer, the woman everyone had loved to hate.

Success any way you looked at it, and she'd hated it. It had been Hollywood on an exponentially smaller scale, but it had been too much Hollywood for her. She'd known it was time to leave when she'd loitered so long in the toilet in the Auckland airport that she'd missed her flight, and neither Geoff nor anybody else had been able to talk her out of it.

"I needed to be where the people live slow and talk fast," she told Geoff now. "You know that."

He sighed. "Josie. My darling. Listen to me. Your Uncle Geoff who only wants the best for you."

"Your fifteen percent, you mean."

"Well, that too," he admitted. "My fifteen percent of absolutely as much as I can get for you. Look at where you are. You've got what any actor would sell his granny for, a starring part on a show that's got the legs only a soap can provide, with some very lucrative modeling on the side. You've just bought a house, for God's sake. What more do you want?"

"What I said. Another type of part. A show where I can try being funny from time to time, where I can be—well, if not three-dimensional, how about two? I think I've got myself half-convinced that I *am* evil, by now. That's not acting, or not the way I want to do it. And besides—I'm not going to be beautiful forever, you know. Almost thirty, aren't I. I don't think the punters are going to want to watch Dr. Eva take her clothes off when she's fifty."

"Referring to yourself in the third person's a sure sign that you're getting above yourself," he warned her.

"See? It's *not* myself I'm referring to. Even you're doing it."

"Anyway." He cast out a dismissive hand. "Just don't have a baby, and you're all good."

"Not in the plans," she said briefly.

"Good. Or if you do get broody, do us both a favor and pay somebody else to carry the baby, too," he said with a grin. "That way, no career break, no nasty stretch marks. Brilliant."

"I'm going to assume you're joking," she said, doing her best to laugh it off. "But keep your eyes open for me, will you?"

"I'll keep them open," he promised. "But, Josie. All joking aside, I wouldn't get my hopes up."

♡

"So, nah," she finished telling Chloe. "No joy. Looks like I'm the Black Widow for the foreseeable future."

"Well, cheers," Chloe said, heaving herself up and clinking her wine glass against Josie's. "To making the most of what we've got."

"Yeh, I get what he said. Fancy me whingeing about what I do. Enough to make me sick myself, thinking about some of the fellas back home. Picking kiwifruit all day, heading to the packhouse to put in a shift there, sleep in the backpackers', just to make sure they can put food on the table the rest of the year. And here I am, not grateful for my success."

"I don't think it's that," Chloe said seriously. "I'd say you're grateful enough. But just because you've done well, does that mean you can't ask for any more? Does that mean you can't keep working to do better? You're not asking anyone to hand it to you. You're asking for the chance to work even harder, to stretch yourself. Doesn't seem like ingratitude to me. Seems like ambition, and why's that bad?"

"Tall poppy?" Josie suggested.

"Nah. Achiever." Chloe smiled. "Star."

"Mm. That's why we're friends. Because you flatter me shamelessly." Josie lifted herself off the couch with an effort. "I should go."

"Stay over, why don't you," Chloe suggested. "If you aren't working tomorrow. We can kill this bottle, if you like."

"I'll stop drinking, but, yeh, I will stay. Get a bit of time with my darling godson. Not to mention that my bedroom reeks of fresh paint, and I can't sleep in it anyway. Shift yourself, then." She gave Chloe a smack. "I'm going to sleep on this couch in about ten minutes, one way or another. And I'd like to do it with a sheet on."

a positive role model

♡

"Hugh."

The woman was calling to him, and he smiled in his sleep, rolled over, and reached for her.

"*Hugh.*" The shove on his shoulder wasn't amorous, and neither was the voice. "Wake up."

"Huh?" He woke up hugging the pillow, rolled to his back and shoved himself up onto his elbows, blinking.

His sister was standing there, hands on her hips, and he could swear her toe was tapping.

"Wake up," she said again. "It's morning."

"Oh. Right." He ran a hand over his jaw and yawned. He'd been up at four the previous morning to give Aunt Cora a lift to the airport, had been seriously drooping after his workout and visit to the physio at midday, had done the washing-up in a fog after a dinner cobbled together from the remnants of the previous evening's meal, and then had once again been unable to fall asleep when he'd finally crawled into bed. Now, his body was telling him in no uncertain terms that it needed rest, but it looked like it wasn't happening. Again. He normally slept until seven-thirty, but it looked like that had changed.

"You're supposed to get up before us," Amelia informed him. "You're meant to be waking *us*. Besides, children who eat breakfast with their families achieve better results in school. We need a committed parental figure providing a positive role model."

He squinted at her. "How do you know?"

"Because I watch television, of course."

"All right. I'm up. Providing a positive role model." When she continued to stand there, he added with exasperation, "If you'd leave, that is, so I can get dressed."

"Fine," she said, and stalked towards the door. "We'll be in the kitchen, eating cereal. Since nobody was available to cook our breakfast."

"Could've made toast, anyway, couldn't you," he muttered as he fumbled to pull his shorts and T-shirt on with one hand.

"Right, then," he said when he'd got himself sorted, had padded barefoot into the kitchen. He flipped the switch on the electric jug, because coffee was definitely required. "Here I am. What's this role model meant to do?"

Charlie looked at Amelia and shrugged. They were both in their uniforms, eating cereal. He didn't appear all that necessary to their progress, in his opinion.

"What does Aunt Cora do in the morning, besides make your breakfast?" he clarified. "Which you could do as well as I can, Amelia. Better. You've got two hands. Can't you fry an egg?"

"No," she said. "Aunt Cora always did."

"Well, time you learnt," he said. "We'll do it together tomorrow, how's that. I'll show you, both of you, for that matter, then we can take turns. How's that for role modeling? Not what you had in mind, is it? Hah."

He got out the bag of coffee, pulled the plunger down from the cabinet, and did his best to hold the bag open with the fingers poking out from the cast on his left hand while dipping the spoon in with his right. He managed it, but not without a fair few grounds spilling onto the bench on their way into the glass carafe. Teamwork was the only way this was going to happen, he decided, because he was halfway to useless just now.

When he'd got the coffee made and taken his first grateful sip, he sat at the table with the kids, watched them working their way through their Weet-Bix, and said, "All right. What else? If Aunt Cora were here, what would she be doing?" He should know, because he'd been around sometimes while she'd been doing it, but he'd never paid that much attention.

"Umm..." Charlie said. "Checking if we have our lunches made, and our homework."

"Well, do you have your homework?"

Charlie shrugged. "I dunno. That's why she checks."

"What else? What else does she do?" Hugh amended when Charlie looked at him blankly.

"Ask us about what happens after school today?" His brother looked questioningly at Amelia, and she nodded.

"So what happens?" Hugh prompted.

"I have rugby," Charlie said.

"I have diving," Amelia said.

"And? What am I meant to do about those things? You just come home later on the bus, right, Amelia?

"Yeh," she said. "But you need to know anyway. You're supposed to *care*. You're supposed to *ask*."

"Asking right now, aren't I. So what about you, Charlie? Just over at the rugby field, right? You'd walk. So, again, where do I come into it?"

Charlie shrugged. "Dunno. Make sure I go, I guess."

"Are you likely not to go?"

Charlie considered. "I guess...you stand there and say, 'D'you have your mouth guard and your water bottle, Charlie? And where did you leave your boots?' Like that."

"Well, that sounds efficient," Hugh said. "Think we can do better than that. I keep my kit in its bag so I know where it is. Why not just do that?"

Charlie put his head on one side. "I could. I s'pose."

"Course you could. Go do it now, soon as you've finished your brekkie."

"But you'll still be here when he comes home from school, right?" Amelia asked. "You have to be here. He's too little to be home alone."

"I'm *not*," Charlie protested.

Amelia ignored him. "Girls who grow up without a father in their lives are more likely to fall pregnant," she told Hugh. "And boys are more likely to join gangs."

"You planning on falling pregnant? You're twelve."

"Twelve-year-olds can be pregnant," she insisted. "I saw a program about it."

"Well, I'll watch out for that, then. And what kind of gang is Charlie meant to join? The gang of eight-year-old schoolboys? Not sure I'd cross the street in fear."

She heaved a mighty sigh and rolled her eyes. "Not *now*. Later. You're laying a foundation for our lives. We're orphans, you know. We need a—"

"A role model," Hugh finished. "What was Aunt Cora, then? You'd think from the sound of you that you've both been begging in the gutter somewhere."

"You *asked*," Amelia said. "What you were meant to do. I'm just telling you."

"And now I'm telling *you*. We're going to sit down together this weekend and make a timetable, so we all know what you're meant to do, not just me. We'll post it on the fridge, and we'll post a list for the two of you as well, so you can check the night before for homework, whatever else you need to remember, get it sorted then. If I'm your role model, we'll do it the way I do.

When I get to training every day, there's a sheet of paper posted with my workout, and I follow it. Nobody's trailing around after me seeing that I do it, and I don't see why I should trail around after you."

"We're *children,*" Amelia said.

"Yeh, well, you're not babies, are you. We've got three months here, and if we're going to get through them, you're going to have to give me some help, take some responsibility." He looked at each of them in turn. "Charlie?"

"OK," he said, looking down again, his face closed. Hugh hadn't meant to scare him, and he smiled, although Charlie wasn't looking, tried to soften his tone.

"Good," he told his brother, and looked to Amelia. "How about you?"

She sighed in martyred acceptance. "I guess. It's not how a mum would do it, though."

"It's how my mum did it," Hugh realized. "More or less. And it's the only way I know. Take it or leave it."

"All *right,*" she said. "I *get* it. *Geez.*"

a big night out

♡

Hugh leant against the railing of Koti James's expansive deck a couple blocks back from the beach in Takapuna, where he, Nic Wilkinson, and Hemi Ranapia were "helping" their teammate with a Saturday-night barbecue. Which actually meant drinking beer and watching Koti barbecue, but supervision counted.

At least somebody else was cooking. They'd been OK on Thursday, because there'd still been some steak and salad in the fridge, some kumara in the pantry, and he'd fixed those, since that was about his skill level in the kitchen. But on Friday, when Amelia and Hugh's own stomach had reminded him that it was dinnertime, he'd been confronted by a pretty limited offering.

"How is there nothing left?" he asked in frustration. "There's not even any bread and cheese in here. And I thought there was some ham." He'd had lunch out after his visit to the physio, hadn't looked until now.

"We took it for lunch," Amelia said. "Didn't you shop?"

"No," he said, only a little sarcastically. "Obviously, I didn't."

She sighed. "You have to *shop*, Hugh."

He could see that. And that he'd have to think about what they were having for dinner before it was actually time for dinner, too. It was quite a bit different from keeping his fridge stocked for himself, and one hell of a lot different from having Aunt Cora keep it stocked for all of them. He'd ended up taking the kids to the pub for dinner, and this morning, he'd taken them to New World.

"Why do we have to come?" Amelia had asked. "I want to go to Pippa's house. We're working on a project for school."

"You'll have to go later," Hugh said. "Right now, we're buying groceries, and you two are helping, no arguments. Because," he'd amended, seeing Charlie's face, "you know what you want to take for lunch, what we're out of. Another list. Breakfast, lunch, dinner, what do we need?" He sat back down at the table. "Come on and help me make it."

So that had been not too bad, though he'd got home and realized they were out of coffee, and nearly out of eggs as well, and had had to go straight back again. He was glad to have been invited to dinner tonight, and even gladder that he'd been able to bring the kids, because he didn't know what he'd have done with them otherwise.

"I don't have a babysitter," he'd told Koti when the other man had invited him a couple days earlier.

"Do you need a babysitter?"

"I do now. Alone with my brother and sister for a bit."

"No worries. Bring them along. Heaps of kids. Your two'll make nine all told, counting the babies. I'll get an extra pizza, and we're all good."

Hugh had accepted gratefully, and Charlie and Amelia had been borne off into the nether regions of Koti's house by Ariana, Hemi and Reka's eldest, with a proprietorial air that suggested Amelia might have met her match.

"Whoa. New blood. Nobody told me there were going to be so many big fellas," Nic said now as Will Tawera, 1.95 meters of hard-kicking, hard-tackling No. 10, came through the ranch sliders onto the deck together with Finn Douglas.

Hugh offered a handshake and a word of welcome to Will, the Blues' much-hoped-for new acquisition from the Queensland

Reds, here in Auckland to discuss a deal for the following season. Hugh meant to do his bit to woo him, because they needed Will. The loss of Hemi this year at first-five, the critical No. 10 position that provided a team with its on-field general, had been a blow from which the Blues hadn't yet recovered. The addition of Will, along with Hugh's own ongoing help in shoring up the forward pack and providing a bit of leadership to a young squad, could make next season look a much brighter prospect.

He could see what Nic had been talking about, too. Will was one of the good-sized breed of 10, and there was even more of Finn than there was of Will. The deck was suddenly looking a bit crowded with rugby muscle.

"Speak for yourself, Nico," Koti said. "The rest of us aren't intimidated by a couple of blokes with a glandular disorder and a suspicious slope to their foreheads. Just because you're such a scrawny fella."

"I am not scrawny," Nic said. "I am a lithe and nimble fullback. Bashing it up the guts may be the only way a musclebound centre like you knows how to do it, to say nothing of the forwards, but those of us with more finesse can pick our routes with a bit more brainpower. *And* I've got the best boot here, I'll just point out. Barring Hemi, of course. Wouldn't want to go up against you even now," he told his former No. 10.

"Nah," Hemi said. "I'm retired. I don't have to prove it anymore. I've earned the luxury of sitting back and criticizing."

"Cheers, Nico," Will complained. "You mean the best boot except Hemi and me."

"Oh, yeh?" Nic said with a grin. "You want a competition for that goal-kicking spot, you know what you need to do."

"No argument from me either way," Finn said. "Because my kicking's always been shocking. And I'm not a forward anymore, am I, slope to my forehead or otherwise. My job now is cracking the whip on you lazy buggers, and I do my best to be an equal-opportunity taskmaster. How's your head, Koti, by the way?"

"You know," Koti shrugged. "Getting there. Be ready to get stuck in when training starts up again, and I'll be on the Tour, no worries. But first, family time. You bring the kids?"

"Yeh. Jenna took them on back to find the pizza. I should warn you, Nico, Harry's got a big Lego book with him he wanted to share with Zack."

Nic groaned. "Exactly what he doesn't need to see. Going to break me. He can hardly find a path to his bed as it is."

"How the mighty have fallen, eh, Koti," Will told his host. "Your entertaining style's a bit of a change from the old days." They'd been teammates when Koti had been with the Chiefs, Hugh remembered, and yeh, he could recall a few parties back in the day, after the Hurricanes had played the Chiefs. Both Will and Koti probably had an incident or two they were just as glad had never hit the press.

"Shh," Koti said with a laugh. "We don't talk about that anymore." He pointed with his tongs to the chilly bin filled with ice, then returned to the huge barbecue, turned over hefty chunks of chicken, added thick rounds of tender eye fillet.

"Does everybody here have kids?" Will asked, helping himself to a beer. "Because I'm getting a bad feeling about this party."

Hugh could relate. He'd been to the odd barbecue or picnic before with the vague knowledge that his teammates' kids were somewhere about the place, but he'd never paid any more attention than that. He felt like he was sitting at the parents' table, and he wasn't at all sure he liked it.

"Pretty much," Koti said. "I asked some of the single boys along tonight, but they realized how family-friendly it'd be, decided on a piss-up instead, I wouldn't be surprised."

"Don't say that," Nic said. "First you invite the conditioning coach, then you tell him about everyone's plans to get out of condition, not to mention having him eyeing us the whole time, counting the beers?"

"If I'm drinking along with you, you're safe," Finn said, popping the top on a Monteith's Black. "And I'm not concerned about the others, not tonight. What I don't know, I can't patrol. I don't have to worry about Hemi anymore, either. He can get pissed, get fat too for all I care."

"Yeh, but I answer to a higher power," Hemi said.

"Didn't realize you were that religious," Will said.

Hemi smiled. "Not the higher power I had in mind."

"Ah." Will looked a bit mystified still, but the other men laughed.

"Anyway," Finn said, "we're all on holiday. Except maybe Hemi. Cheers." He drained what looked like a good third of the bottle, to Hugh's practiced eye. Well, they said there wasn't enough beer in the world to make a loose forward tight, especially not one the size of Finn.

"Where did you say this other party was?" Will asked, a comical expression on his handsome face. "The one without supervision, and with single people?"

"I'm a single person," Hugh pointed out.

"Yeh, well, you're not the exact type of single person I had in mind."

"You just need to get married, Will," Koti said. "Then you'd have the right kind of somebody to bring along, and fewer decisions to make as well."

"I heard that." His wife Kate, a pretty brunette with a personality as large as her frame was tiny, came out onto the deck.

"Close to done here," Koti said. "Everything moving along in there?"

"Are you kidding? What little Reka allowed me to do, I turned over to Jenna the moment she arrived. Couple minutes. We'll give you a shout when we're ready."

She headed back inside, and Will watched her go. "Don't think being married would suit me," he said. "Maybe in ten years or so. When I'm elderly, like certain formerly loose forwards I could name." He gave his prospective conditioning coach a cheeky grin that made Hugh suspect Finn would be setting him right in the gym before very long at all. "Having too good a time right now, and one woman for the rest of my life? Nah. Can't see it. And kids—I'm *really* not ready for that."

Finn leaned against the deck rail, lifted his beer bottle to Hugh. "Speaking of kids, how ya going with yours, Hugh? Jenna was asking."

"Didn't know you had kids," Will said. "Plural kids?"

"My brother and sister," Hugh said. "Back there." He gestured with his own bottle.

"Oh. I thought you meant they were yours," Will said.

"My father and stepmother died a year or so back," Hugh explained, "so I'm living there right now. They're my half-sister and brother, actually."

"That's rough," Will said.

"Not so bad. It does put a crimp in the dating life, though. I like fast women, that's my problem. They used to like me, too," he said with a reminiscent sigh. "But you ought to see them run in the opposite direction now, when they find out. You know that thing when you go out with someone, and you can tell she's sizing you up as the future father of her children?"

"If they are, I'm looking the other way," Will laughed.

"Or they may just not want your dodgy genes in their pool," Hugh suggested with a grin of his own. "But what's worse than that is when you can tell they *don't* want anything to do with the kids you actually do have around."

"May be time to consider a slow woman instead," Finn said. "That little thing called getting to know somebody first? She may even like the kids, you never know."

"Think that'd work?" Hugh asked. "Get one of those sweet, motherly ones, one who wants to be home with kids who aren't hers half the time while I travel, who wants to make those home-cooked meals? And still look good, of course. That's the tricky bit."

"A hot babe who's going to want to take care of you and a couple of kids who aren't hers into the bargain, let you shove them off on her?" Will asked. "That's a pretty sketch plan you've got."

Hugh didn't answer, because he'd got rattled at realizing he'd just described Finn's wife, and that the other man was looking a bit grim. Finn grim wasn't a sight he'd ever relished on the paddock when he'd been playing against him, and he wasn't enjoying the sight of it now.

And then it got worse, because he heard a small voice at his elbow. "'Scuse me."

He turned to see Charlie, and his brother's thin face didn't look happy at all.

"How long have you been standing there?" Hugh asked him. "What did you hear?"

Charlie shrugged. "Dunno."

Hugh closed his eyes for a second. *Shit.* "Something wrong back there?" he asked. "Need something?"

"That baby's crying," Charlie said. "In its room. I thought I should say."

"Which one?" Hemi asked.

Koti had a look at the box set up on the table. Some kind of monitor, Hugh guessed, because it was flashing red. "Whoops. Falling down on the job, aren't I." He handed the tongs to Finn. "Finish this meat, will you? I'll go check."

"So, Charlie," Finn said, turning steaks with a practiced hand. "Think your brother should get married?" Tackling the problem the same way he tackled everything, Hugh realized. Head-on.

"Yeh," Charlie said with decision.

"Got any candidates in mind?" Finn asked. "That can be the best way," he informed Hugh. "Get the experts' opinion. May not be who you're thinking."

"He should marry Josie," Charlie said. "She'd be the best."

"Who's Josie?" Hugh asked. "I don't know any Josie."

"She's Miss Chloe's friend. You know, Miss Chloe, Amelia's dance teacher."

"I know who Miss Chloe is," Hugh protested. "And a dance teacher might be all right." Miss Chloe would be all right, in fact. More than all right. And she taught kids. That could be the sweet, motherly thing right there.

Charlie considered. "I don't think she's a dance teacher herself," he said fairly. "I think she's too big. And she's all...sort of soft-looking. I don't think she could be a dancer."

Hugh was getting the picture. Probably looked like the backside of a bus.

"But she has such a pretty face," Will said. "And a great personality, eh."

"Yeh. She has the kind of face I like. Kind of friendly and smiley," Charlie said. "Sort of jolly."

Definitely the backside of a bus.

Koti came back out onto the deck, his baby daughter wrapped in a blanket in his arms, only an unhappy little face and a halo of black curls visible. She was fussing a bit, gnawing on one tiny fist.

"Can you finish up?" Koti asked Finn. "I need to take her to Kate. Anika's still asleep," he told Hemi. "Clearly, you train them better than I do."

"No worries," Finn said, transferring an eye fillet to a platter. "We'll do our best to save you a steak, though I'm not making any promises."

Kate chose that moment to turn up again, however. "Good to go," she informed her husband. "Oh. Maia wake up? Talk about timing. Just when we're sitting down to eat, as usual."

"All changed and ready for you," Koti said.

"Time to head on back with the rest of the kids, Charlie," Hugh said. He knew he should say something else, something positive, but he couldn't think what.

"I'll come with you," Kate said. "I need to take this little monster back and feed her. That's the only way I ever manage to pry her away from Koti, she's such a Daddy's girl. I can't imagine what she'll be like when she's five."

She took the baby from Koti's arms. "You're going to be toast," she told him.

He grinned. "Pushed around by strong women. It's my curse."

♡

So there he was, Hugh thought as he did the fifteen-minute drive down the North Shore to Devonport after a grand total of two and a half beers over four hours, two sleepy kids in the back seat, barely nine-thirty and his evening, such as it was, over, and what lay ahead not looking much better.

He'd go to training with the others for the bare week they'd put in before the squad left for Europe, offer what help he could, and then they'd be gone, and he'd be spending an unaccustomed and most unwelcome November in New Zealand. The team, some team, anyway, had been his real family for his entire adult life, and missing a tour, particularly such an important one, being left behind, was going to leave a hole that he didn't want to examine and didn't know how to fill.

He knew how he *wasn't* filling it, anyway, and if this were going to be his life, he might as well be married after all. Will was right, it was hard to imagine one woman for the rest of it, but at least he might get lucky now and again. Because unless somebody actually came to his door and invited him to have it off with her then and there, or had her way with him in the vegie aisle of New World, it didn't look like happening. How did single dads do it?

He needed a babysitter, that was all. Then he could try chatting up Chloe again after Amelia's next lesson, invite her for a drink. Or a coffee first, maybe. Take it slow like Finn had said, loosen up a bit of that reserve. If he still remembered how to be charming, which he doubted. He wasn't feeling too charming. He was feeling decidedly grumpy, what with the injury, the kids, and the lack of sleep. Not to mention the lack of sex.

Yeh, a babysitter would help, he thought with more optimism. Maybe the mysterious Josie. Soft, jolly, and Charlie's kind of woman? She'd do.

♡

His more cheerful mood was immediately put to the test when his mum called the next morning and he was forced to explain his new circumstances to her.

"*What?*" she asked, the outrage coming straight through the phone. "How could she possibly expect that of you?"

"Well, she has a point." And here he was, in the middle once again. He stepped out onto the patio so the kids wouldn't hear, because he had a feeling this was a conversation that wouldn't do Charlie any good at all. "She *has* been here doing this for eighteen months, and she probably does need a break."

His mum snorted. "A break from what, I'd like to know. Some of us manage to raise children on our own while we work more than full-time, with a man who can barely be troubled to send a check, much less lend a hand or, God knows, get involved. And there she's been, not a single thing in the world to do except look after two nearly-grown kids and a bit of housework and cooking, with you paying all the bills, and now even that's too much to ask and she can just waltz off for three months, while your hand's broken? It's just so typical of that whole family to leave you holding the bag for everything, it makes my blood boil."

"Mum," he cautioned her. "This doesn't help."

She wasn't listening, though. "I thought it was bad enough when you moved. What obligation did you have? How much was your dad there for you?"

"Not much," he said. "Maybe that's why I had to do it. And it hasn't been so bad."

"It hasn't," she said flatly. "Twenty-seven years old, your whole career, your whole future ahead of you, making a change that did nothing but set you back, sacrificing everything for a couple of kids who aren't yours, who've barely been part of your life, because your dad couldn't be bothered to have you around more than a couple weeks a year? Doing all that for the kids who had everything you didn't?"

"If they did," he said, "they don't have it now." He'd heard it all before, and it was more than time to shut it down. "And the other isn't true either. The move's given me a chance to make a real impact. I've got the opportunity here to help turn a team around. I believe in what we're trying to do, and I'll be in there playing my guts out to make it happen next season. That'll be good for my career, no worries. There's more to this game than winning the championship. There's being a winner when you're losing, too. And that's what the All Blacks are for, anyway," he said, trying to joke. "To give you more of those wins."

She snorted. "And how's that been going for you?"

"Grinding out the tough wins," he said, "coming back strong from the losses, that builds a team too. We're getting there, wait and see. You're going to have to trust me on this one, Mum. I don't need any sympathy, and I'm well suited where I am." Maybe he was and maybe he wasn't, but whingeing about it to his mummy wasn't going to help one bit.

"Do you want me to come up and help?" she asked.

"Uh..." That one took him by surprise. "Would you be able to?"

"Well," she admitted, "it'd be tough. I just got a big commission to do a group of model homes, and they're on a timetable. But I could do some juggling and carve out a few days, maybe even a week."

"No," he decided, "thanks anyway, but I'm here, they're in school, and we'll get through it, one way or another." And he didn't trust the way she'd treat the kids. She wouldn't be unkind, no. She'd be brisk, and managing, and impatient. He wasn't at all sure he knew what Charlie needed, but he could tell he didn't need that. "It'll be three months. May as well start as we mean to go on."

"You could get a nanny," she suggested. "Or even just a housekeeper."

"There's a cleaning service coming in already," he said. "Every week, so that's not too bad."

She snorted. "Of course there is. Why am I not surprised? But still, darling. Hire a housekeeper, somebody to look after them. It's not your job, and really, how fit are you to do it?"

He didn't know if it was the assumption that he was incapable that aroused his admittedly fierce competitive instincts, or something deeper, but he found himself making a hundred-eighty-degree turn from his feelings of the night before. "No," he said. "I'm pretty sure it's better if I'm...well, here, at least, while Aunt Cora isn't. And if they see that I am, too. We're getting the hang of it, anyway. How hard could it be? But maybe I could bring them down at Christmas."

"Oh, dear," she said, and she did actually sound distressed. "I was planning to treat myself to a Samoa holiday this year, and I already booked it, leaving just before the holiday. Maybe just after that. I don't have room for the kids here, as you know, but you all could do a hotel. Or you could come after Cora got back, give us a real chance to catch up."

Without the kids, he didn't need to hear. He couldn't imagine them on her pristine white couches and cream carpets anyway.

Every silk-covered cushion in its place, a disaster waiting to happen. The décor had been a bit more child-friendly when he'd been growing up, but the posh new City pied-a-terre she'd bought once her career had blossomed was anything but.

"All right, then," he said. "We'll plan on catching up after the holiday."

"Call me if you need advice, though," she hastened to say. "I'm always here for you."

"Yeh," he said. "Thanks. Talk to you soon."

the backside of a bus

♡

He was hearing music in his dream. A beautiful Maori woman wearing a flax dress was singing a waiata, bare shoulders and a delicious swell of breasts above the low neckline, appearing and disappearing coyly through the waves of rich, dark hair as she went through the movements of the dance. Her hips were swaying, her rounded arms were swinging the poi, making intricate patterns in the air to accompany her song. She was looking at him, lips curving, eyes beckoning him as she sang and moved so gracefully, yet with so much seductive purpose. It was a good dream.

And then the music changed, and she was singing, for some bizarre reason, "I'm Your Man," by Wham!, and it jarred him out of sleep.

There really *was* a woman singing, he realized, and, yes, she was singing "I'm Your Man." Why? His window was open, and it sounded like she was singing it in his ear. He struggled up in bed, shut the window, tried to go back to sleep and failed, because he could still hear her, and she wouldn't shut up.

Bloody hell. Devonport, at—he glanced at the clock—five o'clock Monday morning. Of all the boring, decorous, ridiculously charming villages in New Zealand, he lived in the most boring, decorous, ridiculously charming one, and yet some drunken woman was singing in the street.

When it didn't stop, when she went straight into "Waterloo," a song he loathed with the burning passion of a thousand fiery suns, and that he knew would now be stuck in his head all day, he swore aloud, threw the sheet back and swung his legs out of bed. He'd been sleeping in his boxer briefs, as usual, and he struggled to pull a gray T-shirt over his head with one hand, grabbed a pair of navy-blue rugby shorts and yanked them up, thought about jandals and his sling but decided not to bother, and left the room.

No sound from the kids. They were asleep in their lovely quiet rooms at the back of the house. Lucky them. He opened the front door, looked out. The street was empty, the dairy across the road still dark as well. But the singing was still going on, although fainter here, and he realized it was coming from the house next door. Mrs. Alberts' house. Since when did Mrs. Alberts belt out bad eighties pop at five o'clock in the morning?

He hesitated, but he was annoyed now. The jet lag had got him again, that and the ache from his hand. He'd tossed and turned half the night, started worrying, despite his words to his mother, about how he was meant to cope with the kids until Aunt Cora came back, especially if Charlie was going to be so withdrawn and Amelia so downright snotty. Then he'd got onto what Luke Hoeata was going to be doing to contest the starting No. 7 spot while Hugh was out of it, and that had chased the sleep away for good, the troubles, as always, seeming insurmountable in the dark of night. He'd finally fallen into a deep sleep only what had felt like twenty minutes ago, and now he was awake because Mrs. Alberts had to sing?

He debated waiting until later, having a civil chat, but she wasn't singing later, she was singing *now*, and he didn't appreciate it. He made up his mind, trotted down the steps, across the narrow drive that separated the villas, and up onto the porch of the house next door.

Mrs. Alberts needed to paint, he reflected as he rang the doorbell. The frame was flaking a bit, he could see in the gray light of dawn. Didn't she have kids, grandkids to see to that? He probably should've been paying more attention.

No answer, and he rang again, knocked for good measure.

Footsteps on the other side at last. "Who is it?" He heard the muffled voice, sounding warier than seemed necessary in Devonport.

"Hugh." He waited, then added, "Your neighbor." She'd been living next door since well before his dad had bought the house, had always looked old enough to have been there since her own tiny villa was built. She ought to know who he was. Had she got senile while he'd been on tour? Was that the reason for the newly acquired musical habit, and the odd hours?

The door opened a cautious crack, the chain on, but he couldn't really see beyond it, because he was standing in the porch light, and the hall behind the door was dark.

He tried to look less thunderous than he felt. Abusing elderly ladies wasn't really on, and he felt a little embarrassed by his temper. "It's your neighbor Hugh," he said again. "I just thought...something might be wrong." He tried a smile. "That you were calling for help." *Or wailing like a banshee.*

The door shut. Oh, no. She really *had* gone senile. Completely round the bend, singing at the top of her lungs in the middle of the night, forgetting who he was, slamming the door on him. Wonderful. Another thing he would probably have to do something about.

He heard the rasp of the chain sliding through the groove, and the door opened fully, and he forgot all about Mrs. Alberts.

Because standing on the other side of the door, still holding the knob, was somebody who most definitely was *not* Mrs. Alberts, and couldn't possibly have been a relation, either. Because she was the woman in his dream, pretty much. The woman, his befuddled mind realized, whom he'd seen at the dance recital the other night. Dark hair falling in tousled waves down her back, glowing, glorious golden skin, huge, wide-set brown eyes and a long, straight, perfectly carved nose, a pair of aristocratic cheekbones that looked like they could slice a man in two. And a wide, lush mouth that conjured up every inappropriate image it shouldn't, all in one single, powerful moment that got a response from his body that Mrs. Alberts had definitely never aroused.

And that was just her face. She was wearing a short, silky robe that stopped at the top of her slim thighs, her legs were long, the sash was pulled around a narrow waist, and there was a fair amount of cleavage revealed in the vee where the two sides of the robe came together. Until she saw the direction of his gaze and yanked the sash a bit tighter, that is.

He jerked his eyes back to her face, shut the mouth that he was very much afraid had been gaping. "Uh...sorry," he said. "I thought you were Mrs. Alberts."

One hand was on her hip now, and the exotically tilted brown eyes were cool, the smile curving the unpainted mouth a bit mocking. She wasn't wearing any makeup at all, he realized, and yet she looked like that. "Well, I'm not. As you see. Can I help you?"

Bloody hell, yes, you can help me. He didn't say it, of course. "Are you...visiting?" he tried next. "Oh. I'm Hugh, from next door." He jerked his head to the left in mute explanation, then realized it was the third time he'd introduced himself, and felt like a fool.

She looked a bit confused herself now. "I thought Cora Middleton lived next door with a couple of kids."

"My aunt," he explained. "I'm those kids' elder brother."

"Ah. Which explains your reluctant presence at the recital." So she remembered him too, though not in the way he could have hoped.

"That's it."

"Well…" She put out a slim hand to him and he took it reflexively, felt her give his a brisk, businesslike shake. He wanted to hold on, but he didn't. Of course he didn't. "Josie Pae Ata," she said, glancing quickly up at him—not as far up as most women, because, as he'd noticed the other night, she was tall—her shoulders relaxing fractionally, for some reason, when he didn't offer whatever reaction she'd evidently been expecting. She probably *had* expected him to keep holding her hand. Probably happened to her all the time.

And she didn't know who he was, he realized. That was unusual.

"Mrs. Alberts moved," she said now. "I bought the house. If you live next door, I'm surprised you didn't know that."

She didn't *believe* him? "I've been away for a bit," he tried to explain.

"Must have been quite a bit. I've been living here for weeks."

"It was. Quite a bit. Wait." His sluggish mind finally made the connection. "You're Josie? Charlie's Josie?"

Her smile wasn't mocking now, it was genuine. "Oh. Charlie's your brother. You really *do* live next door, then."

"Of course I live next door." *The backside of a bus,* he remembered. This was Charlie's idea of "a jolly face?" Not to mention "big" and "soft-looking." His brother needed to work on his communication skills.

"And much as I'd like to stand here chatting with my new neighbor," she said, the cool dismissal back on her face, "it's not precisely visiting hours, so maybe you could move this conversation along a bit."

"Uh…yeh." He tried to remember why he was here. "I heard you singing."

"And you thought I was calling for help," she said, and the smile was *definitely* mocking now.

"Because…five A.M."

"Oh. Sorry." She looked a bit chagrined. "I'm used to sound-proofing, I suppose. Did I wake you?"

"Well, yeh. Because my bedroom must be straight across from yours. Not your fault." It wasn't? It had felt like it.

"It's just…that's how I wake up," she explained. "Singing, and stretches. I'll remember you're listening, do my best to keep it down from here on."

"Got the early shift, eh," he said, not wanting to let her go. Stretches? He'd like to see the stretches.

"Something like that." The cool smile was back, and the door was closing. "And I'd better get on with it. Nice to meet you, Hugh."

weeing round the boundaries

♡

"Morning, Josie-Girl." Clive breezed into the makeup room, gave her a kiss on top of her head, careful not to disturb Gregor, the makeup artist who was brushing the heavy foundation onto Josie's face. "Looks like you're torturing me again today. But I am, of course, resisting heroically."

She smiled. "I'm counting on you to put up a gallant fight against being pulled into my web. For as long as the writers can drag it out, anyway. You know I'll have my wicked way with you eventually. Want me to run lines with you later?"

"Yeh. Got yours sorted already, have you, Encyclopedia Brain?"

"My superpower," she said modestly. She'd always been able to memorize quickly, and in the world of daily television, it was a precious talent to have.

He laughed and flung himself down beside her. "Thanks. You're a love. We'll steam it up, and before you know it, we'll be making Derek jealous, get him coming back across the Ditch to defend your honor."

Josie laughed. "I think he's well beyond jealousy by now. Let's hope so."

"How is Australia's newest and finest talent?" Clive asked.

"Run off his feet, he says," Josie said, careful to move only her lips as Gregor brushed shadow onto her eyelids, blended it with his usual quick expertise. "Fourteen-hour days, already hotter than your dad's cowshed in January on the set, even though it's nowhere near summer, and he said there was a bit of an episode with leeches. Had him shuddering on the other end of the phone, I could tell."

And not happy that she hadn't been quite as sympathetic as he could have liked. "You just pull them off, though, don't you?" she'd asked when he'd told her.

"It isn't quite as easy as that," he'd answered. "We didn't all grow up in the bush, you know. If you had a vampire bat latch onto you, you'd have found out it was some tribal cure and been pleased to have the cultural experience."

"I didn't think we were talking about a vampire bat," she said. "Thought this was leeches."

"Yeh, it was leeches," he said. "And next time they have me go in that water, it'll be crocs, no doubt. Maybe that'll get a reaction out of you."

"When you're bitten by a croc," she said, "I promise to take notice. Sorry, I'm sure it was awful."

"I'm sorry too," he said. "I'm shattered, that's all."

"How's Vanessa taking it?" Josie asked. "Was she in the leeches too?"

"She was, because I was kissing her under a waterfall. Romantic, eh. Sexy. Not too sexy when you have slugs latched onto your legs, swelling up on your life's blood."

She laughed again. "Ugh. Did you cope, though? Manage to be romantic after all? You can be a pretty romantic fella when you put your mind to it."

"*I* did. *She* didn't. Not a hearty country girl like you. I had to carry her out of there, she was shaking and screaming so hard. They're having to scout another location, because she refused to get back in."

"Hard luck. Still, it gave you a chance to be extra-manly and heroic, and that's a good look on you."

"So they say," he said. "Found the bright side, didn't you?"

"That's my job in this partnership," she said. "Designated sunshine."

♡

"Guess you'll find out how he is at the weekend," Clive said now as Gregor finished up and Josie rose from the chair with a smile of thanks, let Clive take her place. "This is the big visit, right? After how long?"

"A month. And no." She sat down beside him, concentrated on the sight of Gregor adjusting the smock carefully around Clive's tanned neck. "They've had so many problems with the filming, they're carrying on with the location work. So it'll have to wait."

"Again?" Clive's eyes darted to hers in the mirror.

"Yeh. Oh, well, can't be helped," she said, pasting a smile on her face. "We'll get it next week. He's suffering more than I am. I'm lonely, that's all, and from the sound of it, he's being eaten alive by the Aussie wildlife."

"Couldn't you go anyway?" Clive asked. "They've got to be giving them a day off, at least."

"Yeh, nah. Too long to get there, and anyway, he says he just wants to sleep."

"You know what I'm going to say," he told her.

"That he's not that into me. That's not it. I've told you, we don't have that kind of relationship. We're easy-peasy. Comfortable."

"I know, you're low-maintenance Josie, comforter of the down-hearted, soup-bringer and plaster-provider. Every man's dream, their fondly-remembered kindy teacher's heart in Angelina Jolie's body. But..." He hesitated, unusually for Clive. "We've been friends a long time, and I hope good ones. Can I say this?"

"Go ahead," she said, and braced herself, her heart pounding a little despite her best efforts at calm unconcern.

"That's exactly why he should be begging you to come, doing whatever it takes to get you there," Clive said. "He should be worried about leaving you over here by yourself, for God's sake. Why isn't he? Not like he doesn't have competition. If I *weren't* actually a married man, you know I'd have tried it on by now."

"Nah, you wouldn't. We know each other too well. Practically brother and sister, aren't we."

He laughed, got a disapproving cluck from Gregor. "Not quite. You underestimate the effect you have. Even on me, sad to say. Not as impervious as that, not yet. Still looking at the menu, even if I'm not ordering. How many times do you get chatted up, anyplace you go?"

"Heaps," she admitted. "But that's been happening since I was fourteen, and Derek knows it. I wouldn't, and he knows that, too."

"That's the problem," Clive insisted. "He knows it. Better if he weren't quite so sure of you. Takes you for granted, doesn't he. How long's it been?"

"Almost three years," she said. "Which you know." Seeing as how their romance had blossomed under the rest of the cast's nose.

"And...sorry, darling, but has he talked about making it permanent? Did you buy that new house of yours together? D'you have a ring I haven't seen?"

She flushed a bit under the heavy makeup. "You know I don't. We haven't got there yet."

"Because you don't want to? Not thinking about kids, staring down the barrel at thirty like you are? That it?"

"You trying to depress me?" she asked him, attempting to rally. "How'm I meant to cheer the place up today if you get me moping about?"

"Well, why hasn't he pushed for it, then?" Clive insisted. "Because he doesn't think he has to, that's why. Men want to have to compete for the prize. We want to win, and we want to beat the other blokes out for it. We want to have to fight for it."

"Is this meant to be a relationship, or a sporting match?"

"I didn't say it was politically correct. I said it was true. Am I right or am I right, Gregor?" Clive asked the makeup artist who was working on his eyes now.

"You're right," Gregor confirmed. "Sad but true."

"Since I've stuck my neck out this far," Clive said, "may as well go all the way. I'd do something about that, if I were you."

"Like what? Have an affair? Start flirting with other blokes? How's that going to improve my relationship?"

"I'm not talking about that. Just a little…uncertainty. We can't actually make him jealous with me, alas. Much as I love you, my darling, I'm not willing to risk my own hard-won marriage over you. But you could mention somebody else, next time you're on the phone. Just casually, get his antennae quivering, get him wondering a bit, give him a reason to think that seeing you might rate above a lovely long sleep. Try Trevor, maybe, eh, Gregor."

Gregor put his head on one side. "Maybe," he said dubiously.

Josie made a little face. "Don't think I could pull that off." Trevor was the show's resident heartthrob, playing a fit paramedic who created almost as much havoc as Josie's character amongst his colleagues at the hospital. Unfortunately, he thought as much of himself as his eager fans did, and Derek knew it.

"Somebody, then," Clive said. "You can't lack for somebodies."

"I could mention my new neighbor," she admitted reluctantly. "He'd do."

"Good?" Clive asked, a look of decided interest on his clean-cut face.

"Oh, yeh. Good."

Good wasn't the half of it. When she'd peered out from behind the chain that morning and caught sight of said neighbor taking up far too much space under the glow of her porch light, looking so incongruous amidst the spindles and ornately curved woodwork of her chocolate-box villa's front porch, she really *had* almost shut the door on him. It had taken some effort to open it again, to assume the amused detachment in the face of masculine interest that she'd been practicing for more than fifteen years now and had down to an art form.

It wasn't that he was so good-looking, because he wasn't, not really. He was a *man,* that was all, in a way that so many of her actor friends, gorgeous as they might be, couldn't match.

The size of him, for one thing. The bulk of his arms, the width of the chest straining that plain gray T-shirt—a chest she'd be willing to bet he'd never waxed in his life—and the extent to which she'd had to look up to see his face.

And what she'd seen when she'd looked. A nose that was probably too big, too uncompromising, a little crooked, too. Eyes that were definitely too deep-set under the brows that nearly met in the middle, but were so dark, their expression so intense. And then that firm mouth in the midst of the dark shadow of beard covering the square chin and jaw. That wasn't bad either.

All in all, it was a pretty potent package, and that was before she'd opened the door the rest of the way and really looked at all of him. She'd restrained herself from glancing below the waist, but she hadn't been able to help wondering. Because he was *big.*

Stop that, she chided herself. It was nothing other than idle curiosity, and anyway, size didn't matter, any more than her own fair-sized breasts offered anything more truly satisfying to a man than any other woman's, once the looking was done. And she didn't do this. She was happily involved in a mutually satisfying long-term relationship, and she'd never got around much anyway. She was reasonably intelligent—all right, more than reasonably—but you didn't have to be a rocket scientist to know that most men had pretty much one thought in their head when they looked at her, and Hugh had been no exception, that was obvious. She hadn't missed the way his eyes had lingered on those same breasts, because he clearly hadn't got the memo about size not mattering. But instead of the faint contempt she normally felt at the attention she inevitably aroused, she'd been...Well, face it. She'd been aroused.

It had been too long, clearly. She had a partner that any woman in New Zealand would have given her eyeteeth to be with. Tall, dark, and handsome, that was Derek, and perfectly satisfactory in the size department as well, if it came to that. If she turned heads, so did he, and it had always been a comfort and a relief to know she was with the one man who wasn't awestruck by her looks, because he was exactly as beautiful himself. They were a matched set, and that had always worked for her. And it still did.

Anyway, what did she know about Hugh? That he lived with his aunt, brother, and sister, some of the time, when he wasn't "away"? That he could barely sit still for his sister's recital piece? Probably dragged there kicking and screaming. Probably on the dole, judging by that shaggy head of hair and the beard. Probably spent his time fishing off the jetty, when he wasn't lifting weights in some mate's homemade gym to build that physique, spending his evenings drinking beer in somebody's basement. Probably broke that hand punching his fist through the wall while he was drunk. She'd gone to school with boys like that, who'd grown into men like that. Responsibility wasn't high on their list, and nor was career focus. And they were definitely, most definitely, not her type.

♡

"Yeh, he looks good enough. Not that I'm tempted. But I couldn't use anybody anyway," she told Clive now. "Not sure I could play this game at all, really. Not fair to either of them, is it, and I don't like women who manipulate men."

"You don't have to use anybody," Clive promised. "You aren't manipulating, or if you are, only a weeny little bit, not enough to count. Just mention him. Just drop him into the conversation. How helpful he's been, how he offered to mow your grass."

"To mow my *grass?*"

Clive waved an airy hand. "If I had a neighbor as fit as you? First thing I'd do is tell her I had the mower out anyway, why don't I do her garden at the same time as mine, because it's really no trouble at all. Take my shirt off while I did it, maybe. Before you know it, she's inviting me into the kitchen, offering me a cuppa, one thing leads to another…"

Josie laughed. "So that offer's a signal Derek will recognize as a threat, and he'll want to come back and wee around the boundaries to let the other dogs know this is his territory, that what you're saying? Because my neighbor offered to cut my grass?"

"That's *exactly* what I'm saying. Mention. And see if I'm not right."

team effort

♡

When he was awoken by the insistent *beep-beep-beep* of a reversing truck, followed by a metallic grinding that boded no good at all, Hugh wasn't, somehow, entirely surprised. This had been his first chance to sleep past seven since Aunt Cora had left, so naturally there would be a truck making what sounded like the delivery of a lifetime to the dairy, first thing Saturday morning.

When he got outside, though, it wasn't the dairy at all. It was Josie's house, and the truck whose liftgate was now lowered to the street, allowing the driver to hop into a forklift and maneuver it onto the road, was apparently delivering her a very large early Christmas present, judging from her look of excitement as she hustled backwards to get out of the way.

More beeping from the forklift, more maneuvering, and the first of two shrink-wrapped pallets was deposited in her driveway with the man headed back for the second.

She caught sight of Hugh, raised a hand in greeting, and he crossed the few meters of footpath to join her, wishing he'd combed his hair. Or even cut it, as Amelia had suggested. Shaved, maybe, because he had a feeling he looked like a wild man. And she looked as choice as always.

Not wearing the silky robe today, unfortunately, but then, if she greeted a deliveryman dressed like that, the bloke would never leave. No, she was in a deep red T-shirt, well-worn brown shorts, and work boots, her hair pulled back in a knot, and she shouldn't have looked nearly as good as she did. She looked like a Hollywood actress playing the part of an undercover cop posing as a site inspector, the casting and the deception both ridiculously improbable.

"Morning," he said with his usual impressive form, once he reached her.

"Morning." She glanced quickly at him, then back at the driver again. "Woke you again, eh."

He raked a hand through his mess of hair, doing his best to finger-comb it into place. "Could be."

"Sorry. This was the only delivery time they had. Least I let you sleep the rest of the week. Did my singing at the back of the house," she explained.

He nodded. He'd looked out for her, actually. But her car, a not-new Toyota Corolla wagon, had always been gone from the drive by the time he'd left the house for his early-morning walk up Mt. Victoria, even though it was only six-thirty. She really *did* have the early shift. Didn't get home early, though, because the car hadn't been back again until seven-thirty or eight. He wasn't proud that he knew that, but he did. The window of the room across from his own was always dark, too, by the time he went to bed. Whether that was because she'd gone to sleep or because she'd gone off again, he didn't know. He wasn't *that* much of a stalker.

He'd wondered what she did to be able to afford to live in Devonport. Something that required long hours. A lawyer, maybe. She had the cool, assessing stare for it. Or, more likely, got the money for the house in a divorce settlement, because she had "trophy wife" written all over her. Although why any man would've let her go, he couldn't fathom. If Hugh had had a woman like that, he'd have held onto her.

The driver was maneuvering the second pallet onto the arms of the forklift as Hugh stood beside Josie and watched. "What is it?" he asked her, trying to see inside the thick layer of opaque plastic surrounding the solid cube lashed to the pallet at their feet.

"Bricks. For my patio," she answered absently, her eyes on the forklift driver, though he wasn't much of a beauty spot. Dressed pretty much exactly like her, shorts, boots, wool socks, and T-shirt, and not looking nearly as good in it.

"Having a new one built, are you?" Hugh asked her. "Sounds like a good idea. I think Mrs. Alberts's husband must've laid that concrete back around the Dawn of Man. Made a dog's breakfast of it, too, as cracked as it's got since then. The spirit was will-ing enough there, but the flesh was weak. You're probably living with a fair few of his subpar DIY projects. He was a banker."

"You could be right. That was why I could afford the place, because it didn't show well. Still doesn't, for that matter, but at least the concrete's gone. First step toward the back garden of my dreams. And this," she said, laying a caressing hand on the plastic, "is the second."

"Who've you got putting it in for you?" he asked.

He had to wait for her to thank the driver, who wheeled his machine sharply round again, headed it back into the truck bed, and commenced to prepare for departure.

"Hope you asked around, got some names," Hugh persisted over the sound of the liftgate slowly grinding back into place. "I could've given you a couple."

She laughed. "Got a name, haven't I. Me."

"You?" He couldn't have been more gobsmacked. "You mean you're helping?"

That detached, amused look was back on her face, to his annoyance. "No, I mean I'm doing it. A couple of my mates came by and gave me a hand with the demo, because that sledgeham-mer's hard to swing after a few goes, but I couldn't really ask them to give me another weekend. But that's OK. This bit's just time and patience."

She'd been using a *sledgehammer?* Yeh, he'd bet it had been hard for her to swing. But that she'd done it at all…"Could be a bit more work than you realize," he said cautiously, feeling his way over what he could tell was shaky ground as she raised a hand to the departing driver.

"No worries. I've got all weekend to do it. More, if it comes to that. Brick doesn't have a time limit. Not like a concrete pour, is it."

"Yeh, nah," he agreed, still bemused. "It isn't. But I'll give you a hand, how's that. Make it go a bit faster." And avert disaster, he hoped.

She looked at him, and he had the uncomfortable feeling that she could read his mind. All parts of it. "A hand would be about what it'd be. Seeing as you've only got one."

He looked down at his cast. "Yeh, well, I'm not too bad with one."

"Oh, wait," she said. "This is cutting the grass."

"Pardon?" What? What grass?

"I appreciate the offer, but before I let you spend your day like that, I should tell you, I've got a partner."

Of course she did. Damn. He looked around. "Where is he, then?"

"Oh, not *here*," she said. "He's in Aussie, working over there."

"So d'you have anyone here to help you, or not?"

"Not."

"Then…" He shrugged. "You've still got the offer of my hand, for what it's worth."

"Good," she said. "Fantastic. Thanks. Come over once you've had breakfast, see what your one hand can bring to the party."

♡

Well, *that* was disappointing, he thought as he headed back to the house. He couldn't really have backed out of it, though. And anyway, he couldn't have listened to her building a brick patio all weekend, known she was tackling that massive project on her own without offering to help. Not possible.

She didn't hear him when he returned an hour later, because she had her headphones in, was singing along to more bad pop, of which she seemed to have a limitless supply, as she crouched and hacked open a bag at her feet. He touched her elbow, and she jumped and whirled on her toes, not losing her balance, he noticed.

"Oh. Hi," she said, and smiled at the kids with none of the distance she kept from Hugh, and her smile was like the sun coming out.

"Thought you could be right about the one hand," he told her. "So I brought five." He looked at the work she'd been doing, and rapidly reassessed. "Did you do all this?" he asked.

The amused look was back. "I did. Surprised?"

He laughed. "Yeh. I'll admit, I am." She had dug out and leveled the dirt foundation for her new patio, he could see, and had about half of the space covered by a lumpy layer of sand in which to set the brick, had been in the middle of opening another sandbag when he'd interrupted her. What was more, the perimeter of the prospective patio was marked by stakes and string, and he could tell at a glance that the string was level, too.

"You know what you're doing," he said.

"Yeh. I do." The look she sent him was challenging. "Glad of the help, though."

"Help, not advice," he said with a rueful smile. "Got it. You open the bags, I'll dump them for now, how's that?"

"With one hand?"

"I can't open bags so well with one, but I can carry and dump with one. And you two can do a bag together," he told the kids.

"Here." Josie finished opening her bag, indicated it to the kids. "Drag it over there between you, and then tip it over, pull it along so the sand pours out."

It was a bit awkward, Hugh found, handling fifteen-kilo bags with one hand, but he was determined to manage it. There might have been a bit of showing off there, too. Just a bit.

And there was *definitely* some showing off after all the sand was poured and raked smooth, and she dragged over the heavy tamper and started pounding away. He watched her for a couple minutes, but when she paused to give her muscles a rest, he took it from her with his good right hand.

"I'll have a go," he said.

He could see her opening her mouth to say the one-handed thing again, but he hadn't spent his life in the gym for nothing. Up in the air, down with a bang to compress the sand, over and over, and she was laughing a little.

"I'm dead impressed," she said, and he grinned at her and kept tamping.

"Here, Amelia." She handed Amelia a pair of heavy kitchen shears. "You and Charlie go out to the driveway and cut the plastic off the bricks, shove it in the bin for me, OK? Because once your brother gets done showing me his muscles, we get to start the fun bit."

Hugh looked at Josie and laughed himself. "Building the patio is the fun bit?"

"Of course it is. That's when the magic happens, when you see that your construction mess is turning into something."

They worked through the morning, loading up, hauling brick barrowload by barrowload to the back garden, Hugh taking one handle, one of the kids on the other side. After the first couple rounds, Hugh sent Amelia back to their own shed for another wheelbarrow and they went a bit faster, Josie deputizing Charlie to help her unload the wheelbarrow and place the bricks in the neat parquet pattern she had designed. She must have measured, because they fit perfectly in the space she'd laid out, with a couple of centimeters of space between each brick.

"I'll put mortar in between here," she explained to Hugh, "so I don't get weeds growing up under," and he nodded.

"You've got the knack of it, Charlie," Josie told the boy as he laid each brick with care, and Hugh smiled to see him puffing up at the praise. Well, there wasn't much a man wouldn't do for a beautiful woman, and he wasn't too surprised that his brother was as susceptible as he was himself.

They broke for lunch in her kitchen, ham and tomato sandwiches and apples,

"You don't have to fix us lunch," Hugh said. "I can take them home to eat."

"Nah," Josie said. "If you're working for me, I'm at least going to feed you. This would've taken me all weekend. Instead, we'll be done today."

Hugh looked around the old-fashioned kitchen. Spotlessly clean, but he'd bet it hadn't been updated in forty years. Cheap cabinetry, laminated countertops, brown vinyl flooring peeling a bit around the bottoms of the cabinets. "I'm surprised you didn't want to fix the kitchen first thing."

She shrugged and smiled. "I'm Maori. Outside's important. Nothing wrong with the stove, anyway, and the whole thing no worse than what my mum's been feeding a family in for thirty years or so. I can wait for a flash kitchen, but I can't wait to have someplace to sit and look at the trees and the sky, listen to the birds."

"Your own patch of paradise," he said.

"That's it. I was in a flat before. No garden, and I was pining. So that's first. And besides," she said practically, "it's the cheapest. That and painting. That comes next, because you should see the rest of the house."

"I noticed that your bathroom was pink," he said with another grin.

She laughed. "*Bright* pink, and look at that godawful bright blue in my lounge."

"Noticed that too," he admitted.

"Somebody must've told Mrs. Alberts that blue would be restful. Not that color, it isn't. I told you I got this place cheaper than I should've, just because of the wallpaper and the paint. No worries, that's all just sweat equity and a bit of paint. Easily fixed. I've already done my bedroom."

And he'd like to see it. But he moved on. "Yeh. My mum's a decorator. The color on the paper isn't what turns up on your wall. She spends a fair bit of time explaining that."

She looked surprised, and he hurried to explain. "Different mums. Mine's in Wellington. Where I grew up."

"Except when you came to be with us, in the summer," Amelia said.

He smiled at her. "Yeh. Except when I came to be with you." He could see the questions hovering on Josie's lips, could see the moment when she decided not to ask them, because it wasn't the time.

"Well," she told them, rising and gathering up plates, it's back to work for me. Sorry I don't have any biscuits."

"No worries," Hugh said. "Charlie, run over and get some, why don't you? Keep us going. I thought I was in condition, but if I'm going to work for Josie, more fuel is definitely required."

She didn't eat any biscuits herself, he noticed, just kept working steadily until the brick was laid, then said briskly, "Right. Time for the mortar."

"Where is it?" Hugh asked. "Tell me, and I'll get it."

"The shed," she said. He went back to her pre-fab shed, which was as neatly organized as any Kiwi bloke's, and pretty well-equipped for somebody who'd only just got her own house, too. He found the heavy bags of mortar and carried them out to her in his good arm.

"Hugh," Amelia told him, "I need to go to ballet. Did you forget?"

"Oh. Right." He *had* forgotten.

"And it's your turn to drive us," she reminded him, not for the first time. "All three of us. So we need to leave in time."

Her and her two friends, and in case he needed to feel any more middle-aged, driving the carpool would do it.

"Right," he said again. "You could take a break too," he suggested to Josie as Amelia shifted from foot to foot beside him. "I could help you finish up when I'm back. At least a couple hours, though."

"Nah," she said. "Only a few more steps to go. Another hour or so, and I'm done. Can't stop now."

He wanted to tell her again to wait for him, because she'd been working as hard as any man would've, all day long, and she had to be tired. But it was her project, not his, and Amelia was making impatient noises now, so he just said, "Come on, then, Charlie."

"I could stay and help Josie," Charlie said.

"That'd be awesome," she said. "Get us through even faster. We could be the first to have a cup of tea on my new patio, Charlie, you and me." And his brother looked blissful at the prospect, so that was that plan sorted.

"Tell you what," Josie said just before Hugh and Amelia took themselves off. "Why don't we all have dinner out here tonight? We built it, we should christen it, don't you think?"

Hugh could think of a better way, but he went with what was on offer. "You don't want to cook dinner after all this," he objected. "We could go out." Not quite the double date of his dreams, the two of them and the kids, not to mention the absent partner, but he'd take it.

"The idea is dinner on the new patio, remember?"

"Well, then, we could get pizza. Amelia and I could even get it on the way back from ballet. Easy as."

"I don't eat pizza," she said. "Alas."

"Not even after laying brick all day?"

"Not even then. The sacrifices we make, eh," she said with another laugh. "But just come on over when Amelia's done with her dancing, and we can have a feed. The least I can do to pay you back, isn't it. If Charlie and I aren't here, we'll have gone to the supermarket. Maybe even for a swim first, hey?" she asked Charlie. "Sounds good about now."

Did she have unlimited energy? He guessed so. And he wanted to come for the swim. Seeing her in her togs would be a fair reward for his work, better than any dinner, especially if it were a bikini.

But his job right now was to drive three twelve-year-old girls to ballet, so that was what he did.

not romantic

♡

"Hugh's nice, isn't he," Charlie offered when Hugh and Amelia had left.

"Yeh, he is." Josie smiled at him, looked at the bags of mortar and allowed herself a moment of fatigue at the thought of this final stage of her project. For a cowardly minute, she thought about accepting Hugh's offer, taking Charlie off for a swim and a shop and finishing the job with Hugh's help when he returned. How easy it was, after all, to look to a man for help, even when that help wasn't one bit his job, or his concern.

Finish it now, she told herself. *Sooner you start, sooner it's done.* Besides, even though she'd been honest with him, this was cutting the grass, and she knew it. And she'd never been one of those women who put off breaking up with a man until after he'd helped her shift house. She'd told Clive the truth. She didn't like manipulative women, and she wasn't going to be one, so she grabbed her scissors and cut open the first bag of mortar, hefted it and began sprinkling its contents over the bricks.

"Cut open the next one for me, will you, love?" she asked Charlie. "And then we just sweep the mortar with this metal broom so it falls between the bricks, see?"

"Hugh's strong, too," Charlie said, reaching for the broom and sweeping with a willing if inexpert hand. "If he was here, he could lift up those bags by himself. He could do it with one hand."

"Mmm. Does he always live with you?" she asked, onto the second bag by now. She was just making conversation, keeping Charlie from noticing how tired he was. Or she was shamelessly pumping an eight-year-old child for information. She'd go with Option A. Sounded much better.

"Just since my mum and dad died," Charlie said. "And only when he's at home. Not when he's away." He laughed a little. "I mean, he couldn't live with us when he's away, could he? But he can't go away now, because he broke his thumb."

"Does he go away for work?" she asked.

"Yeh. But he got an injury, this last time, so he can't go." He opened his mouth, shut it again.

A ship, she thought suddenly. That would explain it. He wasn't a dole bludger after all, she could see that after today. He was a worker, just like her.

"What does he do for work?" she asked, and all right, it was true, she was shamelessly pumping a child. She might as well get her money's worth.

Charlie looked a bit scared. "I'm not meant to talk about his work. If people ask me about him."

"Oh. OK." *What?* She finished emptying her bags, took over on the sweeping from Charlie.

So, all right. Something secret. Either he was an undercover cop, or a drug dealer. *Or an assassin,* her overactive imagination suggested, and she had to laugh a little inside at the thought. He didn't seem much like a drug dealer, or an assassin either. Though drug dealers probably had families. Assassins, she wasn't so sure about.

He did look familiar. Maybe she'd seen him on some TV show about persons of interest? Hard to tell, under all that beard and hair. His disguise, maybe. But no, that was ridiculous. Cora just not mine

Middleton had seemed thoroughly respectable, not somebody who'd leave these kids in the care of anybody that dodgy. In any case, Hugh seemed much too straightforward to be anything that complicated, and anyway, it wasn't her business, not as long as he weren't actually a criminal, and she sincerely doubted it. She gave a mental shrug and concentrated on finishing the job with Charlie's help.

"Here we are," she said when he'd finished spraying the entire surface of the new patio with the hose, concentrating so fiercely on getting every square meter wetted down, his clever little face so intent that her heart went out to him. "Look at you. You helped build a whole patio today. You spread the sand, laid the brick, brushed the mortar. Bet you didn't know you could do that."

He brightened, his chest swelling a bit, and she smiled at him. "Let's put my table and chairs on," she suggested. "And have a look."

He helped her carry them, and they stood together and admired their handiwork.

"Calls for a cup of tea, don't you think?" she asked him. "Lord and lady of the manor, surveying our domain?"

"Yeh," he said. "Except could I have cocoa instead? If you have it," he added politely.

She laughed, light with accomplishment and the satisfaction of a job done. "You could. You can have as much cocoa as you can drink. You earned it."

♡

She and Charlie had their swim, a quick one down the road at Torpedo Bay, because the water was still springtime-cold, but that and a shower renewed her energy for a visit to New World.

"You're a good shopper," she told Charlie when he'd returned to the trolley with a bag of green beans.

"That's because I have to help Hugh," he said.

"Oh. Because of his hand."

"Not just his hand," Charlie said. "It's that he doesn't know how to do things. The sorts of things grown-ups usually know. He forgets to buy stuff, like washing powder. He forgets to *do* the washing. He can't cook too well either. We had pizza two times already this week, and hamburgers one time. Grownups usually cook more grown-up things, but he says he can't. He can do hamburgers, though. And he can do eggs. I have to help him with that, too."

"Well, helping's good," she said cheerfully, selecting tomatoes, throwing in a couple avocados, some spinach and rocket. Salad, that was nice and easy. "I helped my mum and dad growing up, and that's why I *do* know how to cook, and to do the washing, and all sorts of quite handy things. And I should get your brother some beer," she realized as they left the veg aisle. "Bet he likes that."

"I think so," Charlie said. "Not if he's driving, but he hasn't got to drive, because you live next door and we can walk. It isn't good to drink beer if you're driving."

"No, it isn't, but he doesn't have to drive tonight, so I think we'll risk it. What kind's his favorite?" she asked, stopping in front of the extensive selection.

He considered. "Dunno. Maybe that green one. I think he's had that."

"Monteith's Original? Sounds reasonable. Not a big drinker, eh." She pulled a six-pack down and set it in the trolley.

"Nah. Because of work. He can't."

Which made the drug dealer idea less likely, but then, it had never been likely. Still left assassin open, though. Assassins probably had to keep their wits about them.

"Run get me two liters of trim milk, please," she told Charlie, abandoning the question.

He was back with it in a flash. "I think I used to help my mum, too," he told her as he handed it to her. "I don't remember too well, though."

Josie glanced down at him, steered the trolley into the house-wares aisle, selected a packet of ivory candles, then wondered why she was doing it. It wasn't a romantic dinner. Well, no. But it was a party on her new patio, with new friends. So, candles.

"Bet you remember some things," she said.

He was quiet for a full minute as they rounded the corner towards the meat department, and she wondered what was going on in that dark head.

"I remember her doing chicken," he said suddenly. "She'd stand at the sink and reach her hand in the hole and pull the guts out of the inside. And then she'd cut it all up and smash it and cook it a special way that tasted good. It didn't taste like chicken normally does, like Aunt Cora makes it. I remember that."

"Sounds like she was a good cook."

"Yeh. Because she was French. She said if you were French, you had to know how, because you couldn't eat English food. She laughed when she said that."

"See?" Josie smiled down at him. "You do remember."

♡

The doorbell rang while she was hacking away at a pumpkin. "Get that for me, will you, love?" she asked Charlie. "That'll be your brother. And your sister," she added hastily.

She'd resisted the urge to glam up too much, at least, even though she'd found herself putting on a dress, which the apron was covering up just now. Well, it was a *party*. Of sorts. And if her hair was down, and she was wearing a bit of makeup, that wasn't for Hugh's benefit, because she had a partner. But she'd been out and about, and even in casual New Zealand, her image required more polish than she'd been featuring today. Anyway,

Hugh had looked at her all day in her work clothes, and her pride demanded a better showing.

But he was standing just the other side of the kitchen bench now, and she was looking at the depth of his chest, being reminded about the size of his arms, and he was smiling at her, and her hands had stilled on her knife.

"Do the ballet run, then?" she asked him, forcing herself to start cutting through the dense orange flesh again.

"Yeh. I take it you finished the job? Get your swim?"

"Yeh." She smiled herself. "Bet I had a better time."

He laughed. "Bet you did. I was going to say I'd take the kids home, because we all need showers, but d'you need a hand here first?"

She needed to stop smiling at him. "Again, a hand's what it'd be. Don't think you could do too much with one."

"I can do quite a lot with one," he said, the look in his eyes letting her know exactly what he could do, and suddenly, her oven wasn't the only thing warming up. All he was doing was standing there, and he was still sending tingles to places they had no business being, evoking every shivery, delicious sensation that the most heated on-screen kiss failed to arouse, and it took all the training she had not to show it.

She looked down again hastily, resumed her hacking progress. "Nah, got this. Go take your shower. Then come back and help me christen my new deck."

He glanced sharply at her, opened his mouth to say something, then shut it, and she realized what she'd said and very nearly blushed. She never got flustered with men, and she'd worked with, dated, been chatted up by men infinitely more handsome, polished, and urbane than Hugh could dream of being, but she was flustered now.

All he said, though, was, "Right. See you in a bit. Hour or so OK? Enough time?"

"Perfect," she said. "See you then." And kept chopping her vegies, moving around her dark little kitchen in her bare feet, and did her best to pretend that this was about a thank-you and nothing more.

♡

"A feast," he said when she let them back in again, led them back through the kitchen, and he saw the vegies and salad laid out, the fish ready to cook.

"Could you drink a beer?" she asked him, opening the fridge.

"You going to drink with me?"

"I don't drink beer."

"Don't drink beer, don't eat pizza? What do you do?"

"Only low-kilojoule pursuits," she said, pulling out one of the bottles of Monteith's she'd chilled for him, holding it up with a questioning lift of her brows.

"Even after all that work today, not to mention the swim, and as slim as you are?" he asked, taking the bottle from her. "Because my mum would say, get that girl a sandwich. I'd think you could have a beer without fear."

"Your mum's opinion notwithstanding, no, I can't." She realized she was snapping, took a breath. "Sorry. I hear that a lot from people who don't understand, and it can get annoying. I'm an actress, and the camera adds the kilos, even if you don't have any extra. And if you do…forget about getting parts." She took a sip of her own chilled water and tried to pretend it was wine. She'd used up her wine ration for the week already, though, so for tonight, it was water.

"It's me who's sorry," he said, and it sounded genuine, and she relaxed. "None of my business how much you eat. Or drink. An actress, though, eh. Would I have seen you in anything?"

"I doubt it." Somehow, she didn't think he was a regular *Courtney Place* watcher. "Charlie thought ginger beer would be acceptable for the two of you," she told Amelia, pulling out a couple more bottles. "Glasses over the sink," she told Hugh, and watched him reach to pull them down, appreciating the open-necked dark-blue knit shirt he wore, the way it clung to his shoulders and upper back, and the way it didn't cling around the waist and hips, because if any man could be said to have a V-shaped torso, that man was Hugh. Whatever the mysterious profession was, she'd decided it was active, because he hadn't built those layers of muscle in the gym. He'd changed to dressier clothes for tonight, too, dark jeans and that shirt, and she needed to make sure she kept her distance. Asking him to dinner had probably been a bad impulse move, because she'd clearly given him the wrong idea. The only problem was, she very much feared that she had the wrong idea as well.

♡

"Can I do something?" he asked once he'd poured the drinks. "Or can my five assorted hands do something?"

"Carry the plates and cutlery out to our new patio for me," she suggested. "Going to get too cold to stay out there much past dinner, but I need you all to admire it, so we have to at least try it."

"Christen it," he said.

"Yeh." She cleared her throat. "Right." She turned to the stove and turned the fire on under her frying pan. "Less than five minutes."

He got the kids set up out on the patio, she saw with a glance as she added a bit of olive oil, waited for it to heat, and then he was back in the kitchen, leaning against the edge of the bench and taking a careful sip of his beer.

"Looks good out there," he said. "Professional, I'd call that. I like your furniture, too."

"Yeh, thanks," she said. "Suits me, I think." She'd found the café table and chairs in a shop in Parnell, and had known they were hers. The table was a robin's egg blue, the four chairs lemon yellow, cherry red, lime green, and grape, and the entire thing made her smile, looked so cheerful and fun set on the distressed brick, exactly as she'd envisioned it. "I want a fountain next, set in a fern garden. I had that shady spot in mind at the back, under the tree. What do you think?"

"I think you've got it done in your head already, probably got all the steps mapped out, and it's just a matter of time. Planning to put it in yourself?"

"Course I am. But you already knew that."

"Wait till I've got two hands, and I'll help you do it. You're clearly multifaceted. I'm going to have to ask how you do that, too, because it seems like a quick prep." He motioned to where she was setting her dukkah-coated terakihi fillets carefully into the pan, where they immediately began to sizzle.

"Just buy the dukkah ready-made," she said, pointing with her spatula to a plastic container filled with the mixture of pulverized nuts, herbs, and spices. "Pour some into a plate, press your fillets into it, fry them up in a bit of olive oil, and you're all good. Charlie said you sometimes found cooking a bit challenging."

He smiled. "You could put it that way. Or you could just come right out and say that I'm rubbish at it."

"Well, this is a quick option," she said. "Even faster than hamburgers."

He made a face. "Charlie told you about the hamburgers, eh. And the pizza."

"He did." She flipped the fish. "I'm guessing you're a bit new to the full-responsibility mode?"

"Yeh," he said, watching her slide the fillets out onto a platter, then taking it from her and carrying it out to the patio. "You're guessing right."

♡

"I have to say," he said while they were eating, "not only can't I cook like this, I wouldn't have known how to build a patio, not without asking around a fair bit, at least. I'm guessing the trailer in your drive is yours, too, not borrowed off a mate. Genuine Kiwi, that is. Handmade all the way, a few spare boards and two tires somebody took off an old car."

"It is," she said. "I was so excited to find it on Trade Me and have a way to haul all my DIY stuff. Because I've got *projects*."

"Guessing you can back a boat down a ramp, too," he said with a grin.

"Of course I can. I drove a tractor before I did a car. A truck as well, come to that."

"A country girl, eh. Where's your family?"

"Katikati. You know it?"

"Murals," he said. "Close to Mt. Maunganui."

"Close geographically, nowhere near otherwise. Not nearly so flash. But it sounds like you've been there, if you've seen the murals, so you know that."

"What are murals?" Charlie asked.

"Paintings on buildings, or walls," Josie explained. "Almost all the sides of shops, the fronts, all that, in Katikati? Anywhere there's space, really, has got a painting on it, mostly things from the past. They're pretty cool. You could look online if you wanted to see them."

"I'll show you," Hugh told him. "When we go home."

"So you've been there," Josie prompted.

"Well, driven through. On the way to Mt. Maunganui," he said with another smile. "The only other thing I know about it is kiwifruit."

"Josie used to pick kiwifruit," Charlie informed his brother. "That's why she's so strong."

"Does your family have an orchard?" Hugh asked her.

"Only a few blocks. My dad's a contractor. Organizes the teams, sends them around."

"And you picked," he said. "Hard work, isn't it?"

She shrugged. "Everything on a farm's hard work. During school breaks, is all. I blame my lack of a ballet career on that, though. Very convenient excuse, when the truth is that the problem wasn't my broad shoulders, it was my tendency to galumph around the stage like I was on the netball court, and my general lack of talent."

"Did you want a ballet career?"

"Sure. That's how I met Chloe. We were at grammar school together. Boarding school, because I came to St. Theresa's for that, here in Auckland."

He raised his eyebrows, and she added with a laugh, "On a scholarship, of course, as you've guessed. My parents thought I'd be a lawyer."

"I thought that too," he said. "At first, when I met you. That you were a lawyer. Something about the way you stared me down."

"Disappointed you too, then," she said, keeping it cool.

"I wouldn't say disappointed." He was looking at her in the gathering dusk, and she got up, found the matches she'd set ready, and lit the candles on the table, then went around the corners of the patio, crouched and lit the others she'd set ready, careful not to set her floaty white dress alight.

"There," she said with a satisfied sigh, coming back over to the table. "How's that?"

"Beautiful," Amelia said with a sigh of her own. "It's so romantic."

"Candles are always romantic," Josie told her. "Everybody looks better, too, because it's all about the lighting, always."

"I don't think you look better," Charlie said. "I mean, I think you always look nice, doesn't she, Hugh?"

"She does," he said, and Josie looked at him again and got a little flutter, because his eyes were even warmer in the soft glow of the candles. He was leaning back in his chair, smiling at her, big and solid and strong, and she had to remind herself that one day of helping her build a patio wasn't a true test of his character, because a man would do just about anything to sleep with a woman, especially one who looked like her.

And he did want to sleep with her, that was clear. But she had a partner, and Hugh was her neighbor, and she wanted to live in this house until they carried her out feet-first, so that wouldn't have been happening anyway.

She fought to remember what they'd been talking about. "Chloe was the star," she told Amelia. "You should have seen her. She went on to dance with Auckland Ballet Theatre as soon as she left school. Oh, she was good."

"She's awesome," Amelia said. "I want to dance like her. But why does she keep saying I'm not ready for my pointe shoes? I practice every *day*, heaps more than June or Holly, but she still says I'm not ready, and I don't see why. I know all the steps."

"Because you don't look anything like her when you do them," Charlie said with a little brother's frankness. "You look like you're, I don't know, stomping or something. And she looks like she's floating, when she shows you. Like she's on strings, like a puppet."

"I wouldn't say Amelia stomps," Josie said hurriedly, "but I think I did. Sometimes, when you're athletic, it can actually be harder." She had a feeling that Chloe had been referring to Amelia when she'd been talking about being reminded of Josie's own less-than-stellar technique, and she knew exactly what it was like to yearn for mastery that didn't come, for a career that she couldn't possibly attain.

She saw Charlie shiver, realized she was feeling the evening chill through her own lacy sweater, and said, "Much as I'm loving my new patio in the candlelight, it's time to go inside, I think."

Hugh stood, picked up his plate. "We'll help you clear up before we go."

"You've done more than enough today already," she said. "You don't have to do that as well." She didn't press him to stay. She wanted to keep sitting with them, and that was exactly why she wasn't going to do it.

"Yeh," he said. "We do."

They did, loaded the dishwasher too, Hugh brushing aside her protest with, "I may be pretty average in the kitchen, but I can just about manage to bung dishes into the dishwasher," and then they left, and Josie finished clearing up, sat herself down on the couch and turned on the telly for a half-hour of relaxation before a well-earned early night, and wondered why, when she finally had the house she'd longed for, had ticked off one more box toward the life she'd been planning for herself ever since she'd given up the ballet dream, and that other dream, too… why, despite all that, all she felt right now was lonely.

celebrity gossip

♡

She did her best to mention, the next day. Derek called her on Sunday morning, and she was glad to hear from him, glad to remind herself that he was there and that he cared, but she mentioned all the same.

"Wrapping up this week, then?" she started out by asking. "The crocs, the leeches, the heat soon to be a distant memory?"

"Nah." He sighed. "It's been a nightmare, one bloody thing after another. Over time, over budget, you name it by now. Wondering why I signed up for this. You've had your big break, turned your back on it, and that's fine for you, but this was meant to be mine, and I wanted to make the most of it."

She knew her greater success had always nagged at him, so she ignored the dig. "What's happened now?"

"You can't make this stuff up. The kitchen served up some dodgy chicken, that was the latest, most of the cast and half the crew taken ill, spent Friday night hugging their toilets. We were meant to shoot yesterday, and we couldn't do it. Dragging on into next week after all."

"Oh, no. You sound OK, though. You didn't get the bot?"

"Nah. Vanessa's a vegetarian. Says looking at people eating meat makes her sick, and since we were talking over a scene together during lunch, I skipped as well. A heroic effort, but anything for the good of the film, you know. And as it turned out, lucky for me."

"I'd call that very lucky," she laughed. "Looking at people eating meat makes her *sick?* She must do a lot of eating alone."

"High-maintenance and then some," Derek agreed. "Makes me realize what a bullet I've dodged with you. No dramas, that's my easy-peasy Josie."

It wasn't the first time he'd said it, and in the past, she'd appreciated it. Now it made her feel like some kind of a jolly mate.

"So what have you been doing?" he asked. "Got your work boots on, I'll bet, building that patio all weekend. Now you know the real reason I'm over here. Otherwise, I'd feel compelled to help. I don't know why you can't just hire somebody like everybody else does, let me off the hook."

"Because I like to."

"Don't I know it. So how's it going?"

"It's done, actually." Time to mention. "My neighbor came and lent a hand, and we knocked it over in a day." She wouldn't mention the kids. Let him think she'd had a solo work date.

"Your neighbor, eh. Did he try to run the show, put your back up?"

"No, he didn't," she said, and realized it was true. "He just provided the muscle, and as he's got a fair bit of that, we got along well. Probably better than anyone I could've hired, so it's all working out. He said he'd help me with my next job, too," she added, heaping on a bit more mentioning in case Derek hadn't got it. "The fountain and that."

"His partner didn't mind?" he asked, and she smiled. Things were looking up.

"He doesn't have one. A single neighbor with muscles, what could be better?"

"Sounds like I should be worried," he said, but he was laughing again, and she was annoyed, because he so clearly wasn't a bit worried. "But then, if I worried about you every time some fella wanted to help you across the street, I'd be in trouble, wouldn't I? Good thing I know I can count on you. That's what I love about you. Beautiful, and loyal and dependable, too. The perfect woman."

"Or the perfect cocker spaniel."

He laughed. "You know what I mean. And I like cocker spaniels. Just like I like you."

So much for mentioning.

♡

She was pushing her trolley through New World once again. Five o'clock on Wednesday afternoon, because she'd had a couple days where she wasn't called, which meant she'd been able to deal with her bright-pink bathroom, which was thankfully and finally no longer bright pink. It had taken some serious effort with the primer to cover the glaring hue, and it was going to take most of tomorrow to return it to a tasteful off-white that wouldn't assault her eyes every time she walked in.

She was tired, but satisfied, too. A patio, and one-and-a-half rooms painted? Pretty good progress. Anyway, she hadn't wanted to come back from this weekend's long-awaited visit to Derek and face that color.

She rounded the corner now, paint scrubbed off and hair and clothes more acceptable for public viewing, and pushed her trolley into the next aisle. There was Hugh, standing in front of the pie rack with the kids and looking beleaguered. More fuel for mentioning right there, which was why she stopped. Well, that and neighborliness.

"It's not healthy," she heard him say. None of them had noticed her, so intent were they on their discussion.

"It's sausage rolls," Amelia argued. "Everyone eats sausage rolls. You said meat for dinner, and sausage is meat. Anyway, we're *growing*."

"Growing out, that's what you'll be doing if you eat those," he said.

"Hi," Josie broke in. "Having fun?"

All three of them looked around. "Trying to explain nutrition," Hugh told her, "but it's hard going."

"Pizza isn't nutrition," Charlie said. "And we had pizza two times last week."

"Yeh, well, I'm trying to do better," Hugh said. "And if it's not on my nutrition plan, it can't possibly be good for you."

"It's like we're *prisoners,*" Amelia complained, and Josie had to smile. "It's like we're in *jail.*"

"I'll admit my standard isn't too high yet," Hugh said, "but I don't think Amnesty International is actually planning to step in. I got roast chicken. I got this stir-fry packet, too," he told Josie, holding up a foam tray full of prepared vegetables and covered with cling wrap. "Says you just put them in the pan and add the sauce. I thought, not too hard? But how hot should the pan be, d'you know?"

"Pretty hot," she said. "That's the idea, you cook them up fast. And stir the whole time," she thought to add. He had a nutrition plan? She knew some actors with strict diet plans and personal trainers—Derek, for one, had both—but that was because their bodies were their fortune. Hugh's body was nothing to sneeze at, but he didn't look like a professional bodybuilder—too much hair, for one thing—anything close to vain about his looks, which she admitted Derek had a weeny tendency to become.

"Thanks," Hugh said. "We'll just leave the sausage rolls behind, get some yoghurt for pudding. Chicken, vegies, yoghurt. That's all good, and good for all of us, too."

"Oh, joy," Amelia muttered. "You *said* you were going to make up for forgetting to collect us from ballet. I was *so* embarrassed. And yoghurt isn't making up. *Ice cream* is making up."

"You start making up for things with food, that's a slippery slope, eh, Josie," Hugh said.

"Too right," she said. "Next thing you know, you have a hard day and you're into the beer. All downhill from there."

"I'm not asking for *beer,*" Amelia said. "I'm asking for ice cream. Which is a *normal* thing for children to eat. All my friends have ice cream."

"I think if you ask Chloe, you'll find that dancers have a pretty strict nutrition plan themselves," Josie said. But Amelia was right, ice cream *was* pretty normal, though she could see that Hugh was trying his best. Maybe she should talk to him privately about it.

Or maybe she should just stay out of it, since it was absolutely none of her business. An even better plan. "Yoghurt's one of my own treats," she said instead, selecting a small punnet of that very thing, topped with passionfruit. "Even better than sausage rolls, though I barely remember what they taste like." *Liar.*

"*Fine,*" Amelia sighed, and Hugh grabbed a larger container of the same variety.

"Go pick out bread, you two," he told the kids. "Brown, not white," he added, prompting another sigh and flounce from his sister.

"Congrats on trying," Josie told him when the other two were gone.

"I'm making a bit of progress on the food, I guess, but the ballet thing set me back," he admitted. "We've been trying to keep a timetable, but we haven't quite got it down yet. Their schedules keep shifting around, and there are so many different things I'm supposed to know. The activities, and papers I was meant to sign and didn't realize, and then I get that..." He did an exaggerated stomp, flounce, and eye-roll that had Josie laughing, so incongruous did it look coming from him.

"You don't have to let her do it, you know," she managed to say. "You can tell her to stop. And how did you know you were meant to sign?"

"Apparently, Aunt Cora went through their backpacks to find that stuff," he said, still grinning.

"My mum never went through my backpack, I'll tell you that," she said. "Did yours?"

"No. She wouldn't have had time. She was always working."

"Well, there you go. And was there ever anything she was meant to sign that you forgot to give her?"

"I'm sure there was. No, I *know* there was. I can remember a few times…"

"And yet you got your diploma all the same, somehow. You probably got embarrassed into remembering to tell her about the paper next time, too, just like Amelia will."

Amelia and Charlie returned with the bread, and Josie had just decided it was well past time to break this up when she saw the two older women at the end of the aisle looking at them with eager interest, all but pointing and shouting, and that made her decision even clearer. She saw the moment Hugh noticed them too, saw him shifting his trolley along with hers, but it was too late.

"Afternoon," Hugh began, his tone resigned, but the one in the lead, a thin woman with a pugnacious air and tightly curled gray hair, ignored him and went straight for Josie.

"Aren't you Jocelyn Pae Ata?" she asked.

"Yes," Josie said, putting on her best cool, reserved greeting-the-public smile.

"Well, that's exciting, isn't it? I didn't realize you did your shopping here in Devonport. Nobody's ever mentioned it to me."

She looked aggrieved, as if she were planning to have words with whoever had failed to send out the memo. Josie could have told her she lived in Devonport, but she wasn't stupid. Instead, she retained the cool smile and said nothing.

"I have to say, I've always enjoyed *Courtney Place*," the woman went on, "but honestly, you're too awful, and you're getting worse. Couldn't they have had you leave Eric McTavish alone? And what you're doing now…it's really a crime, and I can't think why somebody doesn't put a stop to it. Surely they would, if that actually happened. I get so upset, it's enough to make me stop watching, it really is."

"Oh, when Eric killed himself," the other woman, a softer, rounder version of her friend, put in, "I cried. I'm not ashamed to admit that when he kicked that stool over and I realized he was hanging himself, poor man, I gasped. And then that lovely wife of his, and the wee baby. It was too sad, and so heartless. So cruel, the way he gave everything up for you, ruined his career, and you laughed in his face."

"I wanted to reach right into the telly and slap you," the other woman said. "I know you're acting, but I don't see how you can live with yourself all the same, playing somebody like that every day. He was a joy to watch, too. What a handsome fella he is. It was too bad he had to leave the show at all, especially like that." The look she gave Josie left no doubt as to whose fault *that* was.

"I don't actually do the writing." Josie said, doing her best to project calm relaxation and healthy distance.

"I read that Derek Alverson got a new job in a film," the heavier woman said. "I was so glad to see it."

Josie considered explaining that Derek's—Eric's, that is—dramatic suicide had been a result of that very film offer and his desire to move on, but she'd realized by now that there was no point in defending a character, or in explaining the workings of the entertainment world. She reminded herself that the women's outrage was a compliment to her acting, smiled again and prepared to move on.

But the thin woman was talking again, so she stayed a moment longer, and then was sorry she had.

"Well, he must have forgiven you, anyway," the woman said. "Since you're an item off-screen as well, aren't you? I can't imagine how you film people can keep track, all that chopping and changing you do, shifting partners."

"We manage," Josie said, and this time, she wasn't smiling, and it was time to go.

"How are you, Mrs. Duncan?" Hugh put in, and he'd moved a step forward, putting himself between her and the women. "And Mrs....I'm sorry, I've forgotten," he said to the other one.

"Fiona Garber," she said. "You know Jocelyn, do you? Your aunt never mentioned that. How is she, by the way? How's her butcher doing?"

"She seems pretty happy," Hugh said. "Having a good time, from what I can tell. She's talked more to the kids than to me, though."

"Yeh," Amelia said. "She asked how we were eating." She sent Hugh another accusatory glance.

"Well, I suppose you celebrities are constantly running into each other, functions and that," Mrs. Garber said, Hugh's aunt having clearly been shoved into the less-interesting pile. "How's your poor hand faring, Hugh? My Tom told me about it, said you'd be out of the test matches. In Europe, isn't it? He was sorry to hear it, I'll tell you. He's worried the...I think it's the French, worried that they'll win. I hardly listen," she admitted with a chuckle. "He said that without you, there'd be trouble with the—can't remember again, because I don't really follow it, to tell you the truth, dear."

"The scrum?" Hugh asked

"That was it. What should I tell him?"

"Tell him everybody's ready to get stuck in, that they all know we're in for a contest and that the boys will be playing their guts out, like always," Hugh said. "And that we've got some good cover at 7, too, no worries."

"That's not what he thinks," she insisted, and Josie, who had just figured out exactly what it was that Hugh did for a living, had the feeling that he was as used to awkward, prying questions as she was.

"How *do* you two know each other?" It was Mrs. Duncan this time, back to the more fascinating topic, her sharp eyes darting between Hugh and Josie.

"Josie's a good friend of Charlie and Amelia's," Hugh said. "I only just met her, I'm afraid."

"Well, you'll want to watch out," Mrs. Garber said roguishly. "Not sure you're safe. She likes the big, strong ones. Don't we all know it."

"Is that right. Got to be going, sorry," Hugh said, wheeling his trolley around so quickly that Josie had to grab hers to keep it from getting bashed. "Dinnertime. Come on, you two. See you ladies later."

♡

"Got any more shopping to do?" he asked her when they had put an aisle between themselves and the inquisitive ladies, the kids trailing behind.

"Not anymore, I don't," she said. "I'm done."

"I'm sure. D'you get that a lot?" He still looked upset, she thought. For himself or for her, she didn't know.

"Well, yeh. I play an unpopular character, as you saw."

"And you're not just an actress," he said. "You're pretty famous, apparently. I thought you watched TV, Amelia," he complained to his sister.

"I don't watch *Courtney Place*," she said. "Aunt Cora never let me. My friend Holly does, and she said I should. She talks about it *constantly*. But you're always watching *The Crowd Goes Wild* then anyway, so I can't."

"Not always child-friendly," Josie clarified for Hugh's benefit, in case he hadn't got that point.

"Are you in a show on TV, Josie?" Charlie asked with interest, not following the rest of it. "I didn't know that."

"None of us did," Hugh told him. "And I'm feeling pretty dense about that just now."

"Not so dense," Josie said. "I could hardly expect to compete with *The Crowd Goes Wild,* and I'm guessing you don't have much opportunity to look at supermarket magazines, or pay too much attention to the gossip columns in any case. In other words, you're a man. Am I right?"

"Well, let's hope, or I've been laboring under a fairly serious delusion for some time now. Are you *in* supermarket magazines and gossip columns?"

"World-famous in New Zealand," she said. "That'd be me. A lot smaller fish than you all the same, aren't I? Because I've finally got it. You're a rugby player. You're more than that, you're an All Black. And here I've thought…" She began to laugh, she couldn't help it. "Can't tell you what all I've thought. First on the dole, then builder, then I thought maybe a ship, and the latest was a toss-up between assassin and drug dealer, given the secrecy and all."

"What secrecy?" he asked. "A ship? An *assassin?* I figured you knew what I did. It's no secret. Could hardly be that."

"You didn't know that Hugh was a rugby player?" Amelia asked, because she'd been listening. "Really?"

Josie ignored her, because the penny had dropped. Her eyes widened. "Hugh…Latimer. Hugh *Latimer.* That's who you are. That's why you looked familiar. It's just that I don't watch much rugby, and I *never* watch the Blues, because my dad—Well," she said with a laugh. "Sorry. I grew up in Chiefs country. Anyway, the…" She gestured at his face. "The hair. The beard. I thought it was a disguise, and I was right, wasn't I? And then Charlie."

"Charlie what? How is this about him?"

"Telling me it was a secret," she explained. "Your job."

"You say we aren't meant to talk about it," Charlie said as Hugh looked at him in astonishment. "You always say."

"About what?"

"About you. And about being an All Black."

"I just mean, not go on about it," Hugh said. "Or gossip about me. That's all I meant."

"Gossip's talking about it," Amelia said. "That's what gossip is, talking about people."

"All right," Hugh said. "You can gossip. Geez. It's not a secret, Charlie. How could it be a secret?"

"But you *said*," Charlie said. "You *did*." He was looking distressed now.

"I didn't mean—I meant—" Hugh cut himself off. "Not to share too much with strangers."

Josie glanced at him, realized he was stuck. She'd have a go, then. "It can be hard, when you do something where lots of people know who you are," she explained to Charlie. "Sometimes you don't want to be talked about, things that might be a little bit private. People are interested, even though they shouldn't be, because people who are famous, people like Hugh, they aren't really any more exciting than anybody else, are they? I mean," and she made her smile confiding, cheery, "how interesting is your brother, really?" She heard Hugh's snort of surprise. "Why should anybody care whether he actually eats Weet-Bix for breakfast, or who he goes on a date with? But some people do all the same, and it might make him feel like his privacy's been invaded, do you see, if all those strangers knew all about his life like that? Like somebody was watching him all the time."

"I guess," Charlie said, looking a little less unhappy, but still puzzled. "But I don't think Hugh goes on a date with anybody, so I couldn't tell about that anyway."

"Yes, he does," Amelia said. "Heaps of times. When he stays gone all night? Those are dates."

"Wait," Hugh said. "How do you know those are dates? And not heaps of times. I don't—" He stopped again, and Josie looked at him and could hardly keep from laughing, he looked so uncomfortable. He didn't what?

"Because Auntie Cora said so, of course," Amelia said. "She said, 'Oh, love, he's on a date. He'll be home soon, I'm sure.' When it was Saturday and you weren't at Charlie's game, or something. Or when you dress up, and cut your *hair,* that's how we know," she added. "We're not *stupid.*"

"All right," Hugh said. "I'm sorry I missed the game. I had a girlfriend at the time, yeh. She's not my girlfriend anymore, so you don't have to worry."

"You missed two games," Amelia corrected him. "And you missed mine too, my netball, but it doesn't matter so much for me. Charlie needs a committed adult male in his life, though, or he'll—"

"I know," Hugh groaned. "Or he'll join a gang. I won't miss again, how's that? If I do ever go on a date again, by some miraculous chance, I'll make sure I'm home. Geez. I had no idea you two were watching so closely. And I just decided the no-gossip rule was a good one. Stop talking about me."

"We're just talking to Josie," Charlie said. "Talking to Josie isn't gossip. She's not strangers."

"Well," Hugh said, "not anymore, she's not."

role playing

♡

It was Friday night, another weekend with the kids stretching ahead. No Josie-projects to make this one more entertaining, either, because she was gone.

He'd seen her wheeling her suitcase out her front door when he'd pulled up from his doctor's visit, had jumped out and got over there fast, but not before she'd humped the clearly heavy thing down her front steps.

"Can I give you a hand with that?" he asked her. "And, yeh," he added, laughing at her a little, "a hand is what it'll be. But not for long, because this cast is coming off in two weeks."

"Oh, that's good news." She surrendered the suitcase to him, which made him unreasonably happy, then popped the boot of her little car so he could give the case a heave and a shove from his knee, lodge it safely inside before reaching up to slam the boot again.

"Although you're right," she said, watching him, "you can do a lot with one hand. But I'm sure you'll be happy to have two again."

"I will. Bloody nuisance, and then I can start to work on getting fit again."

She was smiling at him. "Because you're so shockingly out of condition."

"Not fit, and definitely not rugby fit," he said. "Not yet. But I will be, no worries."

"Well, I admit, I checked you out online last night," she said, "and I believe you. It must take some training to be able to go that hard for eighty minutes, and you always do seem to go eighty minutes, don't you?"

"That's what it's all about," he said. "Going hard for as long as it takes."

He saw the faint flush rise, saw her lose the smile, and, even as he felt his blood quicken, was sorry he'd said it, because she so clearly didn't want to hear it. She wanted a good neighbor, so he worked on that. "You off for the weekend? Business or pleasure?"

"Pleasure all the way. Paying a long-overdue visit to my partner in Aussie," she said, and that was a pretty clear message too.

"He's that actor fella I heard about last night?" he asked, doing his best to keep his tone casual.

"Derek Alverson. He's doing a film over there. They've been on location for weeks now, northern Queensland, deep in the bush, but they're back in Sydney, got a weekend off at last, and he asked me to join him."

"He'll be happy to see you, I'm sure."

"Hope so. And I'd best be off. Oh—" She turned, half-into the car. "How were the vegies?"

"Brilliant. Healthy. Have a good weekend." He lifted a hand and watched as she indicated, pulled into the street, and drove away to do it.

♡

So, no. He wouldn't be looking at her, at the golden skin glowing against that white dress, at the waves of hair falling down her back, at the shape of her showing for a moment when she crouched in front of the candle she'd lit, at her turning to smile at him after she did it, making his heart skip a beat. Because she would be with her partner. Because he would be the one taking her to dinner tonight, the one looking at her in the candlelight. And the one taking her to bed, too, which Hugh wasn't enjoying thinking about one little bit.

So he stopped, or he tried to. And asked the kids all the same, after they'd all had their weekly chat with Aunt Cora, and he'd roped them into helping with the washing-up after another reasonably healthy dinner that, he noted somewhat proudly, had been part of the report, "Should we watch Josie's show, then?"

"Yes!" Charlie said enthusiastically, but Amelia looked at him doubtfully and said, "Auntie Cora will say we shouldn't have."

"Oh, I don't think it can be too bad," Hugh said. "It's on at seven, isn't it? You may be bored, but I can't think it's really all that shocking."

They *were* bored, the first fifteen minutes, at least he and Charlie were. The story seemed to be all about an ambo who, for some peculiar reason, was being filmed doing what looked like his entire gym workout as he chatted with some other fellas. He was sweating far too much for the amount of effort he was putting in, from Hugh's point of view, his form was rubbish, and he wasn't wearing a shirt, which was unhygienic and unrealistic to say the least. A paramedic would've known better, he'd have thought. And it was enough that Hugh spent half his own life working out in a gym, he didn't need to spend what was feeling like the other half watching somebody else do it, badly, on TV.

Two of the guys looked like getting into a fight now, though. That was more interesting. Some argument about a nurse that the ambo was shagging and another fella fancied.

"Are they going to fight?" Charlie asked. "Why are they so angry? What happened?"

"Fighting over a girl," Hugh told him. "They both like the same one."

"Oh. That's pretty silly, isn't it? Couldn't they just ask her who she liked best?"

"Somehow," Hugh said, "that never occurs to a bloke when he's in that situation."

"*Shhh,*" Amelia hissed, and anyway, it looked like it was going to come to blows, and Hugh was just getting interested when it ended with the other fella raising a menacing fist—with the thumb inside, Hugh noticed, just asking to get broken as soon as he landed a good punch. And besides, if you fought in the gym, you were sure to be chucked out, have to find another spot to train. Wouldn't make any sense at all. You'd go outside, anybody would.

And then the scene faded out, and it was an advert for some kind of special broom, some woman looking blissful because sweeping was such fun, followed by one for a retirement village, and then the show came back on, and it was Josie.

Except...not.

She was standing next to a rounded desk area full of computer monitors and paper charts—a nurse's station in a hospital, Hugh would say, based on his considerable experience. Wearing a white coat with a name embroidered over the breast pocket, but it wasn't buttoned, and she didn't look like any doctor he'd ever had the pleasure to visit. She had a fitted black suit on under the coat that made the absolute most of her curves, combined with black stilettos that couldn't have been practical for somebody who worked on her feet, though Hugh didn't much care. Her hair was in a businesslike knot, and all she needed was a pair of glasses to become the sexiest librarian any man could ever dream of mussing up.

Until she started to hiss with venom and became intimidating as hell, that is, although the woman standing opposite her looked more than capable of taking her on.

"I'm not going to allow it," her opponent said. She was shorter than Josie, blonde and pretty, a silky terrier to Josie's greyhound. Dressed in scrubs, a stethoscope around her neck. "That's my patient."

"*Your* patient?" Josie scoffed. "Let me remind you that I'm a doctor. You want to swan about and pretend you're important, try it on an intern. To me, you're a nurse. You're here to follow my orders."

"As the *head nurse,*" the smaller woman said with grim determination, "I'm here to make sure my patients—and, yes, they're my patients too—are looked after and go home safely, which includes not being harassed by their surgeon. I'll be filing my report with the Medical Council today."

"Harassed?" Josie laughed, and it was nothing like the merry sound that made Hugh smile just to hear it. This laugh had a mocking edge that made him wince, because she was bloody good at her job. He hated her already, and he knew her. He was beginning to see what those women in the supermarket had been talking about.

"I think if you ask him," she said, a cruel smile curving her mouth, "you'll find he was more than willing. But you wouldn't know about that, would you? You wouldn't know about a man dying for it, gagging for it, willing to do anything, give anything to have it. You wouldn't have a clue, and you know it, and you can't stand it. Why don't you tell them, in that report of yours, what this is really about? That you'd go to any lengths to ruin my career, since I took Shane away from you? Not that it was much of a challenge. Want to know how hard it was?" She snapped her fingers in the other woman's face. "Just…that… easy. He couldn't wait to have me. He couldn't undress me fast enough. He couldn't forget you fast enough."

She stepped closer, lowered her voice, and the dark menace in it made the hairs on Hugh's arms rise. "Thought you'd got yourself a doctor at last, didn't you?" she sneered. "Well, he must not have cared much about you after all, because he was begging me, in the end. We did it right here, did he tell you that? On your desk. Think about that while you're typing up your little reports, keeping your records like the clerk you actually are. He did me hard, *on your desk.*" She leaned closer, and her smile was pure feline as she enunciated every word. "And I...made... him...*howl.*"

Hugh closed his mouth, grabbed for the remote, clicked it, and the screen went dark.

"It's not *over,*" Amelia protested, reaching for the remote, and Hugh held it up out of her reach.

"It is now," he said. "Aunt Cora was right. Not appropriate. I've just declared Josie's show off-limits for both of you, d'you hear?"

"What happened?" Charlie asked, looking seriously upset. "I never heard Josie sound like that before."

"That wasn't her," Hugh attempted to explain. "At least, it was, but it was her acting. That's her part."

"She's not very nice, is she?" Charlie asked.

"No," Hugh agreed, "she's not." He clicked the TV on again, switched the channel hastily to Prime, to *The Crowd Goes Wild,* his lovely safe sport chat show. Mark and Andrew bantering at the desk, anything off-color sure to go straight over the kids' heads. And then the view had switched to cricket, which was safer yet.

"Boring," Amelia sighed. "As usual."

"Just you remember," Hugh cautioned. "Off-limits." Although he'd be watching, he knew that. In his room at night, safely delayed until after the kids were in bed. And able to fast-forward through the rest of it to Josie's bits.

It crossed his mind that it was odd—possibly even a little pervy—to be watching her like that, but then, he'd be watching her along with hundreds of thousands of other Kiwis, most of them women. Most of them probably mums, so how pervy could it be, really? She'd watched him, she'd just told him so. Although he doubted that it'd had the same effect on her as watching her had had on him.

What were they thinking, anyway, having a show like that on at seven o'clock? Weren't kids watching? It couldn't be right.

"D'you think she's pretty? Josie?" That was Charlie.

"Hmm? Yeh. She's very pretty," Hugh said cautiously.

"Then I think you should go on a date with her," Charlie decided. "You said you don't have a girlfriend. She could be your girlfriend."

"No, she couldn't." Hugh turned down the volume on the TV with reluctance, because this was a conversation he could do without. "She has a partner."

Charlie considered that. "I don't think she does. I don't think she goes on dates."

"He's in Aussie, that's why. She's visiting him now," he forced himself to say. "Sometimes your partner isn't right there with you, just like I go away when I have a girlfriend, and she stays here. She's still my girlfriend, even so."

"I still think Josie would go on a date with you," Charlie persisted. "I think she likes you."

"You don't do that," Hugh attempted to explain. "If somebody has a partner, going on a date with them would be cheating, and it would be wrong. That's what the show was about," he realized with relief. Good, an example, because he was damned if he knew how to explain cheating. "Josie's character was cheating. She was going on a date"—well, a date of sorts—"with the nurse's partner, the other girl there. That's what the nurse was so angry about."

"Josie wouldn't really do something like that, though," Charlie said. "Not if it was wrong."

"Nah. She wouldn't," Hugh assured him. "She wouldn't cheat." And neither would he. Unfortunately.

"Then I think you should go on a date with Miss Chloe," Charlie said after another minute's thought. "If you can't go on one with Josie."

"I can get my own dates," Hugh protested.

Amelia cast him a jaundiced look. "I don't think so," she said.

"I beg your pardon?"

"Well, you haven't been," she said. "People who go on dates get babysitters. They stay out all night, like you did before. You haven't stayed out all night in ages, and you haven't got a babysitter, either."

"You don't go out with just anybody," Hugh attempted to explain. "It's not that simple. You have to like the look of the person, and she has to like the look of you."

"Then what?" Charlie asked. "D'you say, 'Do you want to go on a date with me?'"

"Nah," Amelia said knowledgeably. "She asks."

"She does not ask," Hugh said. "Not with me."

"Holly's mum says men are scared," Amelia said. "So the girl has to ask. She has to say, 'D'you want to get a coffee?' Like that. Otherwise he's too scared."

"I am not scared," he said.

"Then why aren't you going on a date? Holly's mum goes on a date on Friday all the time," Amelia saw fit to inform him again. "Sometimes other nights, too. That's why Holly watches *Courtney Place*. Because she and her little brother have to have a babysitter, and she likes it. The babysitter, I mean."

"Like I said," Hugh tried again. "I have to find somebody I like."

Amelia looked at him appraisingly. "Maybe if you cut your hair. Miss Chloe would go on a date with you, I think. I heard her and Josie talking about it."

"You did?" Hugh knew he shouldn't ask, but he did anyway. "What did they say?"

"Josie said Miss Chloe should go out with you," Amelia said with a shrug. "That's all."

"She said this in front of you?"

"Well, I heard."

"You shouldn't go around listening to other people's conversations." He wasn't having much success with his life lessons talk tonight, but he gave it another go. "It's not polite."

"*Hugh.*" She sighed. "I wasn't listening on *purpose.* I heard it after class, that's all."

"Well, what did Chloe say?" Hugh asked despite himself.

"She said, 'Mmm, yeh, not too bad. Pretty fit under all that hair.' That's why I think you should get a haircut, and then she'd go out with you."

"And what did Josie say?" In for a penny, in for a pound, and he wanted to know.

"She said, 'He's a bit clueless, but he's a pretty decent guy.'" Which was a ringing endorsement if he'd ever heard one.

"Well, cheers for that." So much for Josie having any feelings for him, if she were trying to push her friend off on him. All right, maybe he'd done a bit of longing, but it looked like he was the only one.

"So are you going to ask her out?" Amelia persisted. "Maybe I should tell her you like her, too. I could say that she should invite you to have a coffee, like Holly's mum says. I could do that after class tomorrow."

"Don't do me any favors," Hugh said. "If I want to go out with Miss Chloe—*if*—I can ask her myself."

"But get a haircut first," Amelia ordered. "That way, maybe she'll say yes."

♡

"If I did want to go for a haircut today," he said at breakfast the next morning, "would I need to get a babysitter? Or would I just take the two of you into Auckland with me?"

He should have checked that out before, he thought guiltily. He'd texted Vivy last night, had been glad that she'd been able to squeeze him in at the last minute, but he hadn't even thought about a babysitter. He'd got up this morning, though, pulled on his gear as usual for a run, and hesitated. Was it actually all right to leave the kids? He thought Amelia was old enough, but he wasn't sure. He should have asked Aunt Cora, or his mum, but it had never occurred to him.

In the end, he'd written a note and gone. And found himself worrying, which had been annoying. And, of course, had come back to find the house not burnt down, the kids not panicked a bit, calmly eating cereal in front of the TV as usual.

"You're allowed to leave," Amelia pronounced. "For a couple hours. If it's during the day, and if you check with a neighbor first and tell her that we're home alone."

"Or you could come," Hugh felt impelled to say. "If you wanted."

She looked him over critically. "I think it'd be boring. But maybe I should come, so I could say how she should cut it."

"Excuse me? I think between the two of us, we can manage without you. I've been getting my hair cut all by myself for, oh, almost a year now."

"Well," she said, unabashed, "you should shave your beard off, too. Girls don't like beards."

He ran his hand over his jaw. "Oh, I don't know. I think they might."

She sighed. *"Hugh.* I might know just a *little* more about being a girl than you do."

"You know about being a twelve-year-old girl, I'll give you that," he said. "You don't know about being a woman."

She seemed about to argue that point, too, so he turned to Charlie, who looked to have tuned out again. "What about you? Want to go with me?"

Charlie looked up doubtfully through his own shaggy dark hair, and Hugh realized that he should see about getting his cut as well. Where did that happen? Amelia was bound to know.

"Dunno," his brother said.

"Come on," Hugh said. "It'll be good fun. We'll take the ferry over, get you an ice cream, maybe. Take the rugby ball to the park afterwards and do a bit of kicking, practice your passing too, if you like." Because Charlie had finished his season playing at 10, and during the few matches Hugh had managed to get to, he'd seen that his brother had some talent. Besides, that was the one thing they had in common. He had the feeling he needed to spend more time with his brother, try to draw him out of his shell a little. So many things to think about. Pity he didn't know how to do most of them.

Amelia looked at him accusingly. "I thought you didn't allow ice cream."

"That mean you don't want it?" He'd realized after their latest supermarket visit that he might have been a bit harsh. He'd had the occasional ice block growing up, and it hadn't hurt him much.

She put her head on one side and considered. "No. I still don't want to come. I want to go over to June's early and practice for ballet. You're picking us up, don't forget. And don't forget that you need to bring Charlie, too. You can't leave him home alone. He's only eight."

"Which is why he's going to Auckland with me. And I'm not forgetting. That's why it's on the fridge, so I won't forget." That was the whole point of the haircut, after all. That he would be picking them up.

♥

He'd kept the beard, after some reflection, plus a consultation with Vivy that he wasn't going to be telling Amelia about.

"Nah, nice," Vivy had told him. "Give a woman a little mystery, wondering what it'd feel like to...kiss you, if that's what we're talking about, and I think it is. Oh, Hugh, my darling, such a pity I'm married. And streets older than you, of course. Next lifetime." Which had made him laugh, and made him a bit embarrassed, too.

And, when he stayed behind a minute while the girls changed and Charlie waited with his usual quiet patience, fading into the background, Chloe said yes.

She said more than that when they were having coffee the next day, though. He'd started by talking about Amelia, segued, he hoped smoothly, into asking about the school. Asking about her instead of banging on about himself, because that tended to work better, in his experience.

"Must have been quite an undertaking, setting it up," he said. "How long ago?"

"Four years," she said.

"Seems to be getting quite successful. You have some other teachers there as well, don't you?"

"Five."

"Lots of work, organizing all that, teaching as well." Geez, he was dull. He was putting himself to sleep here, and her too, judging by the brevity of her responses.

"Yes, it is," she agreed. "Especially," she said, looking directly at him out of the brown eyes, "since I have a son."

"Oh." Now he wasn't bored. Was *anyone* single and unencumbered? Apparently not. He struggled to find an answer. "How old is he?"

"Nearly two."

"So..." Had she thought this was some sort of parent-teacher conference, then? But the kids had said that she'd talked about him with Josie. He was seriously floundering with reading the signals here. "But not a partner," he said cautiously. "Or...yes?"

"Or no," she said, and there was a little smile there, and his signal-reading was back on track. "Not a partner. Just a child. Like you, I take it?"

"They're not exactly mine," he said.

"Oh?" Her dark eyebrows lifted. "Is that temporary?"

"No," he realized. "Well, temporary in that it won't be forever. New, I guess you'd call it. I've only been living with them for eight months or so," he tried to explain, "and on the road a good half of that or more, and my aunt's been here, so I haven't been in this..."

"The full-on mode," Chloe guessed. "And now you are, and it's new."

"It is."

She nodded. "Imagine what it's like to have a baby, then."

He couldn't, not really, and this wasn't the kind of easy date he'd envisioned, either. But he liked her, and if she had a son, well, maybe that was even better. She wouldn't be running screaming away from the very idea of Charlie and Amelia's existence. She *knew* Charlie and Amelia, she seemed to like them all right, and they liked her, too.

Worth a try, he decided, and asked her to dinner. And she said yes to that, too.

the lucky country

♡

"So how was it?" Clive asked Josie from the makeup chair on Monday. "Did you make a dramatic return to the Lucky Country? Our boy Derek sufficiently re-impressed with your x factor?"

"It was fine," Josie said, looking up from her script. "It was good to see him again."

He raised an eyebrow. Showing off, because he was one of the few people she knew who could actually do that. "Fine? Good? Thought I told you to mention."

"I did. I mentioned like billy-o."

"And? Didn't work? Has he gone off you, then?"

"No, I wouldn't say so," she said. "No. But…he did some mentioning of his own."

♡

Of people, and of places. He'd met her at Sydney Airport, had taken her off for an evening with the rest of the cast in a private area of a popular club. And she'd enjoyed meeting them, most of them, although the pounding music, the laughter and chat and dancing and drinking had all been a bit much after a day of painting her bathroom and the long flight. She'd been glad to leave the club soon after midnight. She'd been to it often enough during her own Sydney days, and she wouldn't have called it her favorite spot in the world, or the best place to re-connect.

"Can you believe Vanessa?" Derek asked, laughing, still excited, still high on the excitement of it all as he pulled her close, his arm around her before the driver jumped to open the door of the private car that had been dispatched to take them back to the hotel. "A little above the *Courtney Place* standard, eh," he added, sinking back into plush leather. "Finally living in the style to which I ought to be accustomed, not having to build my own patio so nobody will think I'm a tall poppy. Why the hell *not* be a tall poppy, if that's what you are?" He laughed again. "I could get accustomed to it, waving my good-looking head up above the rest without fear. But seriously, Vanessa?"

Josie inclined her head toward the driver, shot Derek a questioning look. A studio driver, she knew.

"Oh, don't worry," Derek said. "Rog knows where all the bodies are buried, don't you, mate?"

"You could say that," the driver agreed with a glance in the rear-view mirror.

Josie waited to answer anyway. In her experience, drivers—and the rest of the crew—did indeed know everything, and that was the problem.

"You're so bloody cautious," Derek said again when they'd climbed out of the car, ascended the lift and were in the hotel suite with its stunning, iconic view of the Harbour Bridge and the Opera House. "Not everybody has to like you, you know. But seriously, now you know what I've had to deal with, with Vanessa. Always has to be the center of attention, always something wrong. If it's not the food, it's the heat, or the flies, or her lines. Now, if we're talking about poppies, she's the tallest. And she's been that way the whole bloody time. Makes me appreciate you all the more." He pulled her to him, nuzzled her neck. "Mmm. I missed you. Let's talk about how much."

♡

"Not sure if complaining about somebody really counts as mentioning," she told Clive now, "but he did that, and my mentioning?" She passed her palm over the top of her head. "Just about that much effect. Glad to see me, wanted to show me everything, tell me everything. But jealous? Not so much."

"Hmm." Clive considered as Gregor brushed foundation over his cheeks, blended with the big sable brush. "If he's mentioning, and he's not caring that you're mentioning...I don't know, Josie-Girl. I'd say it doesn't look too good. How was the sex?"

"None of your business. As usual."

♡

But when she was catching up with Chloe on Tuesday night over an early dinner with her friend and her godson, and the subject came up again, she was more forthcoming.

"Yeh, it was good," she told Chloe, taking a bite of the couscous salad they'd fixed and watching Zavy work through his with his usual determination from his high chair. "But it wasn't... great."

"Talking, or...?" Chloe asked with an expressive tilt of her head.

"Both," Josie admitted. "Oh, it happened, but he wasn't all over me like you'd expect after more than a month. Happy enough to wait until the end of the evening. Guess I was hoping he'd be going to the door for the room service we'd finally managed to order, wrapped in the sheet with me hiding in the toilet, know what I mean?"

"Only the faintest recollection," Chloe said. "But the other way around? Yeh, I remember that, from before Rich did his runner.

He said it was because I was pregnant and he didn't fancy me as much, but I think it was just that he didn't fancy me, period."

She caught the red sippy cup just as Zavy dropped it over the side of his chair. "Do that," she warned him, holding the cup in the air, "and no more milk for you. Drink it or leave it. Which is it going to be?"

"Drink," he said, reaching for it.

"All right, then," she said, handing it back. "No more nonsense."

"Yeh," Josie sighed. She'd got the knack a while back of mum-conversation. You had to hold your train of thought through the detours, that was the trick of it. "He said he missed me, but mostly, he just seemed caught up in it all. All the glitz, the money, feeling like a star at last."

"I thought that was how you felt too, though, when you first went to Aussie," Chloe said.

Josie laughed. "This is the problem with having been friends so long. You remember all the inconvenient bits. I did feel that way at first, caught up, holding on for the ride, enjoying the thrill. But then I got over it. Got over myself, more like, and realized that so much of the rest of it that I'd been so impressed by was just…" She skimmed her hand flat over the table. "Surface."

"You thinking that's going to happen with Derek?" Chloe asked, and Josie wished she didn't look so doubtful.

"I don't know," she forced herself to say. "Guess we'll have to see how we go. He's been there for me through my own roughest patch, you know that. I was far from perfect myself, wasn't too sensitive to what he needed. He's due a bit of patience from me."

"Nothing like the same thing," Chloe said.

Josie shrugged. "Another life change. Good change, bad change, all transitions are tough."

"Talking of transitions," Chloe said, getting up and grabbing a face cloth hanging on the towel rack next to the sink and rinsing it under the tap before coming back to begin wiping Zavy down, "your neighbor asked me out."

"Who? Hugh?"

"Got another neighbor like that?" Chloe finished her cleanup of Zavy's plump cheeks and started on the chubby little fingers. "Yeh, Hugh. He seems like what you said, a pretty good guy, even though he did forget to collect Amelia and the other girls once."

"In fairness," Josie said, "I think the kid thing is pretty new to him."

"He said. When we went out."

"Oh."

Chloe lifted Zavy out of his chair and set him on the floor, where he immediately headed for the Playskool bus he'd only reluctantly abandoned for his dinner, plopped himself down on his padded backside and began to pluck out the round plastic passengers, while his mother picked up the dishes Josie hadn't already collected and took them to the sink.

Josie forced herself into patience, and Chloe began washing plates, then finally went on to say, "We went for a coffee on Sunday after I finished up at the studio, since I had Carolyn already. Just a quick one on Victoria Road."

"Babysitter-worthy, you think?" Josie asked, keeping her tone light—and showing some major acting chops in the process, she thought, appalled at the—well, at the jealousy, because there was no other word for it, the crab that nipped its evil pincers into her at the thought of Hugh taking Chloe out. She wasn't, she truly *wasn't* some Black Widow who had to pull every man she encountered into her web, who had to be the focus of male eyes, the center of male attention wherever she went. Hugh wasn't hers to lose, and Chloe deserved a good man, a man who'd spend an entire day helping his neighbor with her patio when there was nothing in it for him. A man who was willing to take on kids who weren't his own, because that was the real test, wasn't it? And the real issue.

"Guess we'll find out," Chloe said. "He asked if he could see me again. We're going out on Saturday night, if I can get a babysitter. Carolyn can't do it."

"Does he know about Zavy?"

"I told him. He seemed a bit…surprised, but he still asked me again, so…" Chloe shrugged. "Worth a try, I thought. Plus, he's fit, isn't he? Got a cast on that hand and all," she said with a smile, "but I figure, by the time I'm ready to see what he can do with his hands, maybe the cast will be a thing of the past, and who knows? Maybe my long drought will be as well."

I can do quite a lot with one. She heard him say it, saw the look in his eyes while he had, and felt another pinch of claws as she imagined him saying it to Chloe, looking at her like that.

But, as Josie had been at some pains to remind him, she had a partner, Chloe would be good for the kids, and Hugh…Hugh would be good for Chloe, she told herself firmly. Her friend had dated little enough since her solo pregnancy and Zavy's birth, all her energies going into the school that was her other baby. She deserved some happiness, and if Hugh could provide it, well, why wouldn't that be just wonderful for everybody?

"I'll be here this weekend," she said, "and I have no plans. Why don't I babysit the kids? You could bring Zavy over to Hugh's, and I could look after all of them there. Easy as."

"Sure?" Chloe asked doubtfully. "Not much of a Saturday night for you."

"Better than the one I'd have otherwise. I'd love to do it." And by Saturday night, she hoped, she'd have convinced herself that it was true.

chemistry

♡

"Hi." Hugh smiled at Josie as she stood outside on his porch, dressed down in skinny black trousers and a purple jersey and still looking pretty bloody fantastic. "Come on in."

"Nice haircut, by the way," she told him as she did.

"Thanks."

"You kept the beard, though," she said.

"Yeh." He ran his hand over his jaw. "After some thought. Should I have shaved it?"

"Mmm, I don't think so," she said. "If you're asking me. Manly, isn't it."

"Not too manly? he asked. "Rough?"

"No. Or if it is…" She smiled into his eyes. "That's not so bad. Chloe will like it, I'm sure."

Right. Chloe. "Come on in," he realized he should say.

"This is nice," she exclaimed as she followed him through the broad rimu-floored passage with its paneled walls that ran, in true villa style, straight back to the end of the house.

"You've never been here?" he asked in surprise.

"Just for a minute, when your aunt was here. That's my ulterior motive tonight," she said cheerily, "get some ideas for how I want my place to look when it's done, or restored, I should say. If they'd had the sense to leave well enough alone, it'd be cake.

Those DIY projects you mentioned, though." She gave an expressive shudder. "Brr."

He'd felt awkward about this, about having her babysit while he went out with somebody else, with her friend. Clearly, though, he was the only one who'd felt that way. "Kids are in the back," he said. "Early dinner."

"Oh, I don't get to cook?" she asked, and actually sounded disappointed.

"Only so much I was willing to ask of you," he said.

"You can ask," she said, and he looked down at her, his eyes met hers, and it was another of those electric moments, or was that just him? Because as always, she looked away first, made a little gesture towards the back of the house, and he led the way into the kitchen, having another talk with himself along the way.

"Oh," she said when they reached it. "This is *nice.*"

Hugh looked around. He guessed it was. White glass-fronted cabinets gleaming with rich paint, pale-yellow walls with glossy white trim, folding glass doors running the entire width of the back wall opening into the garden, onto the wooden deck where the kids were sitting.

"Josie!" Charlie hopped up, came over for a cuddle.

"I was just looking at your mum's beautiful kitchen," Josie told him. "I can see that she loved to cook, just like you said. But then, she was French."

"Yeh, she cooked better than Hugh," Amelia said, poking disconsolately at her dinner. "She cooked better than anybody. But," she added fairly, "Auntie Cora cooks better than Hugh too. And June's mum cooks better than Hugh."

"We made this dinner together," Hugh pointed out. "So if anything's lacking, it's on all of us."

"Shepherd's pie?" Josie asked, looking at the pan. "Moving up, I'd say, mince and potatoes. Looks yum. Got some carrots in there too, I see. Bonus points for nutrition."

"Not *that* yum," Amelia said.

"Have some," Hugh urged Josie. "If you think you can risk it. You can tell us how to improve for next time."

"I don't—" she began, then smiled ruefully.

"Let me guess. You don't eat shepherd's pie."

"Well, no. Mince and potatoes? No."

"You can't eat potatoes?" Charlie asked. "Are you allergic? A kid in my class is allergic to peanuts, but I never heard of anybody being allergic to potatoes. You need to be careful, though, if you're allergic."

"I'm not allergic," she assured him. "Just can't eat potatoes. Make me chubby, eh. But I'll have a wee taste of your pie all the same, give the two of you some pointers if I can. That way, the next time you make shepherd's pie with Hugh, you can put him right, show him up."

"Was your mum a good cook too?" Charlie asked. "Like ours?"

"A very good cook. Not French, nothing flash. But she can turn out dinner for ten on two burners, and make it look easy and taste better."

"Is she alive?" Charlie asked. "Or did she die?"

"She's alive," Josie said, looking a little taken aback.

"That's good," Charlie said. "So she can still cook for you and give you cuddles and things."

She gave him a cuddle of her own, and Hugh thought she might have teared up a bit. "I hope she stays alive a long, long time," she said. "Because you're right, she gives awesome cuddles."

"Then if you had kids," Charlie said, "you'd know how to cuddle too."

She didn't say anything, just held on a moment more, and Hugh had definitely been right about the tears. He realized, too, that neither of the kids ever came to him for cuddles, not these days, not for years, and that he hadn't thought of offering them.

His own mum had never been much of a one for cuddling, though. Always in motion, always on the phone or at the computer, or both, talking and planning, flapping a hand at him to wait, not to interrupt until she'd worked out measurements, coaxed a reluctant client to abandon the "darling" idea she'd found in some magazine, then throwing a dinner together for the two of them before rushing off again. She'd been a fine mum, had done the right things, cared the way a mum should, but she hadn't been much of a cuddler, and she still wasn't.

And neither had his dad been, at least not with him, not as far as his sketchy memory could recall from the early years. He'd mellowed with his marriage to the much younger, effervescent Juliette. A woman who, Hugh realized, Chloe resembled more than a little. No wonder the kids wanted him to date her.

The doorbell rang, and he hustled back through the house, opened the door to find Chloe. Looking, yes, pretty similar to Juliette, elegant in a green-and-white print wrap dress, a chubby toddler on one hip, a heavy-looking bag slung across the other shoulder, both of them seeming like too much weight for her slim frame.

"Hi," he said, stepping back to let her in. "Let me take that from you," he offered, reaching for the bag. "Everyone's on the patio. And introduce me, please," he added belatedly.

"This is Zavy," she said. "Xavier."

"Hi, Zavy," Hugh said. The boy looked at him unblinkingly out of big brown eyes and clung to his mother, and as a buttering-up tactic, Hugh thought, that hadn't gone too well.

"Here we are," he said, taking them out back and seeing Zavy's solemn face light up, his arms go out for Josie. She had the knack, no question.

"Bag's over here," Hugh said, setting it down near the wall. Nappies, he guessed.

"It's got his blanket in it," Chloe told Josie. "And a toy or two. He's already in his jammies. But sorry," she caught herself with a laugh. "You can see that."

"Hi, Zavy!" Amelia said chirpily to the boy. "You get to play with us tonight! And you get to sleep in my bed! Won't that be fun?"

"He's got plenty of minders tonight, doesn't he?" Chloe asked her. "She knows him because I bring him to the studio sometimes with me," she explained to Hugh. "In a pinch. Got a pen in the corner. He's not much of a one for fussing, luckily."

"How about if Charlie and I clean up here," Josie suggested, "and you and Zavy can check out his toys, Amelia? Then we can all watch a film. I rented a couple for us to choose from, and I predict some heated negotiations ahead."

"No princesses," Charlie said immediately. "And no kissing. Amelia always wants to watch ones with kissing. Lame as."

"I do *not*," Amelia said. "You just think that because they have adult themes that you aren't mature enough for."

"Wait a minute," Hugh said. "Adult themes? No adult themes."

"I think she means young adult themes," Josie said with a smile, "which can occasionally include a kiss or two. But no worries, Charlie. No kissing in these, or if there is, only at the end, and I'll alert you if it's looking dodgy, give you a chance to make a timely dash for the toilet."

"Sounds like the entertainment options will be pretty good," Chloe said. "Maybe we should just stay here, Hugh."

He realized that he'd got distracted. He was meant to be kick-starting his love life, not having cozy family time, however appealing that suddenly and unreasonably sounded. He was meant to be concentrating on Chloe. He reminded himself to do just that for the rest of the evening.

He managed it pretty well, in the end. He'd booked them in at Five Forty in Takapuna, close enough to home and her son to keep her comfortable, flash enough to make it look like he was trying. He'd chosen snapper for his meal, because he could eat it with one hand and still look reasonably civilized, had ordered their best white wine, had asked her more questions about her life.

"Josie and I were best of friends at school," she said, which he already knew. "Even though she boarded and I didn't. I took her home, lots of weekends, because she's a home sort of person, and I knew she was lonely. Although of course she'd never have said, and you'd never have known."

"A good actress even then, eh," he said.

"Always a good front," she agreed. "That's Josie. If she's hurting, you don't know it. When my partner left me while I was pregnant with Zavy, that was a hard time for her too. She'd come over and spend the night with me, leave in the morning, and I'd realize that she'd never said anything about herself, and that I'd never asked. Of course, I was such a wreck at the time, between the hormones and the studio and the stress and all, I was in a fog."

"It was a hard time for her?" Hugh asked. "Why?"

"Oh." Chloe looked a little taken aback. "Just some things she was going through herself at the time."

What kinds of things? Hugh wondered. Chloe was right, Josie never seemed fussed. He should turn the conversation back to Chloe, though. He was just trying to think of a smooth way to do it when he heard the voice at his elbow.

"Another wounded warrior on the town."

He turned around, the smile already on his face, because it was Hemi Ranapia, and he had company.

"Fancy meeting you here," Hemi's partner Reka said, and Hugh stood to give her a kiss, nod his hello to Kevin McNicholl, balancing on his crutches in the confined space of the little restaurant, his booted foot stuck out in front of him.

Reka was studying him—and Chloe—with interest, and Hugh made introductions. "Just get here?" he asked.

"Nah, just finished, mate," Hemi said. "Around the back, on the patio. Our usual wild night. Taking Kevvie out, because I took him along to the gym with me yesterday and he was looking like I needed to do something, stop him talking to the walls."

"Join us, why don't you," Hugh said. "We've got a good bit more wine here that needs finishing off, could get another few glasses." He lifted a hand for the waiter and asked for them.

Reka looked at him speculatively. "For a minute, then," she decided, and Hemi and Hugh adjusted chairs, pulled the table out to allow Kevin to get himself and his boot in.

Chloe gave Kevin an assessing look. "I recognized Hemi straight away, so I'm going to guess that you're a rugby player as well, and that that's the source of that injury."

"My sad fate," he said with his cheerful grin. "Hemi and Hugh look like footy players, and I look like the farmer I ought to be, ginger hair and all."

"I didn't say that," she protested, laughing.

"Don't let the false modesty fool you," Hemi said. "Kevvie saves all his flash for the paddock, that's all. Scored some pretty spectacular tries during the Championship. Had a hat trick against the Wallabies a couple months ago, in fact. He'd be on the Tour along with Hugh here if they hadn't been left behind to mend their broken bits."

"Perils of the game," Reka said. "I have to admit, I always enjoyed the injury breaks. I did," she protested at Hemi's indignant snort. "Only way I got to see you. Now," she sighed, "I wonder what I was thinking. Always underfoot, now you've retired."

"Too right," Hemi said. "Looking after the kids, doing the cooking. Bloody nightmare."

"That looks like it was a pretty bad injury, though," Chloe told Kevin. "If you're still on crutches, because it seems like Hugh's had his hand in that cast for a few weeks. Haven't you?" she asked him.

"Yeh," he said. "We both copped it in the last match of the Championship, three weeks ago now."

"You're right," Kevin told Chloe, "feels like I've been in this boot for a good while. Hemi and Reka took pity on me tonight, because it was true, I was going stir-crazy at home. Not being able to drive, it's the worst, eh." He looked appraisingly at Hugh's hand. "You driving with that? Bit of a menace, aren't you?"

"No more than usual," Hugh said.

"Wait a minute," Chloe said. "You both got injured in the same game? Must have been quite a game."

"It was," Kevin said. "I take it you didn't watch it." He was smiling, though.

"Well, no," she admitted, smiling back. "I didn't."

"And Kevvie's foot wouldn't have been as bad as it was," Hugh told her, "if he hadn't kept playing on it almost the entire game. Pounded that bone till it was more than cracked, till it was well and truly broken, is what he did. By the time we got on the plane, it was swollen to twice its size."

"And you'd have done exactly the same," Kevin said. "Anyway, I'll be fighting fit by January."

"If you need a lift anyplace in the meantime," Hugh said, "ring me."

Kevin looked at Hugh's own cast, doubt written all over his good-natured countenance. "Don't think so. What d'you do, club the car into submission?"

"If I'm fit to drive kids, reckon I could drive one whingeing winger as well," Hugh said, "even if he has to cower in the back seat and hide his eyes. I drive the ballet carpool, and if the twelve-year-old girls are brave enough to handle it, there might be hope for you yet."

"Ballet?" Reka asked, looking interested. "Would that be your sister? What's her name again?"

"Amelia," Hugh said. "Chloe here runs a ballet school. Uh..." He looked at Chloe.

"North Shore Dance," Chloe said. "In Bayswater. We do ballet, jazz, tap. Got a class for adults too," she said with a meaningful smile. "Great for fitness."

"Recipe for humiliation," Reka laughed.

"None of my ladies is there to win any scholarships," Chloe said. "Just to enjoy themselves, get a good workout, feel more graceful when they leave, maybe."

"You should do it," Hemi urged.

"Saying I'm not fit?" Reka asked. "Watch it, boy."

"Nah," he grinned. "Saying I'd like to see you in a...what do they call those things?" he asked Chloe.

"Leotards," she said with another smile.

"I've had four kids," Reka protested, but she was laughing again, looking gratified.

"If you've had four kids and are still managing to look that good," Chloe told her, "you should come along to ballet and show the other mums how it's done."

Which was true, because Reka always looked good. Not quite like Josie, because Reka was darker, her features not as sharply carved, and she was even curvier, not confined by some ridiculous standard about how thin a woman ought to be. But with the same air of outsized vitality, that spark of life, of happiness to be here living it that made the room light up a little because she was there.

"A dance teacher, *and* a saleswoman," Reka told Chloe. "Good on ya. I was really thinking about my girls, though. Ariana would love to do ballet. She's nine. That too old to start?"

"Not at all," Chloe assured her. "Hugh's sister is twelve, and she only started a few years ago herself. It's not necessarily about a career in dance, just like every boy who plays rugby won't grow up to be an All Black. Present company excepted, of course."

"I know Amelia won't," Hugh said. "You don't have to be tactful, by the way. Already saw that."

"Well…" Chloe admitted, "It could be her real talent lies elsewhere. Even a different type of athletics."

"I never thought of dancing being athletic," Hugh said, "but I guess it is."

"I have a niece who's dead keen on ballet," Kevin put in. "She likes to inform me that pound for pound, dancers and jockeys are the strongest athletes there are."

"Well, I wouldn't want to arm-wrestle you," Chloe told him. "So I don't know how we'd test that."

"We'll take it as read," Kevin said, smiling at her again, and Hugh's date seemed to be getting away from him.

Reka stood up, pulling Hemi with her. "And we've barged in on your evening out enough, Hugh. We'll be off, leave you to get on with it."

"No rush," Hugh felt constrained to say.

"Oh," Reka said, "I think there may be." As Hugh stood to say goodbye, he saw Chloe reach down to grab Kevin's crutches from the floor and hand them to him, and he saw that Reka saw it too.

"Got a babysitter at home who's probably tacking on the surcharges by now," Reka said. "Good to meet you, Chloe. Hope to see you again sometime soon. Who knows, maybe I'll try that ballet class after all."

"Could be I'll get my leotard after all," Hemi said. "Happy days." And off they went.

♡

"Nice mates you have," Chloe told Hugh when they'd sat down again.

"Yeh. Sorry about that, though. May not have been quite the intimate evening we had in mind."

"No worries. I'm not that used to dating, tell you the truth. It's been a while. Glad to have a little of the pressure off." She smiled at him, her wood-elf's face lighting up, and he laughed.

"I know what you mean," he confessed. "It can be a bit of an ordeal at times, can't it, getting through the early stages, seeing if it'll work?"

"It can. Not that I do it much. Nothing like a baby to complicate the social life. Not to mention thinking about our own babysitter at home, no doubt regretting her kind offer."

He indicated the door. "Ready to put her out of her misery, then?"

She smiled again and stood, accepted his help with her jacket, his hand on the door, with a gentle grace that he enjoyed watching.

When he'd pulled into his drive and turned the car off, though, he was brought up short, realizing that Josie was in his house. Well, this was awkward.

"This was nice," he said across the dark car.

"It was," she agreed.

He reached across the seat for her, grateful that he had his good right arm, at least, turned her face to his, and kissed her, a soft thing. And it felt...nice.

"But not going to work, is it?" she asked when he'd pulled back again.

He laughed, he couldn't help it. "That good?"

"Nah. Just no chemistry, is there? I like you, you like me, but...no. Is it Josie?"

"Pardon?"

She indicated the house with a quick movement of the dark head. "Who you want to be sitting here with? Who you'd rather be kissing?"

"No," he said. "No. Of course not."

"Uh-huh." She opened her door, got out of the car, and he hastened to join her. "Good to know."

just not me

♡

"So," Josie asked, shoving the nappy bag into the back of the car while Chloe buckled a thankfully still-sleeping Zavy into his car seat in the rear of her tiny Fiat, "how'd it go? Hard to tell."

And she'd been looking, she admitted, though neither of them had given anything away. Hugh had offered Chloe the same circumspect peck on the cheek he'd given her. That said something right there, didn't it? Although if it had had the effect on Chloe that it had had on her, there might be more to it than had met the eye.

She'd been wondering for weeks what Hugh's carefully-trimmed stubble would feel like, and just the hint of a whisper against her skin had made heat pool inside her, had had her forcing herself not to lean into him. She'd touched his broad shoulder, her fingers brushing lightly over the layer of jacket and shirt, and had wanted to keep holding him. To have him hold her, because he would have felt so solid. It would be so restful, leaning into all that strength, and yet not restful at all.

But this wasn't about her, it was about Chloe, so she looked the inquiry at her friend.

"No," Chloe said with decision, and Josie tried to still the rush of satisfaction. "Not happening."

"Why not?" Josie asked. "I didn't expect love at first sight, maybe, but I thought you seemed well suited. I wasn't surprised at all when he asked you out." Disappointed, maybe. Surprised, no.

Chloe shrugged. "You'd think, because you're right, he's a good bloke. Who knows why it happens and why it doesn't? It wasn't just me, either. Maybe he minds about Zavy after all. But whatever the reason, there's somebody standing here he wants to get with, and that somebody isn't me."

"Me?" Josie laughed. "I'm just the babysitter. The helpful neighbor."

"I don't think so," Chloe said. "I had my doubts as soon as I got here tonight, because that was a cozy scene. And when a man's having dinner with you and talking about somebody else, that's a pretty sure sign too."

"Mentioning," Josie remembered. "That's what Clive calls it." She considered explaining, abandoned the idea. Too complicated. "Really? He mentioned? Maybe he was trying to make you jealous, though. If he really did talk about me. Trying to up the heat a bit, if he saw it wasn't happening for you."

"He really did," Chloe assured her, "and it wasn't to make me jealous. I don't think he could be anything but straightforward if he tried. I wouldn't say that man's got a devious bone in his body. He'll make a fab partner for somebody, I have no doubt. Just not me."

animal magnetism

♡

He'd gone a bit long at the gym after his visit to the doctor, Hugh thought guiltily on a November Wednesday ten days later. He'd been so excited by the news that his cast was about to come off, though, he hadn't been able to keep himself from doing some extra training in preparation.

Now, his foot touched the brake yet again, and he swore at the unusually bad mid-afternoon backup nearing the approach for the Harbour Bridge. If it didn't let up, he was going to be late to collect Amelia, June, and Holly from dance lessons, and Amelia was going to think he'd forgotten again, he was going to be apologizing and ringing June's mum again, and Chloe was going to think she'd got off easy.

And then he forgot about Amelia, and June, and Holly, and Chloe, and June's mum, too, because he saw it, there to his right, the reason the traffic was slow. Had to be.

It was a billboard. A billboard that, yesterday, had been advertising, what, Tui? Some beer, anyway. And today, was advertising Josie.

Well, probably not Josie, he thought as his attention returned to the creeping traffic ahead. He put on the brake again and slowed nearly to a stop, which gave him the chance to check out the sign once more. It was an attention-getter, right enough, but as a product advert, it was a dead loss, because nobody was going to remember what it was meant to be selling.

She was lying atop a horse, a horse so white it was nearly silver. Stretched out flat along its back, her cheek against its neck, a wreath of frangipani around her head providing one single splash of color. One perfectly shaped golden leg hanging down the horse's side, her long, slender fingers twined in the white mane, her eyes huge and slumberous, the expression on her face, the slight parting of her full mouth saying that lying on a horse was a very pleasurable experience indeed.

Because, oh, yeh, she was naked. No naughty bits showing; her position astride the horse, the strategic placement of her arm saw to that. But they'd made sure the glossy waves of long dark hair didn't obscure anything important, and there was enough swell of bare breast and bottom to allow any man to fill in the blanks. And enough square centimeters of glowing golden skin to ensure that every bloke looking at this would have her in his dreams tonight, with every single luscious bit of her present and accounted for.

Bang. He hit the bumper of the car in front with a jolt that jerked his head forward, followed a fraction of a second later by a second, harder impact that had it going backwards again. He'd barely had a chance to register what had happened when he felt another jolt, then another, and wondered fuzzily if the driver behind was ramming him on purpose, but the impacts were coming too fast.

They stopped, finally, and Hugh pressed the switch for his hazard lights. He couldn't move, jammed between the car in front and the one behind, but he saw the driver ahead staring into his rear-view mirror with a look of panic on his face out of proportion to the severity of the prang. Hugh made a wide gesture toward the side of the road, motioning him to pull over, and the other driver finally got the message and started moving.

They'd been in the right-hand lane, since Hugh had been in a hurry, and there was a shoulder here. Good thing it hadn't happened on the bridge, but then, there wouldn't have been a bloody billboard on the bridge, Hugh thought as he followed the car ahead onto the shoulder and got out, ran forward to where the other driver was exiting his car, the traffic flowing past again now, or maybe inching would have been a better word.

It was a kid, he saw. Skinny and blond, face white, already starting to stammer.

Hugh cut him off. "Put your hazard lights on," he said.

The kid looked confused, so Hugh reached into the car, found the switch, and put them on himself.

By that point, they had company. An older man and woman, with a younger fella bringing up the rear. Four cars, then. Hugh sighed. He was *definitely* going to miss out on collecting Amelia.

"Hang on a tick," he told the others, and sent Christine a quick text.

Sorry held up can you get the girls. Will do 2x next week. He hoped she'd see it. Well, Amelia was twelve, not five, and the girls could walk to the bus stop if they had to, he told his nagging conscience. And he couldn't have helped this. Well, he could, obviously, but he hadn't, so that was that.

And right now, he had something else to see to. The younger fella who'd been in the fourth car along was talking to the kid, and things were getting a bit heated.

"What the hell were you on, stopping bang in the middle of the roadway?" the new arrival was demanding.

"Sorry," the kid said. "It was going so slowly, and I only took my eyes off the road for a second."

"Just like you did," Hugh put in, leveling his best calm-but-intimidating rugby stare at Angry Man. "Or you would've been able to stop in time yourself."

"Yeh, and what's your excuse?" The fella wasn't backing down, not yet.

"No excuse," Hugh said, keeping his tone level. They didn't need a stoush at the side of the road.

The woman snorted aloud and spoke for the first time. "I think we all know what all of your excuse was, and pretty silly you're going to look when you're asked why you weren't watching the road. I *told* you to look out," she reminded the man who had to be her husband, Hugh thought, from the look of exasperation—and a touch of amusement—she was casting his way, a look that said she'd be telling this story at their Golden Anniversary party. "I said, watch the road. What were they thinking, putting up that great thing where every man passing would be bound to gawp at it?"

"Exactly that, I reckon," her husband said. "Hard luck it was us, that's all."

"Look," Hugh cut in. "Let's just exchange details, wait for the police to get here, and get on with our day. Not much harm done, I shouldn't think," he said, casting a glance for the first time at the rear bumper of the kid's car, the front of his own. "Just cosmetic."

"Easy for you to say," the young fella muttered. He'd lost a little of his bluster, though. "Hundreds of dollars, the panelbeaters charge."

"You've got insurance, haven't you?" Hugh asked.

"Well, yeh," the other man admitted.

Hugh shrugged, pulled out his own wallet. "Right, then. Let's get to it."

"Hang on," the kid said. He looked at Hugh's license, then at his face. "You're Hugh Latimer."

"Yeh. Like it says," Hugh said.

"You are, aren't you?" the older man said. "Can't believe I didn't notice, but then, we were all a bit shook up, I'm thinking. There you are, love," he told his wife. "We've just run into an All Black." He laughed at his own joke, and Hugh smiled a bit painfully.

"Thought you were meant to have faster reactions than that," the younger man said, still not having forgiven Hugh for putting him right earlier. "No wonder the Blues were rubbish this season."

"Maybe it was your hand," the kid said, eyeing Hugh's cast. "That must make it tougher to drive. That could be why you couldn't stop."

"I work the brake with my foot, like most people," Hugh said impatiently. "My hand had nothing to do with it. Did it make you..." He glanced at the license he held in his hand, "John, smash into me?"

"Nah," the other man said, grinning a bit now. "The missus is right, I think we all know what happened here."

"My dad's going to kill me, though," the kid, Quade, said in some desperation. "I've only just got my Learner plates off. He's going to say I got reckless, and I didn't. I mean, we all looked, didn't we?"

"We did," John said. "I think we can all agree on that."

"So if you could just say it was your hand," Quade continued earnestly, "that'd make it so much better, don't you see?"

Hugh looked at him with some exasperation. "I'm not going to say that. Sorry and all that, but I'm not." And be disqualified from driving? Yeh, right.

Thankfully, the police arrived and put an end to the discussion, but Hugh didn't much relish the dry look the officer gave the four of them as they attempted to explain their moment of inattention, or the amusement on recognizing Hugh that cracked the professional mask entirely.

It was nearly six before he pulled into his driveway. At least he'd had a text back from Christine saying *OK can do,* which had been a relief, although he had a feeling that Amelia wasn't going to be quite so forgiving, and he went into the house with a fair bit of cowardly dread.

Except that she wasn't there, and neither was Charlie. He could tell they'd come home, because their backpacks were flung

He'd spent all morning with her the Saturday before, had helped her set up her fountain, as best he could with one hand, had even talked her into having lunch with him—and the kids, of course—afterwards, and so far, so bloody good.

"But," he went on, "I was worried myself, when I got home and found the two of you missing."

"We weren't missing," Charlie said. "We were here, visiting Josie."

"Why? You can't just barge in on her anytime. Josie's a busy person, got things to do. She didn't sign on to be your babysitter. And why didn't you leave me a note?" He knew he was snapping, but he *had* got a bit worried, and knowing they'd been next door in blithe unconcern was making him narky.

"We were *helping* her," Charlie said, looking agitated himself now. "She needed help, and we helped, and then she *invited* us."

"They did, and I did," Josie said. "They were helping me unload my new pot plants, out on the patio, and helping me put them into the pots, too. They offered very nicely, and I gave them a few nibbles, and we're all good."

"Well, thanks," he said. "But next time, leave me a note," he told the kids.

"If I had a phone," Amelia said, "you could have texted."

"If you had a phone," Hugh countered, "you'd be texting your friends every few minutes, and I'd be hearing from your teachers that you'd been using it under your desk, and getting one of those shocking thousand-dollar phone bills. No. You're twelve. A twelve-year-old doesn't need a phone."

"I'm nearly thirteen."

"You're twelve and a..." He calculated. "Half. You're not nearly thirteen. No phone."

"*Fine,*" she muttered, looking mutinous, and Hugh sighed. He was right, he was almost sure of it, but being right didn't seem to matter.

"Well," Josie said, "you could give *me* your number, Hugh, and I could text you. I promise to keep it under control. I hardly ever even text my friends under the desk anymore."

He laughed in spite of himself. "If you don't mind giving me yours as well, that'd help. And then we'll be getting on, leaving you to your evening."

They exchanged, and he felt better, though he'd never got a girl's number quite this way.

"Josie," Charlie said suddenly, "it's you! Why are you on a horse?"

"Shh." Amelia flapped a silencing hand at him, reached for the remote and turned the volume up on the telly, and Hugh saw a look he couldn't interpret on Josie's face as he turned and looked for himself.

"UK firm Bain Fantastique's new ad campaign for its *Tropique* bodycare line took an unexpected turn today when a new billboard on the Northern Motorway featuring *Courtney Place's* own Jocelyn Pae Ata contributed to two multi-vehicle accidents and a serious daylong traffic slowdown," the voice of the male newsreader was saying.

He was saying it, but the camera wasn't on him. It was Josie on that bloody horse on the screen, and if Hugh had wondered how he'd got distracted to the extent he had, well, there was the evidence right in front of him, because he was looking again, and he'd bet TVs all over New Zealand were having their volume turned up just now. He still didn't understand why she'd be lying naked on a horse, but it was working for him, so he guessed the advertising people knew what they were doing.

But just now, he had other things to think about, because a police spokesman was on screen now. Must have been a slow news day, and Hugh was sweating a bit. "We've had damage to seven vehicles reported, and the sign's caused a serious bottleneck," he said. "We've also had a number of complaints from the public, which the relevant departments are looking into now, as to whether this is an appropriate image for a public motorway."

"Two multivehicle accidents," the female newsreader said dryly when the cameras were on the news desk again. "Would those drivers have happened to be male?"

"What was the advert for again?" her colleague laughed. "Can't remember."

"Our weather isn't quite so exciting," the woman said, looking at the camera again. "What do you have for us, Sharon?"

"A fine day tomorrow for most of the North Island," the woman standing beside the giant weather map began.

"You can turn it off," Josie said quietly, and Amelia pressed the button on the remote, and the TV went dark, and Hugh breathed a sigh of relief. He was out of the woods.

"Why did they take a picture of you without any clothes on riding a horse, Josie?" Charlie asked. "That doesn't make sense. People don't ride horses with no clothes on."

"It was just for the advert," she said. "It's meant to look... natural. There are some others too, in magazines and such. It's all about being on the beach, in the rainforest, like that, because it's for skin care, you see? So they show...skin," she finished, and she didn't look entirely at ease herself.

"They always show pretty girls in adverts," Amelia explained to her brother. "They picked Josie because she's so pretty. And the horse was pretty too, so that's why they did it."

"You did look pretty, Josie," Charlie assured her. "I just never saw anybody riding a horse with no clothes on, that's all. Or lying down on it either. Was it very comfortable? Weren't you worried you would fall off?"

"It wasn't comfortable at all," Josie said. "It was dead scratchy, and stinky as well. I don't know what they were feeding him, the horse I mean, but a couple times, I'd be lying there and they'd be shooting, and suddenly..." She waved a hand in front of her face, a comical expression twisting her mouth, her eyes wide. "Phew. And I'd be trying to look like I was enjoying myself. Least they didn't have me lying on a cow. Horse poo isn't so bad. Cow, poo, though…" She made another face. "Or pigs. Now, if I'd been on a pig, that would *really* have been an acting job, because pigs smell."

Charlie giggled. "You would've looked so silly, lying on a pig."

"They wouldn't have had her lie on a *pig,*" Amelia said impatiently. "A pig isn't big enough."

"Mmm, I don't know about that," Josie said. "Pigs can get pretty big. I could probably fit. Think anybody'd pay for a picture of me lying on top of a pig, Hugh?"

She was teasing him, he realized. And flirting. She had never flirted before, but she was flirting now.

"I think they'd pay for a picture of you lying on top of anything," he said, and he smiled into her brown eyes, saw them widen a bit at what she was seeing in his. But if she was going to flirt, he was going to flirt back. Partner be damned. If that Derek fella couldn't be bothered to look after the woman of any man's dreams, he'd better start looking for an Aussie girl instead, because Hugh wasn't going to let a little thing like a partner stand in his way.

Amelia was talking again, though, and Hugh did his best to listen. "Of course they wouldn't have her lie on a pig. Or a cow. A cow would just be *stupid,* unless it was meant to be funny. They did a horse because horses are sexy."

"What do you know about what's sexy?" Hugh protested.

She shot him a pitying look. "I'm practically a *teenager,* Hugh. Women know these things."

"They do, eh." Amelia knew what was sexy? Already? Geez. Another thing he was going to have to worry about. Aunt Cora couldn't come home too soon for him.

"Girls like horses, and boys like dogs," Amelia explained. "Everybody knows that. Because dogs are friendly, and horses are mysterious and powerful and sexy, and girls can ride them and be powerful too. That's why there are so many books about girls and horses."

Hugh was losing track of the conversation. That hadn't been what he'd taken from the billboard, that girls liked horses, but if that skin care stuff was for women, he guessed the advert might be for women too, though he still had his doubts. "It is?"

She sighed with exasperation. "Well, duh. Pony club books?"

"Uh…Are there pony club books?"

"Of course there are," she said. "Heaps of them."

"And *Misty of Chincoteague*," Josie put in. *"National Velvet."*

"I don't know those," Amelia said doubtfully.

"Oh, you should read them," Josie said. "They're just wonderful. We can look at the library, if you like. I could show you."

"But there are books about other animals." Charlie was still pursuing the original topic. "Like dogs. There are loads of books about dogs."

"For *boys*," Amelia said impatiently. "Boys like dogs, and girls like horses. Like I *said*. Girls like cats, too," she added as an afterthought. "There are cat books. Cats are sexy, too, I think, though you couldn't lie on one, of course. Anything you can stroke, like a horse, or a cat," she decided. "I think that's what makes it sexy. And that's pretty, of course."

Yeh, pretty things you could stroke, that worked for Hugh.

"And goats," Josie put in helpfully. *"Heidi."*

Goats? Hugh was so confused.

"Animal books for girls," Josie explained, seeing it. "Not sexy animals." Ah.

"I haven't read that either," Amelia said.

"Oh!' Charlie jumped. "Pigs! There *are* ones about pigs. Because *Babe*. Mum read us *Babe*." His face clouded over. "I remember that. We were almost done when she…" He stopped.

"When she died," Hugh said. The kids didn't refer often to it anymore, but of course they thought about it. What should he do about that? What had Aunt Cora been doing about that? He didn't even know.

"You could get that too," Josie suggested. "At the library. I'm not sure how hard it is, but Amelia could read it aloud, couldn't she? Or Hugh could," she said with a glance at him. "Even better. It isn't right to leave a good book unfinished, or a good memory, either."

"I'm not too good at reading aloud," he began to say. But Josie was frowning a bit at him, giving her head an infinitesimal shake, so he changed it to, "but I could try. Course we could read it aloud." She was smiling at him now, so that was obviously the right answer.

"But we'd better go have dinner," Hugh said. "Looks like you two have done your best to clean out Josie's fridge, but I'm starved. And we need to let Josie get on with her own dinner as well."

"Maybe she could come eat with us," Charlie said. "Can you, Josie? Because you said if somebody helped you, you should feed them, and you helped us."

"Nah," she said with a quick glance at Hugh. "You helped me, remember? With the pot plants?"

"Oh, I think it's me in debt," Hugh said. Again, not how he was used to getting his dinner dates, but he'd take her company any way he could get it. "Got a couple roast chickens, some vegies, that's all, but if you don't mind eating that, we'd like to have you come."

"A feast," she said. "Roast chicken? Sounds good to me."

letting your hair down

♡

"Thanks very much for that," Josie said after a dinner that they'd all fixed together, had eaten to the accompaniment of plenty of friendly chat at the kitchen table. Another point on the Hugh as Undemanding-for-Now-Neighbor scoreboard, he hoped.

She got up and carried her dishes across to the sink. "And I should be off."

"If you could stay for a bit," Hugh offered, because this was an opportunity he wasn't going to let go by, "we could put these two on washing-up duty, and we could sit and have a glass of wine. I'm still getting over my traumatic experience, the kids gone missing. I may need a medical professional to sit with me and see that I recover properly."

"Josie's not really a medical professional," Amelia told him. "That's just her part."

Hugh ignored her. "One glass of wine." He held up his index finger for demonstration purposes. "One. In the lounge. Can I talk you into that much excess?"

"Maybe," she said, and she was smiling. "One."

"Good." He was smiling like a fool himself as he jumped up and went for the fridge before she could change her mind. "White OK?"

"White's awesome."

"Washing-up, homework for tomorrow in the backpack, showers, bed," he told the kids, grabbing a couple glasses. "Eight-thirty. I'll be checking."

"Holly's bedtime is nine-thirty," Amelia said, apparently deciding that this was the ideal moment to have this conversation.

"Wonderful," he said. "Tell her I said congratulations."

♡

Josie was laughing when he set the bottle and glasses on the coffee table. "Good job," she told him. "You're sounding more natural at that every day."

"You think?" He grinned at her, switched on the lamp on the end table, then turned the dimmers down on the overhead light. Low, but not too low. He gestured her to the couch, poured them each a glass, handed hers over and sat down in the easy chair at a right angle to her seat. Good distance, good nonverbal communication, he hoped.

"Yeh," Josie said. "I can just hear Amelia complaining about it to Holly tomorrow. Exactly the way it should be. If you're not infringing on their freedoms, failing to understand how mature they are now, you're probably not doing it right."

She leaned forward, touched her glass lightly to his with a murmured 'Cheers,' then settled back again, pulling her long, bare legs up under her. Her eyes smiled at him over the rim as she took a sip, and he blanked for a moment on what they'd been talking about.

"First time I've seen you drink anything," he said. "Next thing we know, you'll be letting your hair down. Feel free, by the way."

She smiled again, but didn't answer him directly. "And now you know why. And why I don't drink beer, and don't eat pizza."

"Or potatoes, or mince, or bacon. Strictly low-kilojoule pursuits, wasn't it?"

"Mmm. More points there, quoting my words back to me. Somebody's been to Dating School."

She really *was* flirting. "We aim to please," he told her, and if he smiled at her a little more while he said it, let his gaze heat up a bit, well, nonverbal communication could work both ways.

She lowered her eyes and took another sip. "Yeh, well, doesn't take too many beers and bikkies to knock the naked billboards right out of the running, and that's the contract that gave me the courage to buy the house at last. Pays heaps better than being Dr. Eva all year, shocking as that is. Although Dr. Eva has to watch the beers and bikkies too."

"I've noticed she can't seem to keep her clothes on," he agreed. "The kids and I had a look," he explained at her questioning glance. "And then I turned it off," he hastened to add, because he had a feeling that otherwise, the points were going to be disappearing from the scoreboard. "You were right. Dr. Eva isn't age-appropriate."

"Mmm. She's not. Good on ya for paying attention to that."

"Yeh, trying. Like we said."

"When is your aunt back?" she asked.

"About seven weeks. We're nearly halfway through, and not too bad, would you say?"

"I'd say not too bad at all."

"You can probably tell, though," he said, "that I've got a ways to go still. That thing about the reading...thanks for that. That would be good, you think, to read Charlie that book?"

"For Amelia too," she said. "She'll probably say she's not interested. But do the reading in here, that'd be my suggestion."

"Yeh? Why?"

"If you sit on the couch," she explained, "right in the middle of it, then Charlie has to sit close, on one side of you. And just that, just having an adult body next to his—he probably misses that. Sometimes having someone to touch is what we miss most, isn't it? Especially for a kid like Charlie who's lost both parents. He needs it more than anyone, and I'm guessing he doesn't know how to ask for it."

"You think?" he asked, startled. "You can tell that?"

"Yeh. I do. I think he's scared to touch you. He's scared you wouldn't want to, that you won't think he's tough enough for you."

"That's not true, though," he said. "He's eight. I know he's eight."

"Maybe you could show him it's all right, then. If you don't make a big deal of it, just sit where he'll be touching you without having to try, that could do it. And then, once you start reading, my guess is, Amelia will come sit too. If you're in the middle, she can sit on the other side, do you see? And then you've got them both close. Read that book, *Babe,* then read another one, and another. Dick King-Smith wrote heaps of them, I know, so that'd be easy, and natural."

He could do that. "Should I be talking about their parents, too?" he asked. "I saw you did that, about their mum, about her kitchen."

"Yeh. Do you really want to know what I think, though? Or is this just..." She waved her wine glass. "Chatting up? Making me believe you do?"

"I really do want to know. And, yeh," he admitted, because he liked her so much, and he didn't want to lie to her, "it's probably chatting up, too. But I really want to know all the same."

"Then here's my wisdom," she said. She laughed a little, then sobered, sat and thought a minute.

"One of the hardest things when somebody dies, I think," she said slowly, "is that people don't mention them again, don't ever say their names. It's because they're embarrassed, because they feel awkward, don't want to show their own pain, maybe, whatever it is, but it can make you feel...it could make Charlie and Amelia feel like their parents aren't just gone, they're forgotten. That's one of the worst things there is, to be forgotten, to have somebody we loved so much be forgotten. Our biggest fear, isn't it? That we'll die, and nobody will care? That we won't have mattered? When people die, as long as they're remembered, they're not really gone, are they? But if nobody ever mentions them again, if nobody remembers...then they're lost. And I think that's how Charlie feels. That his parents are lost, and it doesn't matter to anybody else, and nobody understands how it feels."

"How do you know all this?" he asked, and he wasn't flirting now.

"I'm an actor," she said. "It's my job to know how emotions feel, to read body language so I can convey that. And for me, I have to actually feel the emotions to convey them. Some actors don't, but I do."

"I didn't think Dr. Eva had any tender emotions," he said.

"I wasn't always Dr. Eva, though. And I won't be her forever. And on the loss thing," she went on, "that's being Maori, I guess. I think that's one thing we do better than Pakeha. We keep our loved ones alive in our memories, in our thoughts, and when we say their names, when we honor them, that lets the other people who loved them keep them alive, too."

"Should they be hanging onto the past, though?" he asked.

"That's not it," she said, sounding absolutely sure. "Grieving isn't hanging on. It's letting yourself do what you need to do in order to move into the future. Letting yourself feel the pain and the loss so you can go on and live again. Because the loss and the pain are still there whether you acknowledge them or not, aren't they? If you bottle them so tightly that even you can never see them, that doesn't make them go away. It just means it'll never stop hurting, like a wound that's got infected."

"Ouch."

She laughed, breaking the somber mood. "Yeh. Not the best metaphor, I guess, but that's how it feels, isn't it?"

"You think that's how it feels for Charlie? For Amelia?"

"I'm guessing," she said. "How does it feel for you?"

"For me?"

"Yeh. You lost your dad, too, right? Can't have been easy."

"I was an adult, though."

"Does that make it easy?"

"Well, none of it was easy," he admitted. "But there was a lot to do at the time, so I just got on with it, I suppose."

"Mmm," she said, and took another sip of wine. "Because you weren't living here, obviously."

"No. I was living in Wellington, always, playing for the Hurricanes. Hardly here at all, ever. I wasn't even in En Zed when it happened. I was all the way over in Perth, playing the Western Force. I found out after the match, in the sheds."

It had been a tough loss, a defensive implosion by the Hurricanes against the Force. There'd be some honest talk to come, it had been clear, but at the time, it had been a quiet group stripping down, getting the tape off, showering. Until the two police officers had walked into the room, and then it had gone even quieter.

They'd had a word to the coach, then they were walking through the room with every eye on them, every man praying they wouldn't stop in front of him. Every one of them no doubt running through his recent actions, hoping they weren't there for him.

And they'd stopped in front of Hugh.

"Hugh Latimer?" the elder one asked, his face deadly serious.

"Yeh," he said, his mind a whirl, his mouth dry.

"Got some bad news, I'm afraid. We've just heard from the Auckland Police. They've asked us to come find you."

Auckland. But he lived in Wellington. And he hadn't done anything wrong in Auckland. He hadn't done anything wrong in Wellington, for that matter, but when you were a sportsman, that sometimes didn't make any difference.

Some girl. Shit. Some accusation he wasn't going to be able to defend himself against, some casual thing she'd decided wasn't going to be casual after all. *Shit. Shit.*

"There's been an accident," the man said now, and Hugh stopped swearing inside, because he was past fear.

"What…what kind of accident?"

"Your father and…" The man looked at his pad. "Stepmother, I guess. A road accident. Hit by another car, a drink driver, by the sound of it."

"It's bad?" Hugh managed to ask. He wished he were dressed, that he wasn't sitting on a bench in his underwear.

"I'm sorry," the man said, and paused. "I'm afraid they're both gone. They were clipped on the motorway, went under the back of a truck. They didn't have a chance. It would have been instantaneous. I'm very sorry."

Hugh tried to stand up, but his legs wouldn't hold him. The room had gone dead quiet, he realized in some distant corner of his brain.

"The kids," he managed to say. "Amelia and Charlie. Were they with them?"

"No," the man said. "No kids. I didn't hear anything about that."

"Who's…" Hugh felt his body threatening to shake with the relief of it, tried to ignore it, tried to think. "Who's looking after the kids?"

"I don't know," the man said.

"Then *find out,*" Hugh said. His voice was rising, and he was furious. *"Find out."*

"Calm down," the man said.

"No. I won't calm down. Find out who's looking after those kids." He was up now, pulling on his warmups. "Make sure somebody is. And then ring me and tell me, so I can find them when I get there."

All he'd been able to think about on the plane was that last text from his dad. The one he hadn't answered.

Best of luck tonight. Can't watch this one, but I'll catch it later.

Story of his life, he'd thought when he'd got it. *Can't be there this time. Got a meeting with a client. Got a crew to sort out.* Got these other kids, the ones I wanted, the ones whose lives I want to be part of. Got this new wife, the one I can love, the one whose kids I can love. Got something—anything—to do that's more important than you.

So he hadn't answered. And now it didn't matter. Because both of them were dead.

♡

"So what did you do?" Josie asked quietly when he'd told her. Not all of that, of course. Just what had happened, that the other driver had been killed as well, nobody left to focus his fury on, nothing to be done but move on.

"Stayed with them for a couple weeks," he said. "Until we could decide what to do."

"Weren't there grandparents?" she asked.

"Juliette—my stepmum—she was French," he explained. "Her parents are there. And my dad only had his mum left, in the UK. She was over eighty, and her health's not great, so that was out. In the end, Aunt Cora came, my dad's sister. We talked, decided the best thing was for them to stay where they were, with her. So they could stay in their house, in their school, with their friends. Get as much—normality, I guess—as they could. She was able to do that, stay with them. I still had my contract with the Hurricanes to finish out, and then it was the All Blacks, of course. I was spending most of my time on the road by that point in the season, couldn't shift myself to Auckland and the

Blues until after the Northern Tour, until January, actually. I don't know what I'd have done if she hadn't been able to come."

"But you did move," she said. "You did that."

"I didn't know I was going to," he admitted. "But they had some trouble, the kids. Well, I guess that would happen, wouldn't it. They had some therapy, but it was still rough. The therapist thought it would be better if I were here, even though it wouldn't be all the time, and even though I'm nobody's idea of a parental figure. It seemed like it would be best. So I came."

He'd come, yeh, in the end, and he hadn't been one bit happy about it. He'd signed with the Blues, had gone from a team that was just getting some traction to one that was struggling badly with the retirement of their coach, the loss of so many of their senior players—their senior All Blacks, which had made it even worse. He'd come to a squad that was easily going to spend a year rebuilding, which hadn't been the plan at all, not at the peak of his career, when it mattered most of all.

Not to mention going from almost ten years of living on his own, ten years of doing what he'd liked—everything he'd liked—to living with a middle-aged woman and two kids who weren't his.

"But you didn't grow up with them, I guess," she said. "That's a pretty big age difference."

"More than fourteen years between Amelia and me. Eighteen years for Charlie. And you're right, I didn't grow up with them, because I was in Wellington, and by that time...I wasn't coming up here much."

"It wasn't home, then?" she asked, and he could feel her caution. It wasn't his favorite topic, but if she wanted to sit here with him and talk about it? He'd talk.

"No," he said. "Not that my stepmum didn't try, but by the time you're thirteen, fourteen, and there's a new baby...It was a bit hard."

"Ah," she said.

"And my dad," he surprised himself by going on, "he was…
he was trying harder too, by then. I can see that now. I suspect,
looking back, that Juliette—my stepmum—talked to him about
it. He wasn't very—warm, when I was a kid, but he changed. He
was different, with the others."

"That can happen, I think," she said, "as men get older.
Maybe get a little more secure in their work, stop pushing so
hard, turn to their families a bit more, appreciate what they've
got there."

"Yeh, I'm sure that had something to do with it. And he
and my stepmum were better suited, not that I'd ever tell my
mum that. My mum and dad—well, my mum's a pretty forceful
person, and not shy about giving her opinion. They—clashed, I
suppose you'd say. I don't remember too much, since they separated when I was five, but I remember that, and afterwards, too.
One reason my mum moved to Wellington."

"And took you with her."

"Yeh. She did. Never much discussion around that, from
what I know."

"Ah. Your dad and stepmum were different, though? It's
interesting," she hurried to say when he looked at her. "You
know. As an actor. Plus," she admitted, "I just want to know.
You're so…you're interesting," she said again, and there was a
faint flush on her cheeks now, surely. "But don't tell me if you
don't want to."

"If you want to listen," he said, and he was smiling at her,
because the flush was definitely there, and that had to be a good
sign, "I'll tell you. She—Juliette—was very…feminine, I suppose you'd say. I think she actually got her way more than my
mum ever did, oddly enough, even though she didn't push for
it nearly as hard. I know my dad was a better husband, a better
father with her than he ever was with my mum—at least to hear

my mum tell it. She made him want to please her, I guess. I'd say she made him want to be a better man."

He stopped, ran a hand over his jaw, and laughed a little. "But what do I know about it, right?"

"Oh," she said, "I think you're more perceptive than you give yourself credit for. I'll bet you saw a lot. And felt a little left out, maybe?"

"Maybe," he said. "At times." *At every time.*

"And still, you came. For the kids. You gave up your freedom for them, and came."

Was there anything better, he wondered, than knowing that the woman you wanted admired you? For the first time in ages, he felt like he understood his dad, at least in this one small way. "Yeh," he said. "Well, somewhat. Aunt Cora was here, remember."

"Still," she insisted, "you did."

"Because I needed to. They needed me to. Everybody was pretty clear on that."

He'd assumed that once things were more settled, he'd get his own place again, get some of that freedom back. He could be around, could help out, without actually living in the house, surely. That would be enough, wouldn't it? Surely it would.

He wasn't sure Josie would think so, though. So he didn't say it.

"Well," she said, setting down her empty wine glass with a sigh, "I'd better get home. Five o'clock comes early, every time. Thanks for this, though. Dinner, and the wine, and…everything."

He got up himself, walked her to the door, and she smiled up at him and said it again. "Thanks."

He smiled back, felt the connection as surely as if it were a physical thing, because something had happened here tonight, and he thought she knew it too. He bent and put a light hand on her shoulder to give her a kiss on the cheek, her own hand came up to rest against his arm, and she was staying there for a fraction of a second too long. And then she pulled away, and it took everything in him to stop himself from taking her in his arms and kissing her the way he wanted to. The way he needed to.

"Can I help you with anything else in your garden this weekend?" he asked.

"Oh," she said, busying herself with pulling her jersey on. "No, I'll be in Aussie, actually. I'm off to Sydney on Friday to see my partner."

"Oh," he said, and there was no mistaking what he was feeling now, because it was jealousy, pure and simple. "I hope he's grateful for that."

She laughed a little. "I hope so too."

"If he isn't," he said, his hand going out despite himself to trace the curve of her jaw, "you could think again."

"I couldn't, though." She was stepping away, pulling on her shoes, putting distance between them, and the message was as clear as a bell. "I'm the faithful type. Of course it can get a little confusing sometimes, being so far apart all this time. You must know that, traveling the way you do. It can be hard to maintain a relationship, but that's what you do, because he's still my partner. And I'm the faithful type," she repeated, the words coming out fast. Rushed, because she was flustered. "I don't cheat. So, no. Thanks for dinner, though. See you soon."

And with that, she…well, she fled, because he'd pushed too hard. Damn. *Damn.*

It isn't cheating if you break up first. He wanted to run her down, get in front of her and say it, make her see it too. But he didn't, because she didn't want to hear it, wasn't ready to hear it. Instead, he watched her across to her door and into her house, shut his own door, and went back to check on the kids.

The faithful type. Too faithful, and much too good for that fella she'd been seeing for, what, three years? That's what the magazines said, and it was looking to Hugh like three years too long. Why would any man wait that long to make it permanent, if he had somebody like her? Couldn't he see what he was risking? If Hugh had had Josie, and there had been any way of getting back to her, he'd have been doing it, every single weekend if it had been possible, and Sydney to Auckland was pretty bloody possible. He wouldn't have been leaving that to chance. He sure as hell wouldn't have been letting some other bloke get a look in. And he couldn't understand how any man would do anything else. Not if he had Josie.

enough of a woman

♡

Another weekend, another sunny Australian day, and Josie was back where she was supposed to be, back with her partner, temptation firmly set aside.

This time, she and Derek were doing it more at her pace. They'd got up late, by her standards, on Saturday morning, had gone to Bondi for a walk on the beach, a swim. Now they were having lunch at a café table set on the pavement, and she felt herself beginning to relax at last. Of course it was difficult to get the connection back after such an intense period in Derek's life, so many changes. That didn't mean it couldn't happen.

"This was my favorite part of living in Aussie," she said, stirring sweetener into her skinny flat white and starting in with enthusiasm on her Greek salad. "If it could all have been like this, I might still be here."

"It *is* all like this," Derek insisted. "Once you leave Queensland and the bush, that is, get away from the heat and the humidity and the spiders as big as your hand, back to civilization. And we need to talk about that."

His expression was serious, and all her unease was back, because something was about to happen.

"I'm not going back to New Zealand," he told her, and, yes, they'd gone straight into it. "There's no use thinking I am.

I'm staying here. And who knows? Maybe the UK, eventually. Maybe even Hollywood. Nothing but possibilities, because Bill's got me up for a part in a new show, and he's talking to the film people as well. It's all opening up, and all I had to do was fly across the Ditch to find it. My future's here, I'm sure of it. And what does that mean for us? Long-distance is too hard, and I don't want to do it forever. I don't want to do it much longer, in fact."

"But it's long-distance from my family otherwise," she said. "You know that, and you know how I feel about it. I don't want to move, not just now. Not yet."

"Your partner matters more than your family," he insisted. "Or he should. *I* should."

"So what are you telling me?" She set down the fork she realized she was still holding. The day was warm, but she was cold, had to stop herself from rubbing her hands over her arms, hugging herself. "That if I don't want to move now, we're done?"

"Josie…" He sighed.

"Oh," she realized, and the chill was so strong now she was nearly shivering. "Oh. We're done already, aren't we? Is that what you're saying? Is there somebody else? Is that what this is really about?"

"Wait. Hang on. There's nobody else," he said. "Of course there isn't. That's not what I'm saying."

She scrutinized him, sitting there projecting nothing but handsome, noble sincerity, but then, he was an actor. "I think there is," she decided. "And I think it's Vanessa."

"*Vanessa?*" He laughed, sharp and surprised, and the nobility was gone. "Of course it's not Vanessa. What have I been talking about since I've got here?"

"Not her? But you've mentioned her so much."

"Because I can't stand her, that's why. What, I have a secret passion? Trust me. No."

Trust him? Not anymore, it wasn't looking like. "So it's... who?" she insisted.

"It's nobody," he said, "not really. Well, maybe, maybe there could be, but that's all, because you know I've wanted to make this work between us. It's not about her, it's about you. Or it's about us, I guess. We're going in different directions."

"How? We're both actors. We're both pursuing our career. So we're doing it in different places. How is that different directions?"

He made an impatient gesture. "If you can't see...But it really doesn't matter anyway, does it? Because the real point is, you don't need me, and we both know it."

"Of course I need you," she said, and then stopped herself, because what was she meant to do now, beg? And she was still cold, overcome by numbness that she knew would become pain soon enough, but there was anger in there too now.

"Wait," she realized. "Wait a minute. You call me to talk over your problems, to tell me about your hard, hard day? You want to lean on me like that, tell me I'm so loyal, so cheerful, hoo-bloody-ray for easy-peasy Josie, and now you don't want me because I'm not needy enough for you?"

"You can try to make me wrong," he said doggedly, "but you know I'm right. We're friends, and I hope we always will be, no matter what, because you're a good friend. To everyone. But that's just it. I'm not special, not central to your life. I'm not important enough to you. How much do you miss me, really? If we talk about me, that's because you *ask* about me. And meanwhile, you're just happy Josie, getting along. Everybody's cheerful mum, except that you're never going to be anybody's mum, are you? That's why you have to try so hard."

She flinched as if he'd slapped her. "You know I need you," she whispered. "You *know* it. You of all people." She blinked the tears back, because she wasn't going to let him see her cry.

"I'm sorry," he said, looking a little ashamed. "I didn't want to do this this way. I wanted us just to talk, and have it be all right."

"Have it be all right," she repeated, and now the anger was right there, front and center. "That you're breaking up with me. You wanted me to make that *easy* for you? Because I'm so bloody strong? Because I don't need you even to *think* about me?"

"All right," he said. "All right. I know that once, for a little while, you did need me. You let me in, you let yourself be weak, needed me to be strong, and I was glad to do it. At the time. But that time passed, we got through it, and you're fine now, aren't you? I need somebody who makes me feel like it matters she's not with me, don't you see? Somebody who wouldn't hesitate if I asked her to move so we could be together, someplace that would be better for her too, by the way. Because she'd want to be with me more than anything. Because she'd know there was no real future for two people determined to live in different countries."

"Somebody to cling to you and worship you?" she asked, her voice not in any danger of trembling anymore. "Somebody who thinks the sun and moon rise on you? *That's* what you want?"

"Bloody hell, Josie," he said, reaching for her hand again. "I'm sorry, but I need somebody who thinks I'm wonderful."

She took her hand back. "I do. At least I used to. And maybe I need that too."

"I always have thought so, don't you see that?" he insisted. "I've always admired you. That's the problem. I don't want somebody who thinks she's stronger than me. And you do. Don't try to deny it. You do."

"I should've stayed destroyed, then? I should be weeping on your shoulder still, two years later?"

"Maybe you should," he said. "Because it's a big thing. It's a big problem."

"Ah." She was frozen. Ice. "You've changed your mind. Now it matters."

He gestured helplessly, a straightening of the expressive hands, a shrug of the broad shoulders. "People change. We were so in love at the time, weren't we? And I wanted to be there for you."

"Wanted to see yourself as noble," she said, her lip curling a little. "Holding me up. Playing the part of the supportive partner, loving me through it."

"Maybe," he said. "Maybe I did, and what's wrong with that? And I truly didn't think it mattered then. But I'm getting older, and I'm thinking it might be nice to be a dad someday, and I'm not willing to give up that possibility, not anymore."

"Nice to do it with somebody else, you mean," she said. "With somebody who could do it right. Not with somebody who'd probably have to adopt to make it happen, if it happened at all."

"I want my own kids, it's true," he said. "Does that make me unusual? I don't think it does. A man wants his *own* kids, not somebody else's. He wants his own genes to carry on. That's what being a dad is."

"No," she said. "It's not. That's what being a sperm donor is." She could barely get the words out, could barely hold onto her anger so it would overcome the pain.

She'd thought it hadn't mattered. She'd actually thought so, foolish optimist that she was. That was what she'd clung to after the doctor had changed everything, had dashed all her plans and hopes and dreams, the assumptions she'd made ever since she could remember planning and hoping and dreaming. All of them gone as if the man had waved a wand as he uttered the words.

Cervical carcinoma in situ. Cervical cancer. Hysterectomy.

Derek had sat with her, held her hand, told her that he was there for her, that she was all he cared about. That she was alive, and she'd be healthy again, and they'd be happy. He'd come to visit her while she'd recovered from the surgery, had sat with her and made her laugh, made her feel like her life wasn't really over, that there was still love and laughter to be had, that they still had a future and it was still bright. And that maybe, someday, somehow, she could even still be a mother.

She had told almost nobody. Not the rest of the cast, because illness wasn't something you broadcast, not in her profession, and actors were the worst gossips in the world. Not most of her whanau, nobody but her parents, her grandparents, her youngest brother, because she couldn't stand the pity. For a young, beautiful Maori woman not to be able to have children—they'd call that a tragedy, and she didn't need people to think she was tragic. Some of them, she knew, would even have nodded their heads in grim satisfaction at fate having caught up with the girl who'd been given too much. She'd felt so shaky, the jealous, cold pleasure would have sent her around the bend, and pity would have made her collapse entirely. And she couldn't afford to collapse. Not then. Not ever.

Maybe, if she'd collapsed after all, she'd still have Derek. Except that she didn't want him, not if the price was weakness and dependency. Not if the price was leaving the country she loved, living a life she didn't want.

"All right," she said, standing up, holding herself together. Just until she got to the airport. Just until she got away. "I get it."

"I'm sorry," he said, getting up himself. "That it didn't work out. I wanted it to, but you—"

"Yeh," she said. "I'm sorry too. And I'll say the same thing you did. It's not me, it's you, because I'm worth some sacrifices too. I just have to find a man who's willing to make them. Let's hope not every man is as selfish as you. I don't think he is. I think there are some good men out there, and I mean to find one."

"Selfish? Me? I'm not a good man, just because I want a woman who can have a baby? A normal woman who puts me first?" The dusky color was flooding Derek's tanned cheeks, his sorrow clearly replaced by hot anger, and all his careful phrasing was gone. "Sorry to tell you, but I don't think there are too many men out there looking for an infertile woman. One who's so attached to her mummy and daddy, her precious whanau, her tiny, insignificant little country at the bottom end of the world that she can't bear to leave any of them for more than a weekend. No matter how much that holds her back. No matter how much that holds *him* back. You're not enough of a woman for me, that's what it boils down to. Sorry and all that, but you're not, and that's not my bloody fault."

She wasn't going to cry. She wasn't. Instead, she summoned every bit of technique she had, lifted her chin, and stared him down.

"And you're not enough of a man," she told him coldly, and walked out.

not that kind of girl

♡

He was on a boat. A sleek, modern sailboat, cutting across the clear cerulean waters of Waitemata Harbour under a sun-soaked sky with just a few wisps of white cloud punctuating the blue, catching the stiff breeze full in the sail, then coming about into the shelter of Motuihe Island, the sails flapping as he dropped the anchor. He fixed the handle into its fitting and began to crank, fighting the pull of the wind.

Slap. Slap. He was cranking, but he was also watching Josie opposite him, which made things go a bit more slowly.

"Let's swim to shore," she said. "Race you."

He could tell by the look in her eye that she meant to win, and he was a little worried that she would. She pulled her T-shirt over her head and tossed it onto the blue-cushioned bench beside her, revealing a hot-pink bikini top that he guessed was big enough, but only just. Then she stood, unsnapped the fastening of her tiny shorts, and shoved them over her hips, and, yes, he was watching Josie undress. She wriggled a little to get the shorts off, and he was having trouble turning that handle, because the bikini bottoms were hot pink too, and the vee they made was so tiny, he could tell that what was under there was smooth, and silky, and perfect.

She was decent enough, except she wasn't, because there was nothing decent about Josie in that tiny bikini, all that bronzed skin gleaming, her mass of dark hair tumbling down her back.

She smiled at him, raised her arms to twist her hair back, and her full breasts were lifting, the shadow between them so deep, so inviting, asking him to pull those scraps of fabric aside and feel the weight in his palms, to run his thumbs across the nipples he could see pebbling beneath the fabric, to watch her shiver the way she was shivering right now.

He was staring at them, and then his gaze was moving down her body to her flat belly, tracing the entire delicious path his mouth wanted to take, all the way to that miniscule vee of pink, where he'd stop. Where he'd stay, his hands gripping her, pulling her into him. While he felt her body strain against him, heard the noises she wouldn't be able to restrain, until the moment when her knees buckled and he had to lay her down.

She could tell that he was staring, and he could tell that she knew what he was thinking and that she liked knowing it, and the sails were still flapping.

Slap. Slap. Slap.

He rose slowly to consciousness, and realized as he did that he wasn't on a boat at all. He was in bed, at home, alone, and the slap of the sails wasn't really a slap, either. It was more of a *crunch,* followed by a soft *thud.* Over and over and over, and he thought he knew where it was coming from. But why?

He rolled out of bed, opened his closet door and grabbed a pair of shorts and pulled them on. A quick stop in the bathroom, because these days, he brushed his teeth before he talked to Josie, and he was walking through the back door out into the garden, the grass still wet with early-morning dew under his bare feet.

He stepped onto his Josie-chatting concrete block and leaned his elbows against the top board, dangling his hands over the other side. Her side. He looked across her garden, and there she was. Shoveling dirt as though her life depended on it, in a patch near the side of the house. Her back to him, her hair not tumbling at all but tied up in its knot, her grubby work boots a contrast to the short shorts that were the only thing this scene had in common with his dream.

The shorts were good, though. Covering her beautifully formed backside, but only just, revealing the full length of smooth tanned leg beneath as she worked that spade.

"Burying the body?" he asked.

She stopped in the act of lifting another spadeful of dirt, then tossed it with deliberation before pausing and turning around, one hand hefting the spade, the other forearm going up to wipe her brow, which had a few dark hairs clinging damply to it. There was a smear of dirt across one cheek, her V-necked T-shirt had once been white and wasn't anymore, but it was pretty tight all the same, and shorts and work boots were one hell of a good look on her.

"I wish," she said, and she didn't look cheerful at all. "Digging for a vegie garden."

"At..." He looked up for the sun, but it wasn't visible yet over the roofs of the houses. "Some ungodly hour?"

"Past six," she said. 'Sometime. Yeh."

He looked at her again. "I'll come over and help you dig, shall I?"

"With one hand?"

He held both of them out over the fence, turned his arms so she could admire the finished result. "Two. Just like a normal person."

"Oh. Congratulations. But I don't have another spade." She sighed and wiped her face again.

"I do," he said, and ran to the shed for it, then realized that he wasn't going to be doing much digging barefoot. He went back into his bedroom, grabbed a T-shirt of his own, shoved his feet into socks and boots. He went back to the fence, picked up the spade and dropped it over to her side, tossed his shirt to join it, then shoved off from his block with both hands on the top of the crosspiece and vaulted over himself, landing in a crouch in the grass on the other side.

She needed to mow, he noticed. Or he did. Her grass was getting pretty long.

She stood, still holding her own spade, looking a little dazed. "You know, some people would have walked around."

"Nah. Too slow."

She seemed to catch herself, shrugged, and went back to digging. He looked at her for a moment, then grabbed his shirt from the grass, pulled it over his head and tugged it into place. He picked up his own spade and joined her, and within a few minutes, he was as sweaty as she was.

She didn't stop, because despite her slimness, she was strong, as he already knew, and she was determined, too. She didn't dig like a girl, either. She shoved the metal blade into the ground with decision, sending it on its way with a firm push from her boot, then hefted the whole thing and gave the dirt a good toss, her rhythm steady.

"You've done a fair bit of digging in your time," he said, his own latest spadeful of dirt joining hers on the pile. She was clearing a good patch, a full meter wide and a few meters long. Had marked it out with stakes and string again, too.

She looked up at him. "Sorry. What?"

"Don't want to talk, eh," he said. "I should shut up and dig, you reckon?"

She shrugged again. "You don't have to dig at all. I just need to."

"Because you need to plant vegies. In summer. A bit late, isn't it? But then, you're a country girl. You probably know that."

"It's this or do damage. This is probably better. Doesn't feel better, though," she said, attacking the ground with some real viciousness.

"Going to tell me what?" he asked. "Can't imagine you got sacked on a Sunday morning, so I'm thinking it's something else. And you're angry, not sad, so it's a man. It's him. That'd be my guess."

"Dead clever, aren't you?" She stomped her boot onto the spade, and he could see her, the proud daughter of some Maori chief, shoving that foot right down onto a defeated warrior's neck.

"My partner," she finally said. "If you can call him that. Some bloody partner. Derek." She was shoveling faster than ever.

"You were coming back tonight, I thought," he said cautiously.

"I thought so too. Turns out not. Back last night, late."

"And you're out here working at six the next morning. Something went wrong?"

"Yeh. Something went wrong. On our second visit in seven weeks. You'd think it was the UK, wouldn't you, as big an effort as it seemed to be for him to arrange a visit from me? To *allow* me to fly across the Ditch to see him?" He could see the effort it took her to say it.

"I did wonder," he admitted.

"Bet you did," she muttered. "Bet everybody did. Can't decide if it feels worse that it's over, or that it wasn't over sooner. That he's made me feel such a fool."

"If he doesn't want you," Hugh said, standing up and leaning on his spade to look at her, "he's made himself look the fool."

She sighed and straightened, raking the ground smooth with the back edge of her spade as if she didn't know she was doing it. "You think?"

She was still angry, he could tell, but he thought there might be some tears close to the surface now, and no wonder.

"I know so," he told her. "I don't know what he's thinking, can't imagine, but I'll tell you now, he's not worth it. He's not as good as you, and he knows it, that's my guess. He's finding his own level, that's all."

She laughed, and he could hear the bitterness. "Yeh, well, she's probably blonde, and she's probably somebody in the cast, because the stupid git hasn't got any originality at all. Too lazy to go find somebody at a bar like a normal bloke. Like you probably do." She looked at him, and, yes, there were a couple tears sparkling on those long dark lashes. "Know what he said? That I wasn't enough of a woman for him."

"You're enough," he told her. "And I don't look in bars. I don't need to. I know what I want."

She dropped the wooden handle bang into the dirt beside her and stood there, her eyes glinting with anger and pain and hurt, and he laid his own spade down and put his arms around her.

He'd only meant to give her a cuddle. But he reached a hand to her cheek to wipe the smear of dirt away, and her hands were on his shoulders, her golden-brown eyes raised to his, her gorgeously kissable mouth parting a bit, and he had to kiss her. He *had* to.

He brushed his lips over hers, softly at first, a comforting thing, and tried to tell himself he was being her friend, giving her a sorry-you're-hurting kiss, but she tightened her grip on him with the heavy leather work gloves, her mouth moved under his, and he was holding her sweet, warm body against him and kissing her harder, one hand going for the back of her head, the other around her waist, pulling her even closer, feeling the heat of her through the thin cotton of her shirt.

She opened her mouth under his, he heard the smothered moan, and it wasn't friendly any more, it wasn't brotherly, it wasn't sorry at all. He was glad, fierce with it, and he kissed her some more, dropped down into the darkness of it, into the pleasure of Josie's delicious mouth, into the taste of her, all salt and sweetness, and yeh, she was enough of a woman for him. She was enough of a woman for anybody.

She moaned again, and the sound pulled him back even as it pulled him in, and he stepped back a pace, fought his body and what it was urging him to do.

"What?" she asked, and her eyes were flashing again, angry and confused and hurt. "What?"

He looked down, shook his head, ran a hand through the hair he'd cut, there was no doubt at all now, for her. "Timing," he told her. "Or something, because you don't want me right now, not really. You're not thinking about me. You're thinking about him."

"So?" she challenged. "Even if I am, what does it matter, if I don't care? And I don't. I don't care a bit. Maybe I will tomorrow, but I don't right now."

He smiled a little painfully. "But I do. I do care. I want you to be thinking about me, just like I'll be thinking about you. I want to be in your bed because you want me there, not because you have something to prove."

He did? Since when had he got so choosy? Since now, he guessed.

"You're turning me down too?" She looked incredulous, and he saw the flush moving up the length of her graceful neck, all the way to the fierce planes of her cheekbones. "You've been look-ing at me like you wanted to eat me up since the first day you met me, I'm offering it to you on a plate, and you're turning me down?" She laughed, and it was angry again. "Bloody hell. I really have lost it. Cardinal actor sin, believing I'm what people see onscreen, that every man wants me, even though the one that had me couldn't wait to let me go again. Do you know how many scary letters I get? Men want me to wear boots and tie them up and whip them. And yes, it's true," she insisted, flushing a bit more as he smiled, reflexively, because she'd startled him. "I could show you. And you don't even want to kiss me? Or maybe you *do* believe I'm what you see onscreen, and that's why you don't want it. But that's not me. It's not *me*."

"Josie. Wait," he said, appalled that he'd made her feel even worse, because it was clear that he had. He was rubbish at this kind of emotional stuff. He should have given her that cuddle and been done with it, but he hadn't been able to. He took a breath, blew it out, and tried again.

"Yeh," he said, "I've been looking at you, and yeh, I want to eat you up. I believe you get those letters, too, and no, I don't think you're what I see onscreen." He reached out and smoothed those wisps of hair back, because he had to touch her again. "And I want to kiss you. Everywhere. Believe me, I want it. I won't be asking you to tie me up, though. Ever." He smiled a little, trying to make her see what he felt, what she was to him. "That's a promise. Because you're not that kind of girl."

"How do you know what kind of girl I am?" At least she wasn't looking heartbroken anymore.

He smiled again. "Let's say I have a pretty fair idea. And I can't wait to find out more. But not today."

wings, or not

♡

Hugh opened his eyes on another summer morning, but it hadn't been a dream waking him this time, or any sound, either. He frowned at the quality of the light coming around the edges of the blinds, turned his head to squint at his alarm clock. Then hauled himself up on an elbow, grabbed the clock and stared at it, and swore.

Forty-five minutes late, because he'd been up late the night before, after the kids had gone to bed, watching the All Blacks' game against the French for a second time, and then hadn't been able to sleep afterwards. Keyed up by the victory, and wishing he'd been there. He'd been lucky in the past with the injuries, partly genetics, partly because he trained so hard, and had never missed an entire series like this, and he was hating it. Especially since Luke Hoeata *had* had one hell of a game, had impressed in the 7 jersey, had taken full advantage of the opportunity afforded by Hugh's absence.

In the reasonable light of morning, though, there was nothing new about players competing for their spots, or about the tenuousness of life at the top of the rugby heap, and his unease of the night was overblown and served no useful purpose. Better to spend the energy training. But for all that, he hadn't slept, and then he'd overslept, and why hadn't Amelia woken him up? She'd never been shy about that before.

He walked into the kitchen, and she wasn't there. Just Charlie, eating cereal in his pajamas, and well behind schedule.

"Morning," Hugh said. "Sorry. I overslept. You've got to leave for school in..." He looked at the clock. "Fifteen minutes, so rattle your dags. Amelia already done?"

"Nah," Charlie said, shoveling cereal into his mouth, speaking around it. "She's in bed. She didn't come out to eat breakfast."

"She ill?" Hugh asked with a little alarm. He was doing better at the general feeding and watering, but that would seriously stretch his capabilities.

"She said."

"Well, get dressed," Hugh decided, "and I'll find out."

Her bedroom door was shut. He gave it a rap with his knuckles. "Amelia? You in there?"

"Go away." She didn't sound ill. She sounded unhappy, or worse. What?

He rapped again, then tried the door. Locked. He rattled the handle. "Amelia. Open the door."

"Go *away*," she insisted, and he thought she might be crying. "Leave me *alone*."

What was he meant to do now? "You need to let me in," he said. "If you're ill, I need to see." Not that he wanted to. But it didn't matter anyway, because no matter what he said, the door remained locked.

He went and found the key, which took some searching. Charlie stood in the hall, still in his pajamas, and said worriedly, "I knocked, but she wouldn't come."

Hugh looked at him in exasperation. "Why didn't you come get me? Why didn't you wake me up?"

Charlie shrugged, looked away. "You were asleep."

"That's the point. If something's wrong, you come get me, you don't just ignore it!"

"I didn't..." Charlie said. "You were sleeping," he repeated. "You'd get angry."

"I don't—" Hugh stopped. "Go get your uni on," he said instead. "Get ready for school."

"I'm late, though," Charlie said.

Hugh ran a hand through his hair. "All right. Well, that's too bad. You're late. You still need to go."

"I need a note."

"A note? What note?"

"For school. Saying I'm late."

"Won't they see that by themselves?"

"You have to have a note. So you're excused. Otherwise you're in trouble."

"Just—" Hugh looked at Amelia's door, back at Charlie. Amelia didn't seem to be in dire distress, and her voice had been strong enough, so whatever was wrong, it could wait five minutes, he decided. "Go get dressed," he told Charlie. "I'm going to the kitchen right now to write you a note."

"And I don't have my lunch," Charlie said.

"Well, *get* your lunch," Hugh said with exasperation. "Now. Go."

It took another fifteen minutes, in the end, and Charlie was standing at the front door, note in hand, trepidation clear.

"They're not going to imprison you," Hugh said.

"We have a maths test, though," Charlie said. "And I'll have missed it. Mrs. Anderson will be angry."

"Nah, she won't. Because I wrote 'family emergency,'" Hugh told him, taking the note from him and shoving it into the outer pocket of Charlie's backpack.

"It isn't an emergency, though," Charlie said. "It's because you were asleep."

"Close enough." Hugh opened the door. "Go."

Except that it was raining. Actually, pissing down. Brilliant. He grabbed Charlie's mac off the hook and helped him off with his backpack and into the raincoat, then got the pack on him again. "OK. Now go."

"What about Amelia?"

"I'll look after Amelia."

"If she's ill," Charlie said, still standing on the porch, "you have to take her to the doctor. I mean, if she's really ill. Or you have to buy her ginger beer, if it's a tummy bug."

"I'll figure it out," Hugh said. "Go take your maths test. I've got it."

♡

He didn't knock this time because, truth to tell, he was getting worried himself. He turned the key in the lock and pushed the bedroom door open again. "Amelia? Mel?"

He hadn't called her that since she'd been little, but the fig-ure huddled on her side under the duvet, her back towards him, did look little, and he remembered, all of a sudden, how she'd used to march into his room in the mornings on his rare visits amongst the obligations of rugby and university—not to men-tion his lack of enthusiasm for being a fifth wheel in the happy family that wasn't quite his.

Amelia at three, four, five years old, an imperious little figure with a sturdy body that was all their dad, nothing of her petite, graceful French mother. Her dark hair mussed, still in her paja-mas, she'd climb up to sit cross-legged on his bed, poke him until he woke up, and tell him her dreams. Long, elaborate tales of ponies and kittens and princesses and magic that he'd barely been able to follow, but had listened to all the same, more or less, because her adoration had been flattering. She'd clamored for rides on his shoulders, for him to read her bedtime stories, had come to him at night and demanded cuddles when he'd be watching sport on the telly with his dad, having a rare father/son moment.

Charlie had been shyer when he'd come along, a mummy's boy, and Hugh hadn't been around enough anyway by that point for the attachment to form. But Amelia had worshiped Hugh from the start. When had that changed? When had he lost that, and why hadn't he tried harder to get it back, especially once she'd lost her parents?

Because he hadn't been here, that was why. And by the time he was, she'd been walled off behind her almost-adolescent superiority, and, who knew, probably by her own ways of coping as well, and he...well, he'd been intimidated at the prospect of breaking through all of that. He'd told himself he wasn't necessary anyway. He was doing his part. He was paying, and he was around—some of the time, anyway—and Amelia and Charlie had Aunt Cora for the rest.

But right now, they didn't. Right now, Amelia had him, and that was it, so he was going to have to do his best to make that be enough.

He went and sat on the side of her bed, just as she'd done all those years ago, and put a tentative hand on her shoulder.

And felt her shrug it off again immediately, roll over further, and pull her legs up into a tighter ball. She spoke, her voice muffled by the pillow, or by tears, or both. "Go away."

"Are you ill?" he asked again. He put his hand back all the same. "Mel. Look at me." He kept the note of command in his voice, but tried to soften it a bit. "I need to know. I can help."

"No you can't," she said, and she wasn't looking, either. So much for the note of command.

"Is it something at school?" he pressed, because she didn't seem ill to him. "Or something about your mum and dad, maybe? Or..." He hesitated. "A boy?"

"*No.* You're so *stupid.*"

That set him back a little. He thought a moment, then tried again. "Maybe I am," he said, "because I don't know what's wrong.

But I know that whatever it is, you can tell me. I was a kid too, not that long ago. I know about bullies. I know about exams and feeling like you don't fit in. I know about feeling awkward and about friends who don't want to be your friend anymore. I know how much it all feels like it matters. Try me. Please."

"You can't know about this," she said, "because you're not a girl. Auntie Cora would know, but she isn't *here*. I tried to ring, and she didn't answer. And Mummy's dead. So there's nobody."

"Auntie Cora could be there now," he said. "We could try again, if you like." He pulled his phone from his pocket. "We could do it now."

"I rang Holly and June too," she continued as if he hadn't spoken. He could hear her voice breaking, and she sounded so forlorn. So lost. "I thought maybe June's mum would help, but she said she had to work, and maybe after school. But after school's too *late*. And she said June had to go to school, and I should go too, but I *can't*. I don't have the stuff. I don't even know what to get. So there's nobody who can help."

He was starting to get the glimmer of an idea, because she was twelve. And he was an idiot, not to have thought about this happening. "Is it..." He hesitated. "Is this a girl thing? Is it your period? Did you start it?"

She pulled the duvet all the way over her head, and he thought he'd guessed right.

"Because that's not a disaster," he said, trying his best to sound cheerful and persuasive. "That's normal. All girls have that, don't you know? Didn't you have some class, and all? Didn't they explain?"

"I can't talk to you about it," she said, her voice anguished under the covers. "Go *away*."

"Why?" he pressed. "Because it's embarrassing? I know it is. Bodies are embarrassing. Mine was, too, when I was twelve. In a different way, but still, and I didn't have a dad to ask, so I do know what it's like. And I've known heaps of girls, Mel. They all have periods. Boys your age may laugh about it, but that's just because they're embarrassed too. So get up, and we'll get you sorted so you can go to school, and afterwards, you can ring Auntie Cora, or you can talk to June's mum, and they'll answer your questions. It's going to be fine."

She rolled over at last to face him, only her blotchy face visible, flushed and angry, her hair tangled, one sweaty strand stuck to her cheek, because it was too warm and humid to be under that duvet. "You don't," she said. "You don't know. Because..." She'd begun to cry, an angry sound. "There's blood *everywhere*, and I don't know how to get it out, and I don't have any of the stuff, like I said. I need..." Her color was even higher. "I need the *stuff,*" she said again, and it was a wail.

"We could go get it," he suggested. Oh, geez. Crying. He wasn't good with crying. "We'll go to New World right now, and we'll deal with the blood, too." What did you buy? All those shelves of mysterious boxes—he had no clue. He'd always just gone for the condom packet and got out of there, away from the rows of tampons and pads. Light Days. Heavy Days. Wings. What the hell were wings, and would she need them or not? The women he'd known had all used tampons. Would Amelia know how to use a tampon, though? He abandoned that entire idea pretty smartly. June's mum would have to sort that out. He'd study the boxes, read labels, ask somebody, and find something, something that wasn't tampons, for now. He hoped.

"You can come with me," he said again. "Change your clothes, if there's blood, put some...I dunno, some TP or something in there, and we'll go find the right thing."

"*No.* I'm going to wait for June's mum."

Lie in bed all day and bleed and work herself up? That wasn't the answer, and he sat, helpless, trying to figure out what was.

Josie's car had been in the drive when he'd seen Charlie off, he realized. He'd barely seen her since their garden-digging session more than two weeks ago. Working, he'd guessed, and something else on the weekends. Not hiding from him, he hoped, but then, he didn't seem to be much chop at dealing with distraught girls, so who knew.

He leaned down, brushed the sweaty hair from Amelia's face, and gave her a kiss on the cheek. "I'm going to get you help," he promised. "We're going to solve this. I'll be back straight away."

If Josie wasn't there, well, he'd go to New World on his own, ask one of the clerks what to get, and he'd help Amelia deal with the rest of it, blood and all. Embarrassment be damned.

dr. josie

♡

Josie sat over another cup of tea and contemplated the rain blowing across her back garden. So much for her plan to get the vegies in.

She should have done it over the weekend, when the weather had been fine, but the past couple weeks had taken too much out of her. Projecting supreme sexual confidence, being so devastatingly female when she was feeling anything but, when she was feeling bruised and battered inside, aching and vulnerable. *Not enough of a woman for me.*

She'd done it, because she always did it, because that was what a professional did. She'd convinced herself once again that she was a brilliant surgeon, not to mention a sexual predator who used men as playthings, who was amused by the struggles of her victims, who would never, ever be a victim herself. Had put in the long, hard days, then put her body through its own rigorous workout, the regimen that didn't allow for heartbreak or laziness, that kept her in modeling contracts. Had fulfilled every single obligation, and had crawled into bed at the end of every brutal day too exhausted to cry.

She'd broken the news about Derek to Clive and Val at the studio, had left it to them to spread the word to the rest of the cast, and to her agent to alert the rest of the world, and then hadn't looked to see what the world had thought of it. Had tried, during the rare moments of quiet when she was driving, working out, to sort out her feelings about the breakup, and when they remained nothing but a messy, tangled knot despite her efforts, had given up.

Instead, she'd driven home this past Friday night, since she wasn't called for Monday. She'd gone fishing with her dad at dawn on Saturday morning, had gone to church with her parents and grandparents and had Sunday dinner afterwards with as much of her family as could be gathered for it, hadn't eaten too much of her mum's food, and had watched her mum bite her tongue about that. And, yes, had felt better.

Her parents hadn't seemed surprised at the breakup, and they certainly hadn't been disappointed. At least there was that.

"Best thing that could've happened, you ask me," her dad had said, steering the ute back up the winding road with the boat hitched on behind. He'd been quiet when she'd told him, quiet ever since, but now that he'd digested the news, he was ready to give his opinion. "I haven't said much, because I knew you loved the fella, and he was good to you when you were ill. Credit to him for that. But he's not in your class, and I was always worried he'd ask you to marry him. That would've broken my heart, because I'd have known he was bound to break yours. Better it happened now. Let him find a pretty face, let them admire each other and tell each other that's enough. You're meant for something better. For some*one* better. When I walk you down the aisle, I want to be giving you away to the man who deserves you. I want to know that he'll care more about your happiness than he does about his own. That you'll be his treasure, the way your mum is mine. That's the man I can give you to with a whole heart. The man who'll take care of you, because you're his heart's blood. Because nothing will matter more to him."

"I'm not sure he's out there, Dad," she admitted, the hot tears tightening in her chest, threatening the stoicism that had held them at bay during every disciplined hour of her long work week.

"He's there," he said. "You have faith. God wouldn't have made you so beautiful without making a fit partner for you as well. You wait for him."

"Takes more than looks," she said. "Derek was beautiful too, and you just told me how much that mattered."

"Don't be stupid," he said, his tone sharp, his broad, tough hands so sure on the wheel. "You know I'm not talking about your outside. I'm talking about the part of you that was beautiful when you were a skinny kid, and will still be beautiful when you're an old lady, and afterwards, too, when you're an ancestor. Your spirit, and your heart. That's what the right man will want. That's what I'll never stop loving in your mum, because that's the part of her that will never change. Yeh, your man will care that your outside is beautiful, because he's a man. But that's not why he'll love you. He'll love you because your wairua is beautiful."

"I know you think I'm perfect, Dad," she said, a choked laugh escaping, "but are you remembering that way I'm not? That perfect man who sees my inner beauty, isn't he going to want kids, the way you did? I can't give him that, and that's going to matter. Maybe I can't give any man enough, if I can't give him that."

"Bite your tongue," he told her. "You're more than enough for a good man. When he comes, the right one, he's going to know it. Not a doubt in my mind."

She *had* cried a little, then, had wiped her face on her sleeve, and her dad had backed the boat into its spot, and, when it was done, had held her close and let her cry it out, all the tears she hadn't shared with anyone, the pain and the hurt and the fear of it.

He'd let her show her weakness, and had loved her all the more for it. And still, she hadn't shared her deepest fear, the one that was becoming a conviction now. That no matter what he thought, she'd never find a man who would love her the way her father did. Who would want the complicated, messy, imperfect parts of her. Who would want that most imperfect part of all.

♡

None of that had got her vegies planted, but she'd spend today doing some research, she decided. On kitchen plans, and on some other things as well. Whether or not the right man ever came along, she wouldn't waste her life pining for him. Whatever she'd lost, she'd been given more than her share, and she knew it. She just had to focus on that.

Now, she worked on her third cup of tea, thought about a slice of toast, and abandoned the notion. Tea was good. And afterwards, a smoothie made with nonfat yoghurt and berries and flaxseed and a lot of other things that she'd tell herself were delicious, no matter how much she'd rather have had eggs. And sausage. And bacon, and potatoes, and tomatoes, and mushrooms. And toast. But she'd been a half-kilo over on her latest weigh-in, and a smoothie it was going to be.

She heard the doorbell, went to see who would be calling. Too early for the postie.

It was Hugh. The pretty good man she deliberately hadn't thought about while her dad was talking, because he was her neighbor. He wasn't looking like he'd come by to declare his love, though. He was looking soaked, and harassed, and worried.

"What's wrong?" she asked, opening the door and urging him inside. "Car? Kids?"

"Kids," he said, kicking off his jandals and standing in the entryway, dripping on her floor. At least she'd got a smile out of him. "Amelia. Sorry, I know it's an imposition, but can you help?"

"Of course. What is it? Something at school? She ill?"

"Not ill," he said. "And not at school. Started her period. Last night, this morning, I guess. I'm not sure. Too embarrassed to tell me much, or to have me help her, and I'm not sure what to do anyway. She says there's blood, and she doesn't have any... tampons, I guess."

"Not tampons. Pads, for now. Hang on." She went through into her bathroom, grabbed a few, went and found a plastic bag to stick them into, then came back to join Hugh. "And blood? Underwear, pajamas, sheets? Like that?"

He looked a little appalled. "She wouldn't show me. Huddled up in bed, crying. Would there be that much blood?"

"Oh, yeh. It can look like quite the battle scene if you let it go long enough. And she won't be used to it. She's probably got some cramps, too," she decided. "Did she say?"

"Said she had a bellyache, last night," Hugh remembered. "Didn't eat much dinner."

"Hang on." Another detour for the packet of Nurofen. "Let's go," she said. "Dr. Josie to the rescue. Good thing I work in a hospital."

He laughed, and she heard the grateful relief in it. "Do you actually have any medical knowledge?" he asked when they'd dashed across through the rain, had made it into his entryway. "I've been wondering how many patients survive a stay in your hospital, the way the entire staff seems to be focused on shagging everybody in sight. Bit distracting, I'd have thought."

"That's why they call it fiction," she said. "But I think I've got just about enough expertise for this particular medical emergency. Lead me to the patient."

Hugh took her into Amelia's room, where the girl was still lying in bed, Josie saw. "Right, then," she said briskly, going to the blinds and snapping them up, unlatching a window and shoving it open, making the room immediately appear more cheerful. "Congratulations."

Amelia turned a truly woebegone face to her. "What?"

"You're becoming a woman now, aren't you," Josie said. "And that's a beautiful thing, even though it doesn't feel so beautiful just now. But it will, once we chuck Hugh out, get you cleaned up, and then make him drive us to New World for a bit of shopping so you can get to school."

She turned to Hugh. "Why don't you go make breakfast? Something for Amelia to look forward to, eh. And you too, I'll bet. Go on. Get out. No boys allowed."

She jollied Amelia out of bed, stripped the sheets with a brisk hand, saw the girl's cringing embarrassment at the stains. "I'll show you how to get these out," she promised her. "Not a woman in the world who doesn't have to learn how to remove bloodstains. But first, go pop into the shower. Be quick, now."

Hugh had barely got the bacon cooked when she was hustling Amelia into the kitchen.

"That didn't take long," he said. "All good?"

"Yeh. We'll chuck these in the washer, and we're good as gold, hey, Amelia."

"Yeh," she said, although it wasn't too enthusiastic.

"Cup of Milo, I think," Josie said, went to the kettle to fix it. "And I'll give you something for those cramps that'll set you right. Get Hugh's brekkie down you, too."

That settled her down, as Josie had hoped, although they had a bit more fuss after they'd finished the washing-up.

"I don't want Hugh to come with us," Amelia said.

"Rubbish," Josie said. "He's going to be doing the shopping, and he needs to know what to buy. This happens every month, for our sins."

"He doesn't want to buy those things," Amelia protested. "It's so embarrassing."

Josie shot Hugh a look that, she was grateful to see, he had no trouble interpreting. "Nah," he said. "No worries. Long as nobody thinks they're for me. That's the part that's got me sweating."

That startled a laugh out of Amelia, and Hugh grinned at her and pulled in her for a quick cuddle, gave her a kiss on the top of her now neatly-combed hair. She stood stiffly for a moment, then her arms went around him tentatively, and Josie melted a little.

"It's what Josie said," Hugh told his sister, pulling back and smiling down at her. "Growing up. Being a woman. And it's all good."

♡

"Thanks," Hugh said when they'd dropped Amelia at school after what Josie had dubbed their Women's World Class Trip. To Josie's amusement, Hugh had pulled a little black notebook and pen out of his pocket and taken notes. Which was so...cute.

"Thanks isn't really enough, though," he said again. "Thanks for saving my life? I was in way over my head there."

"Oh, I don't know," she said. "I thought you did all right. More than all right, in the end. But your aunt didn't think about that?" she went on cautiously as he turned out of the Belmont Intermediate School carpark and headed back to Devonport. "I'm a bit surprised, because it's not exactly news that a girl who's reached twelve without her period is bound to be starting it soon."

"Apparently not," he said with a grimace. "Not to the extent of talking to Amelia, or laying in some supplies. What you'd expect, eh. She was a bit preoccupied, I'm starting to think."

"Are you hearing much from her?"

"Every week, and she talks a bit more than that to the kids. She's enjoying her holiday, her romance with the Mad Butcher of Brighton, but...she hasn't called as much as I thought she would. Wouldn't you think you'd stay a bit more involved, in the circumstances?"

"Well, I'd think I would, anyway. Maybe she just had faith in you, though."

"Dunno why she would, so that doesn't really fly."

"Not doing so badly, I'd say. Nobody's starved. Nobody's notified the authorities or taken the kids into care. Learning, aren't you."

"Trying."

"Well, trying counts."

"Thanks. Would you have time to get a coffee? You hardly ate any breakfast, I noticed."

"Because I don't." She hesitated, then made up her mind. "Sure. A quick one."

It was probably best to clear the air. Since they were neighbors, and all.

♡

When they were tucked into a tiny table in the corner of Five Loaves, cozily sheltered from the rain beating down outside, she did just that.

"I wanted to tell you," she said, "thanks for not—well, not taking advantage of my temporary insanity the other week. That would've been a big mistake. You were right."

"Hang on," he said, his cup halfway to his mouth. He set it down and looked at her. "A mistake *then*. At the moment. If I didn't communicate that, let's try again."

"A mistake now, too," she said. "I'm on the rebound, that's pretty clear, and even if I weren't, you're my neighbor."

"And? I'd call that bloody convenient, that's all." It sounded light enough, but his face was serious, and he still wasn't drinking his coffee.

"Bloody inconvenient when it goes pear-shaped and you're ducking out to the curb with the rubbish bags so I won't see you, and vice-versa," she said. "This is my first house, and maybe it won't be my last one, but I'm not planning to move anytime soon, and I'm guessing you're not either."

He looked startled, and not happy. "Who says it's going pear-shaped? Maybe it wouldn't, did you think of that?"

"We live in domestic bliss next door to each other forever and ever? That your thought? That how your relationships generally turn out? Because it wouldn't be a very good description of mine. And if I had Derek next door to me right now, his rubbish bags could be meeting with some serious misfortune."

"Except that I'm not Derek. How about if I promise that, whatever happens, your rubbish bags are safe, and you are, too?"

She had to smile. "A good offer, but no. I don't think you'll be boiling any bunnies in my kitchen, and I can say for sure that I wouldn't do it to you, but still. No flings with the neighbors. That's been a pretty good rule for me so far in life, and I'm sticking with it. So thanks for the cuddle, and we'll leave it at that."

"Thanks for the *cuddle?* Was that what that was?"

"Yeh." She looked straight into his outraged brown eyes, and lied. "That's what it was."

Well, not exactly. She'd finished digging the garden with him that day, because she was an actress, after all. She knew how to play her part. He didn't want her enough to go for it? Fine. She wasn't going to show him how much she'd wanted to do it.

He hadn't talked, thank goodness, and she hadn't either, because casual would have been a hard thing to pull off, actress or no. She'd dug and worked and watched him working beside her like it mattered, like he cared that her garden got dug.

Moe atu nga ringa raupo.

Marry a man with calloused hands.

Her Kuia, her grandmother, had said it often enough. To an auntie, a cousin, clucking her disapproval over a lazy boyfriend. Derek took care of his hands, because they'd be filmed. But then, Derek wouldn't have helped her dig her garden no matter what. He'd have complained that she'd got up so early, have asked her why she didn't hire somebody to dig it, have made her feel ridiculous and completely unglamorous for doing it herself. But she *wanted* to dig it. She *needed* to dig it.

The anger and the hurt were still there, and her thoughts caromed between them and the memory of Hugh vaulting over her fence with his shirt off, because that had been a startling moment. And a good moment.

He was wrong, or he wasn't completely right. She might have been thinking about Derek when Hugh had first kissed her, but she hadn't been thinking about him after that. She hadn't been thinking at all. She'd just wanted more.

And she still did. But she still wasn't going to do it.

star turn

♡

Hugh had been surprised, and not overly pleased, to be summoned to the Blues office for a PR meeting in early December. The All Blacks had just got back from the European tour, and even the uninjured would be looking forward to six weeks without any obligations, the chance to allow nearly a year's worth of accumulated niggles to settle, to recharge for the long season ahead. So what was this?

Arriving in the small conference room five minutes before the meeting's start time, he asked Brenda, the PR, but she just smiled and said, "I'll tell all of you at once. Wouldn't want you to get excited and give it away, spoil the surprise."

Somehow, Hugh doubted it was going to be anything he would be that excited about doing. Part of the surprise, it turned out, was that Koti James and Will Tawera were the other invitees to this party, the new man now signed, sealed, and delivered to Auckland and prepared for what Hugh devoutly hoped would be a well-fought campaign for the No. 10 spot. And once the other two appeared, he quickly found out that he'd been right in his trepidation about the meeting.

"I've got a request from the people at *Courtney Place* to send along three of you for an episode," Brenda said. "Next week, they're hoping, so we need to find a day that'll work for all of you before you start going off on your holidays. They'll shoot around your schedule, no worries. The episode will appear in early February, just before the start of the season. Perfect timing for the Blues, get more women watching the games."

"So, wait," Will said. "This is, what, a TV show?"

"Yeh, the soap opera," Koti told him. "What, you've never seen it? Been running forever."

"Been in Aussie, haven't I," Will said. "And I'm not much in the habit of watching soap operas, so I wouldn't know anyway."

"Here it is," Brenda said. "*Courtney Place,* and an intro to your brand-new co-star, Jocelyn Pae Ata."

She clicked a couple buttons on her laptop, gestured toward the large screen on the wall of the room, and a scene came up. Josie in an exam room with another doctor, both of them wearing their white coats, and looking not the least bit professional.

Whoa. Hugh hadn't seen this one.

"This was last season," Brenda explained over the sound of Josie's smoky voice purring into a dark fella's ear. "When she started on Dr. McTavish. This would be before she broke up his marriage, lost him his job, and drove him to suicide."

"I want you," Josie told the man on the screen. She was unfastening his coat, and if somebody could be said to unbutton somebody else caressingly, that was what she was doing. Her lips were parted, her face hungry, avid with desire. "I need you now. And you need me."

She kissed him passionately, very nearly as tall as he was in her stilettos, and she had both her hands in his hair. His own hands fluttered helplessly for a moment, and then he had grabbed her, was kissing her back as if he were lost and she was the only road home.

She had ripped her mouth away, was kissing his ear, his neck, her tongue just coming out to touch his skin, and he was gasping. "You're burning up," she told him. "You're on fire for me, aren't you? You need it so much, don't you?"

"I…" He gasped. "Eva. Please."

"I know exactly what you need," she told him, her voice promising everything. Every bit of sensation a man could imagine. Ultimate pleasure, and impossible release.

She was dark, and she was deadly. "You need," she said into his ear, her voice a silken tongue licking its way down a man, "a very…*thorough* exam. You need it from a doctor who knows how to treat her most difficult patients. I've got exactly what you need, and I know exactly how to treat you. Get up on that table for me right now, and I'll do it."

Click. The screen went black, and Hugh shut his mouth and tried his best to look detached. Will and Koti appeared slightly stunned as well, he noticed, and Brenda was smiling in satisfaction.

"Bloody hell," Will breathed. "What I've missed. When is this show on?"

"Seven," Brenda said. "Every single weeknight. Did this assignment just start to sound a wee bit more enticing?"

"Too right," Will said. "When do they want me, again?"

"We'll get to that. Maybe you're getting the picture as to why they wanted three of you, too. Because one is never enough for our Dr. Eva. Three good-looking ones, that was the request."

"That's me gone," Hugh said, and made to get up from his chair.

"Not so fast," Brenda said. "We did a quick poll round the office, and you rated up there pretty high."

"I'm not a looker," Hugh protested. "You've got the pretty boys, don't need me."

"Big, tall, tough," Brenda said. "Hard man. Girls love that. All broody and intense, too, like you've got a secret vulnerable side that only they can see. Makes them want to cuddle you."

"They want to *cuddle* me?" Hugh asked in outrage as the other two men burst out laughing.

"You know. Afterwards," Brenda said breezily. "Don't blame me, I just tabulate the results. I could take you or leave you, myself. But you tick all the boxes, no worries. Besides, we need a Pakeha. Diversity, you know."

"So get Nico. He's better-looking than me, I don't care what anybody says."

"I already tried, because like I said, I can take you or leave you. But, A," Brenda ticked off on her fingers, "married. B, won't be here. Taking Emma off on a holiday on their own, he said, last chance for her to travel before the baby. So he's out of it."

"Excuses," Will said with a grin. "Always the excuses."

Hugh sighed. All right, Nico couldn't do it.

"So that leaves you," Brenda told him. "And all those flattering things you didn't want to hear. Oh, well. Probably just that women love a man in uniform, specially a short, tight one, which you'll all be wearing."

"Why on earth would we be wearing our uniforms?" Hugh asked.

"You just came from the game," Brenda said. "Late at night. Or after training the next day, or something."

"Makes no sense at all," Hugh said. "We'd change. And there's no training the day after a game."

"It doesn't have to make sense," she answered. "It just has to make good television. Uniforms."

"I'm married too," Koti pointed out when that was settled. "Why am I here?"

"You're top of almost everyone's list," Brenda informed him. "Well, some said Nic, and one or two said Hugh. And I took a flyer on you," she told Will.

"Better not disappoint, then, had I?" he answered.

"Better not. You did get a fair few second-place votes," Brenda said to Hugh. "Reason you're here."

"Geez, thanks."

"We want to give the ladies what they want, don't we?" Brenda said. "And married doesn't matter for you, Koti."

"Matters to me," Koti said.

"Yeh, well," Brenda still sounded cheerful, not the least daunted by the resistance she was encountering, "that's why they call it acting."

"What do we have to do?" Hugh asked, ready to cut to the chase. If they had to do it, they had to. Might as well get it over.

"Just a couple little scenes," Brenda said. "One day, long as you can learn your lines and make a decent fist of it, because they film fast. One of you's the patient, got an injury on the field, brought in for surgery. Dr. Parker's your surgeon. Lucky you. There'd be that first short scene where they bring you in, groaning in agony."

"We do not groan," Hugh said firmly. "No groaning. No whingeing."

"Clenching your teeth in a manly fashion to conceal your agony," Brenda amended. "Then the two of you visiting your wounded teammate in hospital, and finally one more short one when the injured fella's alone and vulnerable, where Dr. Parker gets a little frisky with her patient."

"Isn't that against the rules or something?" Will asked.

"It's a soap, not a doco about En Zed medical standards," Brenda said. "No worries, you won't be compromised. They want Koti for the patient."

"Oh, no," Koti said. "Like I said. Married."

"And like *I* said," Brenda returned. "Acting."

"No," Koti said, his normally cheerful expression hardening for once. "I told Kate when I married her that I'd never kiss another woman, and I'm not doing it."

"You're not *really* kissing her, though," Brenda said coaxingly. "It's just for the show. And she's more likely to kiss you, from what I know."

"If my lips are touching hers," Koti said, "I'm kissing her. That's how it's going to look to everybody who sees it, and that's how it's going to look to Kate. I'll do the show, but I won't be snogging any doctors. I'm a good-looking visitor, and that's it."

"You're whipped as," Will laughed.

"Have you seen my wife?" Koti demanded.

"Yeh, I've seen her," Will said. "All forty-five kg's of her. And you're, what, a hundred?"

"Trust me," Koti said. "It's not what you've got, it's what you can do with it."

"Not what the girls tell me," Will said with a grin.

"Aw, nice," Koti said. "Brenda doesn't want to hear that. Keep it clean."

"Nah. Fascinating stuff," Brenda said. "I'm making a note. So Hugh takes a step up, as usual. Leading from the front."

"Sorry, not going to be me either," Hugh said. "Flattery or not. Because Josie Pae Ata's my neighbor."

The other three stared at him. "Your *neighbor?*" That was Will. "I knew I should have looked around more before I settled on a place."

"So you already know her," Brenda said. "Even easier."

"No. It'd be too awkward," Hugh said. "She lives next door to me. She's friends with my brother and sister. How'm I meant to explain that, if they see it? Which they would."

"Maybe by saying that you were *acting?*" Brenda suggested.

"I'm not an actor, though," Hugh tried to explain, without saying what he really meant, which was that if he kissed Josie, on camera or off, he wasn't going to be acting, and she'd know it. He didn't need to make this any more complicated than it was, or make her any more skittish than she already was, either. Slow and cautious was working. He thought. He wasn't taking any risks.

"Does anybody here make his own decisions?" Will wondered aloud.

"You do, clearly," Brenda said. "Which is good, because it looks like the job's fallen to you by default. Even better, now I come to think of it, and that's how I'll be pitching it to *Courtney Place* as well. Our new first-five, being introduced to the women of Auckland in all his shirtless glory. I suspect you're going to find you have a shoulder injury that requires a manly bandage that covers as little as possible, and that the hospital's going to be oddly short of gowns."

"Works for me," Will said. "You boys are running away screaming from a potential snog of Miss Jocelyn Bloody Fit Pae Ata, and it's on me to do the hard yards. Yeh, much as it pains me, I think I could just see my way clear to putting my hand up. There's no 'i' in 'team,' eh."

"Right, then," Brenda said. "I'll let them know it'll be you."

"Give her a chance to back out." Hugh wondered if it was too late to change his mind. Yeh. It was. But the only thing worse than trying to be cool about kissing Josie on screen, he very much feared, would be trying to be cool about her kissing Will. "Oh, wait," he said, doing his best on the cool thing. "She's an actress. It's her job to pretend to fancy the unfanciable."

"You wish," Will said.

"Can't wait to see what they do with this one," Brenda said. "Now let's sort out which day, and I'll let them take it from there. We'll email you with the details."

all the live ones

♡

Hugh thought he had everything ready at last. It had been a truly impressive organizational effort, involving togs and towels, sunblock and mozzie repellent and forgotten sun hats. Fortunately not involving food, because he'd got away with supplying the drink, which had stretched him enough. He'd had to ring Reka in desperation for instructions, though he'd concealed that from Amelia by doing it from the back garden. But now, the boot was loaded with bottles and the car was about to be loaded with kids, and their Sunday outing was finally underway.

Until Josie's car pulled into her driveway, and she hopped out and opened her own boot with a wave at them, and he saw that it was loaded down as well and crossed her front garden to find out more.

"I thought we had to go," Amelia said from behind him. "You said we were late."

Hugh glanced back at her. "No worries. It's a picnic, isn't it."

"That's not what you *said,*" he heard her mutter, but he wasn't really listening.

"Hi," he said to Josie. "What's up?"

"Just doing a bit of gardening." She smiled at Charlie, who hadn't hung back one bit. "You look like you're off somewhere exciting."

"A picnic," Charlie told her. "And swimming."

"Looks like you may need a hand before we go," Hugh said. "Now that I've got two and all."

"A few bags of soil amendment and some plants," she said. "I've got it."

"Nah," he said, reaching in for them. "I do."

"Whoa, impressive," she said as he pulled two out at once and hefted the load.

"Why d'you think I have to do it?" he asked with a grin. "Just get the plants," he told her when she reached for another of the heavy bags. "You and the kids."

"Hugh," she sighed, but she grabbed a tray, Amelia took another, and Charlie ran ahead for the gate.

Hugh dumped his bags at the spot Josie indicated, in the shade under the tree at the back of the garden, then went back for the rest.

"So you're going to spend this gorgeous day in your work clothes," he said to Josie when they'd emptied the boot. "Doesn't sound right. I think you should go on our picnic with us instead." Which sounded, he hoped, appropriately casual and child-chaperoned.

"I should get these plants in," she said. "Now that I've bought them."

"How about if I promise to help you with that afterwards? It won't take long with two of us. And I think you need an outing."

"You do, eh." She was laughing a little at him now.

"I do." In truth, she was looking a bit weary, though he wasn't going to say that. Telling a woman she looked tired was a mistake he'd been put right on some years back. "Besides, it'd be a chance to meet another one of your, um, volunteers," he added, "as Koti James will be there. Some of the North Shore boys are getting together, doing a farewell picnic with Hemi Ranapia and his family. He's off to the Bay of Plenty in the New Year to take up a job as the backs coach, working with Drew Callahan. So, farewell picnic. Good fun, and a chance for you to give Koti and me some acting tips so we won't disgrace you."

"Really." She looked interested in that. Or maybe just in Koti, because that was the usual reaction. "I'd heard that that's where Drew had gone."

"And here I thought you didn't follow rugby," he sighed. "My only consolation for my lack of an impression on you's just been shattered."

"Knowing what the captain of the All Blacks is doing isn't following rugby," she said. "It's unavoidable. And I didn't make an impression on you either, remember?"

"Yeh, you did. And former captain."

"Forever and always captain. And no, I didn't. You didn't know who I was either."

"Doesn't mean you didn't make an impression," he said. "Doesn't mean that at all."

"Hugh," Amelia reminded him. *"Picnic."*

"Yeh, so…" Hugh said, and looked at Josie. "Picnic? Long Bay? Swim? Completely safe. Partners, kids, the works."

"You should come, Josie," Charlie said earnestly. "It'll be fun. I'll talk to you, if you feel shy."

She smiled at him. "Thanks. I'd have to get my things."

"We'll wait," Hugh told her. "We've got all day."

♡

It didn't take her long at all. Not more than ten minutes, and they were on the road. Only his second time with her in his car, and very nice indeed to have her there. It might be well chaperoned, but it felt like a date all the same, because she had on her white dress and a pair of oversized sunglasses that spelled glamour all the way, her long legs were folded elegantly together in the passenger seat beside her big straw bag, and there was

nobody he'd rather have had next to him on his way to a picnic.
Or a swim.

They found the picnic already in swing, of course, because
despite what he'd told Amelia, they were late. A couple tables
were shoved together on the wide expanse of grass near the big
play structure, and everyone else had arrived, everyone he'd
expected and then some. Reka and Hemi Ranapia with their
baby, Kate and Koti James with theirs. Not all happy families,
though, because Kevin had come, out of his boot now but still
limping a bit. And, unfortunately, Will had too, and he was
looking all too pleased at the sight of Josie.

"Oh, good, you're here with the drinks," Reka said as they
approached, the kids in the lead, Hugh bringing up the rear with
the big chilly bin. "And you've brought company. Awesome."

"My neighbor," Hugh began. "Josie Pae Ata." He wished
there were some way to introduce her that would make her think
this was a friendly outing and make Will think that it wasn't,
but if it existed, it was eluding him.

Reka took the introductions out of his hands. "Hugh didn't
need to tell me who you are," she said at the end of them, "because
I'm a fan. Come to meet the new recruits, have you? What a nice
surprise for us."

"Not going to be such a nice surprise for her, not when she
sees how stage-struck these two show ponies are," Hemi said.
"Thank goodness Hugh's going to be there to settle things down
like a good solid forward, because otherwise, I'd have felt duty-
bound to come along and keep them from getting excited, deciding they needed more camera time. You get them improvising
all over the shop, and things will be out of control before you
know it."

"Not me," Koti said. "Strictly a bystander in this drama. I
have exactly four lines, and I've memorized them. Will's the one
convinced he's going to be a star. He's been lying about for a

week practicing his barely controlled wincing, asking us for feed-back on his look of noble anguish."

"Nice," Will complained. "She's meant to be overcome by my appeal. How's that going to happen now?"

"Nah, mate," Koti said. "The way I read it, you're meant to be overcome by hers."

"Well, that might be easier," Will said, and Hugh wondered if he were going to regret his impulsive decision to bring her along.

"The other kids are over there on the structure already," Reka told Amelia and Charlie, standing at the edge of the group. "You can head on over there and find them. You remember them from the pizza party, don't you?"

"Yeh," Amelia said doubtfully, "but I'm a bit old for playing."

"Nah," Reka said. "Enjoy it while you can. Don't tell, but I took a turn on the flying fox myself with them earlier. Tried to get these boys to do it too, but they were too scared."

Her husband snorted. "Scared we'd break it, you're right about that."

"Besides," Reka went on, "Ariana's looking forward to seeing you. I've found a ballet school for her, and she wants to ask you about it. She's a bit nervous about it. Be a love and chat with her, would you?"

"Sure," Amelia said, looking a little happier. "I can do that."

"You could help her with Luke, too, if you wouldn't mind," Reka said. "She could use somebody older to lend a hand, just until we go for our swim."

"Thanks," Hugh said as Amelia and Charlie headed over to the big wooden structure that had become a beehive of kids on this warm summer Sunday. "She thinks she's eighteen."

"They swing back and forth at that age," Reka said. "The trick is to give them jobs, make them feel helpful. Plus," she said with a laugh, "you do get their help, that way. That's the upside."

♡

They decided to wait a bit on the alcohol, in the end—well, Reka decided—and have a swim first, and after another effort of rounding up kids and making arrangements, the entire party was headed down to the beach.

"You should swim too," Ariana had told Will once it had been settled that the women wanted a good long swim and the men were being left to mind the kids. "There's a raft and every-thing." Will had already begun to make his mark on the Kiwi women, Hugh thought, because even the nine-year-olds were clearly smitten.

"Well, if there's a raft," Will said, "how can I resist?"

"We'll all go," Hugh said. Especially if he were going to see Josie in her togs at last.

Pity he wasn't the only one looking. It turned out that Josie's bikini wasn't pink, and it wasn't as tiny as the one in his dream, either. But it was black, and it was good. She didn't make any production of undressing, any more than Reka and Kate did, but the three of them stripping down made for a show any man would have been hard-pressed not to watch, though Hugh knew which one he was looking at.

He reminded himself that he was meant to be keeping an eye on the kids, dutifully checked on them, in the water already, splashing and shrieking. They didn't seem to need his help, so he pulled his own T-shirt over his head, tossed it to the sand with the rest of the gear, and sneaked another peek to see that the other two women were already in the water, but Josie wasn't. She was reaching up to pull the pins out of her knotted hair, then working to fasten the heavy mass into a long braid, and it was enough like his dream that his body was threatening to embarrass him.

"You can quit perving any time now," he told Will, because Will wasn't looking at the kids at all. "Weren't we meant to be swimming?"

"In a minute," Will said, sounding abstracted. "Bloody hell. Welcome to New Zealand, Will Tawera."

"You'd think you'd never seen a girl in a bikini before," Hugh said. "Thought they had a few in Aussie."

"Not many like that, they don't," Will replied, unabashed. "Just remembered what I've missed most about the homeland. And I had to rest my eyes somewhere, didn't I, because I'm not looking at Reka and Kate getting their gear off. It always gives me a chill when I realize I've been perving at somebody's mum. And a *hell* of a chill to think about Hemi watching me perve at his wife. Discretion is the better part of valor, or so the man says. And anyway, Josie's got to be used to fellas looking at her. If you're going to be taking your clothes off on camera at every opportunity, it's going to happen. Did you see that billboard with her on it? Fwah," he sighed. "I nearly drove off the road. Pure luck that I didn't crash like those other poor blokes."

Hugh didn't share that he'd been one of those blokes. "Yeh, I saw it," he said.

"I saw she'd broken up with her partner, too," Will said. "I wonder if that was the reason. I might not be too happy to have my girlfriend naked on a billboard for the world and all my mates to see."

"Wouldn't date a lingerie model, eh," Kevin said. "Against your principles."

"Well, now you mention it," Will laughed, "rules are made to be broken, aren't they. So is it true, Hugh? She single now?"

"It's true," Hugh said reluctantly. "Not dating yet, though."

"And 'yet' would be the operative word," Will said. "A lonely woman needs consolation, and I'm the understanding type."

"I have my doubts about that," Kevin said. "You seem pretty clueless to me, I have to say. Does the fact that you're here with Josie," he asked Hugh, "mean something?"

"Means she's my neighbor," he said. "And," he added, "my friend as well. And that you should quit staring at her." He shot Will a look that he thought should get the message across.

"Can't do it anyway," Will said, "not when she's in the water. I'll have to wait for her to come out again, won't I."

"And what about Chloe?" Kevin asked, ignoring him.

"Chloe?" That was Will. "Who's Chloe? You got more than one supermodel you've been hiding from me? It's always the quiet ones, isn't it."

"Josie's friend," Hugh said. "My sister's ballet teacher. Very nice girl," he told Kevin. "But not my nice girl."

"Ah," Kevin said.

"I remember now," Will said. "And I think I ought to have been spending my time with Hugh instead of Hemi, because you seem to have found all the live ones. And to have thrown them back, too. It's not a catch and release sport, you know."

Hugh opened his mouth, but Kevin got there first. "Really," he said. "Because it sounds to me like that's exactly what it is. For you."

destiny breathing down your neck

♡

Josie had had her swim with the other women, and had been glad she'd come, because it was so easy being here.

There was a reason, she thought, striking out for the point behind Reka and Kate, that she'd dated actors for so many years. They understood each other, not just the job, but what it was like to live in the public eye. But being an actor, no matter how well known, was nothing like the pressure and expectations on an All Black, and she had a feeling that Hugh and his mates knew all about the effort it sometimes took to make strangers walk away talking about how "natural and friendly" you were, when you'd actually been feeling unnaturally cross. She suspected that Koti James could teach her a thing or two about being a sex object, too.

The calm spread through her, the pleasant, faint languor filling her as they swam on. Nobody seemed in a hurry to get out of the water, so deliciously cool against their heated skin, such a pleasure to know that there was no need to rush, to get to the next thing.

Finally, though, they emerged from the sea, back where they'd started. They ran for their towels, wrapped up, shivering and laughing, and Josie saw that they hadn't been the only ones who hadn't wanted to leave the water. The older kids were still out there, clustered around the wooden raft set not too far from shore. And not just the kids, because she recognized Hugh hauling himself up onto the structure with a quick, athletic heave, and as she'd already noticed, he had some strength in those shoulders and arms.

Well, of course he did. They all did. He was crouching, reaching a hand down for Charlie and pulling him up to join him, hauling Hemi's son Jamie in as well, while the older girls scrambled up on their own.

She could see Will, too, still treading water beyond the raft, and now the kids were jumping off again, seeing who could make the biggest splash, until Hugh was the only one left standing. He waved off the others' encouragement to jump until they were shouting and beating the water with their palms, then backed up, ran, and took a mighty leap, his arms wrapping around his knees, landing with a truly magnificent shower of spray that drenched everybody and created a commotion Josie could hear all the way from the beach.

"Pretty good bloke, Hugh," Reka said beside her. Kate had already left them to join Koti, Hemi, and Kevin, all of them sitting with the littlies and working on building a castle. And on keeping the babies from stuffing sand into their mouths.

"He's all right," Josie agreed cautiously.

"Taking a real interest in those kids at last too," Reka said. "Good to see."

He was on the raft again, saw the two of them watching and gave her a wave, and she waved back, feeling a little self-conscious.

"Well," she told Reka, "it's a change for him, isn't it?" She shivered, wrapped her towel more tightly around her. "Brrr. I'm going to go get out of my togs." She picked up her bag.

"I'll come with you," Reka said. "Leave the boys in charge a while longer, since they're doing so well."

Afterwards, they ate the picnic to which Josie hadn't contributed one bit, the older kids headed off to the play structure again, Amelia apparently having forgotten her mature status, and nobody else seemed inclined to move too much. Hemi had his baby daughter Anika in his lap, her thumb in her mouth, her heavy eyes continually drifting shut, then opening again. Everyone else lay or sat, pleasantly stuffed and relaxed, on blankets spread on the grass in the shade while family picnics and impromptu rugby games happened around them.

Reka plucked Kate and Koti's daughter Maia out of the bouncy seat where she was kicking her plump little legs, lifted her into the air, then brought her down to sit on her knee. "Oh, I'm going to miss this girl," she said. "What am I going to do without you?" she asked as Maia raised her bright eyes to her, laughed out of her rosebud mouth. "I'm going to have Maia-withdrawal, aren't I, and so's Anika."

"Not as bad as my withdrawal," Kate complained. She was propped back on her hands, Koti stretched out with his handsome head in her lap, looking the picture of domestic bliss. "First Hannah leaves, then you? I'm not going to have a single friend left."

"Got me, haven't you." Koti had turned his head to look up at her, scowling a little in what was clearly a well-rehearsed routine.

"You're all right as far as you go," she conceded. "But you fall woefully short in the companionship stakes about half the time. When you're, you know, *gone*. Maybe you need to get demoted, or whatever you call it, so you can go play ITM Cup rugby for Drew and Hemi."

"Bite your tongue," he said. "Anyway, Bay of Plenty's not my club, so you'd be out of luck there."

"You can come stay with me while Koti's off with the squad, Kate," Reka promised. "As long as you bring my girl along."

"Aw, no," Hemi sighed. "There's my secret plot foiled, the real reason we're moving. Here I'd meant to get Reka out of the danger zone, stop her drooling over other people's babies. I can hear the hormones talking now."

Reka laughed and bounced Maia on her knee, prompting a chortle or two. "I don't think that'd do it. Babies everywhere you go, aren't there, or are you forgetting that Hannah's got one for me to cuddle as well? And I don't make them all by myself, boy. If you're worried about it, you know the answer." She made a scissors-gesture with two fingers. "Snip snip."

"Aw, nice," Koti groaned as everyone laughed. "Ouch."

"You just made every man here cross his legs," Hemi complained. "Snip snip? Geez, Reka. That's me switching off right there."

"Yeh, right," she scoffed. "That's happening. Men are such babies, aren't they, Kate? One weeny little poke either side, and you're done. Twenty minutes, and I'm driving you home with the icepack clamped to the wedding tackle. Just say the word, boy. Say the word, and all your worries are over."

Josie laughed as Hemi groaned again. She couldn't help it, because one thing was sure, none of the five men taking up so much space around her was a baby.

"Four kids," Will said to Hemi lazily from the spot where he lay stretched out on his back, one big arm behind his head, the bicep bulging out in a perfectly satisfactory fashion beneath. Josie had grown up looking at brown arms and broad chests decorated with Maori tattoos, but rugby players, she was rapidly realizing, took it to a whole new level. "That's a fair few. But not as many as you're going to have, sounds like."

"Four's right," Hemi said with satisfaction. "Saw them, didn't you. Or can't you count that high? My hopes for you boys next season just plummeted."

"Making me shudder just thinking about it," Will said. "Four? Too much responsibility for me."

"Aaaand...the bookmakers just shifted the odds again," Hemi said.

"Responsibility on that field is one thing," Will said. "And being responsible at home's another one altogether."

Josie saw Hugh look at Will, could see the agreement he didn't voice.

"How many do your parents have?" Hemi asked. "Tell the truth, now."

"Five," Will admitted with a flash of white grin.

"Uh-huh," Koti said. He sat up and gave the soles of his daughter's bare feet a tickle, making her kick her legs some more, giggle up at him. "The brown boys tend to win this derby. You can run, Will, but you can't hide."

"I don't know," he said. "I'm pretty fast."

"That sound you hear?" Koti asked, giving in to what was clearly a powerful impulse and taking Maia back from Reka, lifting her to give her a kiss on one deliciously rounded golden cheek, making her coo and pat his own cheek with a little hand. "That's destiny breathing down your neck."

♥

Josie smiled and laughed with the others, watched Koti with his baby girl, and pretended that that was all there was. That the pain wasn't there, filling the part of her that was empty, that would always be empty.

She'd come a long way, because even pretending would have been impossible a few years ago. She was a pretty good actress, but there had been no amount of skill that would have hidden what she'd felt then. Taking the long daily walks she'd known were necessary for her recovery, coming home drained every time, because Reka was right, there were babies everywhere.

More babies, surely, than there'd ever been before. In push-chairs, wheeled along by distracted mums who took their good fortune for granted. And the worst of all, the new ones in their prams, or held by a proud dad the way Koti was holding Maia now. Starfish hands waving, tiny fists clutching a blanket, gripping a handful of T-shirt, unfocused eyes blinking at the world around them from the secure haven of their fathers' arms.

Yeh, she'd done more than her share of feeling sorry for herself, until she hadn't been able to tell if the ache in her abdomen was a knitting wound, or a deeper scar that would never heal.

When Chloe had fallen pregnant, it had been almost too much to bear. Especially when her friend had confessed Rich's reluctance, her own doubts. Josie had had to physically hold herself back from begging Chloe to have the baby and give it to her, because it wasn't her decision. It wasn't her life, and it wasn't her baby and never would be, because she'd known Chloe would want Zavy in the end, and she'd been right.

Josie had been a friend, and a godmother, because that was what you did. She'd held Zavy when he was born, minded him as often as Chloe needed the help and she could provide it, had faked pleasure and interest for months—for years, if she were honest—until, now, she could actually feel it.

Most of the time, anyway. Most of the time.

♡

"That was a good picnic," Charlie sighed sleepily when they were in the car heading back to Devonport, the kids clearly as worn out on sun, sea, exercise, and food as Josie was feeling herself. "I like it best when there are other kids and it's not boring. Jamie said they're moving away soon, though. That must be hard, to move away."

"Oh, I don't know," Hugh said. "People do move. Not so bad. I moved to Wellington myself when I wasn't quite your age. New school, new friends. Left my dad behind, too, come to that. And it wasn't bad at all, after a bit. You'd get used to it too."

"Are we going to have to move?" Josie could hear the edge of alarm in Charlie's voice. "Away from here?"

"What? No. Of course not," Hugh said. "That's not the plan. You're staying in the house, in Devonport. That was always the plan. That's why Aunt Cora came, so she could stay with you. That's why she's here, so you don't have to move."

"Are *you* going to move?" Amelia asked, and she didn't sound sleepy herself, the way she had been when they'd got in the car. She sounded very much awake.

"Just moved here, didn't I," Hugh said.

"To play for the Blues," Charlie said.

"Yeh. To play for the Blues, and to live with you. And as the Blues still seem to want me, now that the thumb's all good, that's still the plan."

Josie broke the silence that fell, because it wasn't quite as comfortable now. Had Hugh realized what he'd said—and what he hadn't? "Charlie's right, though," she said. "That was a good day. Thanks for that. And for the chance to meet my costar, of course."

"Right," Hugh said. "Your costar. Will. He going to do the job for you?"

"Oh, yeh," she said. "I wondered, because non-actors are sometimes a little...stiff, but he's clearly got what it takes to carry the day. He'll be fine. You all will."

"Huh," he said. "He's looking forward to it, I'll tell you that. Maybe a bit too much."

She glanced at him. Was he jealous? That was ridiculous, but...good to know. "You could beat him into submission, take his place," she offered. "If you're worried about who I'll be kissing."

She got a glance across the car for her pains before he took the turn onto Vauxhall Road. "Maybe I should."

"Are you going to have to kiss somebody, Josie?" Charlie asked, because as always, he'd been paying attention. "On TV?"

"She's *always* kissing somebody," Amelia informed him. "All the time. All different guys."

"You are?" Charlie sounded doubtful. "Then you should kiss Hugh instead, I think, because you know him better. That would be more comfortable."

Hugh ignored the suggestion. "How do you know who Josie's kissing?" he asked, looking back in the mirror at Amelia.

"*Duh,*" she sighed. "Holly?"

"Don't say 'Duh,'" he said, his tone a little sharp. "It's rude. And if Josie kisses people, it's because it's her job. They aren't 'guys,' they're other actors. It's not real."

"Thanks for that," Josie told him quietly. "And good job on the other, too."

He turned into their street, pulled into the driveway, and she got out, pulled her bag along with her. "Thanks for the day," she told him again.

"Is the day over?" He sounded surprised. "Thought I was helping you with your garden. Or were you planning to wait?"

"No, I'm planning to do it. I'm called every day this week, and I won't get a chance otherwise. But you don't really have to help. It won't take that long."

"Of course I do," he said. "I promised you I would. Besides, we've got Blues pride on the line here. If the boys and I are going to appear on the show with you, we need to make sure you're rested, looking as beautiful as always. We wouldn't want people to say that we'd clearly put you off."

"That's what makeup's for," she said with a laugh. "To make me beautiful when I'm not."

"You don't need makeup, Josie," Charlie said. "You're always pretty."

"That's about it," Hugh said. "I stand corrected. But I'll come help you all the same."

"I will too," Charlie said.

"Nah," Hugh told him. "You and Amelia go have a shower and a rest. I can help Josie."

♡

He scattered the soil from the heavy bags over the ground she'd prepared, worked with her to rake it in. She tried to think of something to say, but everything seemed too weighted, and she was tired, didn't feel up to being chipper. No matter what she told herself, being around babies and happy families still took something out of her. So she was quiet, and so was he.

"How's it gone, with the ad campaign and all?" he finally asked once they were putting her ferns into the soil. "Saw they took that billboard down."

It had been declared a nuisance during the previous week and removed. To full media coverage, of course, the TV cameras lingering one last time on her image as it was stripped away, the cars once again slowing on the motorway to allow the public to watch.

"Yeh," she said.

"Not quite the result they were looking for, maybe, the company," he offered.

"Nah. They're quite happy, even more publicity than they bargained for. Gone over like that in the UK and Aussie too, they said."

"More work for you, then, maybe."

"If I want it."

He was silent a moment more, and she wondered if she should try to explain, but he spoke first. "Not always easy to be out there like that. Or for the people who love you to see you like that, I'm guessing."

"It's been an issue, yeh. You judging?" She rocked back on her heels to look at him. "Because I seem to recall a certain advert with you boys in your undies. Using beautiful bodies to sell products isn't exactly new, not on either side of the gender aisle."

"Sorry," he said, looking up. "Touched a nerve, I guess. No, I'm not judging. I'd be the last, wouldn't I? That's why they wanted us to turn up in our uniforms to do your show, after all. I'm not fooling myself that the ladies will be hoping to see a rugby demonstration, They're hoping to see Koti take his jersey off."

"And maybe you too," she said, relaxing a little.

"Nah," he said. "I've actually got hair on my chest. Nobody wants to look at that."

"I looked today," she said, and neither of them was planting now. "And it's what I thought the first time I saw you, actually. That I would've bet you'd never waxed in your life."

"You'd have won that bet, too. Always been horrified at the thought, tell you the truth. Reka's right, men are babies. Should I, though? Wax the chest, shave the beard? Too hairy for you?"

"No. I told you." She was back to planting now. "Manly. I think most women would think so."

"I don't care about most women," he said. "I care about you."

She felt the shock of it hit her chest, take her breath, looked up again to find his gaze steady on her, and she stood and gathered up the rubbish, buying herself some time.

"Since you're here," she said, taking the coward's way out, "want to give me a hand with the vegies? I bought a few more things to put in, since we got a bit enthusiastic with the digging last month, working through my issues."

"Just show me what to do," he said.

She put him on to planting beans while she worked on the kale, and, finally, she spoke, because he deserved more from her than this. "It's been nearly a month, and that's a while," she said. "But it takes a while, doesn't it."

"It does. Getting over a breakup," he said, understanding her perfectly, she could tell, and she could feel the caution in him.

"But then," she said, tipping the tiny seedlings with a careful hand and placing them gently into the holes she'd dug with her trowel, "It's been nearly three months since Derek and I were together. The one visit I did pay him...all it really did was drive the point home. I see that now, that he'd gone someplace else, in all senses of the word. I spent a lot of time—too much time— wondering if he was with somebody else, too, and then I realized it didn't matter."

"So not too many tears shed?" he asked, placing the long wooden stakes next to the little plants, using the handle of his own trowel to drive them into the earth.

"Oh, there may have been one or two," she admitted. "Angry at him, embarrassed, sorry for myself, facing up to having to start over. All that. May have been more than one or two for a while there. No telling what a person will do in the dead of night."

"Nothing you let anybody see," he said. "Never let them see you sweat, eh."

"I'm guessing you may know a thing or two about that," she said without looking at him, patting the earth around her seedlings with gentle fingers.

"Well, sweat, they see enough of that," he said. "I guess I should say, never let them see you hurt. And yeh, I do know about that one."

"And yet," she said, her hands still busy, "when I think of the people I know with the most mana, like my Kuia—my grand- mother, that is—and my dad. When I think about them, I realize it's not that they never hurt, or even that they never show it. I think, you know, the strength isn't in never getting knocked down. It's in getting up again afterwards."

He'd finished his own planting, was on his heels, watching her. "And that's true too," he said.

"Seeing as you do it all game long," she said, "I guess that's not so very profound after all."

"No. It is, because you're right, that's the hard bit. When you've had a knock or two already, and you're hurting. When you can't win, and you know it. When you're playing for nothing but pride, nothing but that you can't bear to give up. That's when it matters most that you get up again. Anyone can be strong when they're winning, when they've got that rush. But being strong when you're losing, when you've lost...that's the test."

She looked into his dark eyes, and thought that, yes, he probably knew a thing or two about loss. It was easy to forget that when Amelia and Charlie had lost their parents, Hugh had lost his father, and not only that, had lost the life he'd expected to have as surely as she had lost her own. If he seemed to have been having some difficulty adjusting to the change, that was hardly surprising.

"And the relevant point here, as far as I'm concerned," he said, the solemn mood gone, replaced by a hint of a smile, "is that you aren't crying any more over that spilt milk."

"No," she said. "I'm not."

"What good news." The smile was there for real now, and she smiled back, crouching in the dirt across from him.

She caught the movement out of the corner of her eye, turned to see Amelia approaching across the grass, and Hugh saw her too.

"It's dinner time," Amelia announced, her tone, as usual, a little accusing.

"Oh. Right. Why don't you and Charlie get it started, then?" he asked. "Do the salad, at least, turn on the barbecue for me. I'll come over and do the steaks in a minute." He looked at Josie. "We've got menus on the fridge now. Getting more efficient every day."

"You are coming, though," Amelia said.

"Be right there," he promised. "Soon as I help Josie tidy up."

Amelia took herself off with a final backward glance, and Josie began gathering and stacking plastic containers as Hugh picked up the tools, scraped the dirt off and bore them off to the shed for her.

"Thanks for the hand," she said when they'd dumped the rubbish, were standing at the back gate. "I'll run a bit of water over that, and I'm all good. And thanks for taking me along today."

"Glad to do it," he said. "On both counts. And, just for the record? I'm looking forward to Wednesday."

He put a hand on her shoulder, bent down and kissed her cheek, the first time he'd touched her since the breakup. His beard scratched a bit against her skin, felt so male, and she leant into him and enjoyed it for the split second it lasted.

He dropped his hand, smiled down at her. "I reckon it's not such a bad thing I'll be there, either."

"No worries," she said, reading his thoughts without much difficulty. "Will may enjoy himself, I can't help that, but I know how to keep it professional. I can keep my distance when I want to, even if I'm not keeping my distance at all."

"And you'll be wanting to."

"Yeh. I will. And if I can't manage it after all, well, I *will* have you there, won't I?"

"You will," he promised. "See you then."

He let himself out the gate, and she went to the standpipe and unwound the hose from its reel, began to spray her newly planted vegies, and let herself look forward to it too.

To Wednesday.

method acting

♡

Hugh turned up at the *Courtney Place* studios in Henderson three days later feeling a good deal more excited by the assignment than he had been when he'd received it.

He had his lines memorized. Not much to learn, after all, no more than Koti had. Mostly, he was required, in his one brief scene, to stand around in his uniform looking seriously concerned about what seemed to him like a run-of-the-mill shoulder injury. And to look a bit gobsmacked by Josie, which wouldn't require any acting at all.

He saw Koti and Will getting out of Koti's car, went over to join them, and they walked in together. A cheerful young assistant with a swinging blonde ponytail was waiting in the reception area to greet them. She led them down a broad passage and into a big room featuring swivel chairs and one long wall of mirror like a hair salon, along with a table and chairs where a few people were sitting playing cards—people Hugh recognized as cast members, incongruous in casual clothes combined with heavy TV makeup. They looked up from their game, gave a wave to the three of them, standing in their Blues warmups over the uniforms that still seemed stupid to Hugh.

And then he forgot about the other cast members, because Josie had come into the room, and she was dressed in a flouncy little yellow skirt and scoop-necked white T-shirt that had Will paying attention.

"You're already made up," Hugh said unnecessarily after she'd greeted each of them with a firmly offered handshake clearly meant to show that whatever happened here today, it wasn't to be construed as real.

"Been working all day," she said.

"When do you start?" Will asked her. "I heard acting was mostly standing around, a few minutes in front of the cameras."

"Not soaps," she told him. "We film fast, and we start early. I report to my dressing room at seven, finish around six most days that I'm called, and in bed by nine. It's a glamorous life, and that's the truth."

"Sounds about like being a footy player," Will said.

"Except with less beer," Hugh said.

"Oh," she said, smiling at him, "I haven't noticed so very much beer."

"On my best behavior for you, aren't I," he said, smiling back.

One of the makeup artists caught the assistant's eye, the blonde—Erica—stepped forward, and Josie looked away from Hugh and back at Will.

Erica told Will, "As you've got the biggest part, we want to get you started straight away."

"Gregor," the makeup artist said, shaking Will's hand and gesturing him toward a chair in front of the mirror. "You've got your shirt off for this, right?"

"That's what they tell me," Will said cheerfully.

"Well," Gregor said, "we won't need to spray you down, because you're a good color already. But you," he told Hugh, "we'll do you."

"Me?" Hugh asked, taken aback. "What do you mean? I'm not going to have my shirt off."

"No, but the camera will spend some good time on all of you in your short shorts," Gregor said. "And these two are perfect as they are, but you need a bit of color on your legs. We'll do your arms as well, get the girls excited." He nodded at a clearly subordinate associate, and she held up a spray can, pointed Hugh over to a separate area where a tarp was laid out on the floor ready for him.

"Got to get you up to standard, mate," Koti said, "if you're not going to break the camera." He and Will laughed, and Hugh let the girl lead him off, started stripping off the warmups.

"All the way to the undies, please. Don't want any pasty white thigh showing," she said briskly, and he rolled his eyes and complied, grateful that he'd worn the black ones and wasn't going to disgrace himself.

She had him with his arms out by his sides, turning in a circle as she chatted and sprayed like he was a horse she was getting ready for the show ring, and he could see the others laughing at him still. And he could see that Josie wasn't watching him, undies or no.

He heard her saying to Will, "Once you get that done, we'll run through our lines a few times, then the director will block it out. You'll be in bed, just have to turn your head and so forth, maybe do a bit of grabbing with the good arm."

"We aim to satisfy," Will said.

"See you back there, then," she said, "and we'll give it a go."

She turned to leave, and Hugh saw Will watching in the mirror as she twitched off in that little skirt. And despite her words, despite his own, he burned.

♡

It was boring, after that, until it wasn't. Hugh's and Koti's brief scene had been filmed, Koti, of course, lighting up the screen with his hundred-kilowatt smile, and Hugh managing his own four short lines without any difficulty at all, not that anyone would be looking at him. And then more waiting around until, at last, he and Koti were standing and watching the filming of Will and Josie's scene from behind the cameras.

Will was in a hospital bed cranked up high, his shoulder in a sling, a single white bandage stretched across his broad brown chest. Just putting the bandage on had taken forever, because they'd wanted to make sure they had obscured as little as possible of the tattoo decorating his left arm and shoulder.

"That's money in the bank," the director, Mike, had said with satisfaction. But at last, the thing was on, Will and Josie had rehearsed the scene what seemed to Hugh like an unnecessary number of times, and they were filming.

Josie came into the room, jerked her head at the door, and the nurse, the blonde Hugh now knew was, in real life, named Valerie, and very pretty indeed—opened her mouth, closed it again, lifted her chin and stalked out of the room, rebellion written in every line of her tidy little figure. Josie—Dr. Parker—smiled with satisfaction, walked to the foot of Will's bed with the grace of a panther, picked up his chart in a manicured hand, and came around to his bedside, flipping pages.

She sat on the chair beside his bed, opposite the bandaged shoulder and IV bottle, crossed one elegant leg in its sheer black stocking over the other, the tight red dress beneath the open white lab coat riding up a truly incredible distance at the motion, and Will's eyes followed it, as they were meant to do. Not much acting at all required there, because she was swinging that leg a bit now, one black stiletto was dangling, somehow, off her toe, and she was pursing her red-painted lips and sucking on the end of a pen in a performance that would have had Hugh's blood pressure spiking to dangerous levels if she'd ever come near him in a vulnerable state.

"How are you feeling this morning, Will?" she asked him after she'd finished her little oral demonstration.

"Not too bad," he said, attempting to shove himself up in the bed a bit more and stifling the subsequent wince in manly fashion.

"Oh, no," she said, "we don't want you doing that." She leant across him, reached for the remote that operated the bed, pressed the button, and his upper half rose a few centimeters, even closer to the breasts that she'd displayed so tantalizingly close to his face.

She settled herself back in her chair again, taking her time. "Anything you want to ask me?" she purred. "Any questions I can...help you with?"

"What time do you get off work?" he asked with a laugh.

"Now," she said, that crossed leg swinging again, that shoe dangling, "that kind of talk will get you put in the naughty corner, and you don't want that. We surgeons have special ways of dealing with naughty patients."

She picked up his good hand, held it in one of her own, wrapped her fingers around his wrist. "Your pulse is racing," she told him. "Jeopardizing your recovery, undoing all my brilliant work. You're getting me angry, and you don't want me angry."

She leant over him again, propped herself on one elegant hand, her chest very nearly touching his own. And then she brushed her parted lips over his ear, one long, slow journey up, then down again, before murmuring, "You don't want to know what might happen then. You wouldn't want to hear about the kinds of things I can do to very...bad...boys."

His hand came up, dropped to the sheet again, his face showed equal parts arousal and confusion, and again, Hugh didn't think he was doing as much acting as he might have been.

And then the door opened and the nurse was back, and Josie was standing, imperious and forbidding, handing the chart to her like a mistress tossing her coat to a servant. She offered Will one more cool, meaningful smile, slunk her way to the door with that predatory glide, and he watched her go.

"All right?" the nurse asked him, all concern, and he smiled at her, looking a bit shaky.

"Yeh," he said. "Phew. Is she always like that?"

"Oh," she said, her lip curling, "Our Dr. Eva is one of a kind." And that was it. Done.

♡

Erica took them all back to get their makeup off, and Hugh could sense the relief in all of them, even though their gladness at being finished couldn't hold a candle to his own.

"Never had a surgeon do that to me," Koti mused as a wardrobe mistress unwrapped Will's bandaging, while the makeup artist—Gregor—wiped Hugh's face down. "I'd remember that, anesthesia or no. Now I don't think it was enough that I wasn't the patient. I'm thinking having Kate watch this show at all is going to put ideas into her head."

"And that would be," Hugh pointed out, "why they call it entertainment."

"Yeh," Will said. "Entertained me, all right. The rehearsal was good enough, but she took it up a notch there. Had me sweating. This girl's single, right?" he demanded of Hugh. "And your neighbor? And somehow available all the same, because you've failed one too many concussion tests?"

"No," Hugh found himself saying. "Not."

"Not?" Will asked, brows raised. "Not, you hope? Or not, she actually isn't?"

"Not," Hugh said. "Full stop. Find somebody else." He climbed out of the chair to face Will, and he wasn't joking, and Koti studied the two of them for a moment, then jerked his head at Will.

"Get the makeup off, cuz," he told him.

Will gave Hugh one last look. "Not," he sighed, and did as Koti had asked. "Got it."

♡

Erica had gone away once she'd delivered them back to makeup, and now she came back into the room, approached Hugh.

"Josie wonders," she told him, "if you'd like to come on back for a second."

"Yeh," he said. "Of course." He saw the look Will and Koti exchanged, told himself she wanted another chat, and that was a good thing, wasn't it?

He followed Erica around a few corners, down a passage, stopped at the door she indicated, the one with "Jocelyn Pae Ata" printed on a plaque. No actual star, but she didn't need a star, because she was one. The girl left, and he lifted his hand and gave the door a quick rap with his knuckles.

"Come in," he heard, and he opened the door and stepped inside.

She was sitting on a padded pink stool in front of a big square mirror outlined with lights, exactly the way he'd have imagined, creaming off the heavy makeup that had made her look a different person—the hard, cruel person she wasn't. Her heavy hair was down, and she was beautiful.

She smiled at him in the mirror. "How'd you boys go, then? Everyone in one piece? Thought I'd better check."

"Dunno," he said with a grin of his own. "Not sure Will's ever going to be the same again. I think a whole new world's just opened up for him."

She laughed. "Shocked him, did I?"

"Well," he said, "if you get one of those letters, about the boots and the tying-up and all, let me know, because that could be him getting carried away."

"You going to protect me?"

"You know I am."

She smiled into the mirror, finished wiping off the makeup, swung around on the stool, and he saw what he'd been doing his best not to notice since he'd come in, that she was in a dressing gown. Another silky one, long this time, in a sort of bronze color that shimmered in the light of all those bulbs. She was covered from neck to ankle, but that didn't matter, because he could still see that vee of skin at her throat, catch a glimpse of shapely calf above her bare, high-arched brown feet with their pink-painted toenails.

Feet that he'd seen over and over again during the months of their acquaintance, because she didn't like wearing shoes any more than he did. She was wearing more than she'd done when they'd laid her brick, more than she'd done when she'd served him dinner in her white dress on her new patio, and definitely more than she'd done when she'd pulled off that same white dress and gone for a swim in her black bikini. But she hadn't been wearing a silky dressing gown that clung to her curves, held closed with a sash that his hands itched to yank open so he could see and touch what lay beneath. And the two of them hadn't been in an intimate, completely feminine little room with the door shut, and there hadn't been a double row of costumes hanging just to one side of his shoulder, and some of those costumes hadn't been hanger after hanger of bras, undies, and, in some cases, suspender belts. White, ivory, red, black. Silk and lace. Lots and lots of lace.

He glanced at them again, he couldn't help it, and she smiled. "Admiring my wardrobe?"

"Well…" His gaze met hers, and they were both still smiling, but her eyes had widened, her lips had parted, and she wasn't acting now. "How often do you take your clothes off on this show, anyway?" he asked her, the words coming out a bit husky.

"You mean you haven't been watching to see?" Her own voice was low, teasing, and his body responded to it like she'd pushed a button, because she had.

"I have been," he said, "which I'm sure you've guessed. Wondering if I missed the good stuff. Because this…" He reached a finger up to hook a filmy bit of silver lace decorating a scrap of pale pink, let it fall. "This would be the good stuff."

"I don't always show them," she said. "But I usually wear them, because Dr. Eva does. Because she's always aware, no matter what else she's doing, of what she's got to offer, what she's got that they all want."

"This would be what they call Method acting, then," he said, and she shifted on her stool, the carefully closed neckline of the gown opened a little wider, and he could see an edge of ivory under there, scallops of lace against the golden brown of her skin.

"You *have* been studying," she said. "Want to see the rest of it?"

Hell, yeh, he did.

"Come here and I'll show you, then," she said.

She stood, a graceful movement, turned to open a drawer in a cabinet beside her, and he saw the shape of her under the gown and covered the space between them in two strides.

He was looking down into a shallow drawer divided into diamond-shaped compartments, each containing a filmy mass of…something. Black and gray and nude this time, with black heavily represented.

"These are my other secret weapon," she told him, pulling out one black bundle and unrolling it. "Dr. Eva's stocking collection. These are fishnets," she added unnecessarily. "Always effective." She rolled them up again, put them back into their spot. "The ones with the seam running down the back are good too, and these." Another silky length dropped from her hand, black again. "Don't need the suspender belt for these, which is helpful when Dr. Eva's wearing knits. And when she finds it more convenient to do without her knickers."

"You go out there," he managed to say, "without your knickers on? Wearing those?" They had lace at the top, were nearly transparent beneath, and he needed a dress rehearsal. Right now.

"I do," she said, her smile inviting him to share her secrets. "Want me to tell you next time that happens? Increase the entertainment value?"

He didn't answer. Instead, he took the stockings from her hand, dropped them back into their drawer, and shoved it shut with his knee. Then he reached for her shoulders.

"I think we both know the entertainment value I want," he said, just before he lowered his mouth to hers.

This time, it didn't start out gentle. It started out hot and hard, and it got hotter, because her mouth was opening under his, welcoming the invasion of his tongue. His hands were tight on the backs of her shoulders, until she reached up to grab his upper arms. Her hands were gripping him hard, then, and she was making noises into his mouth, little smothered sounds deep in her throat that were rapidly pushing him past the point of thinking.

He had to plunge a hand into her mass of hair then, because he needed to pull her head back to kiss that throat. His other hand was at her waist, and she was holding on, gasping, turning her head to the side so he could do it some more. He found a spot that made her squirm, and stayed there, the sound of her breath with its keening undertone competing with the roaring in his own head. His hand moved down a perfectly curved hip, his fingers closing over the roundness of her, and he didn't have a choice. He had to give her a stroke or two there, to run his hand over her curves, and she was sagging at the knees now.

He couldn't have that, so he let go of her hair, put a hand on either side of her waist and lifted her onto the top of that chest of drawers, which was exactly right, because her knees parted, and he was standing between them, grasping the edge of the dressing gown and pulling it aside so he could touch her, his hand stroking higher over the silk of her skin, his thumb drifting up over the soft, secret flesh of her inner thigh.

He wanted to watch, but she had her own hands in his hair, was kissing him with a hunger he needed to satisfy, because that was what he was here for.

He did his best, took his time, kissed her until she was melting into him, until her own tongue had come out to play. He explored the curve of her upper lip, gave the deliciously plump lower one the nip he'd been imagining for weeks now, drawing a gasp from her, a little whimper that had his blood heating. And eventually, he found his other hand reaching for the opening at the front of the dressing gown as if it had a mind of its own, and he was parting it, breaking the kiss and pulling back from her to look.

He'd been right, because she was wearing an ivory bra underneath. Low-cut, the swell of her upper breasts showing above, so tantalizingly close to revealing the treasures beneath.

"Aw, Josie," he groaned, his fingers lightly tracing those scallops. "You're beautiful."

He felt her shiver as he touched her, as he reached down and yanked that tie loose from around her waist, and the bronze fabric parted completely, revealing the tiny undies that matched the bra, more ivory scallops decorating their top edge.

He took another step back to appreciate the picture she made, ran his fingertips delicately across the edge where lace met firm brown flesh, so far beneath her slit of navel with its winking diamond, and he could actually see her flesh quiver.

"I'm going to kiss you everywhere," he warned her, his voice hoarse in his ears. "I'm going to do it now."

"Huhhhh." It was a sigh, or a groan, and her eyes were closed.

"Open your eyes," he told her gently. "Know who I am?"

He watched the lashes flutter, saw the delicately carved lids opening to reveal dilated pupils, the flush that had risen on her cheeks.

"Hugh," she sighed. "Hugh."

"That's right," he said, his fingers continuing to trace their slow path, then, just for a moment, sliding down, touching her through the silk, one fingertip gliding lightly over her, finding the spot. He felt the moisture that had soaked through the fabric, the spasm as she jerked against him, and he smiled. Oh, yeh. This was going to be so good. He was going to make her feel so good.

Knock knock knock.

The rapping at the door was so sudden, they both jumped.

"Josie?" the feminine voice came through, muffled by the wood. "Excuse me."

Hugh expelled his breath in a curse, and Josie hastily pulled her robe together and tied it shut with hands that he saw were shaking. Then she shook her hair back, stood tall, and walked to the door to open it, and Hugh turned toward her dressing table and tried to pretend a fascination for her cosmetics he definitely wasn't feeling.

"Sorry," he heard the assistant saying. "The other fellas are leaving, thought I should let you know. I think they wanted to say goodbye."

Hugh would bet they did. Especially Will. Well, goodbye was all right. Goodbye was perfect.

"All right," Josie said. "Tell them I'll be right out, and Hugh will be too."

"Will do," the voice said, the door clicked shut, and Hugh turned around again to see Josie shedding the dressing gown with nothing but efficiency this time, pulling the little yellow skirt on over the undies, the white T-shirt over the bra before adding her high-heeled brown ankle boots and zipping them up with a couple quick motions, the whole thing taking her about thirty seconds.

"Ready?" she asked him.

"No," he said. "Nowhere close to ready, because we're nowhere close to done."

"My recovery period's over, you think?" she asked, a faint smile curving the lips he wanted to be kissing again. The ones he *would* be kissing again.

"I think," he told her, "your recovery period just came to a crashing end."

stamping on it

♡

She walked back out into the makeup room, so aware of Hugh walking behind her, and used every bit of her training not to show how shaken she still felt.

"Thanks," she told Will and Koti, shaking hands all around. "You did awesome," she said to Will. "Good job acting terrified."

She gave him a smile and a wink, and he laughed back at her and asked, "Who says I was acting?"

"You'll have picked up a few new fans, anyway," she said, "this side of the Ditch. I predict a good turnout for your first appearance at Eden Park."

She dropped his hand, turned to Hugh, standing there staring at Will, and if that wasn't a warning-off glare, she'd never seen one. "See you, then," she told him.

He shifted his frowning attention back to her. "You're not coming?"

"Nah, got a few more things going on here, now we're done filming."

"Right," he said, and she held out a hand to him, but he didn't take it. Instead, he took her by the shoulders, leaned down, and brushed his lips over hers.

"Be good," he murmured in her ear, just loud enough for the others to hear, then turned and walked away.

♡

"Uh, Josie?" Clive asked from his spot at the table with Valerie when the others had left. "Something you want to share with the group? Thought you were still getting over Derek. You done getting over?"

"Could be," she said. "Or I'm going to be."

"With a bit of help, I take it."

"Well, yeh," she said. "Maybe. Working on it. Or he is. Or..." She sighed. "Something."

"Uh-huh," Clive said with satisfaction. "Looks to me like he's ready to start working hard. Remember our little talk about weeing round the boundaries? That, my darling, was a champion exhibition. That's our boy Hugh saying he's won, and letting everybody know it."

"He's *won?*" Josie sat down with them, grabbed Val's cup of tea and took a swallow, trying to laugh it off. "Because he kissed me goodbye?"

"Because he put his stamp on you," Clive said, "in front of Will Tawera, and anybody here who needed to know it, too. That was the point."

"His stamp," Josie said. "That is disgusting."

"Then my work here is done," Clive said. "Men *are* disgusting. That's what I've been trying to tell you."

"And here I was," Val complained, "letting myself get excited to see him in his undies this morning. Thought you didn't care, when you didn't look. You could've warned me so I wouldn't have wasted my energy flirting. Though Will's more than all right too. Pity I didn't get a chance to check out what was in *his* undies."

"You didn't check out what was in Hugh's," Josie protested.

"Well, not *check,*" Val said. "But I got the chance to take a pretty good guess. And my guess is, it'll do."

"Maybe women are disgusting too," Clive said. "Or maybe that's just you, Val."

"Oh, you know you love it." She stuck out her little pink tongue at him, and he laughed.

Mike walked in, all efficiency, and cut to the chase, as usual. "Ready for you, Josie," he said.

"Break a leg," Clive said, his voice low, and Josie saw Val lose the smile and give her a meaningful look that she knew meant the same thing, and she forgot about Hugh.

"You've got maybe ten minutes," Mike said as they walked. "Make them good."

She longed to ask him what they'd thought of her idea, to attempt to get some last-minute reassurance, but it sounded needy, so she didn't. She took a breath, put her shoulders back, and channeled Dr. Eva as she stepped into the writers' room ahead of Mike.

"Mike says you have an idea," Victor, the head writer, said without preamble once she'd sat down, and his expression in the heavy black glasses didn't look welcoming. He shoved his stocky frame back from the conference table, gestured with a meaty hand to the other three writers, and added, "Actors telling me how to write my characters aren't my favorite thing, but he asked us to hear you out, so we're all ears."

Josie gave him a cool smile, then made eye contact with each of the four others at the table. "I do have an idea," she told them, "thank you. We've had Dr. Eva being Dr. Evil for three years now. I thought it might be interesting to show a different facet to her character."

"Such as?" Victor asked, his unkempt beard bristling pugnaciously.

"Nobody's ever suggested she's anything but a good surgeon," Josie said, keeping her tone level, impersonal. "In fact, I've always thought a lot of her confidence comes from knowing she's a *great* surgeon. If she's arrogant, well, surgeons are. It's just that most of them are men, and arrogance in men is called 'confidence,' isn't it?"

She saw the nod from Samantha, the youngest writer on the team, and went on. "She's sexually aggressive, she's arrogant, she's cold, and she's unpopular. But she also does right by her patients, at least in the operating room. Even if it comes from her pride in her skill rather than her humanitarian instincts, she does care. So what if somebody else wasn't providing that level of care? How would she feel about that? I think she'd hate it."

"Go on," Victor said, his expression giving nothing away.

"What if there were a surgeon who was stuffing up," Josie asked, leaning in, looking around again, ramping it up a little bit, impressing her personality, her own confidence in her idea on all of them, "and Dr. Eva was the only one who saw it? What if he was a man who'd refused her, and everyone knew it? Say he had a drug problem, or an alcohol problem. You all would know what would work best, could give him a tortured past. Make him complex, a tragic figure. Nobody better at that." Buttering them up couldn't hurt. "Say Dr. Eva brought it to the chief medical officer's attention, and he brushed it off, because of her reputation. Thought she was trying to get revenge because he—the other surgeon—had turned her down. Say patients started dying, and some of the hospital staff were covering up. And she couldn't get anyone to care, and didn't have any allies to call on."

"That'd mean a new character," Mike pointed out.

"Yeh, and one people could change their minds about, gradually," Josie said. "Just like they could change their minds a bit about Dr. Eva. It'd get the viewers talking. Get them thinking. I got the idea from a headline about a surgeon like that, big news at the time. You may have seen it yourselves, because it's a horror story everyone can relate to, isn't it? Dad going in for a heart op, your partner going in for a Cesarean, dying because the doctor was drunk. The baby dying, too. Pure drama. Cue the tears."

She stopped, because it was time to listen, looked around the room, and saw them considering. Well, considering was good.

And then Victor ruined it. "So you want your character to be more sympathetic," he said. "All the work we've put in to make her not be, and you want to take out the villain of the piece?"

"I put in a bit of that work myself," she said, "and I'm not saying to take out the villain. I'm just saying, add a bit of nuance. A spin."

"I like the spin," Samantha said, which was brave of her as the newest writer on the team, and Josie shot her a smile of gratitude, got a smile back. "I think Josie's right, it'd get people talking. How many men is Dr. Eva going to be able to work through? She's shagged half the cast already. Unless she starts in on the women as well, there's only so far we can take that storyline."

"An alcoholic surgeon's not a bad idea," Ian, the other junior writer, said with a judicious air. "But I'm not so sure about the other. You're meant to hate Dr. Eva, full stop. And nuance? This isn't a BBC costume drama. It's a soap."

Victor looked at the fourth writer, Rose, an older woman and the second-most senior member of the team, but she only shrugged. "Sounds good to me, but I'm not fussed either way," she said.

"But would you want to watch that?" Josie pressed a bit, because she could feel the tone of the meeting shifting away from her.

"I don't want to watch any of it," Rose said. "I just write it."

"And I don't like the idea much at all," Victor said. "Turning your villain sympathetic isn't a recipe for ratings. Mike?"

"It's your call," Mike said. "I could do something with it, yeh. I think it's good. But I'm not going to shove it down your throats if you don't want to do it."

"We'll think about it," Victor said. He looked at Josie. "And let you know."

She nodded, stood up with a smile. *Never let them see you sweat.* "Good. I'll look forward to hearing more," she said, and left the room with her head high.

♡

Mike followed her out. "Sorry that didn't go better," he said when they were walking down the passage again.

She tried not to let the exasperation show. He hadn't exactly stuck his neck out for her. "Thanks for getting me the meeting," she said. "If it doesn't fly, well, there's always next time. And who knows, maybe Victor will change his mind."

"Yeh. Maybe." Mike sounded about as convinced as she felt.

Clive and Valerie looked up inquiringly as she entered the makeup room again. They'd stayed, she knew, just to see how her meeting had gone, and she felt a rush of gratitude.

"No joy," she told them, not sitting down with them again.

"Ah," Clive said. "Hard luck."

"Yeh. Win some, lose some," she said. "Thanks for hanging around. But it's late. See you both tomorrow."

♡

Her thoughts on the drive home in the thinning post-six-o-clock traffic caromed between the disappointing meeting, her optimism taking a hit as she contemplated the dashing of an idea on which she'd pinned too much hope…between that, and Hugh. Down, and then, oh yeh, up again.

It was such a good diversion to think about Hugh making those slow turns in nothing but his black boxer briefs. No matter what Val had thought, Josie had looked, and it didn't seem to matter that she'd seen him in his togs just a few days earlier. He was what she wanted, and she couldn't get enough.

She'd looked at broad thighs defined by heavy muscle, at the wide shoulders and deep chest with its light furring of dark hair, all of it narrowing so satisfactorily to his trim waist and hips, at the arms he held out from his sides, so much of them it seemed like it would need some strength just to hold them up like that. At everything she'd been looking at for weeks now, so tantalizingly close to being fully revealed. When he'd pulled his jersey over his head again afterwards, tugging it into place down his torso, she'd wanted to take it off again. To stroke her hands up his sides, over his chest in its wake, listening to him groan out her name, her real name. Not because he was acting, but because it was real.

She'd had a quick image of doing just that, of him in her bed, every beautiful naked bit of him sprawled there while she worked on him, while she drove him wild. And then he'd kissed her in her dressing room, and it had been exactly the other way around, and she'd been lost.

What was she meant to do now, though, turn up at his door tonight and ask him to finish the job? She'd got reckless today, but he was still her neighbor, and this was, suddenly, going much too fast. All the arguments that had made sense yesterday still did. It was just that their voice was being drowned out by something else. By the sound of his voice, low in her ear.

Be good.

She didn't have a clue, so she went to the gym, did her workout and took a quick shower, and picked up a takeaway salad at the café afterwards.

"Thirteen-fifty?" the girl behind the registered prompted.

"Hmm?" Josie looked up, startled, from her mobile.

"Thirteen-fifty," the girl said again with a sigh, and Josie swiped her card, punched in her PIN, took her salad out to the car, and sat and looked at the text again.

Still going to do it.

Five words on a screen, and her body had gone on Full Alert. The problem of her professional future had been shelved, because she wasn't thinking about it anymore. But then she drove home, saw his car in the driveway, the lights on in the house, knew he was with his brother and sister, doing the washing-up, probably. And again...now what?

She let herself into her own dark little villa, switched the lights on, sat at the kitchen table and ate her Thai chicken salad, for once not noticing the hunger that remained afterwards, the yearning for one of her mum's roast meals, kumara and potatoes and lamb that stuck to your ribs. Which was why she didn't eat it, because she didn't need anything sticking to her ribs.

And by then, it was after eight-thirty, and it was time to get ready for bed, because no matter how many sexy rugby players she kissed in her dressing room, the alarm was still going to ring at five o'clock the next morning. And Hugh was with his family.

She went into her bedroom, raised the blind all the same and looked across at what she knew was Hugh's window. Dark. Of course it was, because he didn't have to be asleep by nine.

They could go out, she thought, switching on the bedside light and switching off the overhead one. He could ask her to dinner. She could start dating again. She could start with Hugh. As long as they kept it…friendly, what was the harm, after all? He was decent, she was sure of it. And as for her, she never lost her head, and she wasn't going to start now. If it didn't work out, it didn't, and they could move on.

She walked across to the closet, pulled the T-shirt over her head and tossed it into the hamper, undid the side zip on her skirt and clipped it onto its hanger. Unfastened the back clasp on her bra, wriggled out of the undies, and couldn't help feeling his fingers sliding over the lacy scallops with a deliberation, a delicacy she'd never have imagined, leaving a trail of tingling nerves in their wake.

When she was naked, she pulled her dressing gown off its hanger and shrugged it on, then walked across the room to sit at her dressing table, where she pulled the pins out of her hair one by one, dropping them into the green pottery bowl with its koru design that she'd made in primary school, and began to brush her hair.

She didn't really need to, but she liked to. She loved the long, rhythmic strokes, the sensuous grace of it, liked to watch herself in the mirror while she did it. The one time she allowed herself to look in the mirror and not worry that that was a wrinkle developing beside an eye, a spot forming on her chin.

At night, she gave herself a pass. So she sat and did her hair, taking it slowly, then set the brush down and massaged lotion into her face, her neck, her chest, focused on the touch of her fingers, the silkiness of the cream dissolving into her skin. And the memory of Hugh's mouth on her neck, of his hand whispering up her thighs, over the tops of her breasts.

When she was relaxed, her body humming, she stood up again, went over to the bed, unfastened her robe, dropped it at the foot of the bed, and crawled under the duvet. Crawled under it naked, because she loved the feel of the cotton sheet against her skin, the freedom of nudity in this one place where it was just her and her body. And because she and her body were going to have a long, slow, delicious date tonight, while she thought about Hugh, about what had happened today and all the things she hoped would happen next.

She heard her phone ding, because she'd forgotten to switch it off, sat up again, picked it up from the bedside table and read the words.

Unlock your back door.

Her eyes flew to the window. To the blind that, she realized, she hadn't shut again. To the figure she could barely make out, a shadow against the shades of black behind him. To the man who'd been standing there watching her this entire time, because he'd thought she'd meant to do this, that she'd been inviting him to watch her, asking him to come to her.

She was frozen, sitting up in bed, the sheet around her waist, the phone in her hand. And the figure still standing there. Waiting. Watching. The phone was silent, and all she could hear was the sound of her breathing, audible in the stillness.

She slid out of bed, pulled on her dressing gown, and left the room.

over the fence

♡

She hit the light switch in the kitchen, then wished she'd left it off, because she could see nothing beyond the glass sliders but the reflection of the room and the impenetrable blackness beyond. He could be standing outside right now, looking at her, and she wouldn't even know it. The thought made her breath come shallow, her body tighten with shivery nerves. But this wasn't really some demon lover she was waiting for, some anonymous visitor in the dark. This was her neighbor. This was Hugh.

It was the Hugh who'd kissed her the way he had in her dressing room, though. That Hugh had been a different animal from her friendly, helpful neighbor. That Hugh unnerved her.

She hesitated a moment more, then turned the lock and slid the door open, her heart pounding.

To find...nothing. Nothing but the darkness of her back garden, the looming bulk of Mt. Victoria beyond, the musical trill of the cicadas.

And, after a moment, the movement at the top of the fence. A dark shape suddenly appearing above it, then dropping to the grass. Hugh, coming across to her. Coming fast.

"You know," she started to say, "some people would have just walked around."

She didn't finish the sentence, because he was on her. One arm wrapping around her shoulders, the other hand at her waist, his big body backing her through the door.

His mouth was hard on hers already, forcing her lips open, his tongue invading. She was dimly aware that she was whimpering with surprise and excitement, that her hands were at his shoulders, grabbing at him, and still he pushed her backwards, until her back hit the wall and there was no retreat. One hand was behind her head, cushioning it, threading through her hair, the other was at her waist, and she was on her toes, his body pressing into hers.

"I need to do this," he groaned, his hand between their bodies, pulling at the sash of her dressing gown. He yanked the edges apart, and then both hands were cupping her breasts, his thumbs moving over them, sending jolts of pleasure straight to her core. His mouth was at her throat, his teeth closing over her skin, and she was gasping, her hands pulling his shirt up, sliding over the skin of his sides, his back, greedy for him.

When he lifted his mouth from her neck and took his hands from her, it took a moment for it to register. He was yanking the dressing gown from her shoulders, dropping it to the floor, and she pulled his T-shirt over his head with desperate haste, ran urgent palms over the heft of his shoulders, down his broad chest, around to his back while he shoved his shorts over his hips, kicked them aside, then reached for her again, hauling her up against him with one arm, the other hand sliding down her back, and down further still, gripping her, holding her even closer. The wall was cold against her upper back, and he was hot against the rest of her, hot and urgent and big and hard.

His mouth trailed over her cheek, biting her earlobe, his teeth scraping the skin beneath, and she was shuddering. He shifted her in his arms, and his hand wasn't on her leg anymore. It was over her, moving, stroking, and he had her bent backwards a little over his arm, and her gasps had turned to moans.

"Take me to bed," he told her, his voice coming out strained, "or you're on the floor."

She didn't answer, because she barely heard him, and he didn't ask again. He was pulling her with him, down onto their knees, laying her down on the rag rug in front of the kitchen sink. Coming down over her, his hands on her breasts, and then his mouth was moving over her throat, down her breast, settling on her, teasing out a response her body was completely willing to give, while his hand roamed, dove, held her, and began to stroke, finding the perfect spot, the perfect way to touch her.

Her head thrashed, her hands reached for his shoulders, and she clung to him so tightly as he worked on her, drove her higher.

"That's right," he said as she began to cry out, her hips bucking into his hand, because she couldn't help it. "Come on, Josie. Arch that pretty back for me. Show me how much you want it."

He kept on until all rational thought had left her, until every bit of her had become pure need, pulling her toward a peak she needed to climb with everything in her. And then he let go of her, lifted his head, and she trembled and jerked against him.

"More," she begged, opening her eyes to look at him, her hands pulling at his shoulders. "Please. More."

"You're going to get more," he promised, moving down her body so she lost her grip on him. "Right now."

There was nothing subtle about it. He had a thigh in either hand, had spread her legs wide. He set his mouth to her, the rasp of his beard providing a delicious friction against the tender skin, his mouth and tongue doing the rest. Doing so much, she could barely stand it. Her breath was coming in loud sobs, her hands were scrabbling, reaching for a hold they couldn't find, until she gave it up and her fists clenched shut, pressed against the cold linoleum, and began to slide back and forth in a frantic rhythm.

He slowed down, and she rose into his mouth and begged again.

"Please," she gasped. "Please. Don't...stop."

"I'm not going to stop," he promised, his hands under her now, lifting her into him. "I'm never going to stop. I'm going to make you come so hard. And then I'm going to make you do it again."

He sped up, and she got louder, then slowed down until she was begging again. Over and over, cranking the tension up so deliciously slowly, and she'd forgotten that she was lying on her kitchen floor, was aware of nothing but his hard mouth on her, his strong hands gripping her.

"I can't...I can't..." she got out, straining against him as the flames licked her, consumed her, devoured her.

He wasn't listening, though. He held her tight, kept on and on, merciless, until her back was arching so strongly she was bent like a bow, until her head was thrown back, her mouth open, her arms flung out from her sides, and she was gasping for air.

He made her shake. He made her burn. And then he made her howl.

She was still trembling, her legs parted, her body limp, when he came back over her, took her mouth in a deep, drugging kiss. Her eyes were closed, and then he slid home, and they weren't.

Size mattered. Oh, it mattered. She was filled so completely, even her eyes stretched wide at the astonishing sensation of it. He began to move, slowly at first, and that was even better, and she grabbed the bunched muscle of his shoulders, wrapped her hands around his biceps, flexed to support his body weight, and held on for the ride.

He was so solid over her, inside her, around her, and she drew her legs up, twined them around his broad back, and urged him on. He was on his palms, driving so hard he was moving her across the floor, and all she could do was hang on and keen out the hot pleasure of it.

It was fast, and it was hard, and it was all the way over the top. They rode the dark wave together, more and more, higher and higher, until it pulled them under, tumbled them, rolled them. Until it very nearly drowned them both.

demon lover

♡

"Whoa," Hugh exhaled when he'd got back enough breath to say it, had rolled off her so he wouldn't crush her. "Bed, don't you think?"

"Yeh. Bed." She sounded about as shaky as he felt.

He stood, reached a hand down to pull her to her feet, grabbed his clothes and her dressing gown off the floor and let her lead him down the hall.

He came out of the bathroom once he'd got rid of the condom he'd barely managed to remember in the heat of the moment, followed the pathway of light to her bedroom, and found her. Sitting up, the white sheet pulled to her waist, the heavy waves of her dark hair streaming over her golden skin.

"What a view," he said, sliding in beside her. "Thought so earlier tonight, and I haven't changed my mind."

He leaned over, pushed her hair away from her face with a gentle hand, and gave her the soft kiss he hadn't managed yet that night, then sat back and smiled into her eyes, his hand still on her face, his thumb stroking over her cheek, feeling her leaning into it.

"Have I mentioned," he asked her, "how beautiful you are? And what a lucky man I feel tonight?"

"Mm, I don't think so," she sighed. She was smiling too, soft and sweet, sliding down to lie against the pillows, and he was going with her, as if he'd ever had a choice. He got an arm under her so he could pull her into him, stroke the skin of her shoulder, and she settled against his chest, and it was exactly where he needed her.

"But, Hugh," she asked. "What about the kids?"

He had to laugh. "What about them? Was I meant to be thinking about them? I realize I don't know all the rules, but I'm pretty sure that's not one."

"No," she said. He could feel the curve of her lips as she smiled against his skin, and that was good too. "But you shouldn't leave them alone too long. Even to come here. Even to be next door. Not at night."

"Ah. Means I get points," he told her.

"You already got points," she said, and she was smiling again, he could tell.

"More points, then, because I left a note on the kitchen table and put my phone in my pocket. On second thought, considering the kind of pressure I was under, I reckon that earns me a medal."

"Could be," she said, sounding a little sleepy. "More thinking than I was doing."

"Oh, I thought you did some fairly good thinking. That was a pretty good invite you sent me."

"Well, actually," she said, "it wasn't. Not exactly, because that wasn't…it wasn't the result of thinking. When you texted me, when I saw you at the window…well, you startled me. That's putting it mildly."

He pulled away, looked down at her with a frown. "What?"

"Because I didn't mean to do that," she said. "I didn't know you were watching."

"Aw, shit." He lay back down again with a groan, his arm flung over his eyes. "I've been a bloody Peeping Tom."

"No, you haven't," she assured him. "I think you just gave me a real-life Demon Lover fantasy, that's all."

"A *what?*"

"You know. A stranger coming out of the shadows without a word. Rushing me, taking me over the way you did."

"You saying I attacked you?" He pulled himself up to sit, an icy chill replacing the hot blood in his veins, and stared down at her. "That doesn't sound like a demon. That sounds like a rapist. You were allowed to say no. You were allowed to text me back and tell me to get the hell out of your bedroom. All you had to say was no."

"And if I'd wanted to, I would have." She was sitting up too, her hand on his upper arm. "Hugh. No. That wasn't what I meant, not at all. I'm saying, when you texted me, when I saw you, I realized that I must have wanted you to watch. I raised my blind to look for you, and then I didn't close it again, because I must have wanted you to see, and then I wanted you to be my Demon Lover. I wanted you so much. I wanted you to come."

She leaned over, kissed him softly on the mouth. "And you did, didn't you?" She'd pulled back a little, had herself propped over him, her body so irresistible, her smile so slow, so seductive, and he was falling again. "And so did I. How many times was that? You had me so far gone, the last thing I was doing was counting."

"Three," he told her, smiling back, the relief filling him. "Because I *was* counting. And next time, it'll be more. Now that I know what you like."

"Oh, big promises," she mocked, and her eyes were sparkling, her gorgeous mouth was curving, and he laughed, rolled her over, got her under him again.

"Well, maybe," he said, "just one more. For tonight. Going to rock you nice and slow this time, just because I want to. Because your Demon Lover isn't done with you yet."

dr. eva takes a turn

♡

She woke to the sound of the alarm, struggled out of sleep and rolled to switch off the annoying buzz, not feeling one bit ready to wake up.

And then she remembered why. She sat up, pulled her tangled mass of hair from around her face, and listened for him, but of course he was gone, had left sometime in the minutes or hours after she'd fallen asleep with her head pillowed on his chest, his hand stroking her hair. He'd gone back home, leaving not so much as an indentation in the pillow. Nothing but the faint ache between her thighs, the hum in her body to show where he had been.

♡

"Somebody got a shag at last."

Clive was scrutinizing her from the chair in which he was sprawled with his script. She had arrived in the makeup room not first, or even second this morning, because Val were already there too.

"And that somebody isn't me," Clive continued. "Sadly, the only love affair Steph's got going right now is the one with the toilet bowl."

"Still sick?" Josie asked, taking her own seat in the next chair along.

"Yeh. Never fall pregnant, that's my advice," he said, and she kept the smile on her face. "But you're trying to change the subject. Hard Man Hugh living up to his name, eh."

"Good one, Clive," Valerie said without turning her head as Gregor continued his ministrations, added another coat of mascara to her big blue eyes before stroking blusher onto the apples of her porcelain cheeks.

"Absolutely none of your business," Josie said. "And how would you know anyway? Not like I've got an 'Engaged' sign lighting up in the pertinent area. You're not nearly such a Clever Clogs as you'd like to believe. He's my neighbor. I told you."

"Oh, yeh, I'd say you've got the sign," Clive said, unperturbed. "Wouldn't you, Gregor?"

"Well…" The makeup artist paused in the act of blending Val's blusher and cast a speculative eye over Josie. "Let's say you've given me more work to do than usual. The beard burn, darling," he said at her look of outrage. "That's put us all on notice. Not to mention the wee baggies under your gorgeous eyes. Get on with it and get your sleep, please, sweetheart. For my sake."

"Didn't even notice the beard burn," Clive said. "You're good, Gregor."

"Just doing my job," he said modestly. "Honestly, Josie, tell him to go easier on you next time. You're going to look well and truly preserved by the time I cover all that up."

"Will you *stop?*" she protested, though she couldn't help laughing. "Leave a girl a bit of dignity."

"Nah, got to let us live vicariously," Val said. "If you're going to have that much fun. Because he did look like a bloody good time to me. All that smoldery burn when he looked at you? Mmm. And I take it the undies didn't lie, either? That wasn't a sock stuffed in there?"

"Glad one thing went right last night, anyway," Clive said more seriously when Josie didn't dignify Val's question with a response. "Since the meeting didn't, I guess."

"No," Josie said, and she'd gone from being a bit embarrassed to being a bit gloomy now. "Haven't heard for sure, but

I'm thinking, not a chance. And Dr. Eva's character's looking thinner and thinner, isn't she? You can see right through her by now, she's so shallow. Only so long you can milk a story line, and I think we're about there. That's what worries me."

"Good thing you've got the adverts, then," Val said bracingly. "Keep that wolf from the door. Wish I had that many offers, but all I ever get is washing powder. Or, for a real treat, running through a scratchy field full of tall grass with some bloke tenderly holding my innocent hand. Not paying the mortgage with that."

"Sex sells," Clive said. "And our Josie's sex on wheels, or sex in heels, more like. You can write your own ticket, can't you."

"Long as I want to focus on the sex," Josie said.

"Trust me," Val said. "Do it. Or you'll find yourself smiling with loving Mummy patience at some spoilt brat of a two-year-old who's just undone the entire roll of loo paper and tied the dog up in it, with some fella doing a voiceover. 'So strong, and still so soft. Because little bums can use a little help.'"

Josie laughed. "That's how much fun you had last week, eh."

"Yeh," Val sighed. "Just that exciting. The kid was a bloody nightmare, too, and his mum was worse. I wanted to tie both of them in the loo paper by the time we'd done, and leave them there. The dog was the best actor of the lot."

Gregor pulled the smock off from around Val's neck, and she got up and collected her script from the table. "So if anybody rings, asks me to lie in all my glory on top of a horse and look shaggable for a few hundred thousand dollars?" she asked. "Tell them I'll be in my dressing room, running through my virtuous lines, preparing to keep the hospital pure for another day. And that I'm very good with animals."

♡

Josie didn't have much time to think about Hugh after that. Not with two hefty scenes on her plate, first pitching a fit during a surgery, and then pitching something else at Clive's Bruce Dixon in Dr. Eva's continuing bid to get herself out of disciplinary hot water. Which all made for a very long day of rehearsal, filming, and jollying the others along.

Not to mention a bit more complication added as well, when she was called into the writers' room at the end of the day to meet with Mike and the writing team, which definitely caused her heart to beat a little faster.

"We're not going for your plan," Victor said as soon as she sat down, and she saw the look of satisfaction on his bearded face at being able to say it. *You may be the star out there, but you're not the boss of us. I call the shots here.*

She didn't allow the disappointment to show, gave a casual shrug instead. "Right, then. Thanks for letting me know." She began to get up, because all she wanted was to get out.

Victor held up a broad hand. "Wait. We've got another story idea instead, and we're going to be using this one."

"And as you started us on the track of it," Rose, the other senior writer, said, "we thought it was only fair to let you know."

Victor shot her a glare, but she ignored him, gave Josie a little smile that told Josie whose idea this had actually been, and that Rose wasn't quite as detached and uncaring as she'd seemed the day before.

Josie smiled back, then turned her attention to Victor again. "I'd love to hear it," she said politely.

"Dr. Eva's too one-dimensional," Victor began. "We need to shake things up, have her confronting a situation she can't control."

Josie bit her tongue to keep from retorting that that had been her own suggestion, and kept the attentive expression on her face.

"Everyone would like to see her get a taste of her own medicine," Rose put in, earning her another exasperated look from

Victor. "With people like that, that's what you want to see most, don't you? You want to see them pay, to get what's coming to them. You want life to give them a swift kick in the arse."

"You do," Josie agreed, because she needed to say something.

"So," Rose said, "she falls in love. Or at least," she amended, "she gets obsessed, because even I may not be able to make Dr. Eva fall in love."

Or even me, Josie didn't say. "No," she said instead. "I don't think she would, not really. I don't think she's capable of it, not real love. Not caring for somebody."

"But she could be obsessed," Victor said, ignoring her. "And that's the plan. We get a new character in, a new surgeon. Dr. Eva in reverse. He's brilliant, has shot up fast, comes in senior to her from the start, which will get her pretty knickers in a twist. Arrogant, too, as bad as her. And, of course, tall, dark, and deadly handsome. He's an alpha male, and as we all know, in any dog pack, the alpha female still has to answer to one dog. The top dog."

Nice, Josie thought. Clearly Victor's ideal world.

"So," Rose took over, "Dr. Eva tries her tricks on him straight away. Once she's had time to pack a sad at the whole idea of him, of course, make life miserable for the rest of the staff. But does he fall for her? I'm guessing you know the answer."

"No," Josie said. "He laughs at her."

The other woman pointed a finger at her and grinned. "Got it in one. And she's rocked. Thinks she just hasn't tried hard enough, keeps having a go. And at some point, when he chooses, at a medical conference, maybe, our new Dr. Deadly takes her up on it. Not in her usual style, either. She's not in charge this time."

"Got to keep it seven o'clock appropriate," Victor warned.

"Oh, I'm very good," she assured him. "I'll manage it."

Or I will, Josie thought, because she could do so much with a look, the tone of her voice.

"So he gives her the ride of her life," Rose said. "Leaves her wanting more."

"And then doesn't give it to her," Josie said.

"That's the idea. Laughs at her again, tells her she wasn't that good. Not enough of a woman for him."

Josie flinched involuntarily at the sting of it, and Rose laughed. "Yeh, that's just how she'd feel, isn't it? Am I good, or what?"

Josie summoned a smile. "You're very good," she assured the other woman, because she was.

"I know," Rose said. "Got some more work to do on it, how it all plays out, but as a twist for next season, yeh. Bloody good. I think it'll put the ratings through the ceiling, eh, Mike," she asked the so-far-silent director.

"It's good," he agreed.

It wasn't her preferred outcome, Josie thought as she left the room. But it was good television all the same.

♡

Finally, she was back in her dressing room, changing her clothes, changing her personality, weariness gaining a hand now, because it had been a long day. And a long night, Gregor had been right about that.

She looked again at the text she'd got from Hugh that morning. *Ring me when you get a chance.* She pressed the screen, and heard the buzz. Two rings, three, and he was picking up.

"Hi." She heard his deep voice at the other end, and despite her fatigue, got a thrill of remembered excitement at the sound. "Is this a beautiful woman, by any chance?"

"Mm. Maybe," she said, feeling the smile curving her lips. "May just be your lucky day."

He laughed. "I think yesterday was my lucky day. How'd you go at work? You're ringing me at five-thirty, so I'm guessing it was another long one."

"Yeh," she said with the hint of a sigh. "You'd be right."

"And somebody kept you up last night," he said. "Bet the alarm came early. I know it did for me, not that I'm complaining. So can I tempt you to come by and have dinner with us tonight? Not sure I'll be able to impress you much with my skills, but I'm hoping for points for effort."

"I'd like to," she said, "but no. Got to go work out still, and you're right, I'm a bit tired. I need to make sure I get to bed on time."

"Ah. So does that mean no visit over the fence tonight either? Even if I take it easy on you?"

"Wish I could say yes, but...no."

"Disappointing," he said. "As it happens, though, I've got another suggestion, because Amelia's got an end-of-term dance tomorrow night."

"Ballet?" Josie asked with surprise. Chloe hadn't said anything about a recital.

"Nah. Dance-dance. You know, boys and girls staring awkwardly at each other from across the room, until the girls finally take the boys in hand in desperation."

"Really," she said. "Well, I guess that's about right."

"Doesn't seem possible to me," he said, "but as she keeps telling me, she's twelve. But the pertinent part of all this is that she's staying the night with friends tomorrow, and that I used my new skills to get Charlie sorted that way as well. Which means that, from about seven tomorrow night until nine-thirty on Saturday, your Demon Lover's all yours, if you want him."

"I want him," she said, because, oh, yes, she did.

"Good," he said, and she could hear the satisfaction in his voice. "That's good. We'll have a proper date this time, dinner and all, how's that? Think you could see your way clear to dressing up for me, maybe even wearing a bit more of that secret armor of yours? You started a whole new train of thought there, I have to tell you. If you don't satisfy me soon, I may just explode, and wouldn't that make a mess in the neighborhood."

"Sounds like you want it," she said, and saw the smile spreading across the face in the mirror. She wasn't Dr. Eva, and that was the truth. It was one thing to be desired by strangers, but it was a whole different thing to be desired this much by the one and only man she wanted.

"Oh, I want it," he assured her. "So, what? Collect you at seven-thirty? Dinner, wine, dress, pretty undies I get to look forward to taking off you?"

"All of the above," she said, a rush of unaccustomed recklessness overtaking her at the thought. "I'm all yours."

playing with fire

♡

"Ah," Hugh sighed when Josie opened the door to his knock the following evening. "That's what I love to see."

She was wearing a black dress. Nothing low-cut, nothing short, not even too tight. Sleeveless, with a neckline that barely showed her delicate collarbones, a skirt nearly to the knee. But skimming every delicious curve of her, showing off the golden skin of her shoulders and arms, and every bit of it worked. Her hair was down, too, pulled straight back off her face and falling down her back in lustrous waves, her makeup was low-key and perfect, her heels were high, and she was gorgeous.

He leaned in for a kiss, felt her hands come up to clutch at his shoulders, and that was even better.

"You look very handsome, too," she said when he'd managed to pull himself back. She looked at his white shirt with its subtle stripe, his black trousers and shoes. At the effort, he hoped, she could see he'd taken, new haircut and all.

"I'm just the backdrop," he assured her.

"Not to me."

He had to kiss her again after that. Well, maybe he just had to kiss her again.

"Got my undies on, too?" he asked, once his mouth had made its slow way across to the underside of her jaw, once he felt the way she was leaning into him.

"Mmm," she sighed, "you'll have to find that out for yourself, won't you?" Her hand was stroking the nape of his neck, and he wasn't at all sure he was going to make it through dinner.

"I think you need a challenge," she told him, her voice promising so much. "Something to look forward to, and I'm going to give it to you. But I will show you this." She turned in a graceful circle, spinning on a toe, the other foot cocked up in the wicked black stilettos. He saw the stockings, and they weren't the least little bit decorous.

"You liked the seamed ones," she said when she was facing him again, "as I recall. Aren't they pretty?"

"Not the word I'd use," he managed to say, "but they're bloody effective. What's holding those up, that's what I'd really like to know."

"And...another challenge for you," she said, her voice full of smoke. "Another mystery for you to solve. Later. Think you can handle that?"

"Oh, I know I can," he assured her. "I can handle you, no worries. But before I do, I'm going to take you to dinner."

♡

He didn't even have to remind himself to listen to her, to ask questions, he realized when they were sitting at one end of the low-ceilinged Auckland pub with its dark wood paneling, the doors open to the cobbled courtyard beyond. She was just so much fun to be with, her face so alive, her hands moving as she talked. He asked about her day, listened to her account of her two meetings with the writers, and was swept irresistibly into her world, frowning and laughing in equal measure as she talked.

"What do you think?" she asked when she'd finished. "I thought, pretty good, though I'm a bit disappointed."

"Why?" he asked. "Because it sounds like a pretty good stretch, a chance to be a bit...different, eh. And that's good, right? Seems like you'd want to keep...moving?"

"Yeh," she said. "Exactly. I'm surprised you know."

He shrugged. "That's how it is when you're playing, too. You can't stay in one place. Get overtaken by somebody else then, for one thing. You have to keep getting better. In our case, you can lose a bit of edge with the years and the injuries, once you're aimed at thirty. But if you've got the skills, the experience, the mental game, as well as training hard, you're still better, on the whole, then you were five years earlier, at least you hope so. Must be about the same for you."

"You're right," she said. "Getting older matters, but it's more than what you look like, when you're an actor. At least the kind I want to be. If it were just the face and the body, I could've stayed with the modeling, made the most of the early years, although I'd be more worried about the age now if I'd gone that route."

"So..." he pressed. "Why wasn't this good news, today?"

"It was," she said. "Just not my preferred outcome, I guess. It doesn't really expand Dr. Eva's character, doesn't show any other side of her. And it certainly doesn't offer me a chance to play anything but evil, even if it's evil thwarted. And evil's a bit limited, isn't it? I've always thought of Dr. Eva as a sociopath, and sociopaths are boring, aren't they? No real emotions but anger and frustration, no ability to care about anybody except themselves. I guess I wanted to think she was more than that."

She paused, took a final bite of fish and vegies, a sip of white wine while she thought, and he waited.

"What it is," she finally said, "is that I've been playing these brilliant, heartless—well, these horrible characters, really, for five years now. My Aussie lawyer was pretty much Dr. Eva with a law diploma. I was thinking I might be able to do more, but it's hard to turn your back on a good thing, isn't it."

"What would that look like, doing more?" he asked. "What would you like to play, if that's the right word?"

"Somebody totally different," she said immediately. "Mad, I know, but...I'd like to do somebody who could be funny. A whole person. Women aren't one thing or the other, you know, not really. Not sexy," she said, gesturing with both hands, a chop on one side of the table, "or complex. Complete." Another chop on the other side. "At least I hope they're not."

"They're not," he assured her. "At least this one isn't. What else? What else do you want to do?"

"Well..." She hesitated. "I had an idea. But it's for a show that doesn't exist."

"What kind of show? Funny? A comedy?"

"Not strictly. Not just that. Everything."

He made a beckoning motion with one hand. "Let's have it. I can tell there's a whole world worked out in that clever brain of yours."

"You think I have a clever brain?"

"Oh, I don't just think. I know. So...what's the show?"

"Well," she said, "it's this. It's somebody—well," she said with a laugh, and he liked her so damn much, "it's me. Guess you know that. My character. Somebody making a big change, what that's like. And not in the direction you expect. She was living a glam life before, that's my idea. In Aussie, maybe, or just in Auckland. Living the dream, you know, in the Big Smoke. Trophy wife, maybe."

He didn't share that that had been his own guess, at the beginning. "And?"

"And something happens. Hubby dumps her, or she loses the glam job, gets humiliated somehow, whatever. Not sure. So she goes back to the homeland, back to her roots, her whanau. Because, of course," she said with another sparkling smile, another sip of wine, "she's Maori. You probably guessed that. She has a primary school qualification from her beginnings, before all the flash happened. And now she's back, in Northland, or the Eastern Cape, maybe. Someplace picturesque, lots of gorgeous, exotic location shots. Very Maori, very remote. Because she grew up like that. Simple."

"Again, like you."

"Yeh. And then it's just funny, and tender, and maybe a bit dramatic. With the schoolkids, and the parents, and the blokes, because of course, she's a hot property, right?"

"Right," he said, smiling at her. "Again, because she's you."

"And being back with her family," she went on, "all the conflicts and exasperation of it, trying to date, having her dad sitting up for her, wanting to have a chat with the bloke beforehand. The whanau, the marae, the songs. It's all just normal to me, but I think it could be interesting to other people, that whole aspect. I think it could work really well in En Zed, but other places, too. Aussie, the UK. Even," she said, taking a breath, "the States. *Whale Rider* was a hit, why couldn't this be? Why wouldn't people enjoy something as different as that?"

"No reason," he said, "especially with you doing it. Sounds fun, and interesting, and pretty awesome, really. I guess you know that I'd watch you in anything, but I think everybody would watch you do that. I think so."

"You do?" she asked, her eyes searching his. "You're not just saying that to—" She stopped, smiled. "To get my knickers off? Because it's working, for that. I'm liking you a lot right now."

"Nah," he said, smiling back. "Not that that's not good news, but I'm pretty sure I'm going to be able to get your knickers off all by myself. But, yeh. I think it's brilliant."

"Thanks," she said with a sigh, and he realized how much his opinion had mattered to her, and how much he cared that

that was true. "I haven't told anybody about it," she confessed. "You're the first."

It was a new way to be a woman's first, but it was a good way.

"All I need," she said, "is somebody to write it. I've got the whole pilot worked out already, half the first season too. I wake up with the characters talking in there, like it's a show already, projected in my head."

"Well, why don't you?" he asked.

"Why don't I what?"

"Why don't you write it? It's your show. You're the one with the idea, the characters. Why wouldn't you do it?"

"Because..." She seemed to be groping for an answer. "Because I'm not a writer."

"How do you know? Have you tried?"

She laughed, a surprised sound. "No."

"Then..." He shrugged. "You don't know. What have you got to lose? Why not try it and see? If nothing else, seems like you'd get your ideas better fixed, be better able to tell somebody else about them. Whoever it is that you'd tell about something like that to make it happen. So why not?"

"Wow," she said blankly. "I never really thought about it. Not seriously."

"Aren't there actors who write as well?" he asked. "I know there are some who are directors, right? So why not writers?"

"Yeh," she said. "A few, I guess. I guess I could try."

"You can always try," he agreed.

"Then I will," she said. "I'll have a go." She blew out a breath. "Phew. Not what I expected to be talking about over dinner with you."

"That's why we've got all night," he said, and smiled at her again.

He realized they'd finished eating long ago, and that his beer was gone, her wine nearly so. "Need another?" he asked her, gesturing to her glass.

"I usually don't drink two, but…" She laughed a little. "This is too good. All of it. You going to carry me home if I get too wild?"

"I am," he promised. "I'd carry you anywhere."

He couldn't believe he'd said it, but her expression had softened, so it had clearly worked, and that was good enough for him. "And I'll get you another glass of wine, too," he told her.

He crossed the room to the crowded bar, placed the order. The bartender nodded, his hands and feet moving fast on this Friday night, and Hugh resigned himself to a wait and thought about her. About her face, telling him her plan. About how much more she was than what she appeared. About all the surprises of her.

♡

"It's her. I'm sure of it." The voice came from the closest of the three raucous blokes next to him. "Can't mistake those tits, eh. Bet I've spent more time looking at hers than my girlfriend's."

Hugh looked up, startled, and realized that Josie was sitting facing them, looking beautiful, and looking alone, and that they were all staring at her across the long room.

"Because she actually shows you hers," one of his mates said, "and we all know your girlfriend's not giving you any. Watch a lot of *Courtney Place,* do you, while she's got you doing the washing-up?"

"Only the good bits," the first man said with a loud laugh. "And our Jocelyn's got the best bits in the business. Wouldn't mind having a squiz at them, up close and personal."

"I wouldn't mind having more than a squiz," the other one said. "I'll have the whole lot, thank you very much. And it'll take a while, because I've got a whole list to get through."

Where the hell were his drinks? He was meant to be wining and dining Josie tonight, not doing some bastard over, but that was what was going to be happening if this took much longer.

"Yeh, right," the biggest—and the loudest—of the three mocked. Pissed as a fart, too, Hugh saw. "She'd have you bent over the bed, giving you six of the best with her riding crop, before you could say Bob's your uncle. And have you thanking her for it and begging for more."

"Nah, mate. Other way round. Got to be the other way round, when it's my turn," his friend said.

And that was it. That was enough, and Hugh had shifted to face them, invaded their space. "Shut up. Now," he told them, and he made sure they could hear it.

"Who invited you, mate?" the loud man said. "Piss off."

"I invited myself," Hugh said, keeping his hand with difficulty off the other man's collar. "Shut up, or I'll do it for you."

One of the others was talking, low and urgent, to his friend, and they were both looking hard at Hugh now, but all Hugh's attention was on the loud man.

"I'll shut *you* up," the bloke said, and that was a fight that would be over in about five seconds, if it started at all. Which it wasn't going to, because Hugh stood a little taller, shifted his weight, and stared hard. He watched with satisfaction as the fella broke eye contact, had one of his mates grabbing his arm, talking fast in his ear.

"Excuse me, Hugh."

He whirled. Josie. What the hell?

The men gawked, but she merely cast them a cool glance that seemed to sum them up and dismiss them in a instant, then turned away with that panther's stalk, and Hugh offered one more challenging look around and walked around the corner with her.

"Everything all right?" she asked him.

He pretended it was. "Yeh. Fine."

"I'll be back in a moment, then," she said. "Ready to have that drink with you." She smiled at him, put a light hand on his arm, and stretched to give him a soft kiss on the lips.

"See you soon," she murmured before swaying across in the direction of the toilets, and he went back to the bar, shot another look at the three blokes, who'd moved about as far away as they could get, and picked up his beer, because he was going to stay there until she got back. When she walked across the room again, she wasn't going to be walking alone.

"All right?" the bartender asked him.

"Yeh," Hugh said.

"I've got a proposition for you," the bartender said, pulling a beer from the tap for another customer. "I get them chucked out, and you don't get into it in my bar, because you don't need that and neither do I. Fair enough?"

"Yeh," Hugh said again. "That works for me."

♡

"What was that about?" Josie asked when they were seated again and his blood pressure was more or less back to normal.

"Oh, just…" He shrugged. "I took exception to their topic, let's say."

"Ah. Thought so. Defending my honor, eh."

"Well, starting to. I'd have enjoyed it, too. Pity you came along and broke it up, because there was a face there that needed my fist in it."

"Probably be a good idea for you to get used to that," she said. "It comes with the territory."

"Not happening," he said briefly. "Not if they say it around me, it's not."

"Then you're going to be a busy man."

"I'm already a busy man. And intimidation," he said with a smile for her, "is what I do."

She looked at him, and then she smiled, slow and sweet. She put a hand out, began to trace the muscles of his forearm with delicate fingers, and the evening had suddenly taken a whole different turn, leaving him reeling along in its wake.

"It looked like you were doing it pretty well, too," she said, her voice, her eyes so soft. "I wouldn't want to be facing you like that. In fact, you've got me a little scared now. You going to intimidate me too?"

"Never," he promised, his heart hammering. "You, I've got other ways of dealing with." Her hand was caressing, and his beer was half-drunk, and half was enough.

"Oh, yeh?" she asked, and took another careful, deliberate sip of wine, kept smiling at him. He could tell she knew exactly what effect that sip, that smile, had on him. And then she put the tip of her tongue out and licked the rim of her glass, just the faintest touch, and it was as if she'd put her hand straight onto his groin under the table. She looked at him, tipped her head back, and drank, and he watched the movement of her golden throat as she swallowed.

"I think," she said, setting her glass down, drawing a slow circle around its rim with one long finger, "that you should take me home and show me exactly how you're going to deal with me."

"I'm going to do that," he told her over the pounding in his head. "In about two minutes. But only if you stop making love to that wine glass so I can walk to the door."

"You want me to stop?" she asked, her finger still moving. "Not touch it anymore? That doing things to you?" She was caressing the stem now, her fingers running lightly over its length, stroking it. "This bothering you too?" she purred. "Poor Hugh. How can I make it better?"

"You're not going to make it better," he said. "That's going to be my job. And if you want to know how..." Now he was the one smiling, and her eyes had widened a bit, and she wasn't being

Dr. Eva anymore. "All I'll tell you is this," he said. "How? In all sorts of ways. Ways you'll remember next time you're doing that act of yours. Ways that will remind you not to play with fire, because you just might get burned."

a maori thing

♡

She'd walked out the door with him, had taken his arm, had wondered in a detached corner of her mind why her legs weren't actually shaking.

He hadn't taken her back to the car after all. Because he'd taken her straight into a hotel lobby.

"Wait here," he told her, leaving her in the corner next to the lifts, and she knew why. So this wouldn't make it into the papers.

She stood, pretended to study the menus for the hotel restaurant on the wall, and didn't see a thing. She should have worn some less microscopic undies tonight, too, because the ones she had on weren't doing the job. She shifted her weight in the high heels, felt the throb, and it was as if she could already feel his hands, his mouth on her.

He was back, punching the button for the lift. And not reaching for her when they got inside. She looked at him, and he said, "Camera," and she nodded.

"But no microphone," he said, "so I'll say this. Your clothes are going to be coming off slowly tonight, but the first thing that's going to be happening is that pretty dress hitting the floor."

She couldn't help it. She actually shivered, a delicious sensation, and he saw it and smiled a little. "You like that, don't you?

You're so used to doing the talking, nobody ever tells you the good stuff."

He was leaning closer now, and his mouth touched her ear as he murmured, "No worries, though. I'm going to tell you all the good stuff tonight. And this would be the night when we find out how many times you can come."

The doors opened, and he stepped back and smiled at her, then led the way to the room, and she followed and tried to think of something to say, but for once, she couldn't come up with a thing, because, if the truth were known, she was having a hard enough time breathing and walking.

He opened the door, held it for her, switched on the lights, but he didn't take her into the bedroom, and he didn't reach for her, either. Instead, he walked across the lounge and turned on the lamp set on the end table next to the window, then came back and turned the rest off, leaving him behind her, in the dark.

"Thought I was getting the Demon Lover," she said, trying to get a little control over the situation. "And here you are, not rushing me. But I see we've got the lights down. I didn't think that was your style. I thought you were a watcher."

"There are ways and ways of watching," he said. "And there's no rushing tonight. I told you. We're going to take it slow." He walked across to the window again, pulled the drapes, and the Auckland night sky was revealed in all its glory, the Sky Tower glowing purple tonight, the skyscrapers dropping away down the hill to the blackness of the Harbour beyond.

"Pretty," she said. "We star-gazing, or what?"

"I'm star-gazing," he said, coming back around her, then reaching to pull her against him from behind, wrapping his arms around her. "The difference is, I'm only looking at one particular star. My favorite one."

He reached a hand out to pull her hair back, kissed her cheek, and then his lips were moving, warm and firm, over her ear, down the side of her neck, the rasp of his beard adding so much more stimulation, wakening every nerve fiber it encountered along the way.

"So pretty," he murmured, and she realized what he was doing. He wasn't looking at the view. He was looking at their reflection in the window that stretched almost from floor to ceiling, from wall to wall, revealing them nearly as clearly as a mirror, but so much darker, all glowing light and mysterious shadow, so much more exciting than a mirror could ever be.

"Watch this," he told her, "because it gets even better."

He had brushed her hair over one shoulder, and both hands were on the back zip of her black dress, pulling it slowly down, all the way to her hips, his hands easing the garment over her shoulders, down her body.

"Step out," he told her, and she did, and his hands went around her shoulders, pulled her back against him.

"Look at that," he said. "Aw, that's so nice. Look what I've got." His hands stroked over her arms, and then they were cupping her breasts, his thumbs tracing lightly over the mesh of her demibra, and she watched her reflection, saw his hands on her, saw the woman with her waves of hair cascading over one shoulder, eyes half-closed, wearing a low-cut, nearly transparent black bra, a tiny thong, and a suspender belt, its thin black straps circling her hips, holding up the sheer black stockings, her body rocking a little in the cruel black stilettos under the influence of his hands.

"Want a little more, don't you?" he asked.

"Yes," she whispered. She watched his hands slip inside the mesh, and moaned as he stroked her.

"So pretty," he said again, dragging the fabric down, exposing her full breasts, lifting them for him. "And that's even prettier. Look at that." He was rolling her nipples between finger and thumb, pinching, at the very edge of too much, and her mouth had opened a little, her head was back against his chest, and she was breathing hard.

"Look what else we have," he said, his voice low. "What a present for me. You're all wrapped up with ribbons. What a good surprise." One big palm glided over her belly, traced the edge of the belt, his fingers exploring the intersection where ribboned straps met firm golden flesh, all the way across her belly.

"Turn me around," she got out, "and you'll see the rest of it."

"Oh, I'm not turning you around," he said. "Then you couldn't watch, and you're enjoying watching, aren't you? But I'll have a look all the same." He kept his hold on her hips, took a pace back, and she missed the press of his body.

"Ties," he said, his hands tracing them, moving over the curve of her cheeks. "You're all tied up for me back here. And as you have the most gorgeous arse I've ever seen in my life, I'm going to have to spend some more time looking at it. Later."

"This one…" she said, shivering at his touch, "I can't wear on TV. This one is just for you."

"Oh, I think it's all just for me, don't you?" He got a hand under the crisscrossed straps, pulled her back by them until she was pressed against him again. "Especially this. This is all for me, every bit of it." His hand had moved around, had edged lower now, was gliding over the top of the minuscule triangle of sheer black mesh. "Hardly seems worth wearing, does it?"

"You wouldn't want me to come out without my knickers," she managed to say. "You wouldn't want a bad girl like that."

"I've got a bad girl just like that, though," he said, "and you know it." His hand was still moving, touching her through the thin mesh, finding the dark seam that ran straight up the middle of that tiny vee, and he was running his fingers over it, up and down, over and over. "And we both know she's not going to be wearing these much longer. But since she is, I'll make the most of them. Touching this little line—that feels so good, doesn't it? This is what you like."

His other hand was cupping her breast again, and she was watching him in the black expanse of glass, watching her body straining against his hands as he worked on her.

"No," he decided. "On second thought, I don't think I want them after all." And then she jumped, because he had both hands around the whisper-thin string at one side of the undies, had snapped it with one quick yank, pulled the tiny thong from around her and tossed it to the floor.

"So much better," he told her. "Because now, you're dressed exactly appropriately for this date. Ready for anything."

His hand was back again, and she was completely exposed to his gaze and her own, watching as he rubbed, stroked, explored, and she wouldn't have been able to stand at all if he hadn't been holding her up from behind, one big arm wrapped around her waist.

"Look at you," he said. "You're a prize worth fighting for, aren't you? A prize worth winning. And I've won you, haven't I?"

"Yes," she sighed, squirming in his grasp. "Yes."

"You make me think these things," he said, his voice husky in her ear. "Things I shouldn't say, but I'm going to say them anyway. About what I'd have done if you really were the Maori princess I've always thought you were. About how I'd have fought for you, and how, once I'd won you, I'd never have let you go. How I'd have kept you forever, no matter what."

"What if…" she managed to say, because she was almost past the point of talking, "you'd lost, though?"

"I wouldn't have lost," he said, and he sounded so sure, so dark and dangerous. "I'd have won you, and I'd have kept on winning. I'd have fought all the way to have you. I'd have done whatever it took. And then I'd have showed you what that meant."

"What would…it mean?" The thrill was strong now, a shudder coming from someplace deep inside, and she was so close.

"You really want to know?" he asked her. There was real intent in his touch now, and she was burning.

"Yes. Yes."

"Then once you come for me," he said, "we'll find out." His hand was moving harder now, faster, and she couldn't talk anymore, because he knew so well how to touch her. "Come on, now," he said. "Come on, Josie. Show me you belong to me. Show me what you'd do for me."

That was it. She was crying out, spasming against his hand, watching the woman in the glass being pushed over the edge, her body stiffening, shuddering with the dark, hard pleasure of it.

He held her until she finished, and she could see from his face in the window, the press of him against her just how much he was enjoying watching. And then he turned her in his arms and kissed her at last, deeply and so possessively, his hands going down to cup her cheeks, pull her up against him, trace the straps, the ties, and she was still shaking.

When he lifted his mouth from hers, she reached trembling fingers for the buttons of his shirt, began to unfasten them, one slow hole at a time, her mouth closing over the side of his own neck. She sucked at him there, bit and licked, heard him groan deep in his throat, his hands tightening over her bottom. He'd excited her to a point she'd never reached, but two could play at this game, and she was a very good player.

"If you'd won me," she told him, her voice low and full of promise, pulling his shirt off and tossing it to the floor, running greedy hands over his broad chest, the bunched muscle of his shoulders, "I know one thing I'd have had to do for you. And if I'm yours, I need to do it now."

Her hands were at his belt, and Dr. Eva had never worked a strip of leather through a buckle with any more intent, any more slow, seductive purpose than Josie used on Hugh right now. She got it unfastened, held the little tab of his zip between thumb and forefinger, and slowly lowered it, then looked into his eyes and smiled, stepped back, and carefully removed one high heel, then the other.

"Don't want you to take them off," he said, and she could see from the rising and falling of his chest how far he'd come already. She might be his, but he was hers, too, every hard centimeter of him.

"I can't be on my knees, though, in those," she told him softly. She got her hands under the waistband of his briefs and paused a moment. "And you want me on my knees, don't you? Wouldn't that be one of the requirements?"

"Yeh," he groaned. "That's one."

"Then I'd better obey, hadn't I? Because," she said with another lick at his neck, "who knows what you'd have done to me if I hadn't."

"Uhh..." he sighed, because she'd eased the briefs, his dark trousers over his lean hips, had brought them to the floor along with her, and she was kneeling in front of him, taking off his shoes and socks, then settling herself in front of him, holding the length of him in one hand.

"This is what I'd have done," she told him," if you'd won me. I'd have showed you what that meant. How glad I was that I belonged to you."

His hands were fisting in her hair, and that was a yes, so she leaned down, gave him a long, slow lick, felt his grip tightening. She took her time, and she wasn't the one moaning now. She knew exactly how to do this, and she was making the effort to do it absolutely right, and he was loving it.

"You need..." he got out when she'd wound him up almost to breaking point, "you need to stop now."

She sat back, looked up at him, kept her hand going, felt how close he was, because if she had a talent for reading body language, this was her ultimate gift.

"You sure?" she asked. "Because…" She stroked him again. "There's more I'm willing to do. I'm willing to do it all."

"Aw…" He groaned. "Get the condom out of my pocket and put it on."

She did it, and he dropped to his own knees, reached for her. "I want it all," he told her. "And I'm going to take it tonight. So turn around," he whispered in her ear, his hands going for the hooks at her bra, taking it off at last, tossing it aside. "I've got some straps to look at."

He looked at the straps, and by the time he'd finished, she'd come a couple more times, just as he'd promised, and her delicate stockings were a thing of the past. He undid the bow tying the suspender belt together, then, pulled everything off her, and took her into the shower.

They used the shower, and they used the bedroom wall, and, finally, they used the bed. And he got it all.

♡

"I should have guessed," she sighed when her head was pillowed on his chest, his hand moving over her hair, and she was so sleepy and sated that she felt drugged, "that you had a Maori thing."

"I don't have a Maori thing," he said, and she felt the rumbling vibration of his voice from deep inside his chest. "I've never had a Maori thing. I have a Josie Pae Ata thing."

not boiling the bunny

♡

He woke slowly, looked at the plain expanse of white ceiling overhead, and was disoriented for a moment. And then he remembered. Josie.

Who wasn't in bed with him anymore. He rolled out of bed, moving a little fast, and stopped at the door to the lounge. There she was, of course. In one of the hotel's white dressing gowns, legs curled beneath her on the couch as she gazed out at the street scene far below. Her hair was knotted tidily at the back of her head, she had a cup of tea in her hand, and he took a breath.

She looked up at him and smiled. "Hey, good-looking."

"Hey yourself. I thought for a second..." He ran a hand over his jaw and laughed. "That you were gone. Stupid."

"Can't sleep past seven, that's all. No matter what's happened in the night." She was still smiling, and now she got gracefully to her feet, went across to the kitchen. "Want a cup of tea?"

"Yeh. Sure." He looked down at himself, had to laugh a bit about that too. "Maybe I should put some clothes on for it, what d'you reckon?"

"Oh, I don't know. Seeing as how I don't have any undies to wear myself, or any stockings either, since somebody destroyed all of them. I'm going home with about half the clothes I started with."

"Dangers of getting carried away in the middle of the date, I guess," he said. "But if you're going to turn me on that much, you may just have to put up with having your undies ripped off you."

That made her pause in the middle of her tea-making, he saw with satisfaction. "It was a good thing I had a few emergency supplies in my bag," she said after a moment. "No extra undies, alas. If I'm going to have a Demon Lover, I can see I'm going to need to be better prepared. Want a disposable toothbrush, though?"

"If you've got one." She was making him smile again.

"Here." She picked her bag up from the kitchen bench, pulled out a tiny little thing. "So we can actually kiss each other good morning without worrying we'll put the other off for good."

"Cheers." He took it from her, along with the cup of tea, and headed for the bathroom, and his shower.

Mornings-after could be awkward. He should have guessed, though, that they wouldn't be awkward with Josie.

♡

"Christmas coming up," he told her when he'd taken her out to breakfast and was watching her keep herself to two eggs, a coffee, and not a thing more.

"What alerted you?" she asked with a little smile. "The giant reindeer head on the corner of Whitcoull's?"

"Yeh, that helped. I wondered what you're doing, that's all."

"Two more days of work, then ten days off," she said. "And back shortly after the New Year."

"That's all?"

"We get a proper break at the end of the season," she explained. "But meanwhile, the public wants its entertainment. I'm going home, of course, for a few days. What about you? What will you and the kids be doing? Got to be a bit rough for them, only the second one."

"Yeh, I'm thinking that too. Last year, Aunt Cora was here, and I was still in the process of moving. I spent the day with my mum, came up on Boxing Day, and they'd had their dinner and all. But it's up to me this time, I guess."

He should have discussed it sooner with Aunt Cora, in time to do something about it. Got a bach somewhere, maybe, gone to the beach. But as usual, it hadn't occurred to him. They'd talked about the kids' school holidays, and Aunt Cora had signed them up for a couple camps, had told him she'd take care of their shopping for the new term, which was something Hugh hadn't even thought of. But nothing about the holiday itself, and he should have asked her. She'd probably assumed that he'd know how to do it, but he didn't.

"And? What have you done?" Josie asked.

"Uh—not much, would be the answer. That's why I brought it up."

"Not going anywhere?"

"No plans. I should have made some, I see that. I was thinking it was all sorted, with Aunt Cora due back, and that I was managing pretty well."

"She quite happy to come back, then? Is it not working out with her fella?"

"Yeh, nah, sounds like it is, actually. He's coming out to visit again as soon as he can take another holiday. A few months, she said. They've even looked into the possibility of him buying a shop here, and she's excited about that, so I'd say it's all going along swimmingly. And that's all good, and I'm happy for her, but meanwhile...there's this day. Christmas. I missed that I should be planning something for that, something special. What *should* I be planning, though? I'm not sure I could manage Christmas dinner, no matter how hard I tried. I've barely got past pizza and shepherd's pie, you know that. The ham would probably be beyond me, much less the pavlova. And...the day."

"Uh-huh. Did you do gifts yet?"

"Not much," he admitted. "Aunt Cora did send some, but I wasn't sure what to buy. Ordered a couple books, but that's about it."

"Want to do some shopping with me, then?" she asked. "Maybe I could help, and I still have a few things to get myself. We could go tomorrow, if you like."

"That'd be awesome," he said with relief. "And if you'd give me some ideas on the day, too. How to do the dinner at my skill level. How to make it…all right."

"I'll have a think. One idea—you could do a beach day. Start your own tradition with the kids, as long as you make it special. Take them fishing, have a barbecue. Or," she said, and he could see her hesitate, "you could do something completely different. You could take them to my family, if you liked, come along with me."

"That would be quite the unexpected descent on your mum and dad," he said, and that was the least of it.

She waved a hand. "Doesn't matter. They won't mind, I'll tell you that. We'll put the three of you in the caravan outside, and three more for my mum to cook for? She'll hardly notice."

"I wouldn't be sharing your bed, eh. That's pretty disappointing."

She smiled. "Not happening, sorry. You haven't met my dad. But it'd be good fun, just like you told me when you took me along to your picnic. And," she said, her gaze steady, "no pressure. You wouldn't be making a statement, to my family, to me, to anybody, any more than I did by coming with you then, and I wouldn't be making a statement to you. Just taking some friends home with me for Christmas, because one of them's a fairly clueless fella who didn't make any plans."

He wondered if he should say that he wouldn't mind the statement, but that might fall into the category of bunny-boiling after exactly two—dates, so he didn't. "Sounds perfect," he said instead. "Getting away on the day, doing something different—that may be best anyway, eh. Not trying to do the Christmas they've had, and not having it work out."

"You're right," she said.

"Then, if you're sure it'll be all right," he said, "I'll say yes. For all of us. Christmas in the caravan with Josie."

"Christmas in the caravan *without* Josie," she reminded him. "My dad, remember?"

"All of a sudden," he said, "the hair on the back of my neck is rising. I can almost feel that patu coming down on my skull."

"No worries," she said. "I have a feeling you'll do just fine."

complications

♡

"Tuck. Bee tuck."

"That's right," Josie said as she helped Zavy pull the rest of the wrapping paper away. "It's a very big truck."

It was a log truck carved out of wood, and the logs came off, which Zavy was discovering right now. As Christmas presents went, it looked like being pretty successful, because Zavy had gone to collect his round plastic people now, and it looked like they were going to be taking a very unsafe ride in the back of a log truck.

"You off to your mum and dad's tomorrow?" Josie asked Chloe, settling back on the carpet against the base of the couch and taking a sip of her Officially-on-Holiday glass of wine.

"Yeh," Chloe said with satisfaction. "No tact, no scheduling, and no patience required for two long weeks. Well, except with my mum. But I'm getting around that by only staying with them for a few days. I wish she'd child-proof. She keeps saying that she didn't do it with me, and how I was quite happy to sit and play in one spot without touching anything I shouldn't. I don't remember, but it's hard to believe."

"Mmm," Josie agreed.

"Even if it were actually true," Chloe said, "it's not true for Zavy, that's for sure. And following after him to keep his fingers out of the sockets and off the breakables wears me thin. So, short visit, then back here for some Mum Time. And an early bedtime, too. Funny how you grow up wishing you could stay up past ten, and then, once you have kids, heaven is lying in bed with a book at eight-thirty."

She stopped herself. "Sorry. I keep forgetting."

"Nah," Josie said, even though it hurt. Of course it hurt. "It's your life. You get to talk to me about your life. You let me talk to you about mine."

"Yours is a bit more exciting at the moment, though," Chloe said. "Except that I've got news myself on that score. You may just get some competition in the Rugby Dating Stakes."

"Really." Josie sat up a little straighter. "Tell. Who?"

"I got a call the other week from Reka Ranapia, asking me about classes for her daughter in Mt. Maunganui, about whether I could recommend anybody, what she should look for. And she came and took me to lunch, Zavy too, to chat about it. Quite nice, I thought."

"And she wants to be your girlfriend?" Josie asked. "That *is* exciting news. You *are* getting around."

Chloe laughed. "I'm not that adventurous, though I'll admit, it has its appeal. At least I understand women. Pity I'm not attracted to them. But she brought attractive company. Will Tawera, the latest victim of your deadly charms, and I can only imagine how many viewers that's going to get tuning in, because he's quite the looker, isn't he? She *said* it was because he was new in town, getting situated, but I can't think he has a burning desire to become acquainted with dance studios."

"But maybe with the owners of dance studios?"

"Yeh," Chloe said with satisfaction. "A setup, I'd say. He asked me for my number, at any rate."

"Good-looking," Josie agreed. "A bit of a handful, though, you ask me."

"I'm not going to marry the bloke," Chloe said. "Just brush up on my dating skills, because my sadly tame outing with Hugh told me it was time to get out there again, especially if there's a hot rugby boy on offer. I could stand to have some sex, and as I nobly restrained myself from having it with your man, I need to find one of my own. I'm not eager to take a walk down the aisle, or even get close, but I'm guessing that he could show me a good time. What do you think? Think I can juggle one more rather *large* priority?"

"With everything else you're juggling," Josie said, "I guess I'd either say, of course you can, or, don't get your life too complicated. Which is it?"

"I don't know," Chloe admitted. "I guess I'll find out. A chance to get pretty, anyway, have somebody else buy me dinner, and maybe a little more. No reason I have to get involved."

"Famous last words," Josie warned.

"Look who's talking. I'm not the one taking a man to bed, then taking him home to my parents a week later. I thought you were going slowly, because of the neighbor thing."

"I thought so too," Josie admitted. "Somehow, though, it just...slipped out, and before I knew it, I'd invited him. But it's casual."

"Uh-huh. Right. Casual. Does he know about the—" Chloe gestured at Josie's midsection.

"No. Of course not. Way too early to talk about that. He'd be running in the opposite direction for sure then, wouldn't he, if I started talking about the kids we could or couldn't have together."

"When would you do it, then?" Chloe pressed.

"*I* don't know," Josie said, heard the irritation in her voice. "Sorry. It's just...I don't know. This is my first time dealing with it, remember? Not after one date, I'm sure of that."

"Spending Christmas together may qualify, though," Chloe said.

"I told you. It's not like that."

"It's not? Really?"

"No. It's just...they're alone, and those kids need something more than a day mooching around the house with a brother who doesn't know what to do with them. They need dinner, and family."

"They need your family?" Chloe asked, and her voice was gentle now.

"I—" Josie stopped. "Yeh. They do. But that's a separate thing from Hugh and me."

"I'd think that'd be pretty hard to separate."

"Complicated," Josie agreed with a sigh. "Like you say. But all I can do is see what happens. Go slow."

"The way you've been going so far. Uh-huh."

"Oi. We have gone slow."

"You may have started slow," Chloe said. "But I'd say you're on the express now."

♡

"Do your mum and dad have animals at their house, Josie?" Charlie asked from the back seat of Hugh's car the next morning. His, because it had room enough for four. She'd had to remind herself, climbing in, that she wasn't taking her family to her parents' for Christmas. She was taking *Hugh's* family to her parents' for Christmas, and Chloe had been right, there was a big, big difference that her heart seemed to be having trouble accepting.

"Not many. Just chooks," Josie said. "Not that kind of farm, I'm afraid. More about the fruit and vegies."

"Oh." He sounded disappointed. "I was hoping pigs, like *Babe*."

"Our neighbors have pigs," she said, "if you'd like to visit. Not quite like *Babe*, heaps bigger and stinkier, I'm afraid, not nice clean little pink piglets, but they quite like to have their backs scratched, and they're quite clever, too, pigs. Horses as well," she said, twisting around to look at Amelia. "Would you like to try riding a horse, or have you tried already?"

"D'you really think I could?" Amelia sounded more excited than she'd seemed about the excursion up to now. A bit of nerves, Josie thought. Well, her mum would soon put that right. No kid could be uncomfortable for long with her mum around.

"I know they would," she told Amelia. "We'll get onto that straight away."

"What other things are there to do at your house?" Charlie asked.

"Well, let's see. Swimming, and my dad will probably take you fishing, and heaps of playing with the cousins. There'll be all sorts of other kids around, Christmastime. It'll be good fun. Some cricket on the beach, probably, and I'm guessing Hugh may find himself playing a bit of rugby with all of you, and with the bigger cousins as well. May not be much of a holiday for you," she told him.

"Nah. All good," he said. "You can have them take it easy on me, eh. Tell them I'm still getting fit."

"Yeh, right," she snorted.

"Is your partner coming too, Josie?" Charlie asked. "The one that's in Aussie?"

"Uh…no," she said. "He's not my partner anymore."

"He's not? How come?"

"That's a bit rude," Hugh said. "You don't ask that, Charlie."

"Oh. Sorry."

"We decided we weren't suited," Josie said. "No worries. Sometimes it happens that way."

"So does that mean you can go on a date with other people?" Charlie asked.

"Of course it does," Amelia said with exasperation. "Honestly, Charlie, you're so *dim.* You break up, and then you go out with another guy. Although sometimes, then, the first guy gets jealous and comes back and says he still loves you and wants to get back together again. Kids at my school break up and make up again all the time. That's romantic, especially if it's in the rain."

"Wait," Hugh commanded. "Kids at your school are dating? What?"

"Going out," Josie told him. "It's different. You say you're going out, and you walk around together, and the girl writes the boy's name in her notebook, hey, Amelia."

"That had better be all it is," Hugh said with a frown in the rear-view mirror for Amelia. "Geez," he said quietly to Josie, "am I going to have to have a talk about what boys want?"

"Probably," she said. "Probably pretty soon, too."

He shook his head. "I am so not equipped for this."

"Oh," she said. "I'd say you've got exactly the right equipment to speak with the voice of authority. Welcome to the wonderful world of fatherhood."

He glanced sharply across at her, opened his mouth, shut it again, and turned his attention back to the road.

Charlie had clearly been distracted. "If it was raining, though," he said obstinately, "Josie would just get wet. I don't think getting wet is romantic. I don't think Josie would want to get wet, either. That doesn't make any sense."

"The *girl* doesn't have to get wet," Amelia said impatiently. "The boy stands outside her window, or outside her door, or something, and *he* gets wet, because it *is* romantic that way. Everybody knows that. Or sometimes it's out on the street, like in *Bridget Jones.* It doesn't matter. The point is, he comes to find her and says he loves her, and they kiss, and they're made up again."

"What have you been watching?" Hugh asked. "Bridget *Jones?* Where?"

"Duh," she said, and Josie could fairly hear her eyeballs clicking in their sockets. "Holly's?"

"Don't say 'Duh,'" he said. "We've had this. And I think I need to have a little chat with Holly's mum."

"But if Josie doesn't have a partner anymore," Charlie said, clinging to the original topic, "she could go on a date now."

"Yeh," Hugh said, "she could."

"Then I think you should ask her to go on one," Charlie told his brother. "You should ask her now, in case that guy does come back and kisses her."

"That's a good plan," Hugh said. "But I'm a couple steps ahead of you. I already asked her on a date. I kissed her, too." He took a hand off the steering wheel to pick up one of Josie's and squeeze it briefly. "So actually, she's got a partner again. And it's me. So no kissing in the rain, unless she's kissing me. Right, Josie? We clear?"

"Well…" she said, and she couldn't help it, she was laughing. "If it were in the *rain*…I don't know. That'd be pretty tempting." She got a scowl from Hugh for her pains that made her laugh harder.

"Really?" Amelia asked. "Did you really ask her, Hugh, or did she have to ask you?"

"I asked her," Hugh said. "Amazingly enough. It was a bit scary, it's true, but I summoned up the courage in the end."

family ties

♡

Hugh woke to the sound of a knock at the metal door of the caravan. Christmas Eve, and not yet dawn.

The door opened with a creak. "Time for my fishermen to shift themselves," Josie's father Tana called into the little space, and Hugh saw Amelia and Charlie stirring in their bunks.

"Right," Hugh said, sitting up himself. "Out in a flash."

"It's *early*," Amelia moaned as Hugh switched on the light at his bedside, began to pull on his clothes. "It's *dark*."

"Yeh," Hugh said. "It is. And I'll bet Josie's mum has a cup of Milo and a bit of brekkie ready for you before you go out on the boat, and that she'll have something even better when you get back." Based on the roast meal she'd provided the evening before, he'd have put money on it.

He was right, he saw when Tana had declined his offer of help hitching the trailer to the ute and he'd taken the kids on into the house instead. He'd found not just Josie's mum, but Josie, too, already in the big, old-fashioned kitchen. Not Milo at all, but genuine cocoa in big white mugs, a chocolate fish on each saucer, and a big plate of toast cut into fingers, a jar of Marmite and one of jam, and the inevitable Weet-Bix and milk, all of which the kids got stuck into pretty quickly.

"Mum," Josie said from where she sat at the big rectangular table, sorting avocados, mandarins, and lemons from bins into plastic bags, twisting them shut with ties, and marking the bags with a black felt pen, "you'll spoil them. Chocolate fish for breakfast? And here's Hugh trying to maintain some level of nutrition and all."

"Nah," Arama Pae Ata said. She was a handsome woman with Josie's lustrous eyes and hair, her bone structure, too, softened by the lushness of figure Josie had dieted away. It was easy to see where Josie had got her looks. "They'll need their energy, out there on the water at dawn. Besides, it's Christmas. If you can't spoil the mokopuna at Christmas, where's the joy in living? Even you may be able to have a chocolate fish on Christmas Eve, my darling."

"Or not," Josie said.

Hugh sat down beside Josie, accepted a cup of tea from Arama with a word of thanks. "Looks like you've both already been busy, and the sun's not up. What's all this?"

"Getting things ready for the honesty box," Josie said. "Like old times, eh, Mum."

"Oh, Josie was my little helper," Arama told Hugh. "On a stool at six helping with the washing-up, getting breakfast on the table by the time she was ten, filling the box every morning just like she's doing today, taking her brothers to school on their bikes. I can't tell you how I missed her when she left for Auckland."

"Mum," she protested. "I wasn't that good. Ask Rodney. He'll tell you I was dead bossy, and that he wanted to chuck things at me half the time. You should tell Hugh that I was cooking breakfast because you were doing the midnight meal for two hundred at the packhouse. And look at me now, still having to get up at five. That would've been loads harder if I hadn't grown up doing it. Funny how the things that happen in your life prepare you for the rest of it, isn't it, hard as they seem at the time?"

"Or make you able to do what you have to do in the rest of it," Hugh said. "That could be it."

"You said you helped your mum, Josie," Charlie said, happily dipping toast fingers into his cocoa. "You said that's how you learnt to cook. She said I had to help you too," he told Hugh. "And then Amelia and I could learn."

"And have you learnt?" Arama asked him.

"Yeh. We make dinner all together, usually," Charlie said. "And breakfast. I can't do too many things by myself," he admitted, "but I can do eggs now, and I do the salad too, most times."

"Well, that's a good thing," Arama said. "That's a start."

"Right, then," Tana came into the house, wiping his hands on a bit of rag. "I need a couple of keen fishermen out on the boat with me, and they'd better rattle their dags, because if we don't get some hooks into the water sharpish, those snapper aren't going to be biting anymore. We won't have any fish for tea then, will we, and Josie's mum will give me that look of hers."

His wife swatted him with a tea towel. "What look's that? Here I am, got up to cook your breakfast, and you're talking about looks? I don't give you any looks."

"The one that says you still love me," he said with a grin and a wink for his daughter, "disappointing as I am. I want the one that says I've impressed you, coming home with fish for your tea. That's the one that gets me up in the dark."

Josie finished shoving her plastic bags into a big pasteboard box, stood up and hefted it. "Have a good time, you two. No worries, Dad always brings home the tea. And now we know why."

Hugh got up himself and took the box from her. "I've got it."

"I carried this box when I was twelve," she protested, but she was smiling all the same.

"Yeh, I heard. That doesn't mean you have to carry it now."
He saw the look her parents exchanged, and he was just fine with
that.

♡

She had more surprises in store for him, he discovered a few
hours later. After her two brothers and the elder one's partner
had come downstairs to join the others, after the kids and Tana
had returned with four good-sized snapper, "and we helped clean
them, too," Charlie had reported proudly. After Josie and her
mum had produced pancakes and caramelized bananas and bacon
and sliced kiwifruit for nine.

"We're going down to Moore Park in a bit, meeting the cousins and some mates, chucking the footy around," Josie's younger
brother Aaron told Hugh, pushing back from the table with a
sigh of satisfaction. "Want to join us?"

"Sure," Hugh said. "What about the kids?"

"Let them stay here with us," Arama said. "There are sure to
be some cousins around."

"And Mr. Anderson said I could ride the horse again today,"
Amelia said. "I want to do that."

"Right, then," Hugh said. "You coming, Josie?"

"Oh, yeh," she assured him.

"Someone should stay and help Arama," Rodney's partner
Charmaine, a slim brunette whose prettiness was marred by a
petulant expression around the mouth, put in with a glance at
Josie. "Never mind, though. I'll do it."

Hugh wanted to ask exactly what Charmaine had been doing
while Josie had been cooking breakfast, but it wasn't his family,
so he bit his tongue.

Arama didn't, though. "Oh, Josie's earned a bit of a break,"
she said easily. "She's been up since sparrow fart. Go on and show
Hugh your skills, darling. Bet he doesn't know you've got them."

"What skills?" he asked.

Arama laughed and gave Josie a nudge where she stood beside her drying dishes. "He won't know what's hit him, eh. You just wait, Hugh. You'll see."

He did see. When she was on the field with her brothers, her cousins and their mates, a few girls mixed in there too, teenagers, mostly. When he was coming at her, not too fast, and watching her kick the ball away with a boot that would have done Charlie proud, then flashing him a challenging grin before jogging back into position. Or when she was lunging to grab the ribbon hanging from a hefty cousin's waistband to save the try, with an effort that sent her sprawling onto elbows and knees, heedless of her scrapes and bruises.

She was fast, and she was fearless, and if he slowed down on purpose so he could watch her dive across the tryline, slide across the grass with the force of her momentum, then be pulled up, laughing, into the embrace of her teammates—well, he was just a man, after all.

"Aw, mate," her cousin Martin said, puffing up beside Hugh. "You're letting us down here. Last time we let you play opposite Bug. I thought you lot were meant to have the competitive fire no matter what game you were playing."

"Sorry," Hugh said, his hands on his hips, grinning at Martin, then looking back at Josie, doing a little dance now that was making him laugh. "I can't help it. She's prettier than you. There's a reason we don't play with girls." Because there were some flames that burned even hotter than the competitive fire, and he was discovering exactly what they were.

Another cousin, Conrad, was clapping Josie on the back. "And that's five more to us," he said unnecessarily. "Put it between the posts, Bug, and you'll have Hugh well and truly thinking twice."

"He's already thinking twice," she said with a saucy smile for him, then took the tee from her brother Aaron, set herself up, and took the kick.

The others hooted when she slotted the ball through, and Aaron picked her up in a hug that took her straight off her feet. "Haven't lost your touch, have you?" he said exultantly. "First to twenty, that's what we said, and I'll tell our All Black here, in case he's forgotten how to keep score by himself, that Josie's just got us to twenty-one."

Hugh laughed himself. "I guess I know when I'm beaten."

♡

The beer came out of the chilly bins then, and they were on the grass, and it was Christmas Eve, sun and beer and good mates, and Hugh couldn't remember when he'd felt more relaxed.

"You know I have to ask," he said, looking at Josie, lying on her stomach with her pretty ankles crossed in the air—and, of course, no beer. "Bug?"

"My nickname," she said, putting a cheek on a folded hand and smiling at him. "Feminine, eh. Awkward childhood revealed."

"Because she looked like a stick insect," Martin explained with a grin. "All skinny arms and legs, huge eyes and a great wide mouth. Tagging around after the boys, wanting to play our games. And the worst part was, being good at them. I'll tell you," he said, taking another hefty swig of beer, "I was happy when she went away to school in Auckland."

"Nice," she complained.

"Because," Martin said, ignoring her, "when she stopped being a stick insect—bloody hell, she was even more trouble. Us cuzzies had to have an eye on her every minute. Fourteen years old at the beach, and some thirty-year-old arsehole trying to chat her up, get her over next to the toilets. Can't tell you how many of them we had to run off, eh, Conrad."

"Too right," Conrad said. "A girl's school was the only place for her. Or maybe a convent."

"You make me sound like I was man-mad," she complained as everyone laughed. "I wasn't even looking, you know that."

"You looking wasn't the problem," Conrad said. "It was who was looking at you."

"Worked out all right for her in the end," her brother Rodney said, and his voice wasn't quite as lazily good-natured as the others'. An estate agent, Josie had told Hugh, and a rapidly rising one. The one who'd achieved the kind of career she'd been meant to have.

"Still looking at her, aren't they," Rodney went on. "The difference is, she gets paid for it now."

That got Hugh's attention, and he could feel the mood of the group shifting a bit.

"That's right," Josie said calmly. "I do. Hard to do my job without people looking at me."

"Maybe you could get a part where you keep your clothes on," Rodney said. "I've heard there are actresses who do. Could be less embarrassing for your family."

"Oh? You embarrassed?" She was still in her relaxed pose, but she didn't look as relaxed as she had a minute ago.

"Well, when every fella who comes into my office wants to ask me about my sister," Rodney said, "not to mention talk about seeing an advert where she had not a stitch on, yeh, it can get a bit embarrassing. For everybody."

"Funny nobody else has said anything yet, then," she said.

"Maybe because they're proud of her," Aaron put in quietly, and Hugh looked across at Josie's younger brother, sitting up now, his expression serious. "Like me, and the rest of us, too."

An assenting murmur greeted his statement, but Rodney wasn't done. "Speak for yourself," he told his brother. "You really think the grandparents, the uncles and aunties are all rapt about it? Huh. I wonder. But Josie will choose for herself, I'm sure. She always has. And if you're quite happy to have men stare at you naked, Josie—well, good on ya, I guess. I'm pretty sure Charmaine wouldn't enjoy it, and it wouldn't be all right with me either, but not all men have the same standards, I suppose."

If Hugh's temper was still in check, and it was debatable, it was only because this was Josie's brother, and it was Christmas. "Seems to me," he said, and he wasn't lounging anymore, "that most men would think they'd won the Lotto if they had a partner as beautiful and talented as Josie. But when I find the man who's anything but envious of me, I'll let you know."

"You saying that doesn't bother you," Rodney said. "Huh. Interesting."

"If it bothered me," Hugh said, "I guess I'd remind myself of what Josie told me. That there's a billboard or two where you can see my teammates and me in our undies, and I don't think it's because the men of New Zealand are interested in studying our muscular development. My family hasn't disowned me yet, and none of my mates have told me that their partners are packing a sad because the girls enjoy looking at them with their jerseys off."

"There's a difference, though, isn't there," Rodney said. "And the difference would be, Josie's a woman. You've got a sister, eh. You saying you'd be happy to see your sister naked on a billboard, looking like she's just been...looking like that?" he finished, because he'd probably recognized the expression on Hugh's face.

"If my sister turns out to have half the heart and brains and courage that yours does," Hugh said, not even pretending to be calm anymore, "I hope I'll be as proud of her as you should be of yours. I hope I'd be able to see that there was more to her than a beautiful face and a beautiful body, and that I could see the woman she was and love her for it. Because she'd be my *sister*. And I'll tell you another thing I'm dead sure of. Any man who had anything to say about her? He could say it to me."

Silence greeted him, and he saw the rigid stillness that had settled over the others, the only movement that of their eyes as gazes darted from face to face. He could feel the adrenaline trying to take over, trying to push him the last little bit of the way past self-control, could see, too, how white Josie had gone, how her hands were shaking, and how she was trying to hide it.

He got up, put a hand down for her, and pulled her up with him. "Come on," he said. "We can walk home from here, can't we?"

"Yeh," she said, and her voice was shaking too.

"Then that's what we're going to do." He didn't look around again, because he didn't trust himself to. He just got her out of there.

a bigger star

♡

She walked across the field with him, and he didn't let go of her hand. Instead, he threaded his fingers through hers.

He'd never done that, she realized. Never held her hand. And she hadn't realized how solid, how comforting that simple contact would be.

Her own hands still wanted to shake, and she didn't talk, because she was afraid that if she did, she would cry.

"Let's sit a bit," he said when they'd left the others behind. He found a bench set in the shade under the trees and pulled her down with him.

"Thanks," she managed to say.

"I'm trying to figure out what to say right now," he told her. "I want to say that your brother's a dickhead, and I don't know if it's all right."

She had to laugh a little. "It's all right. Right now, it is. I never knew..." She took a shaky breath, blew it out. "I always knew he was a bit...jealous. More since he married Charmaine, because I think she is too. He's always thought I was the favorite, and now he's got her saying it as well, I'm sure. And being what he said. Embarrassed, both of them. And I don't want..." She had to stop for a moment before she could go on. "I don't want to embarrass my family. I don't want to think that my mum and dad, my grandparents, are ashamed of me. I don't know what to do about it. If I shouldn't have done those adverts after all. If I shouldn't be doing what I'm doing, not if it's bringing shame to them."

The tears were threatening now, her throat closing around the words. "I want my family to be proud of me. I can't stand..." She tried to go on, but she couldn't, and she made a helpless gesture with her free hand, tried to turn away so he couldn't see.

"Josie." He had an arm around her now, was turning her into him. "Sweetheart. Don't cry. It's all right."

She did cry a little then, of course, and he held her until she pulled back, tried to laugh, wiped her cheeks and nose as best she could. "Sorry," she said again.

"Nah." He still had his hand running over her back, and she leaned into his chest and let him hold her some more, just because it felt so good to be there.

"I don't think your family's ashamed of you," he said at last. "If you want my opinion. I don't know all of them, but one thing's obvious, your mum and dad are nothing but proud of you. I don't think you could disappoint them if you tried. I think that's what's really bothering your brother, but that's not your problem. It's his."

"You don't think..." She hesitated, then tried again. "You aren't embarrassed yourself to have people know what I do. To have them know you're with me. You don't wish I were playing Val's part, being the good girl."

"I meant what I said. I'm proud to be the man who's with you. That would be one way of putting it. And I'm a big boy, aren't I. I can handle your being special. I don't have to be more of a star than you are to feel like I'm enough."

"Well, but," she said, and she was laughing again herself despite her shakiness, "that's because you *are* more of a star than I am."

"Or because it's not a contest. And maybe because I know what it means, and what it doesn't. That it's more than having more money than the average bloke. That it's pressure, people judging you every day, writing about you, and, yeh, being jealous because you've got what they don't, and they don't see how much effort it took you to get there. I don't think that's a bit different, and I know it's not always comfortable."

"But the naked thing," she pressed, because she needed to know. "That isn't…eating at you."

"Well, wanting to see you naked again, maybe," he said, and she could see the smile. "That's eating at me, no worries. And it makes me want to be there with you when you go out, I'll admit that. But it's what your cousins said. Men would look at you whether you were a star or not, because you're beautiful. Most of what's bothering your brother doesn't have a thing to do with how many clothes you're wearing, though, no matter what he's telling himself. And that's true for his partner as well. It's that you're more successful than he is. It's that he feels like he's in your shadow. That's easy to see."

"I know," she said bleakly. "I know you're right. I don't know how to fix it, though. I don't know what to say, or what to do. I've never known."

"Because there's nothing you can do. Because it's not you, it's him. It's his problem to get over, or not. It's not yours."

He'd walked home with her, had held her hand, and it had been a comfort to walk through the front door with him, not to have to face her brother by herself. Rodney didn't say anything, but Josie could tell by the aggrieved look on his face, and the way her sister-in-law wasn't looking at her at all, that neither of them had forgiven her. It was a relief to have the kids there, to have Christmas Eve dinner to cook with her mum. And to have Hugh beside her for all of it. He didn't say any more, because he didn't have to. She knew when she looked at him, when he looked at her that he'd meant it. And she knew that, as long as Hugh was there, Rodney wouldn't be saying it again.

ringing the changes

♡

They'd gone to church on Christmas morning, and then Hugh had gone with the others to the beach, had swum and played cricket with the kids, kicked the footy around with Charlie and some of the other boys, while Josie and her mum and sister-in-law had done Christmas dinner. He'd come back and helped Tana and Josie's brothers set up the tables outside, had had dinner with Josie's entire family, grandparents and aunties and uncles and cousins, and there had been a mountain of food of which Josie had eaten very little, and Charlie and Amelia had pulled crackers and eaten Christmas pudding and pavlova and had very nearly been sick.

He'd got the gifts right, too. Josie had helped with some clothes for Amelia, and they seemed to have been successful.

"That's such a cute color on you," Josie had said when Amelia had tried on the purple skirt that Hugh still thought was too short. Josie had given her a certificate for a manicure and had promised to take her to get it. "We'll have our makeup done, too," she said. "Maybe a consult with my stylist as well for your hair, what do you think? Time to glam you up a bit, now that you're about to start Year 8. We can make a Girls' Day of it, get you all sorted before term begins."

"No," Hugh said immediately. "Makeup? No. She's too young."

Josie looked at him in surprise. "Really? A little lip gloss and mascara, getting her eyebrows shaped? That's what I had in mind. Pretty harmless, eh, Mum?"

"Well, I'd say," Arama said, "but it's Hugh's decision, after all, Josie. Are you saying you don't remember the fuss your own dad made?"

"Too right," Tana said. "Dads never want their little girls to grow up, I suppose. I always told her she could start dating boys the minute she turned thirty. As long as they came to me for vetting first, of course."

"All the other girls at my school wear makeup already," Amelia assured her brother. "They wear eyeshadow and blusher and do nail varnish and everything. I *told* you, Hugh, I'm nearly thirteen. You act like I'm *five*."

"Wait," Hugh said, "what? No. That I'm sure of. No. No… eyeshadow and blusher."

"A little lip gloss, though?" Josie asked him. "Under carefully supervised circumstances?"

"If Josie shows you," Hugh decided, because he was clearly outnumbered here, "it's all right. But *only* what she says is right for a *twelve*-year-old to wear."

"*Fine*," Amelia sighed.

"Thank you, Hugh," he corrected her. "That would be the right answer. And thank you to Josie for showing you how to do it so you don't look like…so it's all right."

♡

"Makeup," he said to Josie that evening. "Geez. Did you have to spring that on me?"

He'd read Charlie the start of a story out of his new book, had actually had Amelia join them on the double bed for it, had seen them into bed. Now, he was walking with Josie in the kiwifruit orchard, just because they had a bit of privacy there. "You could have warned me," he told her.

"Well, it's going to get worse," she said cheerfully, "because I'm planning to buy her a razor and show her how to shave her legs and underarms, too. What was your Aunt Cora *doing?*"

"She can't be old enough for that, surely," he objected.

"Uh-huh. Have you heard of this little thing called puberty? She's old enough, Hugh. How old were you?"

"Before I started wearing makeup? At least twenty-five. And the state of my underarms is still shocking."

"Yeh, right. Never had an impure thought or noticed your body changing, either, I'll bet. Trust me, it's time. And time for you to have that talk about boys with her too."

"Oh, geez," he groaned. "I don't know who'll be more embarrassed."

"All right," she said. "Practice on me. Say I'm Amelia." They'd got to the end of the last block of the orchard, and she sat down on a rough bench set at its edge, crossed her arms, tucked her chin, and scowled up at him in such a good imitation that he laughed.

"Go ahead," she prompted. "Here I am, all embarrassed and reluctant."

"Yeh, that's helping."

"If it were easy," she said, "you wouldn't need to rehearse." She rolled her eyes, turned her body away from him with an exaggerated flounce as he sat down beside her. *"Hugh,"* she sighed with exasperation, "I don't want to *talk* about this. I already *know."*

"Uh..." he said. "We need to discuss it, though. Because men are...different from women."

Another eye-roll, which he couldn't see but knew was there all the same. *"Duh.* Like I didn't *know* that."

"And sometimes," he went on doggedly, feeling embarrassed on one hand, and wanting to laugh out loud on the other, "your body gets away from you a bit. Girls as well as boys, I'm sure, but I know about boys. Those feelings can be pretty powerful.

You want to try things, touch each other, maybe kiss each other, in ways you aren't necessarily ready for. And boys will sometimes act like they like you more than they do, because they want to... um...touch so you badly."

"This is *so embarrassing*," Josie said, shifting farther down the bench. "I *know*. My friends talk about this all the *time*, OK? Can I *go?*"

"In a minute. I just want you to know," Hugh continued, "that if you have any question at all about whether something is all right to do, you can say no. Any boy who really likes you will respect your right to say no. And if a boy tries to pressure you to do more—he doesn't really like you, no matter what he says. You tell him no anyway, and don't worry about his feelings, because you won't be hurting them. And then you come tell me," he said, and he didn't have to fake the grim tone in his voice. "If you have any questions, if you wonder whether he really likes you, come ask me. Oh, and no dating yet," he went on hastily. "I mean, if going out is walking around together, like Josie said, all right. But no going places with boys alone, not yet. Not when you're twelve, and not when you're thirteen either," he thought to add. "Not until you're..."

"You don't have to decide that now," Josie said, back to being herself again. "Just say, not yet, if you're not ready to decide when it's OK."

"Good," he said. "Because I don't have a clue. So how'd I do? All right?"

"Pretty good," she said, "for the first time. Although you may want to sound a bit less like you're going to be beating the boy to a bloody pulp. That was a little scary."

He laughed. "Nah. Whatever it takes. Bet your dad and your cousins had a few talks like that."

"Bet they did," she conceded. "My cousins, for sure. And my dad—I think the boy would have fainted before it ever got that far. My dad can be a little scary. Just like you."

"Mmm," he said, and it was a good thing she wasn't being Amelia anymore, because he had his arm around her, was pulling her a little closer on the bench, feeling her scoot in as well. "Luckily, I'm never going to be intimidating you, remember?"

"I remember," she said, and her hand was stroking over his jaw, moving around to the nape of his neck, because she could tell how good that felt to him. "I thought you made a very, very good big brother," she said. "The big brother every girl should have."

"Good," he said, and Tana had been right, the smile a woman gave you that told you she was proud of you, that she was impressed by you—that was the best one of all. He kissed her in the way he'd been waiting to do all day, gently and sweetly at first, her body curving so softly into his.

He pulled back, smiled down into her eyes in the light of the setting sun. "Merry Christmas. Thanks for sharing it with me."

"Merry Christmas," she said. "Thanks for being here so I could."

"And this," he told her, "is the other thing I've wanted to do all day." He reached around behind her, slowly began to pull the long stick of carved jade out of her hair. He could feel the knot loosening with every centimeter, and then he had the thing in his hand, and her hair was falling around her shoulders, down her back.

"Ah," he sighed. "Just as good as I thought. It's like undressing you, watching your hair come down for me."

She reached her hands up, lifted the heavy curtain of hair and shook it so it fell around her, smiled at him in the slow, seductive way she knew made his temperature rise, then pulled him towards her with a gentle hand at the back of his neck and kissed him exactly that slowly, exactly that seductively.

"If you're going to give me such pretty things," she said, her tongue coming out to lick into the corner of his mouth, both hands in his hair now, and he was burning for her, "you're going to get everything you want."

After that, he couldn't have let her go if he'd tried. He kissed her, held her, touched her as the light vanished, as the stars began to appear, the full moon struggling to make itself known through a mask of cloud. It was so good, and it wasn't nearly enough.

"I feel like a teenager myself," he said at last, kissing her delicious mouth once again, just because it was there, and it was his, and he needed it. "Kissing you in front of your parents' house, feeling you up in the car, dying to have more, but knowing your dad would kill me."

"Mmm," she said, her hands stroking over his shoulders, down his arms. "I love your arms, have I ever told you that? You're so strong. You excite me so much."

He groaned. "You're making it worse, you do realize that, don't you? I'll just say this, and then we're stopping, because there's only so much of this I can take, now that I'm *not* sixteen and I know exactly what I'm missing. I love all of your body, and in a couple days, when we're back home again, I'm going to lay you down on your bed and show you exactly how much I love it. Very, very slowly. And very, very thoroughly. I'm going to do it until you're telling me exactly how good it feels, because you'll have no choice, because you won't be able to stop yourself telling me. I'm going to do it until you're begging me for more."

He had a hand under her T-shirt, stroking over a breast, and she was gasping. "I'm about to tell you right now," she said, and wriggled a little, and he was dying. "You're killing me."

"You like the dirty talk, eh," he said, his teeth at the side of her neck, finding her favorite spot and biting a little, feeling the way she strained against him, what it was doing to her.

"You know…I do," she managed to say. "I like everything you do."

He took his hand from her with reluctance, lifted his head again. "Supposed to be stopping, and here I am, getting carried away again. Come on." He got up, put out a hand to pull her to her feet, kept hold of it as they walked back toward the house. "One more kiss goodnight, and something to think about for a couple more days. Make us really want it by the time we get it."

"I already want it," she said, and he had to laugh, and had to kiss her again, and it was a while before they made it to her door.

He went back to the caravan in the end, because he had no choice. Even though all he wanted to do was to keep kissing her, to take her to his bed, to lay her down and love every golden centimeter of her with his hands and his mouth and his body, to listen to her sigh, and moan, and, finally, cry out her pleasure, and know he was giving it to her. To feel her arching into him, and know that she was his.

But he couldn't do any of it, not now. So he went back to the caravan.

He moved quietly so as not to wake the kids, used the bathroom light for its modest illumination, keeping the door open a crack. He got ready for bed, pulled his phone out of the pocket of his shorts to set it on the table, and saw the notification.

1 missed call.

It was Aunt Cora. They'd talked just this morning, a quick one, and she'd wished the kids Merry Christmas already, so why would she be calling now? He debated waiting until the morning, but if she was calling again…And she hadn't sounded quite like herself earlier. Probably worried about how it was going to work out with the Mad Butcher of Brighton after all, now that they were down to the wire.

He left the caravan, started up the drive toward the front garden so he wouldn't wake the kids, and pushed the *Call* button.

"Hello," he heard. "Hugh. Oh, good."

"Merry Christmas again," he said. "How ya going? Having a good day?" He could afford to be cheerful, now, because she was coming back, and everything was going to get easier. And because he *was* cheerful.

"Yes," she said, and laughed. "You could say that. Because..." She paused for effect. "Henry asked me to marry him last night. And I said yes."

"He...Really?" It had sounded increasingly serious, but—so soon? "Whoa. That's awesome. That's...whoa, *quick.*"

"No, it's not," she said. "It hasn't been quick at all, it's been much too long. When it's right, it's right. We're both old enough to recognize it, that's all, and take our chance."

"So he's, what? Coming back with you? Or following you, still? Or what? What have you got planned?"

"No," she said, and the excitement was gone, replaced by caution, and something else. "That's not what we've decided. We had a long talk about it, were up half the night deciding. And what it comes down to is, we've realized that's not what's best for either of us, and it's not going to work. This is my home, and it's his. He's built up his business here, his family's here, and so is the rest of mine. He wants to stay, and so do I."

"You're staying *there?* For good, you mean?" It wasn't that it had never occurred to him, it was just that he hadn't thought it was possible. She'd never even hinted at it. She'd leave the kids? No, that couldn't be it. That wasn't what she was saying, and his heart had begun to pound. "So, wait," he said. "Wait. You're wanting to take the kids back there after all? Because I don't think that's best. They're doing all right, but they're not out of the woods. I thought we agreed that they'd be best off here. That was the whole idea."

"No," she said. "I'm not. I'm not taking them, because we did agree. They're better off staying where they are."

"So…what are you saying?"

"I'm saying…" She stopped, then began again. "I'm saying that I want all of you to come for the wedding, and Henry and I will come out and visit too. Every year, I hope. And I'll call. I'll help out as much as I can, talk to them, all that, but that's it."

"What?" He was standing in the middle of the front garden, in the dark, and it didn't feel warm anymore. It didn't feel anything. "That's it? You're moving back there, and that's *it?* You're just going to leave them? Alone?"

"Of course I'm not going to leave them alone," she said. "I'm going to leave them with you. If they were really alone, that would be different, but they aren't. They've got you. That was always the plan, that they'd have you."

He began to pace now, the agitation demanding release. "No," he told her. "That was *not* always the plan. That was nowhere close to the plan. They were meant to have both of us. They were meant to have you, because they need you. You're their aunt, and their guardian. We agreed."

"I'm *one* of their guardians," she said. "You're the other, and it's your turn to step up. I helped out as much as I could, for as long as I could. And, Hugh, come on. Think about it. What am I, really? I'm their aunt, who'd seen them a few times in their life, and I came all that way all the same, stayed a year and a half, did my best to love them and care for them and help them through the worst of it. But you—you're their brother, and you're a Kiwi, and you belong there. They're your responsibility, in the end, aren't they? My life has always been here. Even more so now, because I've got this chance, and I can't give it up. I *can't.*"

"And you're not willing to take them at all." He'd refused to consider this, because he hadn't thought it was possible. She wouldn't turn her back on the kids altogether, surely she wouldn't. She would change her mind. She'd miss them too much, surely, and they'd miss her. "Not even half the time? You could have them some of the time, surely."

"Some of the time? What, half their schooling here and half in New Zealand? Or away from their friends for their holidays? There's no way that works. That's no life for them. You have to think of what's best for them."

"Yeh, right," he said, and the cold fury was there now, making his hands shake. That she'd do this to him. That she'd do it to Charlie and Amelia. "Like you are."

"Like I've done for nearly eighteen months, while you've still been able to live your life and have your fun." She was getting angry too, it was clear. "Now I need to do what's best for me, what's best for Henry, too. I deserve that. I deserve some happiness myself."

"And what about what's best for me?" he demanded, hearing his voice rise. "What about when I'm back playing again? I've barely been able to manage while I've been out of it, while I've been home every night. What am I supposed to do then, gone half the time, out of the bloody *country* as often as not, training the rest, and just about useless with them when I am here?"

"You'll cope, that's what you'll do. They've sounded fine to me so far, and so have you. You hire a nanny to care for them and stay with them while you're gone, what do you imagine? You're a grown man, you can figure it out. And once you've done it, no doubt you'll go on exactly the same as when I was there. It's not like you can't afford to hire someone, is it? The kids will have their stability, their home and friends and schools. And nobody's asking you to take on a pair of delinquents. They're good kids."

"They're great kids," he said. "They're fantastic kids. They're just not *my* kids, and if you think all they need is a nanny and my job's done, then I…well, I don't even know how to answer that. They don't need a nanny, they need someone who can be a mum to them. Somebody who's a lot closer to that than what I can be, at least. They need somebody to listen to them and talk to them about their mum and dad and help Amelia figure out about being a teenager. They need a *parent,* and I can't be that."

"Well, you're going to have to be," she said. "Why ever wouldn't you be able to do it? If I could, you can. They need somebody, of course they do. And they've *got* somebody. They've got you. But I need something too. I need a life, and I deserve to have one."

"And so do I," he insisted. "I'm twenty-seven years old. How am I going to have any kind of normal life with two kids who aren't mine bang in the middle of it? What if I find a woman and want to have my own kids with her? What woman in her twenties is going to want to be a mother to teenagers? It's too much to ask of any woman. And it's too much to ask of me, because God knows, I'm not equipped to do it."

He'd been pacing faster and faster in his agitation, and now he stopped, took a couple deep breaths, and tried to start over.

"Look," he said. "I understand you're feeling pressed. I understand it's a lot of responsibility. Believe me, I do. If I never did before, I do now. And I understand if Henry's got doubts himself, and I'm willing to help with that. I'm willing to help with everything. If the problem's starting a new business, I can give him a loan, help him with the contacts, help him get set up with a shop here. You say he's built up a good business, so why can't he do the same thing here? Devonport could use a good butcher's, and he'd be able to price as high as he liked. Everyone else does. It'd be a good investment for all of us. And the two of you can keep living in the house, too. That'd save you heaps on rent, or keep you from having to buy a place, and you know what that house, what that rent would cost you. You wouldn't need to work yourself, either. How else would you get that kind of deal? That's even less pressure on the business, on either of you, right from the start. It's a win for everybody."

He racked his brain, tried to think of something else. "And I'd stay around," he added hurriedly. "I'd stay in Auckland. I'd help, but I need you here. I can't take this on by myself. I didn't sign up for this, and it's not fair to me, and it's not fair to the kids, either. I can't *do* it."

"I'm sorry," she said, and he could hear the distress, but he could hear the finality in her voice too. "You're going to have to, because that isn't going to work. The kids can visit, and I will too. But Henry won't do it. I'd lose him, and I can't let that happen, not after all this time. I can't give up my chance of happiness now I've finally found it. I'm not coming back, and that's that. I'll ring again tomorrow and tell the kids, or you can. It would probably be best coming from you. But Henry's been standing here for an age waiting for me to go with him to visit his mum and tell her our news, and I need to leave. We'll talk more tomorrow."

"And that's it?" he asked, incredulous. "That's *it?*"

"I'm sorry," she said again. "Try to understand. I have to go."

"Wait," he started to say, but she'd rung off.

He shoved the phone back into his pocket, barely aware of what he was doing. *Shit. Shit.* What was he meant to do now? He couldn't believe it.

It was bad. And then it got much worse.

life happens

♡

She'd broken away from Hugh at last, had gone back into the house, even though she'd wanted nothing more than to stay with him. Rodney and Charmaine had been sitting in the lounge, had looked up with a start at the sight of her, and she'd known they'd been talking about her. She'd known she should sit down too, try to mend this fence, but not tonight. And for once, she hadn't been ready to go to bed, although it was late. So she'd gone straight through the house and into the back garden instead, listened to the cicadas in the bush, and thought about Hugh. And eventually, had wandered around to the front, had lain down on one of the lounge chairs in the dark shadow of the big pohutukawa, wrapped her sweater around her, looked at the stars, and dreamed.

Until she'd heard his voice. At first she'd decided to wait until he'd finished talking to his aunt, had had some idea of sharing her chair with him, getting some more of what he'd left her aching for. And then she'd forgotten all about that.

He was silent, finally, and she lay where she was for another long moment. She wanted to stay there and wait for him to go back into the caravan, wanted to go to bed and pull the duvet over her head. But she'd never been one to run away. So instead, she swung around in the chair, put her feet on the ground, and spoke as she rose.

"That was your aunt."

"Josie." He sounded startled, and no wonder.

"Yeh, Josie. You're bloody lucky it was me. What if it had been the kids? What if they'd heard you say all that?"

"What? Why would they have heard me? They're in the caravan." He sounded distracted. "Bloody *hell*," he muttered. "I can't believe it."

"So you didn't say it in front of them," she said, and his attention was back on her, because she'd moved close. She needed to see his face, needed to be up *in* his face for this. "Not now, you didn't. You really think that helps? You think they won't know how you feel, when you tell them about this? You think they're that stupid?"

"What?" He was staring at her, and the moon, out from behind its cloud, showed him to her in all his distress.

"Because they aren't," she said. "They already know. They've always known."

"Known what?"

"You think it's funny, don't you," she demanded, willing her voice not to shake, "how bossy Amelia is? How she's always telling you what to do, telling you what children need? Telling you what you have to do so she doesn't fall pregnant, so Charlie doesn't join a gang?"

"What are you talking about? I know I'm no good at this. And if you're saying she knows it too—well, she wouldn't have to be that clever, would she? That's my point, don't you see?"

"Oh, I see. I see fine. It's you who doesn't see. Why do you think she does that? I'll tell you why. Because she sees you there, one foot out the door, and she's desperate to keep you somehow, any way she can. But she doesn't know how to do that, how to ask you to stay, how to make you want to stay. And why do you think that is?"

"I don't know," he said. "I don't have a bloody clue. But I have a feeling you're about to tell me."

"Because she doesn't have a dad, that's why. She doesn't have a man who loves her, a man to tell her she's beautiful, she's precious, she's lovable. She doesn't know how to get what she needs from you. She can't *be* lovable and precious and hold you that way, and she knows it. So instead, she's trying to *tell* you. She's trying to hold onto you any way she can, boss you into doing what you need to do for them both. But it isn't working, is it? She's failing, and she knows it. What do you think is going to happen to that girl when she's fifteen, sixteen? When she's still desperate for a man to love her, and she's given up on getting that from you? I can tell you what's going to happen."

"What? She'll fall pregnant after all?" He was getting more than angry, she could tell, and she didn't care. "And that's going to be my fault, somehow?"

"Maybe she won't," she said, wishing she could slap it into him. "Maybe she'll just get her heart broken, over and over, because she'll keep giving it—and her body, too—to a boy, to any boy, in hopes that he'll be the one who'll make her feel special. But that won't matter to you, will it? Because she's not yours. Because you didn't sign up for this."

The words were tumbling out, and she couldn't have stopped them if she'd tried. "And Charlie. What about him? He's so afraid to do something you won't like, to be something you won't want, how's he ever going to have the courage to be himself? How long's it going to take that sweet boy to give up on you? How long's it going to take before he looks for some other way to make the pain stop?"

"And that'll be my fault too?" he demanded. "That's what you're saying? I know I'm not what they need. That's what I've just been saying. That's the point."

"No," she told him. "It won't be your fault. It'll be your missed opportunity. It'll be the chance you've lost. Don't you *see*, Hugh? *Can't* you see? Those kids aren't your burden. They're not some millstone around your neck. They're your blessing. They're your gift."

"My *gift*," he said, and he actually sounded stunned.

"That's right. Your gift. You say they're not yours. Who else's do you imagine they are? Kids don't become yours because you give birth to them, or because you father them. They become yours when you care for them. They become yours when you love them."

"Maybe you think you'd have done better, if they'd been dropped on you?" he asked, his own voice rising now. "Maybe you'd say, 'Thank you so much for this opportunity? Thank you for the unexpected gift? I guess I don't need to worry about having my own kids now, because I've got these?'"

"Yeh," she said, the anger so strong now she could barely speak to tell him. "I would. I can tell you right now that I would. If I got two like Charlie and Amelia, I'd know God had answered my prayers. But then—" She laughed, and heard the bitterness, because the old pain was there, and the new one, too. That Hugh really didn't see. That he really couldn't do this, couldn't be the man she'd thought he was. "But then, that's me. Because I know that's the only way I can have kids. Because I'll only ever have them if somebody gives me the gift of them."

"What?"

"That's right. I can't have children," she told him. "I can't have—what you call *mine*. You know. *Real* kids. But luckily for me, I know that's not the only way to be a parent. And if I get an opportunity like you have, I won't waste it. I won't hurt those kids by not wanting them, by whingeing about them. I won't try to push them off on somebody else, somebody who doesn't want them enough to sacrifice for them. Somebody who can't wait to get away from them and give them up. *I'll* love them. If I get the chance, I'll love them. But like you say," she told him, feeling all the desolation of it, "that's me."

"Josie," he said. "Josie, wait. Hang on. I didn't know."

"No," she said, the tears threatening, "of course you didn't. I don't go around advertising it. It doesn't exactly add to my appeal."

"I'm...I'm sorry."

"Yeh," she said, and wiped her face with the back of her hand. She'd done more crying in the past two days than she ever allowed herself, and this time, there were no strong arms to hold her, no deep voice to tell her it would be all right. Because it wouldn't be. Because she'd been wrong. "I'm sorry too."

"I've got..." he said, and she heard the sigh, saw his hand running over his jaw, saw the helplessness, the fatigue. And despite everything, she ached for him, that he couldn't do this. And for herself, too, because she loved him, and she'd fooled herself into expecting too much from him, had wanted so badly for him to be the man those kids needed. The man *she* needed.

"I've got too much here," he said helplessly. "I can't sort it out. Too many things. I need to...I need to think about it. Can you give me a chance to think?"

"I don't know if I can," she said, the sorrow a black shadow, smothering her, weighing her down. "I don't know."

But, she thought bleakly as she left him there and walked into the house, walked straight past Rodney and Charmaine without a word, she was afraid she did know. She was afraid she already knew what would happen when he'd thought. She was afraid the answer was no.

home truths

♡

Josie woke early—well, as much as she'd been asleep—and was downstairs already by the time her mum appeared in the kitchen. Sitting at the table drinking her tea, because it had to be better than lying in bed.

"I thought, big brekkie today," her mother said, turning on the kettle for her first cup of tea. "Anything Hugh especially likes, that we should make him?"

"I don't know," Josie said, "and I don't think it matters."

Her mother looked at her, took in the state of her, and came to pull up a chair at the table. "Why not?"

"Because..." Josie shrugged helplessly. "Because I think we may be done. I think it's over already, and I shouldn't have brought him after all. It was too soon, and he's...he's not what I thought."

"He's not, eh," her mother said. "In what way?"

Josie told her, reluctantly at first, then picking up speed. What she'd heard, what he'd said, what she'd said, what he'd said in return, the words pouring out, desperate for release.

"He doesn't want those kids," she told her mum when she'd finished, "and it's pretty clear that he isn't going to want me, either, now that he knows. Maybe he would have, if I'd waited to tell him, but I *couldn't* wait, not after what he said, and anyway..."

She stopped, having run down at last. "It's all such a mess," she tried to explain, "and I can't believe I've got myself into this. I thought I wasn't on the rebound anymore, but of course I was. I must have been, mustn't I? I wanted to have somebody, so I made myself believe it was right, and now I've stuffed up so badly, Mum, because he's my neighbor, and I'm going to have to go on living next door to him, and I don't know if I can. I rushed into it, exactly what I didn't want to do, and now I have to pay the price."

"But what is it," her mum said slowly, "that you actually know? Here's what you know, seems to me. That his aunt talked to him, and he was startled, and scared. That you told him you can't have kids, and he was startled again. Is that about it? Because if it is, I can't quite make out what he's done that's so wrong that you're ready to give up on him."

"*What?* Mum, come *on.* He's had a year and a half to accept his responsibilities. A year and a *half.* He's been living with them for nearly a year, had full charge of them for three months, and he's *still* trying to run away from them? What am I supposed to think about that? How am I meant to judge that?"

"So he disappointed you," her mum said.

"Yeh." Josie laughed, and the bitterness was back again. "He disappointed me. You could say that."

"Were you expecting to have a relationship where your man would never disappoint you, then?" her mother asked her. "Where you never disappointed him either, for that matter? Do you imagine that relationship exists somewhere? Do you think that your dad and I have never disappointed each other?"

"Not like this," Josie said. "I know it was never like this."

Now her mother was the one snorting. "And exactly how do you know that? You know what you see now, what you see from us after more than thirty years together. Do you imagine it was always that way? Do you think there weren't things we didn't let you see, because you didn't need to see them, because they were none of your business? Do you think it was always easy?"

"I—" Josie didn't know how to answer. *Yes,* she wanted to say. "But you always loved each other. You were always there for each other, and for us."

"Were we? Are you so sure of that? Could you see into our hearts? Do you imagine that there were never times we failed each other? Because I can tell you for sure that there were. Times when I was too focused on you kids to make the time I should have for your dad, give him the attention and the affection he needed. And times he was too focused on the work to notice how I was feeling, what I needed. All of those times. When we didn't tell each other what was on our minds, didn't trust each other to listen and work it out and make it better. When we forgot to be lovers, and even sometimes forgot to be friends."

"But…" Josie began, even though she didn't know what she would say.

Her mother went on, though, without waiting for her answer. "Sometimes a relationship, a marriage is so bad, you have no choice but to leave. There's nothing to stay for, and the only answer is to walk away, to save yourself, or to save your kids. You know what those times feel like, because you did it yourself not so long ago. You could have tried to fight for it with Derek, tried to salvage it somehow, but you didn't, you walked away, and I thought that was the right choice, because he wasn't the right man, and he wasn't worth fighting for. Is this one of those times, though?"

"I don't—" Josie said, and wished she could finish a sentence. "I don't know. It feels like it."

"I'll tell you what I think," her mother said. "I think that when you have a good man who's having a rough time, who's lost his way? That isn't when you cut and run. That's when you get stuck in."

"But, Mum," Josie said desperately. "This is different. Dad never did anything like this. I don't care what you say. He never wanted to give us up, I know it."

"Because it wasn't anything like the same thing. Not even close. He had a good dad himself, and I wonder if Hugh did. Did he grow up with his dad? He can't have, can he? What do you think he really knows about how to be a dad?"

"I don't know," Josie said again.

"You don't know, because you haven't asked him, have you? I'll bet he doesn't know much. Or at least he didn't, because it seems to me that he's learning, and that he's willing to learn more. And it's more than that, too. Your dad knew what he was getting into, and having kids was our choice. But were there times all the same when he felt overwhelmed, when he wondered if he could do it, when he even wished he was free to do what he wanted, go wherever he pleased, not have to carry the responsibility for all of us, at least for a while? I'll bet if you asked him, if he told the truth, the answer would be, of course there were."

She paused a moment, considering. "Let me ask you," she finally said. "If it had been you. And I know—" She put up a hand to forestall Josie's protest. "You're going to tell me what you'd do, knowing what you know now, going through what you've been through. You've got the wisdom, *now* you do, because you've had the pain, and the time to take the pain in, sort through it, see what it all meant. But what if you hadn't?"

"I don't understand," Josie said. This was nowhere close to what she'd imagined her mum's reaction being, and she was reeling. "What?"

"You're an actress," Arama said. "That's your job, imagining how people feel, eh. So imagine. Imagine you've just had the kind of loss Hugh did. Imagine your dad died. Right now, today. Yeh, that's right," she said when she saw Josie flinch. "Hurts even to imagine it, doesn't it? Hurts me even to say it. Now think that it's actually *happened.* An accident, no time to prepare for it. And then you don't just have that to cope with, because the very same day, today, you get the charge of two kids, kids who are your brother and sister, but kids you've never lived with, that you barely know. You're used to living your life, going your way, and, yeh, having a good time, too. And now you're told you have these kids. Would you be able to turn your life around straight away and take them on—and do it right?"

"Yes," Josie said. "I hope so. I hope I would."

"No," her mother corrected her. "You wouldn't. Stop and think. You hated living in Aussie, didn't like that show, that part much, either. You hated almost everything about it."

"What—"

"So imagine," her mother went on, "if that's what you were told. There you are, your dad gone, and half your money too, I'll bet. Because if Hugh hasn't been supporting that whole family since the minute it happened, I miss my guess, or I don't know men, and I know men. And now, on top of all that, and the kids too, you've got to give up your job that you like so much, your show, all those friends of yours. Got to leave the place that's home, leave me behind, too, and go to Aussie to be on a show that's not doing so well, where you don't know anyone. You're thinking, maybe it's temporary. You're telling yourself that just to get yourself through, even while you're changing, even while you're falling in love with those kids. Even while you're learning to be a mum, whether or not that was your plan. And you're falling in love with somebody else, too. You've met a good man at last, one you can see a future with, and your mind starts making plans whether you like it or not, starts to imagine a life with him. Because that's happened too, hasn't it. That's happened to you."

"Yes," Josie said, because there was no denying it, not to her mum.

"You fall in love," her mother went on. "And then it's all ripped away again. A second time. Your temporary change? It just got permanent, and you're scared. Not because you're not good enough, not because you don't care enough. But because you are, and because you do. Because you care too much, and you're afraid you don't have what it takes to do it right. And on top of that, that person you fell in love with? He just told you that because you're scared, and you've been honest enough to say so, he doesn't want you. He's not willing to hang around and share that load with you, help you through it. He only wants you if you fit his perfect image of what a woman ought to be. How do you feel now?"

The tears were there, and she wasn't sure she could hold them back anymore. "Mum. Stop. Stop."

"I'm not going to stop," her mother said. "I'm going to tell you, because you need to hear. What did Hugh tell you, when you told him that you couldn't have babies? Did he say, well, good riddance, then?"

"No," she managed to say. "He said…" She took a shuddering breath. "That he didn't know. What to say. He asked me to wait and give him a chance."

"And did you give him a chance?"

"No," Josie whispered. "No."

"Did you say, 'I understand it's hard, and I'm here to listen, the way you listened to me? I'm here to believe in you? I'm here to support you, to stand up for you the way you stood up for me in front of everyone when my brother said hurtful things and made me cry?'"

Josie's eyes flew to her mother's face. "Yeh," Arama said. "I heard about it. What Rodney said was true for him, I guess, and he'll have to sort it out, and his dad will be helping him do it, no worries. But it was a load of rubbish, and you know it, because we're nothing but proud of you. And your man is too, and not afraid to stand up and say so, even though Rodney's right about one thing. That probably isn't easy for Hugh, not a bit of it, knowing men are looking at you the way they do. And even so, he's proud of you, and willing to tell anyone so. He'd defend you to the death, I'm sure of it. But how proud are you of him?"

"But he said—" Josie began.

"He said," her mother said contemptuously. "He said. Of course he said. He's not perfect. He's a *man*. But what has he *done?* I'll tell you what he's done. He's done all that. Supported his family. Moved for them. Done whatever it took to be there for them. And he'll keep doing it, too, no matter how hard it is, because that's the kind of man he is. Any man can say pretty things that a woman wants to hear. But a man who *does* the right thing, even when it's not the easy thing, even when it's the hardest thing, the last thing he wants to do—that's a man worth having. That's a man worth keeping. He may not be your fantasy. He may not be perfect. But he's a good man. He may not have ridden up on a white horse to sweep you away from all the pain and trouble in your life, and he may be the right man all the same."

"I don't—" Josie said. "I don't know what to think. "I can't—"

Arama's face softened. "Isn't that what he said to you?" she asked gently. "That he didn't know what to think? That he needed time?"

Josie nodded miserably, and her mother sighed and, at last, pulled her into her arms, let her lay her face against her shoulder so the tears could come.

"You give him time," she said, smoothing a hand over Josie's hair. "You let him sort it out. And, if you're lucky, he'll do the same for you. You won't be perfect, and neither will he. You won't have the perfect love, or the perfect life. But if you forgive each other, if you love each other, and if you keep on doing it? If you love harder when it's hardest to do it? You may just be lucky all the same. You may just be happy."

ready or not

♡

Hugh woke to a warm morning, a heavy, humid feeling to the air that heralded the arrival of the remnants of the latest tropical cyclone, supposed to make its sweep through the North Island later that day. Not any heavier than his own state of body and mind, though.

He'd had no choice the night before but go back to the little caravan, to climb into bed, because there was no place else to go. He couldn't exactly pack the kids up and steal away in the middle of the night. So instead, he'd lain on his back through the long hours, heard the even breathing of the kids, deep in the blameless sleep of happy fatigue. His own fatigue on waking from the few disturbed hours of rest he'd finally managed, though, was anything but blameless, and nothing like happy.

♡

The kids weren't happy themselves when they found out they were leaving a day early.

"But *why?*" Amelia demanded again, not even making an attempt at packing. "I was going to ride the horse again today."

"It's supposed to rain," Hugh pointed out, grabbing his own things and stuffing them haphazardly into his bag. "You probably couldn't have ridden anyway. And we need to go back. Josie has...something she needs to do, and so do I, and we need to leave."

Charlie said nothing, just packed up his duffel, his face closed in a way that Hugh realized he hadn't seen for a while now.

He'd wished they could just creep out, but of course that wasn't possible. At least Josie wasn't in the kitchen when he took the kids over for breakfast, and he thought, from the look Arama gave him, that she might know why.

"She's taking a walk," she told him. "She went off up the bush track. D'you want to go after her, say goodbye?"

"No," he said. "She'll be needing her walk. We'll see her when we're back in Devonport." He hoped. "As long as she'll be all right getting back," he realized, and could have smacked his forehead. "Seeing as she doesn't have her car here."

"That's what buses are for," Arama said. "You go on and do what you need to do. Give her time to think about things." Which made it pretty clear.

After he'd got a quick breakfast down the kids and got the car packed up, he found out for sure. Arama and Tana walked out to see them off, and Hugh said his thank-yous, had the kids say their goodbyes as well.

Arama gave both the kids a cuddle and a kiss, and then, to Hugh's surprise, pulled him in for his own warm hug, squeezed him tight.

"Give her a chance," she said, keeping her voice low. "She's been hurt so much, it's hard for her to believe. Give her a chance to believe in you."

"I—" He wasn't sure how to answer. "I'll try," he said, and if that sounded lame, well, he *was* lame. He didn't think Josie was the one who needed the chance, anyway. How could her mother think so?

Tana reached a hand out, shook Hugh's. "We'll hope to see you again," he said, his gaze direct.

"Yeh," Hugh said. He wanted to ask, and he wanted to leave. "I hope so too."

Both kids turned to wave as they left, kept waving until they had turned from the drive onto the road, and Josie's parents were no longer visible.

"I wish we could have said goodbye to Josie," Charlie said. "I wanted to tell her goodbye. I wanted to tell her about the parrot story we started last night, too. She'd want to know about that. She'd think it was interesting."

"*I* wanted to ride again," Amelia said. "It's not fair."

"Well, maybe you can ride again another time," Hugh said. "Maybe there's a camp or something, who knows."

"Really?" she asked, and for once, she actually sounded like a twelve-year-old, one who wasn't sure she had all the answers. "I want to, because I like it better than anything, even better than ballet."

"Huh." He tried to think what to say about that. "I thought it was all about the ballet."

"It *was*," she said. "And I *wish*...But Miss Chloe said I'm still not ready for my pointe shoes. She said..."

"What?" Hugh prompted.

"That maybe I won't be ready," Amelia said reluctantly. "That maybe ballet isn't my best thing. She said it's a good thing to do, and I shouldn't stop trying, but maybe I should do netball too."

Hugh shot a look across at her, and he could see how hard it had been to tell him. "Well, netball's good," he said. "As far as I'm concerned, netball's better." He tried a joke. "I know which one I'd rather come watch you do."

"I like netball all right," Amelia said. "But I liked ballet best, if I could do it the right way, and riding is a bit like ballet. It's the feeling I want to have, like the horse is moving like I want to move in ballet, except I *can't*."

"You could do tap instead of ballet," Charlie suggested from the back seat. "I think tap would be more fun anyway, and there's only one kind of shoes."

"What's tap?" Hugh asked.

"*You* know," Amelia said. "Tap shoes with metal plates."

"Ah," Hugh realized. "Where it makes all the racket."

"Yeh," Charlie said, "because your feet are going so fast. You can go in circles, do heaps of moves, and it's more…jumpy. Amelia wouldn't have to be floating, like she can't do."

"I can too do it," Amelia said. "I just can't do it *enough*. And I don't like tap."

"Oh," Charlie said. "I thought it would be fun, that was all."

"Just because you like tap," Amelia said, "that doesn't mean *I* like tap. If people like to do things, *they* should do them. Other people don't necessarily want to do them."

"Wait," Hugh said. "Charlie likes to do tap?"

"Yeh," Amelia said.

"I do not," Charlie said.

"You *do*," Amelia insisted. "You do it all the time. I've seen you."

"No I don't," Charlie said again. "Boys don't do dancing."

"Don't they?" Hugh asked. "That tap thing—haven't I seen some fella doing that on TV sometime? Going up and down the stairs, things like that?"

Charlie didn't answer. "So you like it?" Hugh prompted. "When do you do it?"

"While he's waiting for me to change after class, and they have tap class next," Amelia said. "He copies."

"I *don't*," Charlie said again, sounding a little frantic. "Boys don't *do* dancing. I just…if I'm bored, because I'm *waiting*."

Hugh was starting to get the picture. "If you want to do tap," he told Charlie, "if you think it'd be fun, why couldn't you do it? You wait through Amelia's class often enough, why couldn't she wait through yours? I don't see why a boy couldn't do it, if he wanted to."

"Because everybody would *laugh* at me," Charlie said. "They'd say it was for girls, and that I was..."

"Why should they?" Hugh asked. "The time I saw it, it looked pretty athletic to me. Looked like some good footwork, like it'd make you a pretty good stepper. Good for rugby, eh. Just like some of the boys do yoga to stay flexible. Somebody could laugh about that too, but if it helps them play better, why not? And if they did laugh at you," he said with inspiration, "you could show me how, and I could try, and they could laugh at *me.*"

"You couldn't do dance," Charlie said, and he still sounded doubtful, but Hugh thought he might be smiling a little too.

"Well, no," Hugh conceded, "probably not. That'd be the point, wouldn't it? Tell you what. We'll ask Miss Chloe, you can take a class or two, teach me some moves, and the next picnic we go to, we'll try it together. Get my mates falling about laughing at me, and all the more impressed with you. It's all in the comparison, eh."

"Wouldn't you be embarrassed?" Charlie asked.

"Nah," Hugh said. "Nobody thinks I'm graceful now. It's not like they'd be surprised. Bet we could get Koti James up there tapping, though. I'll bet he could do it, and there's nothing a back likes better than showing up the big boys."

"If kids at my school found out, though," Charlie said.

"Then you tell them I tried it, and was rubbish at it," Hugh said. "That'd stop them, I'll bet. And they'd like to hear that."

"That's gossip," Amelia pointed out. "That's talking about you, telling people things about your life."

"Sometimes," Hugh said, "gossip's OK. I'm telling Charlie it's OK this time."

"I don't know if Aunt Cora would want to take me," was Charlie's next objection. "She doesn't like waiting for Amelia already. She complains because the traffic's bad, and it takes too long."

"Ah." No time like the present. They still had a couple hours to go, and talking about it in the car could be the best. Nobody could go anywhere, and everything that needed to be said could be said. He hoped. If he knew how to say it. "Aunt Cora isn't going to be here, so that's not an issue."

"Yes she is," Amelia corrected. "She comes back next week."

"Well, no," Hugh said. "She doesn't. She's marrying that fella, Henry. She'll tell you herself today, but she rang and told me last night, and that they're planning to stay in the UK. You'll visit, and she'll visit here," he hurried to say, "but she's not going to live here anymore."

"Then what happens to us?" Amelia asked, and Charlie hadn't said anything at all. Hugh glanced in the mirror, and Charlie's face had gone white and shuttered again.

"You stay with me," Hugh said, and he said it absolutely as firmly as he'd ever said anything in his life.

"But she's our *guardian*," Amelia persisted.

"She's been one of them. I've been the other, and now I'm doing it, and that's all there is to it, because it's all sorted. So," he went on, and tried to lighten it up a little, "I'm afraid your days of fixing dinner and doing the shopping aren't over after all, because I'm going to need your help. We can get better at it, if we work at it. And if you have problems, things you want to ask Aunt Cora about," he realized he should add, "you can call her and ask them. Or if you just want to complain about me, because that could happen. If I won't let you buy ice cream, you can tell her how mean I am, eh."

"But what about when you're gone?" Amelia asked. "You still have to play. You still have to leave."

"We get a nanny for those times," Hugh said. "Somebody to stay with you. I'll get onto that straight away. You two can help me with the interviews. We'll make a list of questions to ask, make sure we get the right one."

"What if you leave too, though?" Charlie asked. "What if you get married too? What if you go back to play for the Hurricanes again?"

"It doesn't matter what happens," Hugh said, "because I'm not going anywhere, or if I do, you're both coming with me. We're going to work it out."

"What if..." Charlie began, then stopped.

"What if what?" Hugh prompted when he didn't go on.

"What if you die too?" Charlie asked, his voice small. "Then there's nobody."

That one threw Hugh, he had to admit. "I don't know," he finally said. "I make a plan for that too, I guess, and I tell you what the plan is. I'm pretty healthy, though, and people don't normally die when they're young, do they. I could break another bone and need help with the washing-up, get concussion and need help remembering the shopping list, but I'm not likely to die."

"Mummy and Daddy died," Charlie said. "They weren't old, not *very* old, but they died anyway."

"We'll make a plan," Hugh repeated. More therapy, maybe, he decided. With him there too, because he was going to need some help coming up with answers to questions like these. "All I can promise is that I'm here," he said. "And that I'm not going anywhere. And with the three of us working on it, we'll make it happen. I'm ready to get stuck in if the two of you are."

"Really?" Charlie asked.

"Really," Hugh promised. "I'm ready."

Maybe he was, and maybe he wasn't. But he was going to do it anyway.

what's in front of you

♡

The cyclone had threatened, the wind had blown, the rain had come in fits and starts all through Boxing Day, and now, on the twenty-seventh, it was here in force. The rain streamed down the windscreen of the big bus, forcing the wipers to work in frantic rhythm to keep it clear enough for the driver to see. Traffic on the motorway was so slow it was crawling, and Josie felt as if she were stuck in a dream, trying desperately to reach her destination, one obstacle after another in her way, never able to make it, never able to quite get there.

She'd come back from her walk in the bush the day before, her thoughts still whirling, sure of only one thing, that she needed to talk to Hugh again and tell him how she felt, find out what he had to say. She'd walked up the steep path for nearly an hour, sorting it through, had reached her decision and turned around, and by the time she'd got back to the road, she'd been running, because she was too far away.

But when she'd made it back down the drive, his car had been gone. She'd pounded on the caravan door, but had received no answer, had opened it and found they were gone. She'd run the rest of the way to the house, and known all along it was useless.

"They *left?*" she panted, standing sweaty in shorts and T-shirt and bare feet in the kitchen.

Her mother continued sorting the washing into the machine. "About a half-hour ago."

"But…I can't get back," she realized. "I don't have a car. And I need to go too. How could he just *leave?*"

Her dad looked up at her from his spot at the table, where he'd been going through paperwork. "How could he have stayed?" he asked her quietly.

"Oh." She sank down into a chair opposite him, and her mum poured her a glass of water, set it in front of her. "Mum told you."

"She did."

Josie popped up again, unable to be still. "Then I need to go after him. Right now. But I don't have a car. Can I borrow your car, Mum?"

"No, darling," her mother said, shoving the soap dispenser into place and slamming the machine shut, twisting the dial. "Sorry. Better to give Hugh some time, anyway. Wasn't that the idea?"

"The bus," Josie said, because she wasn't listening. "I can take the bus. That's what I'll do. When does the bus leave?"

Except it had turned out that she couldn't, because the bus had been booked solid during the rush of Boxing Day, the car hire firms closed for the holiday, and it wasn't until an interminable twenty-four hours later that she climbed on board for the frustratingly, grindingly slow journey back to Auckland.

She descended at last at the Sky Tower, pulled her wheelie bag down Queen Street through the late-afternoon crowds, her parka an insufficient shield against the blowing rain, her hair quickly growing soaked, and found she had just missed the ferry to Devonport.

Another twenty-five minutes on a bench looking at the gray chop of the Harbour, the boats rolling and bouncing in the swell, another queue to board, a stomach-churning ride across the narrow channel with holidaymakers who had decided, for some obscure reason, to sample the delights of village life on a day wholly unsuited for it, and she was on the other side at last. Through the terminal building, down the path past the play structure, and then along the waterfront, the waves crashing, the wind buffeting her, moving as fast as she could pull the little suitcase, and it was nearly two full days now since she'd talked to Hugh, and she should have rung him after all, because it was too long to wait, and what if he'd changed his mind?

She saw his car in the drive, the glow of light in the house, left her bag there at the bottom of the steps to get wet—to get wetter—and climbed up to ring the bell. Then stood there, her heart pounding, her entire body shaking, and waited.

The door opened, and it was Hugh. Hugh, looking down at her in apparent shock, and she couldn't tell. She couldn't *tell*.

"Josie," he said. "What…what happened?"

Her teeth were chattering, her hair streaming wet, her clothes dripping around her. "I came…I came…" she tried to say.

Charlie and Amelia were there now, staring at her from behind Hugh, and he reached for her, pulled her into the entryway. "Come inside. You're freezing. You're soaked."

"The bus," she said. "I was on the bus, and then the ferry, and then it was raining, and I…" She wasn't coherent, and this wasn't at all the speech she had intended to make.

"Why didn't you call me?" he demanded. "I'd have come and got you."

"I didn't…I didn't know if you…if you would," she tried to tell him.

He was smiling, and still frowning, all at the same time. "Of course I would. Don't you know that by now?"

"I came to tell you," she said, "let me try again. Let me try to say, I know it was asking too much. I was too…too hasty. I came to ask…to tell you…"

"You really need somebody to write your lines for you this time, sweetheart," he said, and he was pulling her into his arms, not caring how wet he got, and she was hanging onto him as if her life depended on it, and she couldn't tell what was tears and what was rain.

"Come on," he told her. "Let's take you over to your place, and get you warm and dry, and then you can tell me, and I can tell you too."

"Josie came in the rain," Charlie said. "She came in the rain, Amelia."

"I know," his sister said. "And I was right. It *is* romantic. It *is*."

She was still trying to tell him, trying to think of the right way, but he wasn't listening. He was helping her pull off her wet things, and she was shivering with cold, and nerves, and exhaustion from two sleepless nights, and he had turned on the shower and shoved her into it.

"Stay in there," he told her. "Stay in there until you warm up."

She cried a little more in the shower, because she'd stuffed up utterly, and all she'd been was pathetic, and she'd never know how he really felt now, because how could a man be honest with a woman who was clearly too distraught, too needy to hear the truth?

She climbed out at last because she had to, her head feeling dull and stuffed but her body no longer shaking, toweled herself off and pulled on a warm dressing gown, combed her hair out and left it hanging, long and wet, and went out into the lounge to find him.

He was sitting on the couch, but he smiled at the sight of her, stood up and put out a hand to draw her down with him.

"I even made tea," he said. "Sit here with me and drink it, and listen, because I have a few things to tell you."

"I want to tell you too, though," she said.

He shook his head. "I promise, from now on, you can go first. But right now, you need to listen to me. You've known what was right all along, and I haven't, so I have more to say."

"But I *haven't,*" she protested, and her chest was filling, her throat tightening, and she could hardly dare to breathe, but with joy this time. With hope.

"Me first," he said. "Please, because I've been waiting so long to tell you. I thought about the phone, but I wasn't sure you'd want to hear it, and I thought, better to wait until I was with you again. I thought I had a better chance," he said with a little laugh that didn't sound very steady, "if I could hold your hand while I said it." He took it lightly in his own, ran his fingers over the backs of hers. "This is my speech. It's a bit corny, maybe, but it's the best I've got."

He took a deep breath and began. "There are these things you say in sport. People think they're clichés, and I guess they are, but you say them so often, for so long, they sink in all the same."

He paused, and she waited, her eyes on his face. "One of them is," he said, "you play what's in front of you. What it means is, yeh, you've got a game plan. You train, you study the other team during the week, you do your very best not to leave anything to chance. But then you turn up on the night, and you play what's in front of you, whether it's what you planned or not. Somebody gets injured, you've got a man in the bin, doesn't matter. You don't get to stop and ask the ref to start again because you didn't plan for this. You just keep playing. You may win, and you may lose. But if you stop playing, if you stop trying, you're sure to lose, aren't you? So you don't stop trying, not until the ref blows the whistle. Because even if you lose the game, you didn't lose..." He stopped.

"Your self-respect," she suggested.

He shook his head. "I guess...yourself. And your team. You don't lose them, you don't lose each other. Next time, you know they'll be there. You know they'll front up, be there all eighty minutes for you, the same way you will be for them. And if it's hard, well, it's always hard. Anyway, you'd think you'd want the easy game, and maybe you should, but you don't. You want the tough ones. Those are the ones you want to play, the ones you want to win. That's why you play, to put yourself to the test, see what you're made of."

"And that's what this is," she said. "With you and the kids. Since your dad and stepmum died. You've been playing what's in front of you."

Another shake of the head. "No. I haven't been. That's what this is."

"But you *have*," she insisted. "Of course you have. I see that now. When your father and stepmother died, you told me you were here the next day. You flew all night to get to your brother and sister. And you've been with them ever since, as much as you could be."

"Helping," he said. "I always thought I was helping. Paying the bills, being there—when I was able to. But not fronting up, not really. Somebody needed to step up."

"And you *did.*"

"I'd say that Aunt Cora and I each took a half step up. That's not fronting. Not even close. You were right. I'm not good enough, I know it, but I'm what they've got. So it wasn't the game plan. So I have to readjust. Doesn't matter. It's what's here. It's what they need. It's what *I* need. Because I've realized, in the past couple days, what if Aunt Cora had rung to say that she wanted the kids with her in the UK? What if she'd said, put them on the plane, and I'll meet them, and I'll love them, and you're done? I thought about that, and I realized I'd have said no. I'd have fought to keep them. I realized—that I could love them, I guess. Both of them. That I may not be their dad, but in a way…I am, now."

"Of course you are," she told him, and she couldn't believe she had ever doubted it.

"I'm the closest thing they've got, anyway," he said, "and even if Aunt Cora came back, it wouldn't matter. They need one person who puts them first. That person's going to be me. Because that's what's in front of me, and because that's what I want. To take care of my family."

"I know it's going to be hard, though," she said, "half the time away."

"The other boys do it. I can find out how. There must be a way. A nanny, or whatever. But also—give them what they've been missing. A brother who's willing to step up and be a dad. Whatever that means, and however rubbish I am at it at first. I can get better, and that's what I mean to do."

He looked at her again. "And you know the other thing I realized, all this time I've been thinking?"

"No," she said, and her heart was pounding now. "What?"

"I realized that I want you, too. That if this isn't what loving someone is, I can't imagine what more it'd be, because what it is—it's knowing that I'd do anything I could to keep you from hurting, but if you are, I want to be there to soften the blow. I want to know that I'm there for you, and I want you to know it too. I need you to trust that if you need me to come pick you up because it's raining, I'll do it, no matter what, no matter how angry you are with me, no matter how angry you think I am with you. And if that isn't love," he repeated, "I guess it's close enough for me. I hope it's close enough for you."

"I can't..." Her chest was tighter than ever, the tears pricking behind her eyelids, and she couldn't have kept from showing him how she felt if the most important role of her life had been riding on it. "I can't have children," she managed to say.

"That's all right," he said, and he was smiling. "I've already got children."

"Your own children," she insisted.

"You told me," he said, "that children were yours when you cared for them, and when you loved them. I reckon you were right."

"So you don't want...babies?"

"Maybe I do," he said. "Maybe I do, if you do. But aren't there other ways to have babies?"

"You'd do that?"

"Don't you know by now," he asked her, "that I'd do just about anything for you?"

"You may change your mind, though," she said, wanting so much to believe him, wishing so much that she dared to trust that he meant it. "It happens. It's what happened with Derek. You can say it doesn't matter, but you may get older, and in the end, it will."

He sat a minute, thinking, and she waited, hardly managing to breathe. She waited, because his answer mattered. His *honest* answer.

"You said once," he told her at last, "that you weren't planning on moving. That the two of us weren't likely to live in domestic bliss next door to each other, forever and ever."

"You should be an actor," she said, trying to joke, because she wasn't sure where this was going, and she so desperately wanted it to go in the right direction, "the way you remember my lines."

He didn't respond to that. "Maybe," he said, "what we need to do is try that. Try living in domestic bliss next door to each other for as long as we need to. For as long as it takes for me to convince you that I can love you, that I *will* love you, and that this is the real thing. That this is forever. I know it already, but I can see you need some telling, and some showing, too, and I'm willing to keep telling you and showing you until you believe it. All I'm asking is that you give me the chance to try, and that you try too. And that, whatever happens," he said, his face filled with so much tenderness, "whatever happens, you promise me that my rubbish bags are safe."

She was laughing, and she was crying, and she was in his arms.

"So is that a promise to try?" he asked after he'd held her and kissed her and wiped her tears away.

"That's a promise," she told him, both hands on his face, her fingers smoothing over the dark rasp of his beard, and she'd never wanted anybody or anything more in her life. "To keep your rubbish bags safe, and you, too. To keep you safe, and cared for, and loved. That's my promise to try."

epilogue

♡

One year later

Another December day, a fair one this time, the pohutu-kawa just coming into bloom in Katikati, and there was music in the air.

"Are they coming?" Charlie asked for what must have been the tenth time.

Hugh looked down at his brother, whose hand was going up to tug at the unfamiliar constraint of the gray necktie for what must have been the *twentieth* time, and reached out himself to give the thing a quick straighten. Charlie was nervous about doing this, and about the dance he was doing later, too, he guessed. His brother tap-dancing at his wedding reception. That was one he could never have imagined a couple years ago, and here it was, and how lucky was he?

"Wait," he said. "Almost. Got the rings for me?"

Charlie swallowed with nerves, gave a quick bob of his head. "Yeh."

"Then we're all good," Hugh said. "Hang in with me here, mate."

The music changed, and he looked up fast and saw his sister standing at the end of the aisle, clutching her bouquet, saw the figure in ivory leaning down, a graceful shape, to give a tug to the skirts of the pale green dress Hugh hadn't yet been allowed to see. He saw a hand lift a veil for just a moment to allow a kiss on Amelia's cheek, and could imagine the smile, the encouraging word before Amelia had turned to face him, had started her slow march down the aisle, concentration evident in every fierce line of her thirteen-year-old body. Josie's maid of honor.

And this was it. This was the day. The villa next door was on the market again, because when he and Josie came back from their three-week honeymoon in the Cook Islands, she wouldn't be living there anymore. The kids would have another Christmas with Josie's parents, her mother would be spoiling the moko-puna, truly hers now, with chocolate fish every day, no doubt, and then they'd be together. All of them. A family, complete at last.

His sister continued her achingly slow progress down the aisle, and Hugh waggled his fingers at her, got a nervous little waggle in return, and offered a smile to his mum, sitting in the front row with Aunt Cora and her Henry. However much any of them had to give now, it was going to be all right, because he and Josie had enough. He and Josie had it all.

Everything was coming together, except Dr. Eva, because Dr. Eva had disintegrated about as thoroughly as a woman could. She'd met her nemesis at last in the cliffhanger to end all cliff-hangers, to be revealed in the first episode of the following sea-son, when her obsession with her brilliant colleague had reached crisis point, the woman scorned had demanded revenge, and a plot had been hatched involving a highly improbable assassin and a car bomb gone horribly wrong.

Dr. Eva was no more, because the new series had been cast by the network, Josie's script for the pilot was being refined even now by a team led by Rose, wooed from *Courtney Place* as head writer to everyone's satisfaction, and the men of a fictional Northland town weren't going to know what had hit them.

But Hugh forgot all of that in the next instant, because the music had changed again, the congregation of the little church was standing, and everyone had turned to watch the woman starting down the aisle on the arm of her father. The big, broad figure beside her radiated sober strength in his black suit, his eyes looked straight into Hugh's, and the message was about as clear as it could be.

Take care of my little girl, her father's set gaze said, *or I will kill you.*

No worries, he told the other man. *I've got her.*

Josie was a slim ivory column, and just like always, there was nothing too tight, nothing too low. The veil obscured her face and hair, leaving nothing but her own beautiful shape visible, coming towards him without a falter in her step. So sure, and so right. All his tomorrows.

Amelia reached the altar, and Hugh smiled at her, made an "OK" sign with finger and thumb, and she smiled back and took her place. And then Josie's father was there with his daughter, placing her hand in Hugh's, giving him one final sober nod before going to sit with his wife.

Hugh wasn't looking. He waited for Josie to hand her bouquet off to Amelia, then reached out with hands he could have wished were steadier, gently picked up the ends of the veil, and lifted the gossamer thing over her head.

And there she was. Smiling up into his eyes with the warmth, the life, the light that was Josie, and he could have sworn that his heart actually stopped for a moment.

"Hi," he said, and smiled at her.

"Hi," she said, and smiled back.

He took her hand, twined his fingers through hers, and turned with her to face the altar.

"We're ready," he told the priest. "We're all good. Let's go."

The End

Sign up for my New Release mailing list at
www.rosalindjames.com/mail-list to be notified
of special pricing on new books, sales, and more.

Turn the page for a Kiwi glossary and a preview
of the next book in the series.

a kiwi glossary

A few notes about Maori pronunciation:
- The accent is normally on the first syllable.
- All vowels are pronounced separately.
- All vowels except u have a short vowel sound.
- "wh" is pronounced "f."
- "ng" is pronounced as in "singer," not as in "anger."

ABs: All Blacks

across the Ditch: in Australia (across the Tasman Sea). Or, if you're in Australia, in New Zealand!

advert: commercial

agro: aggravation

air con: air conditioning

All Blacks: National rugby team. Members are selected for every series from amongst the five NZ Super 15 teams. The All Blacks play similarly selected teams from other nations.

ambo: paramedic

Aotearoa: New Zealand (the other official name, meaning "The Land of the Long White Cloud" in Maori)

arvo, this arvo: afternoon

Aussie, Oz: Australia. (An Australian is also an Aussie. Pronounced "Ozzie.")

bach: holiday home (pronounced like "bachelor")

backs: rugby players who aren't in the scrum and do more running, kicking, and ball-carrying—though all players do all jobs and play both offense and defense. Backs tend to be faster and leaner than forwards.

bangers and mash: sausages and potatoes

barrack for: cheer for

bench: counter (kitchen bench)

berko: berserk

Big Smoke: the big city (usually Auckland)

bikkies: cookies

billy-o, like billy-o: like crazy. "I paddled like billy-o and just barely made it through that rapid."

bin, rubbish bin: trash can

bit of a dag: a comedian, a funny guy

bits and bobs: stuff ("be sure you get all your bits and bobs")

blood bin: players leaving field for injury

Blues: Auckland's Super 15 team

bollocks: rubbish, nonsense

boofhead: fool, jerk

booking: reservation

boots and all: full tilt, no holding back

bot, the bot: flu, a bug

Boxing Day: December 26—a holiday

brekkie: breakfast

brilliant: fantastic

bub: baby, small child

buggered: messed up, exhausted

bull's roar: close. "They never came within a bull's roar of winning."

bunk off: duck out, skip (bunk off school)

bust a gut: do your utmost, make a supreme effort

Cake Tin: Wellington's rugby stadium (not the official name, but it looks exactly like a springform pan)

caravan: travel trailer

cardie: a cardigan sweater

chat up: flirt with

chilly bin: ice chest

chips: French fries. (potato chips are "crisps")

chocolate bits: chocolate chips

chocolate fish: pink or white marshmallow coated with milk chocolate, in the shape of a fish. A common treat/reward for kids (and for adults. You often get a chocolate fish on the saucer when you order a mochaccino—a mocha).

choice: fantastic

chokka: full

chooks: chickens

Chrissy: Christmas

chuck out: throw away

chuffed: pleased

collywobbles: nervous tummy, upset stomach

come a greaser: take a bad fall

costume, cossie: swimsuit (female only)

cot: crib (for a baby)

crook: ill

cuddle: hug (give a cuddle)

cuppa: a cup of tea (the universal remedy)

CV: resumé

cyclone: hurricane (Southern Hemisphere)

dairy: corner shop (not just for milk!)

dead: very; e.g., "dead sexy."

dill: fool

do your block: lose your temper

dob in: turn in; report to authorities. Frowned upon.

doco: documentary

doddle: easy. "That'll be a doddle."

dodgy: suspect, low-quality

dogbox: The doghouse—in trouble

dole: unemployment.

dole bludger: somebody who doesn't try to get work and lives off unemployment (which doesn't have a time limit in NZ)

Domain: a good-sized park; often the "official" park of the town.

dressing gown: bathrobe

drongo: fool (Australian, but used sometimes in NZ as well)

drop your gear: take off your clothes

duvet: comforter

earbashing: talking-to, one-sided chat

electric jug: electric teakettle to heat water. Every Kiwi kitchen has one.

En Zed: Pronunciation of NZ. ("Z" is pronounced "Zed.")

ensuite: master bath (a bath in the bedroom).

eye fillet: premium steak (filet mignon)

fair go: a fair chance. Kiwi ideology: everyone deserves a fair go.

fair wound me up: Got me very upset

fantail: small, friendly native bird

farewelled, he'll be farewelled: funeral; he'll have his funeral.

feed, have a feed: meal

first five, first five-eighth: rugby back—does most of the big kicking jobs and is the main director of the backs. Also called the No. 10.

fixtures: playing schedule

fizz, fizzie: soft drink

fizzing: fired up

flaked out: tired

flash: fancy

flat to the boards: at top speed

flat white: most popular NZ coffee. An espresso with milk but no foam.

flattie: roommate

flicks: movies

flying fox: zipline

footpath: sidewalk

footy, football: rugby

forwards: rugby players who make up the scrum and do the most physical battling for position. Tend to be bigger and more heavily muscled than backs.

fossick about: hunt around for something

front up: face the music, show your mettle

garden: yard

get on the piss: get drunk

get stuck in: commit to something

give way: yield

giving him stick, give him some stick about it: teasing, needling

glowworms: larvae of a fly found only in NZ. They shine a light to attract insects. Found in caves or other dark, moist places.

go crook, be crook: go wrong, be ill

go on the turps: get drunk

gobsmacked: astounded

good hiding: beating ("They gave us a good hiding in Dunedin.")

grotty: grungy, badly done up

ground floor: what we call the first floor. The "first floor" is one floor up.

gumboots, gummies: knee-high rubber boots. It rains a lot in New Zealand.

gutted: thoroughly upset

Haast's Eagle: (extinct). Huge native NZ eagle. Ate moa.

haere mai: Maori greeting

haka: ceremonial Maori challenge—done before every All Blacks game

hang on a tick: wait a minute

hard man: the tough guy, the enforcer

hard yakka: hard work (from Australian)

harden up: toughen up. Standard NZ (male) response to (male) complaints: "Harden the f*** up!"

have a bit on: I have placed a bet on [whatever]. Sports gambling and prostitution are both legal in New Zealand.

have a go: try

Have a nosy for…: look around for

head: principal (headmaster)

head down: or head down, bum up. Put your head down. Work hard.

heaps: lots. "Give it heaps."

hei toki: pendant (Maori)

holiday: vacation

honesty box: a small stand put up just off the road with bags of fruit and vegetables and a cash box. Very common in New Zealand.

hooker: rugby position (forward)

hooning around: driving fast, wannabe tough-guy behavior (typically young men)

hoovering: vacuuming (after the brand of vacuum cleaner)

ice block: popsicle

I'll see you right: I'll help you out

in form: performing well (athletically)

it's not on: It's not all right

iwi: tribe (Maori)

jabs: immunizations, shots

jandals: flip-flops. (This word is only used in New Zealand. Jandals and gumboots are the iconic Kiwi footwear.)

jersey: a rugby shirt, or a pullover sweater

joker: a guy. "A good Kiwi joker": a regular guy; a good guy.

journo: journalist

jumper: a heavy pullover sweater

ka pai: going smoothly (Maori).

kapa haka: school singing group (Maori songs/performances. Any student can join, not just Maori.)

karanga: Maori song of welcome (done by a woman)

keeping his/your head down: working hard

kia ora: welcome (Maori, but used commonly)

kilojoules: like calories—measure of food energy

kindy: kindergarten (this is 3- and 4-year-olds)

kit, get your kit off: clothes, take off your clothes

Kiwi: New Zealander OR the bird. If the person, it's capitalized. Not the fruit.

kiwifruit: the fruit. (Never called simply a "kiwi.")

knackered: exhausted

knockout rounds: playoff rounds (quarterfinals, semifinals, final)

koru: ubiquitous spiral Maori symbol of new beginnings, hope

kumara: Maori sweet potato.

ladder: standings (rugby)

littlies: young kids

lock: rugby position (forward)

lollies: candy

lolly: candy or money

lounge: living room

mad as a meat axe: crazy

maintenance: child support

major: "a major." A big deal, a big event

mana: prestige, earned respect, spiritual power

Maori: native people of NZ—though even they arrived relatively recently from elsewhere in Polynesia

marae: Maori meeting house

Marmite: Savory Kiwi yeast-based spread for toast. An acquired taste. (Kiwis swear it tastes different from Vegemite, the Aussie version.)

mate: friend. And yes, fathers call their sons "mate."

metal road: gravel road

Milo: cocoa substitute; hot drink mix

mind: take care of, babysit

moa: (extinct) Any of several species of huge flightless NZ birds. All eaten by the Maori before Europeans arrived.

moko: Maori tattoo

mokopuna: grandchildren

motorway: freeway

mozzie: mosquito; OR a Maori Australian (Maori + Aussie = Mozzie)

muesli: like granola, but unbaked

munted: broken

naff: stupid, unsuitable. "Did you get any naff Chrissy pressies this year?"

nappy: diaper

narked, narky: annoyed

netball: Down-Under version of basketball for women. Played like basketball, but the hoop is a bit narrower, the players wear skirts, and they don't dribble and can't contact each other. It can look fairly tame to an American eye. There are professional netball teams, and it's televised and taken quite seriously.

new caps: new All Blacks—those named to the side for the first time

New World: One of the two major NZ supermarket chains

nibbles: snacks

nick, in good nick: doing well

niggle, niggly: small injury, ache or soreness

no worries: no problem. The Kiwi mantra.

No. 8: rugby position. A forward

not very flash: not feeling well

Nurofen: brand of ibuprofen

nutted out: worked out

OE: Overseas Experience—young people taking a year or two overseas, before or after University.

offload: pass (rugby)

oldies: older people. (or for the elderly, "wrinklies!")

on the front foot: Having the advantage. Vs. on the back foot—at a disadvantage. From rugby.

Op Shop: charity shop, secondhand shop

out on the razzle: out drinking too much, getting crazy

paddock: field (often used for rugby—"out on the paddock")

Pakeha: European-ancestry people (as opposed to Polynesians)

Panadol: over-the-counter painkiller

partner: romantic partner, married or not

patu: Maori club

paua, paua shell: NZ abalone

pavlova (pav): Classic Kiwi Christmas (summer) dessert. Meringue, fresh fruit (often kiwifruit and strawberries) and whipped cream.

pavement: sidewalk (generally on wider city streets)

pear-shaped, going pear-shaped: messed up, when it all goes to Hell

penny dropped: light dawned (figured it out)

people mover: minivan

perve: stare sexually

phone's engaged: phone's busy

piece of piss: easy

pike out: give up, wimp out

piss awful: very bad

piss up: drinking (noun) a piss-up

pissed: drunk

pissed as a fart: very drunk. And yes, this is an actual expression.

play up: act up

playing out of his skin: playing very well

plunger: French Press coffeemaker

PMT: PMS

pohutukawa: native tree; called the "New Zealand Christmas Tree" for its beautiful red blossoms at Christmastime (high summer)

poi: balls of flax on strings that are swung around the head, often to the accompaniment of singing and/or dancing by women. They make rhythmic patterns in the air, and it's very beautiful.

Pom, Pommie: English person

pop: pop over, pop back, pop into the oven, pop out, pop in

possie: position (rugby)

postie: mail carrier

pot plants: potted plants (not what you thought, huh?)

poumanu: greenstone (jade)

prang: accident (with the car)

pressie: present

puckaroo: broken (from Maori)

pudding: dessert

pull your head in: calm down, quit being rowdy

Pumas: Argentina's national rugby team

pushchair: baby stroller

put your hand up: volunteer

put your head down: work hard

rapt: thrilled

rattle your dags: hurry up. From the sound that dried excrement on a sheep's backside makes, when the sheep is running!

red card: penalty for highly dangerous play. The player is sent off for the rest of the game, and the team plays with 14 men.

rellies: relatives

riding the pine: sitting on the bench (as a substitute in a match)

rimu: a New Zealand tree. The wood used to be used for building and flooring, but like all native NZ trees, it was overlogged. Older houses, though, often have rimu floors, and they're beautiful.

Rippa: junior rugby

root: have sex (you DON'T root for a team!)

ropeable: very angry

ropey: off, damaged ("a bit ropey")

rort: ripoff

rough as guts: uncouth

rubbish bin: garbage can

rugby boots: rugby shoes with spikes (sprigs)

Rugby Championship: Contest played each year in the Southern Hemisphere by the national teams of NZ, Australia, South Africa, and Argentina

Rugby World Cup, RWC: World championship, played every four years amongst the top 20 teams in the world

rugged up: dressed warmly

ruru: native owl

Safa: South Africa. Abbreviation only used in NZ.

sammie: sandwich

scoff, scoffing: eating, like "snarfing"

second-five, second five-eighth: rugby back (No. 9). With the first-five, directs the game. Also feeds the scrum and generally collects the ball from the ball carrier at the breakdown and distributes it.

selectors: team of 3 (the head coach is one) who choose players for the All Blacks squad, for every series

serviette: napkin

shag: have sex with. A little rude, but not too bad.

shattered: exhausted

sheds: locker room (rugby)

she'll be right: See "no worries." Everything will work out. The other Kiwi mantra.

shift house: move (house)

shonky: shady (person). "a bit shonky"

shout, your shout, my shout, shout somebody a coffee: buy a round, treat somebody

sickie, throw a sickie: call in sick

sin bin: players sitting out 10-minute penalty in rugby (or, in the case of a red card, the rest of the game)

sink the boot in: kick you when you're down

skint: broke (poor)

skipper: (team) captain. Also called "the Skip."

slag off: speak disparagingly of; disrespect

smack: spank. Smacking kids is illegal in NZ.

smoko: coffee break

snog: kiss; make out with

sorted: taken care of

spa, spa pool: hot tub

sparrow fart: the crack of dawn

speedo: Not the swimsuit! Speedometer. (the swimsuit is called a budgie smuggler—a budgie is a parakeet, LOL.)

spew: vomit

spit the dummy: have a tantrum. (A dummy is a pacifier)

sportsman: athlete

sporty: liking sports

spot on: absolutely correct. "That's spot on. You're spot on."

Springboks, Boks: South African national rugby team

squiz: look. "I was just having a squiz round." "Giz a squiz": Give me a look at that.

stickybeak: nosy person, busybody

stonkered: drunk—a bit stonkered—or exhausted

stoush: bar fight, fight

straight away: right away

strength of it: the truth, the facts. "What's the strength of that?" = "What's the true story on that?"

stroppy: prickly, taking offense easily

stuffed up: messed up

Super 15: Top rugby competition: five teams each from NZ, Australia, South Africa. The New Zealand Super 15 teams are, from north to south: Blues (Auckland), Chiefs (Waikato/

Hamilton), Hurricanes (Wellington), Crusaders (Canterbury/ Christchurch), Highlanders (Otago/Dunedin).

supporter: fan (Do NOT say "root for." "To root" is to have (rude) sex!)

suss out: figure out

sweet: dessert

sweet as: great. (also: choice as, angry as, lame as...Meaning "very" whatever. "Mum was angry as that we ate up all the pudding before tea with Nana.")

takahe: ground-dwelling native bird. Like a giant parrot.

takeaway: takeout (food)

tall poppy: arrogant person who puts himself forward or sets himself above others. It is every Kiwi's duty to cut down tall poppies, a job they undertake enthusiastically.

Tangata Whenua: Maori (people of the land)

tapu: sacred (Maori)

Te Papa: the National Museum, in Wellington

tea: dinner (casual meal at home)

tea towel: dishtowel

test match: international rugby match (e.g., an All Blacks game)

throw a wobbly: have a tantrum

tick off: cross off (tick off a list)

ticker: heart. "The boys showed a lot of ticker out there today."

togs: swimsuit (male or female)

torch: flashlight

touch wood: knock on wood (for luck)

track: trail

trainers: athletic shoes

tramping: hiking

transtasman: Australia/New Zealand (the Bledisloe Cup is a transtasman rivalry)

trolley: shopping cart

tucker: food

tui: Native bird

turn to custard: go south, deteriorate

turps, go on the turps: get drunk

Uni: University—or school uniform

up the duff: pregnant. A bit vulgar (like "knocked up")

ute: pickup or SUV

vet: check out

waiata: Maori song

wairua: spirit, soul (Maori). Very important concept.

waka: canoe (Maori)

Wallabies: Australian national rugby team

Warrant of Fitness: certificate of a car's fitness to drive

wedding tackle: the family jewels; a man's genitals

Weet-Bix: ubiquitous breakfast cereal

whaddarya?: I am dubious about your masculinity (meaning "Whaddarya...pussy?")

whakapapa: genealogy (Maori). A critical concept.

whanau: family (Maori). Big whanau: extended family. Small whanau: nuclear family.

wheelie bin: rubbish bin (garbage can) with wheels.

whinge: whine. Contemptuous! Kiwis dislike whingeing. Harden up!

White Ribbon: campaign against domestic violence

wind up: upset (perhaps purposefully). "Their comments were bound to wind him up."

wing: rugby position (back)

Yank: American. Not pejorative.

yellow card: A penalty for dangerous play that sends a player off for 10 minutes to the sin bin. The team plays with 14 men during that time—or even 13, if two are sinbinned.

yonks: ages. "It's been going on for yonks."

Find out what's new at the **ROSALIND JAMES WEBSITE.**
http://www.rosalindjames.com/

"Like" my <u>Facebook</u> page at facebook.com/rosalindjamesbooks
or follow me on <u>Twitter</u> at twitter.com/RosalindJames5
to learn about giveaways, events, and more.
Want to tell me what you liked, or what I got wrong? I'd love
to hear! You can email me at **Rosalind@rosalindjames.com**

by rosalind james

Cover design by Robin Ludwig Design Inc.,
http://www.gobookcoverdesign.com/

Read on for an excerpt from
Just Once More
Available December 1, 2014

in the tunnel

♡

Drew Callahan sat bolt upright in the dark, his heart hammering, his body wet with cold sweat.

"Shit."

It was nothing more than an explosion of breath, but it woke Hannah anyway.

"Drew?" She struggled to heave her body up, and his arm went out reflexively to support her. "Is something wrong?"

"Nah." He had himself back under control now, his galloping heart finally slowing. He lay back down, pulled her gently along with him. "A bad dream, that's all. You OK, though? Baby not coming or anything?"

"What?" She still sounded sleepy. "Of course not. I'd have woken you up. Why?"

He shrugged, tried to shove the dream aside. Its dark tendrils still lingered despite his efforts, sticky cobwebs of fear and dread brushing across his mind. "Just a bad dream. Sorry to wake you. I know sleep's coming hard now."

"What kind of dream?" She settled herself a little more comfortably on her side, put a hand onto his chest and stroked him there. The touch of her hand, the sound of her voice began to smooth the jagged edges left by the nightmare. His muscles released some of their tension, his body settling into the mattress.

"People who tell their dreams, gah." He felt nothing but foolish now. "Anything more annoying than that? Never mind. Doesn't matter."

"Tell me. Because it scared you. Your heart's still beating so hard."

He tried to laugh. "Can't hide anything from you, I guess. OK. It was...I was in this...tunnel. With you. And somebody was coming. I couldn't quite hear, but I could tell. Somebody who meant to hurt us, I knew that."

Because he had known. He'd known it for sure, and it had scared the shit out of him. Not for him. For her.

"I was waiting," he went on. "Couldn't stand up—too low. Too narrow. In this little space, with somebody coming. Crouched down in the pitch black, listening and waiting, seconds going by, holding my breath so I could hear him breathe."

He stopped, forced himself to relax again, but the tension took hold all the same. "And then I felt him come, just this whisper in the air, and I was grabbing for his hair. Stabbing at his eyes, punching at him in the dark as best I could, trying to bang him into the rocks, and he was fighting back. Fighting so hard. He was so strong, and I was scared..." He swallowed, the fear gaining the upper hand again, tightening his muscles, shortening his breath even as he told himself it was a dream. Only a dream. "Scared that I'd lose. Scared that he'd get through me. That he'd get through me to you."

"Sounds terrifying," she said softly. Her hand was still there, stroking over his skin. "I'll bet you saved me, though."

"No." He felt her hand still for a moment in surprise. "I mean, I did, I guess, because he was gone, and I was lying there, beat to hell from having my head bashed against the rock and that. But I'd had my hands around his throat, and I'd either killed him or he was gone, don't know which. You know, dreams. But then I was still there, in the dark, in the tunnel, and I couldn't find you.

And I knew you were having the baby. Right there. I knew it, and I couldn't get there. I couldn't get to you." His body remembered exactly how it had felt. Because she was right. It had terrified him.

"Which has happened," she pointed out practically. "Twice now. Though without the tunnel, thank goodness. And I've had them all the same. I know you think you're necessary, and no question, you're pretty important at the start, aren't you?"

She was trying to tease him, doing her best to ease his unquiet mind, and he was embarrassed. She should be the one being nervous, and he should be the one doing the comforting, not the other way around.

"But when it gets to that point, you know," she reminded him, "I pretty much have to do it myself. An anxiety dream, that's all it was. But it's all right."

"Going to be there for this one all the same," he told her. "Shouldn't have missed the last one. Should never have gone, not after the first time."

"No," she said instantly. "How could we have known it would be that fast?"

Because it had been fast. Too fast. He'd been here, talking to the Bay of Plenty club about the coaching job, and she'd been back in Auckland with their three-year-old. And his mum and dad, thank God.

"It's only three hours away," she'd told him when he'd vacillated about going. "It's not going to happen faster than that, for heaven's sake. You need to talk to them, I'm not due for more than ten days, and the midwife says nothing looks imminent. Go."

So he'd gone, and once again, he hadn't made it back in time, because three hours had been too long after all. He'd broken every speed limit to get to her, and it hadn't mattered. He hadn't made it.

"It's going to be me holding your hand this time," he told her now. "Not my mum. Me. So don't be thinking you're going anywhere without me for the next couple weeks, or that I'm going anywhere without you. No arguments."

"I'll be happy to have you there holding my hand, believe me," she assured him. "I want you there. And meanwhile, I guess we probably shouldn't go caving for the next couple weeks after all. Better cancel that blackwater rafting booking, you think? Shoot. I was really looking forward to that." She still had her hand on him, and she was smiling, he could tell.

He laughed. Reluctantly, but he laughed all the same. "Stupid, I know it. It's just..." He said it, in the dark. "My biggest fear, isn't it. That I won't be able to take care of you. You and the kids."

"And you might not be able to, someday, somehow," she said, no laughter in her voice anymore. "You're not always here, even now. But I manage all the same. And I would manage. To take care of myself, and the kids too, no matter what. Don't worry, Drew. It's all right."

"I know," he said. "I know. It's just..." He rested a hand on the taut roundness of her belly. "Too close, I reckon. I'm always nervous when you're this close. It matters too much. And besides, I'm used to being able to do things, to take care of things, and when you're having the baby, I can't. So hard to know you're hurting, and not be able to help."

"Somebody said that. That when you have a child, you give a hostage to the world. When you love somebody that much."

"A hostage. Yeh." He felt his son kick under his hand, held safe there under his wife's heart, and knew how true it was. "You, and the kids."

"True for me too, you know," she said. He'd turned onto his side to face her, and he could see her now that his eyes had adjusted to the darkness. The gleam of her pale hair, her eyes on him, her face so gentle. "True for both of us. Love is a risk. But you're worth it, Drew. Always."

He did his best to speak around the lump in his throat. "Yeh. So are you."

acknowledgments

My thanks to Kirsten Iiams for her assistance with choreography, dance, and dance studios.

To my husband, and my sons, too, for listening and reading. An extra thanks to James for watching so much rugby with me!

And, as always, grateful appreciation isn't nearly enough for my awesome critique group: Barbara Buchanan, Carol Chappell, Anne Forell, Mary Guidry, Kathy Harward, and Bob Pryor.

Cover design by Robin Ludwig Design Inc.,
http://www.gobookcoverdesign.com/

16199155R00215